# DAY
# ZERO

# DAY ZERO

# MARC CAMERON

**PINNACLE BOOKS**
Kensington Publishing Corp.
www.kensingtonbooks.com

PINNACLE BOOKS are published by

Kensington Publishing Corp.
119 West 40th Street
New York, NY 10018

All Kensington titles, imprints, and distributed lines are available at special quantity discounts for bulk purchases for sales promotions, premiums, fund-raising, educational, or institutional use. Special book excerpts or customized printings can also be created to fit specific needs. For details, write or phone the office of the Kensington special sales manager: Kensington Publishing Corp., 119 West 40th Street, New York, NY 10018, attn: Special Sales Department; phone 1-800-221-2647.

This book is a work of fiction. Names, characters, businesses, organizations, places, events, and incidents either are the product of the author's imagination or are used fictitiously. Any resemblance to actual persons, living or dead, events, or locales is entirely coincidental.

ISBN-13: 978-0-7860-3527-4
ISBN-10: 0-7860-3527-7

First printing: February 2015

10 9 8 7 6 5 4 3 2 1

Printed in the United States of America

First electronic edition: February 2015

ISBN-13: 978-0-7860-3528-1
ISBN-10: 0-7860-3528-5

*For Martha Cope, Charlotte Skidmore,*
*Bill Witherspoon, and Gene Reynolds—teachers*
*who inspired and expected.*

*Violence isn't the answer. Violence is the question . . .*
*The answer is yes.*
—Anonymous

# Prologue

*June*
*Razika village, northern Pakistan*

Emiko Miyagi was not accustomed to wearing so many clothes. Considering the deeply conservative Islamic practices in this part of Pakistan, the muscular little Japanese woman was fortunate to be wearing her head. Defending herself was not normally a problem she worried about. At forty-four, she could have killed any three men in the village at one time without batting an eye. Still, she knew that enough wild dogs could bring down even a powerful lioness, so she covered her body—and kept her plans to herself.

Tugging at the heavy, earth-colored robe she wore over her slacks and long-sleeve cotton shirt, Emiko pulled her black head scarf tight against the breeze and heaved a five-gallon plastic water jug onto the uneven wooden bed of a donkey cart with a dull thump. In truth, forty pounds of water was nowhere near too heavy for her, but she had to keep up appearances.

She used the back of her arm to mop the drops of sweat from her forehead and paused from her work at the communal well to gaze through the crystalline air of the broad river valley. She could have been in Montana were it not for the slumping stone houses and terraced green fields. Dark stands of spruce and oak spilled down the boulder-strewn mountains that rose up on either side. The ever-present smell of wood smoke, human waste, and burned trash, common to underdeveloped countries, also provided a clue that she was a long way from any amber waves of American grain.

A rusty diesel engine and the series of belts and pulleys that served as a pump for the community well stood alongside the knock-kneed beast. Two black weatherproof Pelican cases containing Emiko's water-testing equipment sat in the back of the cart. There was other gear too—sure to get her head sawed off with a dull knife if it was discovered.

The warped wheels on the ancient cart listed heavily to the right just like her hovering warden, Ismail. The village headman had assured her the bent old man was her protector, but Emiko knew better. The man was little more than her guard—who seemed much more intent on catching her in some minute violation of Sharia law than protecting her from danger.

It was unheard of for a woman to move about the village unaccompanied by a male escort—even a woman who was supposed to be a Japanese NGO scientist assisting with a clean water initiative. Japan and Pakistan had a special arrangement, with the former sending great sums of money and aid while the latter agreed to protect the people administering the aid . . . for the most part.

Traditions ran deep here in the untamed wilds of the Kohistan Province, where every household was required to have a male leader. Lone women were such a danger to religious sensibilities that local clerics had threatened female NGO aid workers with forced marriage to village men—or on occasion, simply dragged them into the street and shot them.

A recent outbreak of dysentery had paved the way for this male-dominated society to allow Miyagi into the valley—because of her supposed scientific background in potable water systems.

Had they known her real intentions, the villagers would have cut her down on the spot.

Ismail canted sideways, leaning on his knotted elmwood cane beside the sun-bleached timbers of an old well house. The ribs of the long-gone building, with timbers curved upward, were gray and weatherworn, like something out of an ancient sailing ship. They were taller than the old man by a head and leaned inward, surrounding the communal pool of the well. A round pakool hat, common in the tribal areas of Pakistan and Afghanistan, slumped over Ismail's wizened brow. The long, pajamalike shirt and pants known as *shalwar kameez* clung to his bony body. He looked as if he might topple over at any moment. Surely in his seventies, he was a dinosaur in this impoverished area of an impoverished country where fifty-five was considered elderly. Presumably too old to have unclean thoughts about a female infidel scientist, he did his job without speaking. He watched her every move, ensuring that she committed no blasphemy or insult to the village. It was a tall order for a tribal area where, just months before, a minority Christian woman had earned herself a death sentence for drinking out of a village well and then dipping that same cup—that had touched her infidel lips—back in the water.

A soft breeze tumbled down from the blackness of the Karakorum Mountains, bringing welcome relief from the mid-morning heat. The wind pulled the old man's wisp of a beard to one side, adding to his tilted appearance. Emiko kept an eye on Ismail while she moved around the well, inspecting the pump. It made her belly burn that he could stand there in his light cotton clothing while she baked in a layer of robes that covered her from head to ankle—all in an effort to shield him from lascivious thoughts.

The water loaded, she returned to the well. A stone wall, a little taller than her knees, formed a circular reservoir pool roughly fifteen feet across. Water dripped from a rusted pipe beside the engine. Patches of green grass and lush weeds grew around the edge of the pool, taking advantage of the shade and consistent supply of water. Miyagi took a small glass vial from the folds of her robes and leaned over the wall and dipped it into the pool. A slurry of stone and mortar from the decaying wall skittered over the lip and sank into the dark water.

Miyagi muttered under her breath as if she cared about the water, while she paid close attention to the reason she was actually in the village. Fifty feet away, under the sprawling branches of an ancient oak tree, seven bearded men sat in council. The men spoke with animated gestures over mid-morning tea. Now and again barking voices carried over on the breeze, loud enough that Miyagi could tell they were having a heated conversation about something.

Ismail gave Emiko a long, chastising look, before hobbling off toward the meeting-tree without a word of explanation. He was apparently satisfied that she could not possibly fall into serious mischief while merely filling glass vials with water. He was probably hoping the men under the tree would give him a handout of *naswar*, the local snuff made from tobacco, lime, and indigo. It was already a slight to his manhood that he was assigned to watch the female foreign devil all day long anyway. Emiko frightened him, and as she well knew, the worst of all insults a woman could pay a man was to make him aware of his fears.

Emiko Miyagi had been in Pakistan for four months, ingratiating herself with a Japanese NGO, Helpful Hands, an organization that funded water testing and the building of tube wells in rural Pakistan. She was smart enough to learn enough about the process to look like an expert to all but the most trained eye, and when one of the scientists had to return to Japan because of an illness, Emiko had assumed her identity and slid into her place.

Far from any sort of scientist, Emiko was a hunter, and found herself in this lawless area of Pakistan for one reason alone. She was looking for a man named Qasim Ranjhani. She'd discovered his name in a book during her last trip to Japan—a journey where a close friend had lost her life. Ranjhani was the key to unraveling the plot that put a foreign mole into the US presidency.

For months, her work had yielded nothing, but now, in this remote valley, she'd heard the other women speak of a meeting of Al Qaeda and another terrorist group known as the Jundalla—or Soldiers of God. The Jundalla had claimed responsibility for many atrocities in northern Pakistan over recent years—including the murder of eighteen passengers on a bus for the crime of being Shia rather than Sunni Muslims. The driver, a Sunni, was killed because he didn't answer quickly enough when quizzed about *Fajr* prayer. Later, this same group had slaughtered sixteen international mountain climbers at the base camp to Nanga Parbat in Gilgit Baltistan.

Miyagi continued filling vials with water samples as the men gathered under the shade of the tree, some sitting back on a large woven rug, others squatting on their haunches in the manner peculiar to Asian men. One, a large man with a full black beard that doubled the size of his face, appeared to be the guest of honor. He sat at the head of the blanket, where he could rest his back against the oak. He would be Ali Kadir, a close associate of Ranjhani—Emiko's target. She had learned that his parents lived here in Razika village and he'd come to visit them and pay his respects. With any luck, he would lead her to Ranjhani.

Miyagi knew the great oak was a customary place for men to hold a *Jirga* or sit in council. The day before, she had placed two listening devices in the crooked branches as she'd walked by, feigning the need to lean against the tree to fix her sandals. The bugs were small gray-brown sticks, barely two inches long and made to blend into wood or stone backgrounds.

With Ismail safely talking to the gathered men, Emiko reached beneath her robes and took the small earpiece from the pocket of her khakis. She flicked open the latches on the smaller Pelican case to activate the receiver that would boost the signal from the listening devices. The receiver was nestled in the foam padding of the plastic case and difficult to distinguish from her other test equipment.

Men's voices resonated in her ear. Amazingly clear, they spoke in the singsong cadence of Urdu. Though not fluent, Miyagi was conversant enough to know the men were speaking of their journeys in and the hardships of simply "being men these days," what with their government of weak-minded American puppets. Ali Kadir told fantastic tales about beloved brothers who'd martyred themselves in the war against the Great Satan. Miyagi's ears perked up when he spoke of an upcoming mission "to spill infidel blood." He gave no specifics but mentioned only vague allusions when pressed for details by the other men.

Miyagi used a Sharpie marker to label her test vials in order to appear busy. She tilted her head when a round of crackling static filled her earpiece. When it didn't go away, she adjusted the gain on the receiver inside her Pelican case and glanced toward the oak.

A flash of movement caught her eye. At first she thought it was a bird, but there was something different in the way the thing moved, like a bee or a humming-bird, only bigger. It flitted back and forth, hovering for a moment in one spot before zipping to another, as if working a grid. Whatever it was, it was searching for something—or more likely, someone. The static in her ear grew louder as the object came closer. Five more of the little things zipped in from nowhere appearing nearer the oak, barely visible against the blue sky.

The men sitting in *Jirga* under the tree would pay the tiny drones no mind, thinking they were birds or in-sects. Miyagi recognized them for what they were. Known as a Black Hornet, the tiny radio-controlled heli-copter could have fit into her palm. Each was outfitted with a nose-mounted camera that fed images back to its handler. They were also capable of remotely "painting" a target for laser-guided munitions.

It was no secret that the US military employed all sorts of Unmanned Aerial Vehicles for everything from forward observation to assassination. Targeting a ter-rorist leader like Ali Kadir and the other men under the great oak certainly met the drones' mission description of work that was too "dull, dirty, or dangerous."

Miyagi cursed the irony of her luck. The man who would lead her to the terrorist responsible for trying to topple the US government was about to be killed by the US military.

She moved instinctively to the far side of the stone wall that surrounded the well reservoir, putting as much distance as she could between herself and the men. Once the target was found, it would be only a matter of seconds before a larger Predator drone or even some manned aircraft sent a Hellfire missile screaming into their position, reducing them to a crater of ash.

Miyagi watched as the Black Hornet spun on its axis, following her as she moved. The nose of the hellish little thing continued to point directly at her. A moment later, two more of the tiny pocket drones zipped in from the direction of the oak and settled in a tight formation next to the first—hovering passively against the pale blue sky.

A cold realization crept over Emiko Miyagi, chilling her even under the heavy robes. A half a breath later, a screaming hiss split the air and a Hellfire missile impacted dead center on the donkey cart, fifteen feet away. The drones weren't looking for Ali Kadir.

They had come for her.

# DAY ONE

*My wife handed me my rifle, saying,*
*"Here's your gun . . . fight."*
—CHIEF JOSEPH

# Chapter 1

Jericho Quinn used the back of a bloody hand to wipe windblown spray from his eyes. Behind him, the growl of a single-engine airplane brought a familiar twist of concern to his gut. He turned from his spot at the steering post of an open aluminum skiff to watch a newer-looking Cessna Caravan emerge from a line of low, boiling clouds to the south, on the other side of the Yukon River. Quinn nudged the throttle forward and leaned against the console, bracing himself against the constant chop brought on by a fresh breeze that worked against the current of the mighty river. Water hung in droplets on his thick black beard. A tangle of wet hair escaped a camouflage ball cap, framing the portions of his face not covered by the beard. Even after a long, lightless winter in the north, he was deeply tanned—a trait inherited from an Apache grandmother—and chapped by wind and weather. His knees ached from the constant bouncing on the river—one of the several new pains to which he'd resigned himself over the past half year.

The ripping *blat* of the approaching aircraft drew his attention away from his aches. Even the most experienced bush pilots steered clear of weather like this. Quinn tamped back the nagging uneasiness in his belly and coaxed the skiff around to cut the current diagonally. A hundred meters away, in the lap of rolling hills, low and covered in willow, white birch, and spruce, a tumble of weather-worn buildings spilled from the fog. It was *Asaacarsaq* in traditional Yup'ik, but to the United States Post Office it was known as Mountain Village.

Behind Quinn, standing at the stern of the little skiff, a big-boned Eskimo leaned back to watch the airplane pass directly overhead, less than five hundred feet off the water. The big man shook his head in amazement. His name was James Perry, but Quinn had known him since high school and had never called him anything but Ukka. When Perry was nine, his grandfather had given him the Yup'ik nickname, *Ukkatamani*—"*a long time ago.*" It was the Eskimo equivalent of "once upon a time."

Quinn looked back over his shoulder from the steering pedestal while he turned the boat in a slow arc. "You see something in the water?"

Ukka's eyes were locked off the stern. "Never know," he said, cocking his head to one side in concentration. He was a broad man, standing an inch over six feet and weighing in at nearly two hundred and fifty pounds. "We'll have to get in close if we see one so I can stick it. You can't just shoot 'em out here. Freshwater doesn't float them as well as seawater . . . so they sink fast." He glanced up. "I ever tell you about the time my grandfather caught that beluga whale with a harpoon from his kayak down by Alakunuk?"

"You have not," Quinn said, smiling to himself.

Five months of stories had made it easy to see why James Perry's grandfather had called him "Once Upon a Time." No matter his nickname, Ukka certainly held the short weapon like he knew how to use it. When he wasn't bringing in his family's winter supply of meat, he made his living as a village public safety officer. In the Alaska bush, a VPSO was often the only law out here on the rough edges of the world. Ukka carried himself with the attendant swagger of a man in charge.

Like Quinn, Perry wore rubber knee boots and a blood-smeared orange float coat against the rain and wind-driven spray of his open boat. Beside him, in a slurry of rain, river spray, and fish slime, lay a mound of white Styrofoam football floats and green gill netting. A heavy rubber tub at the transom held a shining heap of the catch from their last drift—forty-six Chinook salmon.

Perry and the others in settlements along the Yukon were not the Eskimos of the icepack whose life revolved around heading out on the ice for polar bear or hunting the bowhead whale from skin boats. They caught seal and loved good whale *muktuk* when they could get it, but the Yukon River Eskimo were people of the salmon. When the fish arrived, everything else took a backseat.

"That guy's an idiot," Ukka shouted over the sound of the skiff's motor. He gnawed a piece of black, wind-dried meat with one hand while he clutched the wooden shaft of a harpoon in the other. "Man makes the rules. God makes the laws. You can break one and maybe you survive. Break the other—like flying in this shit—and it don't turn out so good."

The plane overflew the village, and then dipped a wing, banking toward the gravel runway a mile to the east. Quinn watched until it sank out of sight beyond the tree line, and then shot a glance over his shoulder at his friend. "Was there another flight coming in today?"

"Not that I know of." Ukka mused over his seal meat. "Everything was supposed to be weathered in all the way to Bethel. Must have cleared up some down there." He turned to scan the churning vee of water off the stern and took another bite of his black meat. "Sure you don't want a hunk of this? Tastes like chicken."

Quinn had learned the hard way about his friend's palate. To James Perry, even the clams, shrimp, and other stomach contents of a freshly killed walrus, flavored with nothing but seawater, also tasted like chicken.

"Think I'll pass," Quinn said, "My doctor says I should stay away from fermented seal meat."

"Suit yourself." Ukka licked his lips. Dark eyes darted toward the airport. "You think we should be worried?"

Quinn groaned, thinking through the possibilities. "It's probably nothing," he said. But his gut told him otherwise.

Quinn was a hunter by nature, not wired to hide behind anyone, least of all his friends. Yet, that is exactly where he'd found himself for the past five months— badly wounded, wanted for murder, and so helpless he could do little but depend on friends to protect him.

In order to stay safely hidden while he'd healed, Quinn had had little contact with the people he cared for the most. His ex-wife was getting used to a new prosthetic leg, he knew that much. And their seven-year-old daughter, Mattie, had just lost a front tooth. It killed him that he wasn't there to watch her grow up, but he realized he never really had been. Middle East deployments, long investigations, the heavy responsibilities of work had taken him away from home since she was a baby. That was the chief reason Mattie's mother was now Quinn's ex-wife.

On the brutally long winter nights, Quinn had sat with James Perry and his family watching the news while Hartman Drake, the new president of the United States, slowly but surely pushed the country toward ruin. The double assassinations of both the President and Vice President sent a shock wave through the American public not seen since September 11th. Near panic allowed newly appointed President Drake and his cronies to chip away at personal privacy and curtail press access, on the grounds of the need for tighter security. Taxes were slashed but welfare went up. High-level leaks from the White House led blogs and political news shows to place blame for the killings at the feet of the Chinese government. Diplomacy was kicked to the curb in favor of bellicose saber rattling with the US spoiling for a fight.

Hartman Drake, the bowtie-wearing former congressman from Wisconsin then Speaker of the House, had been thrust into the presidency. Quinn was certain Drake had something to do with both the President and Vice President's deaths. And he was equally certain the man was a terrorist. Drake had admitted as much, right after Quinn had put a bullet through the bottom of his foot— a big reason Drake wanted to see Quinn very dead.

Quinn was under no illusions that he was the only man in the world who could save the day. He knew his old boss, Winfield Palmer, would have others working on some sort of coup, but it went against everything in his makeup to sit on the sidelines while others did the dirty work. He was built to run toward the sound of gunfire—and if this new airplane carried the sort of people he thought it did, he might get his chance to do just that.

He moved his left arm, feeling the familiar tightness in the long scar that ran diagonally along his ribs. Considering that the wound had been made with a full-size Japanese sword, it was a wonder he was even able to stand. It was pink and raw and would be for many more weeks.

Quinn peered through the line of fog at the willows that separated Mountain Village from the airstrip, flexing his hands against the steering wheel. He was still far from completely healed. It would be at least another month, maybe two, before he'd be back in true, fighting shape. But deep down, he hoped this unscheduled arrival would force his hand.

A chilly wind stiffened from upriver, prompting Quinn to pull his head down, turtlelike, into the collar of his bright orange float coat. He watched a milling crowd of villagers and other fishermen come in and out of view in the fog as he neared the processing plant. A half dozen skiffs crowded along the steep gravel bank, working their way forward when a spot opened up on the docks of the drab blue building where they could offload their catch. Even in the flat light, Quinn could see huge Chinook salmon—called "kings" by Alaskans—flashing silver-blue as they were passed from boats to waiting plastic tubs.

Willing himself to relax, Quinn breathed in the sweet scent of fir and willow as they mingled with the odors of boat fuel and fish. He'd spent so much of his life in sandy, war-torn deserts that he couldn't help but smile at the freshness of the Alaska bush. All but the closed-mouth grin and crow's feet disappeared behind his beard.

He'd been little more than bandages and bones when he'd arrived in the village, wounded and sick, but five months of work and Perry's good cooking had added nearly twenty pounds and a fresh outlook on life. Even with the added weight, the baggy float coat his friend had loaned him still swallowed Quinn up like a child wearing his daddy's clothes. Far from the tactical colors he was used to, the combination life vest and raincoat was meant to facilitate a quick rescue if he fell overboard and into the bone-numbing water. Perry, the practical Eskimo that he was, reasoned that the water was so cold that the bright colors would aid more in body recovery than in saving anyone's life.

Quinn's rough-and-ready life in Air Force Special Operations as a combat rescue officer, and then later as a special agent with the Office of Special Investigations, or OSI, piled on top of the injuries he'd sustained from years of boxing and riding motorcycles to make him feel decades older than his thirty-seven years. A life of dangerous work and play had seen him endure hour upon hour of physical therapy. But hunting, hauling nets, lugging tubs of fish, and just living away from the clamoring city, had produced better results than any rehab he'd ever experienced. His movements were still slower—from one too many beatings. He'd lost some range of motion in his left arm, but an active winter of helping Ukka run traplines and bringing in moose, firewood, and fish worked wonders.

As his body had begun to heal, Quinn added exercise to the chores—push-ups, pull-ups, skipping rope, and a run up Azachorok Mountain above the village at least once a day. After he was well enough, Perry sparred with him in a makeshift boxing ring in the family living room. The matches were good natured but fast paced. Ukka's wife rooted for him, while his daughters cheered for Quinn. Invariably, at least one of the men got a bloody nose. At first, it had been Quinn, but as time progressed and he began to regain his legs and at least part of his reach, Ukka felt the sting of his gloves more and more.

Firearms and fighting were both perishable skills. Perry hand-loaded .45 ammo so they were able to practice shooting out at the dump a couple of times a week during all but the coldest days of winter. More than anything, the training helped Quinn's mood.

Less than fifty meters out, Quinn eased back on the throttle, pointing farther upriver to let the current push him toward the crowd of milling boats that jockeyed for position at the fishery plant. Everyone on the beach at the present moment held a commercial permit. Their own fish, they'd take to fishing camps up and down the river, away from the village itself, where they'd cut, smoke, and dry it for the winter. Even now, the smell of burning alder from their smokehouses hung along the crumbling riverbank, mingling with the fog.

Closer now, he could see the round faces of the villagers, family groups working to offload their boats. Colorful *kuspuks*, the thigh-length hooded blouses favored by Eskimo women, peeked out from blood-smeared rain gear and fleece jackets. Some were dressed in rubber boots and gloves, while others wore soaked cotton hoodies and muddy tennis shoes. Many worked with bare hands, pinked by the frigid water. Wet and cold, they all smiled because the fishing was good.

The single wiper blade thwacked back and forth on the small windscreen atop the steering post of the open boat. The wiper did little to stay ahead of the rain and spindrift blown off the great river. Quinn peered over the top as he drew closer to land, scanning for threats as much as picking where to dock.

"I wouldn't mind seein' a fat seal out here," James Perry said from the stern. Quinn glanced back to see the big Eskimo aim his spear at an imaginary target in the wake of the skiff. It was not unheard of for seals or even the occasional beluga whale to make the seventy-five-mile journey up the Yukon from the Bering Sea, as far as Mountain Village or even beyond.

At five feet long, the harpoon was relatively short, not nearly as heavy as the big ones used to catch bowhead whales. Yup'ik Eskimos rarely said they'd "shot" a moose or "killed" a whale—preferring to describe the act as "catching." A length of half-inch steel rod was fixed into the business end with a polished brass barb that toggled at the point. The barb was sharpened to a razor's edge and as big as a crooked thumb.

Ahead, eight other skiffs jockeyed for position along the muddy gravel, lining up for their turn at the wooden docks. Bowlines crossed. Aluminum gunnels banged into one another in a happy riot of mud, rain, and the beautiful catch of salmon—the lifeblood of the Yukon.

Beyond the thick stands of willows, the new airplane's engine gunned as the pilot taxied to the parking apron. Ukka stepped to the steering console beside Quinn, passing him the harpoon as he grabbed the wheel. "Better let me take over," he said. "People here like you, but they won't be so quick to let us in if a *gussak*'s drivin' the boat." His face darkened as he looked at Quinn, squinting over round cheeks. "You're armed, right?"

"Of course." Quinn let his elbow tap the Colt 1911 in the holster over his right kidney. As an agent with OSI, there had been very few times he didn't have a sidearm. Lately, as a fugitive, those times were fewer still. Opposite the pistol, a Severance hung from a Kydex sheath on his left side. It was as much a tool as it was a weapon; Quinn found uses every day for the heavy seventeen-inch blade.

Ukka leaned around the windscreen of the steering

pedestal to shout at his two daughters. Both in their teens, the girls sat on Yamaha ATVs halfway up the bank, waiting to accept the load of salmon. They were dressed in blue cotton hoodies that bore the "Strivers" mascot of their school. Their forest-green Hellys hung unbuttoned to vent the heat while they worked.

"You girls bring your Hondas down here closer to the boat," the big Eskimo said, eyes darting back toward the airstrip. Quinn had learned early on that in the Alaska bush, all ATVs were "Hondas" no matter the brand, just like every soft drink was a "Coke" in the South.

"We'll give the girls the fish," Ukka said. "They can take care of getting them weighed and recorded while I go see what's up."

Quinn hated hiding in the shadows while someone else did his dirty work. But they had planned for this—going over and over the possibilities during the long winter nights in the Perry home while they listened to Molly Hatchet on Ukka's vintage stereo system. Quinn had always known he couldn't hide out forever—and in reality, had never planned to.

Up the bank, the girls gunned their engines and began to slosh their way down the steep gravel.

Quinn stowed the harpoon along the side rail of the skiff and took several deep breaths of the chilly air to clear his head. Logic said this new aircraft was likely nothing to worry about. Unscheduled planes had sometimes landed in Mountain Village over the course of the last five months. But his gut told him this was different. And if he'd learned anything in his thirty-seven years, it was to trust his gut.

His parking spot assured, Ukka passed control of the skiff back to Quinn and then hopped off the bow into the shallows by the bank. No sooner had his feet hit the gravel than the throaty burble of a boat prop in reverse caught Quinn's attention. He turned to find a shiny new aluminum riverboat bearing down on them from upstream.

"*Gussaks,*" Ukka hissed. He gave the bow of his skiff a mighty shove, turning it outward, toward open water.

Three men crowded under a canvas cover peered out through a foggy windshield. Quinn could see at least one of them had a gun—and if one did, they all would.

Quinn kept the skiff at idle. Parallel to the bank now, it was still nearly beached. The hull crunched softly against the gravel bank, nudged by the waves.

The driver of the new boat appeared to be unaccustomed to maneuvering a boat at all, let alone working a river as large as the Yukon. He struggled in the strong current, constantly throwing the engine in and out of reverse in an attempt to bring it under control. Too far downriver on his first attempt, he gunned the motor and made a quick circle to try again.

On the banks, people stopped with fish in their hands to watch the debacle, grinning at the hapless driver's problem of simply bringing the boat to shore.

He was finally able to bring it to heel in a small eddy of slower current thirty feet out. The swinging door in the center of the walk-through cabin swung open and a middle-aged man stepped to the bow. Baggy rubber knee boots covered half his khaki slacks. A tight, muscle-mapping turtleneck showed he spent a good deal of time in the gym. The skiff's bow dipped in the water at the added forward weight and the man had to grab the brow of the canvas cover to steady himself. Dark eyes that had surely seen plenty of the world methodically scanned the crowd.

A second man, younger than the first by a decade, but dressed the same and every bit as fit, emerged behind him and stepped to the rail. This one wore a black wool watch cap snugged down over his ears. Both men carried MP7 submachine guns on slings.

The older man cleared his throat to get everyone's attention. He held the submachine gun barrel up, elbow resting against his hip, as if it might release a string of fire into the air at any moment.

"My name is Rubio." He addressed the people along the bank in a deep, pharaohlike voice. "I am here representing the government—and I'm looking for a man named Jericho Quinn."

# Chapter 2

Rubio paused, letting his words sink in. Quinn sized the men up in a heartbeat. Rubio had introduced himself not as an agent, but as a representative of the government—a contractor. Quinn had worked with many during his deployments to the Middle East. With the US involvement overseas winding down, many of these companies had come home to roost and landed lucrative private security contracts on American soil. Some were salt of the earth—former special operators who'd moved on to ply their very special skill sets in the private sector for exponentially more money than they were making wearing the uniform. But some were little more than thugs in khaki slacks and black T-shirts. Unable to cut it in their old units, they were still highly trained and capable of dishing out all manner of death and destruction, then ducking behind a convoluted corporate bureaucracy whose ethics stopped where the bottom line began.

Rubio and his men looked straight through the villagers gathered along the bank. Their fingers were far too cozy with the triggers of their weapons for Quinn's taste. Drifting now, the new boat crossed directly in front of Ukka's open skiff, less than fifteen feet away. Quinn's Apache heritage and heavy rain gear would make it difficult for them to differentiate him from the rest of the villagers at first glance.

Along the river's edge, people froze in place, nets, buckets, and even fish in their hands. All stared at the ground avoiding the question. Quinn had made many friends over the last few months, but he was also certain there were a few who would be glad to see him leave the village. Thankfully, none of those were on the bank at that moment.

"Let me be clear on this," Rubio barked. The cadence in his voice made Quinn guess he'd spent time in the military. "Hiding this man is not an option. I know he's here. Your guilty looks are enough to tell me that. Jericho Quinn is dangerous, wanted for murder."

Skiffs' bottoms scraped gravel, motors chugged, and the Yukon gurgled along, but no one on the bank said a word.

Rubio screwed up his face like he was going to spit.

Ukka started to move, but Quinn caught his eye, giving a slight shake of his head. The two had ridden motorcycles, boxed, and chased girls through junior high and high school. There was zero doubt the man would die for him.

Quinn had just made up his mind to raise his hands when Rubio spoke again.

"Listen up!" he barked, lips frozen in a dismissive sneer. "I tried to play nice. Now, I'm going to shoot one of you *muktuk*-eating sons of bitches every thirty seconds until someone digs the—"

"That's enough of that." Quinn stepped forward, hands well away from his waist.

"It's him!" the younger agent yelled—and opened fire.

Quinn dove beneath the gunnels as bullets thwacked into the aluminum steering pedestal, stitching their way up to shatter the glass windscreen. The fickle Yukon current nudged the boat sideways, just enough to keep Quinn from taking any rounds on the first volley.

Trapped between the bank and the shooters, Quinn crawled on his hands and knees toward the steering console. Bullets continued to stitch the side of the boat as he reached up and shoved the throttle all the way forward. The aluminum gunwales provided some concealment but no real cover, and he watched as dots of light appeared with each new bullet hole in thin metal. Mired in the shallows, the prop ground against a slurry of gravel and mud before Ukka gave the boat a mighty shove and pushed it away. With only Quinn and the salmon on board, the little skiff jumped forward, chewing up the distance to Rubio's boat before he or his partner could adjust their aim.

Rather than try to avoid them, Quinn held his course, bracing his shoulder against the aluminum pedestal as the bow took the other boat in a direct broadside, riding up to put Ukka's skiff nearly vertical in the water. Metal shrieked and motors roared as both props cleared the surface.

Rubio staggered to the side, arms flailing as he teetered against the forward rail. He was smart enough to let the MP7 fall against his sling, giving him both hands to hold on. Regaining his balance, Rubio launched himself over the bow and onto Ukka's skiff like a boarding pirate. He brought the machine gun up as his rubber boots hit the slanted deck just forward of the steering post.

Thrown forward by the crash, Quinn met the new arrival a half step in, surprising him with two quick shots to the chest from the .45. Rubio was wearing a vest, but the blunt force of two 230-grain slugs shattered his collarbone. He backpedaled instinctively in an attempt to get away from the pain, toppling over the bow rail into the waiting river.

The rubber boots filled instantly, dragging him along with the current. Rather than relaxing to simply remove the waterlogged boots, the man thought he was strong enough to fight against the unbeatable current of the mighty Yukon. The boots acted as a sea-anchor, towing him sideways in the swift water. A frantic gurgle caught in his throat as the Yukon tugged his head below the surface.

With Rubio no longer a threat, Quinn focused on the others in the skiff. Pistol up and ready, he chided himself for being so focused on the new airplane that he'd missed the threat right in front of him.

Welded together in a sort of twisted tee, the two boats caught the current and began to spin downriver. A great gash had opened up along the front quarter of Ukka's boat below the waterline. Gallons of brown water gushed through the ripped metal. Dead salmon bobbed in the rising brown water around Quinn's boots.

Stunned by the sudden death of his partner, the younger man regained his senses and sent a wild volley from the MP7. Quinn dove sideways, splashing to the relative safety behind a thick plastic tub full of drift net to avoid another string of fire. Frigid water rushed beneath his float coat, soaking him to the skin.

Fortunately for Quinn, the younger agent fell victim to dependency on the machine gun and used spray-and-pray tactics. Quinn, with only eight rounds, had to be more judicious and actually aim.

Peeking around the corner of the steering pedestal, he put two rounds in the youngster's left shoulder, outside the vest. He knew his shots were on target, but as he'd expected, in the heat of the fight, the kid didn't even know he was hit.

Regaining his composure after the crash, the driver of the other boat threw his motor into reverse in an effort to free it from the rapidly sinking skiff. The yank of the larger vessel sent Quinn sliding backwards in a soup of fish, fuel, and river water. His shoulder slammed hard off the unforgiving aluminum transom, knocking the .45 from his grasp. The younger agent fell directly on top of him.

Quinn was keenly aware of the MP7 wedged between them, digging into his ribs. It was sideways, for now, but the kid still had a good hold and worked feverishly to wrestle it away. The .45 was lost and useless somewhere under a foot of brown water.

On his back and nearly submerged, Quinn felt a low growl grow in his belly. Quinn gave the kid a vicious head butt. The blow brought a torrent of blood, but failed to get him to release the grip on the gun. Fear and adrenaline caused the kid to kick into high gear, flinging himself into the fight. The head butt was no more than a stunning injury, but soon he'd feel the effects of blood loss from the bullet wounds in his shoulder. His face just inches above the water, Quinn wondered if it would be soon enough.

Quinn's legs trapped the young contractor's body against his, heels hooked behind the small of the young man's back. Snaking his left arm through the MP7's sling, he jerked the kid in close. It constricted his movements, but wasn't quite enough for a proper choke.

Rising water lapped at Quinn's ears, and he had to crane his neck to stay above the surface. In a matter of seconds, the river would be above his face and do the kid's work for him.

Quinn held what he had while his right hand searched desperately under the surface, shoving aside dead salmon and coils of gill net. The Severance was on his left side, useless for the moment. Now with just his nose above the water, his fingers wrapped around the wooden shaft of the harpoon just as the silhouette of the boat driver appeared on the bow above the younger shooter. Backlit by the gray clouds, he loomed above for a split second, MP7 in his hands. The man shouted something but water lapped around Quinn's ears, making it impossible for him to make out the words.

Quinn was vaguely aware of pistol shots, and at first thought the boat driver may have shot directly through his partner. Instead, the man toppled over the side and into the river.

*Way to go, Ukka*, Quinn thought. Bucking his body upward to create the needed space, he drove the point of the harpoon through the young contractor's ribs.

The kid's eyes flew wide as he tried to make sense of what was going on. Blood covered his teeth by the time Quinn had swiped the MP7 out of the way and dragged him sloshing onto the bow of the other boat. His rattling wheeze said the shaft of the spear had gone through the vest and pierced a lung. Quinn used his hand to try to seal the foaming wound as best he could. The bullet wounds on the opposite shoulder were not life threatening in and of themselves, but taken together, shock and additional loss of blood only sped up the inevitable brought on by the harpoon.

"What's your name?" Quinn asked, cradling the young man in his lap.

"Lane . . ." The kid said, choking on his own words.

He looked up, blinking terrified eyes. "We came to kill you . . . and you're trying to save me?"

"You're too far gone to save." Quinn gave a slow shake of his head. "But I'll sit here with you while you die."

"Thank you . . ." His face tensed at a sudden shot of pain. Tears welled in his eyes. Quinn had seen many men die and often thought how they looked like little boys the nearer they got to that moment.

Lane's pulse grew faster as he fell deeper into shock. More blood oozed from the wound around the shaft of the harpoon. Quinn leaned in so the kid could hear and understand him. "How many on the plane?"

Lane swallowed. He didn't have long. "Five, counting the pilot, I think. . . ." His body began to shake uncontrollably. "They're . . . picking us up." A wave of pain brought on a twisted grimace. His words came in short, panting breaths. "This . . . is so . . . wrong. . . ." The boy gave a rattling cough, and then fell slack in Quinn's arms. Pale blue eyes stared up blankly at the mist.

Ukka had commandeered his cousin's battered skiff and now motored up alongside the two wrecked boats. He sat on an ice chest at the stern, working the tiller to keep the boat steady in the current. Quinn pulled the earpiece out of the dead kid's ear and took the radio off his belt. He grabbed the MP7, checked the chamber, and then slung it around his neck.

Ukka held up his hand. "Don't forget the harpoon. It was my grandfather's."

Quinn looked back over his shoulder at the dead contractor. "The barb's going to make it tough to pull out."

"He can keep that for his trouble," Ukka said, frowning. These men had attacked his village and he felt no sorrow for them. "It comes off anyhow. I can make a new one." Quinn gave the harpoon a quick yank, freeing it from the body, and hopped over the gunwale and onto the deck of Ukka's new ride.

The big Eskimo threw the boat in reverse, and then turned to take it upstream, free of the drifting wreckage of the other two vessels. "You know the plane that just landed is full of another hit team," he said, once Quinn was on board.

"No doubt," Quinn said. "The kid told me five more."

Ukka's lower jaw pushed forward and stayed there, the way it did when he was angry. "We need to haul ass up to the village. That first bunch didn't care much who they shot—and my family is back there."

"I appreciate your help." Quinn nodded, shaking his head. "Seriously, James, I am sorry about bringing these guys down on your family."

Ukka pushed the throttle forward, bringing the boat up on step. He pointed it toward the bank a half a mile downriver, well below the fish processing plant where they would be closer to his house. "I ever tell you about the time I left my good friend out to die on the tundra?" He raised his voice to be heard over the drone of the motor.

"No," Quinn answered. "I have to admit, you've skipped that story."

"That's because I don't do stuff like that." Ukka twisted the throttle and laid on the gas.

Inside the pocket of Quinn's float coat, safely wrapped in a plastic Baggie and barely audible above the sounds of wind, water, and the outboard engine, his phone began to chirp.

Far from anything close to a "smart phone," the little Hershey Bar–size device was a prepaid "burner." It was difficult, but not entirely impossible, to trace, given the right set of circumstances. In the five months since he'd had the phone, Quinn had received a grand total of three incoming calls. Considering the fact that men were trying to kill him at that very moment, the timing of this fourth call was no coincidence.

# Chapter 3

*Las Vegas, Nevada*
*McCarran International Airport*

Tang Dalu stood outside the security zone and watched his wife work her way toward security screening with the snaking queue of passengers. The Chinese man was thirty-nine years old and dressed for travel in gray cotton slacks and a short-sleeve white button-up shirt. He was short enough that he had to stand on tiptoe in order to keep an eye on his wife. Her name was Lin. They had been married for eleven years—long enough for him to know, even from nearly a hundred feet away, that she was crying.

Hers was a silent, anguished cry, manifested only by glistening red eyes that seemed ever on the verge of tears—and the periodic shudder of frail shoulders.

Tang had wept too, in the beginning, great choking sobs that wracked his chest and threatened to detach his lungs from his throat.

He could not eat. He could not sleep. He could not bring himself to touch his wife. The sadness was too much to bear. At first, he'd thought he might die. Then he'd watched the light vanish from his wife's wide brown eyes and he feared he might have to live forever to witness her despair. She'd depended on him, on his position—and he had let her down.

Allah, it turned out, was not nearly as merciful as he had once supposed.

Only the man from Pakistan had saved him. Lin had never been devout, but she had listened to the man's message and he had saved her as well. In her misery she did not seem to care.

Tang craned his head as he watched her move to the front of the line. He could feel his jaw tighten as a TSA agent ordered her forward with a dismissive flick of his fingers. All around her other agents barked orders at passengers to remove their shoes and empty their pockets. *Keep it moving, slow down, stop right there, step forward, quickly, slower, this not that.*

*Do it my way.*

Bewildered or just plain numb, passengers plodded along like sheep. If they wished to fly there was no alternative but to submit to the will of the officious security agents who squawked and scolded like so many angry blue jays, steadfast in their own moral superiority. Such power always brought oppression—and under oppression the weak had no choice but to give in to despair or fight back. The man from Pakistan had taught him that.

Though Tang had been born to Hui Chinese parents and raised under the tenets of Islam, he had never heard of Ramzi Yousef. The man from Pakistan had explained that in 1994 Yousef had smuggled nitroglycerin and other components on board a Philippines Airline flight from Manila to Tokyo. Using a simple Casio watch as his timer, he'd assembled his bomb in the bathroom while in flight. He'd placed the bomb under a seat in the life vest compartment and then gotten off the plane in Cebu. The device had exploded on the way to Tokyo, blowing a Japanese sewing machine maker in half and ripping a hole in the floor. Security technology had progressed since then, but as the man from Pakistan explained, so had the technology of making bombs.

Tang felt the knot in his stomach grow as Lin put her camera bag on the X-ray conveyor. To her right, in an adjacent line, a red-faced passenger began to argue with his TSA overlord about a water bottle filled with vodka.

Most of the security staff on scene converged around the sputtering drunk, leaving Lin to pass through the scanners without a hitch. Relief washed over Tang as she retrieved her camera bag from the belt on the other side of the X-ray. She turned to wave, a hollow look of resignation weighing heavily on her sallow face.

The detonator was in.

# Chapter 4

*Alaska*

Quinn pressed the phone tight against his ear, straining to hear over the wind and roaring motor.

"Hello," he shouted.

"'Mariposa' hasn't called in." The caller started right in without introduction—par for Quinn's former boss, even though he hadn't spoken a word to the man in two months. There was a tense note of despair in the man's voice that Quinn had never heard before.

It was Winfield Palmer, national security advisor to the recently assassinated president, Chris Clark. A West Point alumni and confidante of Clark, Palmer had served with him in various posts from their military academy days, including director of national security and then national security advisor. As such, he'd recruited Quinn as a blunt instrument, a sort of hammer to be employed when more diplomatic or traditional means failed.

Now, under the new administration, Palmer was unemployed and followed everywhere he went.

Living under constant surveillance, he had resorted

to layers of security with his communication—proxy servers, shadow e-mail accounts, remote log-in to computers located in various safe-sites around the world, burner phones—and, of course, code. *Mariposa*, the Spanish word for *butterfly*, was the code name he'd chosen for Emiko Miyagi, Quinn's martial arts instructor and friend. The name signified something beautiful and delicate. Miyagi was one, but certainly not the other.

"How long has it been?" Quinn asked.

"Five days," Palmer said, uncharacteristically silent.

Both Quinn and Palmer knew Miyagi was 115 pounds of highly skilled badass warrior woman. Quinn, a more than talented fighter himself, had tasted defeat at her hands each and every time they had sparred. If she hadn't made contact in five days, she was in serious trouble.

"Maybe she's close to something?" Quinn offered.

"Maybe," Palmer said, hollow, unconvinced. "She gave me a name last time we spoke. I have 'Sonja' looking into it now."

"That's good," Quinn said, nodding to himself. "She still has resources." "Sonja" was Palmer's code name for CIA agent Veronica "Ronnie" Garcia. Apart from hair color, the buxom, sword-wielding fantasy heroine Red Sonja was a perfect ringer for Garcia—who also happened to be Quinn's girlfriend. At least she had been, before he'd dropped off the grid. Quinn was smart enough to know that girlfriends needed care and feeding—and he'd been around to do neither for nearly half a year.

"Maybe she can get us something to go on," Palmer said. "I don't mind telling you, though, I'm worried."

Behind Quinn in the boat, Ukka shouted from his position at the tiller. "Nearly there!"

Quinn gave the Eskimo a thumbs-up to show he understood, and then turned back to the phone. "Listen, I've got to go. Things are heating up out here."

"Anything that I can do?" Palmer said, more out of habit from the old days than any ability to actually help. Even with his little ad hoc resistance movement, as a private citizen in suburban Virginia, there was nothing he could offer Quinn in Alaska beyond good wishes.

"No," Quinn said, careful to not to use military trigger words like *negative* and *affirmative* that might trigger closer scrutiny from the NSA. "Looks like I'm burned, though. They've sent what looks to be contractors."

"Contractors?" Palmer said. "That's not good."

"Yeah, well," Quinn said, "they're three down from when they started. Watch yourself. Looks like the gloves are off." Quinn ended the call. He made certain the phone was on silent—a ringtone at the wrong moment could get him killed.

Twenty meters away, Ukka took the skiff out into the current to make a wide turn back toward the bank. The white crosses in the cemetery on Azochorak Hill ghosted in and out of the fog above them. They were coming in downriver, about a quarter mile from the village proper. Quinn traded his float coat for a more neutrally colored Helly Hansen raincoat he'd found in the borrowed skiff. The jacket was tattered and stunk of fish and mildew, but its olive green would be far less noticeable against scrub willow or even the open tundra. He slung the MP7 over his shoulder and stuffed the cell phone and the dead man's radio in the pockets of the raincoat. He stood at the rail, ready to jump and run as soon as the bow touched gravel.

\* \* \*

Cut, broken, and bruised to the point he could barely walk, let alone run, Quinn had come to Mountain Village one step ahead of US authorities. The marshals had taken him off their Top Fifteen wanted list for all of about ten minutes, until someone in the new presidential administration had caught wind of it and insisted he be made a priority. Thankfully, a deputy named August Bowen, an acquaintance of his from his boxing career at the Air Force Academy, had been assigned the case. Bowen had been in Japan and knew much of the truth about Quinn, so he dragged his feet as best he could. Still, Top Fifteens were worked by many hands. Quinn had to keep his wits about him to keep from getting captured—which under the present administration would surely mean a speedy trial and quick backroom execution.

He'd made too big a splash in Japan to stay there, leaving a wide and lengthy trail of bodies in his wake while looking for the assassins responsible for shooting his ex-wife. Even with friends in Japanese law enforcement, security footage of his face had already made it onto every news feed and blog in Asia, branding him the murderer from the US who typified the Japanese view of American bloodlust and gun craziness.

It killed him that he was too banged up to follow leads to Pakistan. He'd lived much of his life gutting it out through the pain. But this time was different. Miyagi took him to a doctor in Japan who asked few questions and patched him up well enough to travel. When Quinn argued or tried to do too much, she reminded him that "though a concentrated mind could pierce a stone, it was a long process."

Fellow OGA "Gunny" Jacques Thibodaux pointed

out the reality that "that which does not kill us makes us weaker for the next thing that tries to kill us."

Quinn had needed a place to hide out, to heal from the many wounds he'd gotten in Japan—both physical and mental. His friends in the tiny Yup'ik Eskimo settlement of Mountain Village provided exactly what he'd needed.

He'd made the long trip by oceangoing car hauler from Tokyo to Seattle, just one step ahead of Interpol. A barge going up the inside passage had taken him to Anchorage, where he'd caught an Era flight to the bush. He'd not chanced seeing his parents or his daughter, or going to any of his old haunts. They were all certainly being watched.

Once he arrived in Mountain Village, Ukka's wife and mother-in-law had tended to his wounds with traditional herbs as well as antibiotics they got from the clinic and school by feigning illness themselves. Of course, nothing went on without everyone eventually finding out in a close community like Mountain Village, called simply "Mountain" by locals. Soon, the entire village became accessories to the crime of harboring a fugitive. Few knew what he was wanted for, or his real name, but they knew he was wanted by the United States government, and that alone was enough of a reason for most to hide him.

Ukka threw the skiff into reverse just before they scraped gravel. Quinn hopped to a clump of willows, using them to keep his feet on the slippery mud and vegetation along the eroding cut bank. Gnarled limbs and bits of wood from upstream littered the area from the recent "breakup" when thousands of tons of ice melted enough to crack and give way ahead of the pressure of meltwater building upstream. Great, frozen slabs scoured the riverbed as they were shoved downstream by the tremendous pressure that built up behind them.

"Ukka," Quinn sighed as he watched his friend jump to the bank beside him. "I'll never be able to repay you for—"

"So help me, Jericho"—the Eskimo shook his head—"you're gonna make me cry. And if I start crying, the next thing you know, I'll be picking berries and cutting fish with the women."

The Eskimo's cell phone played the snippet of "Old Time Rock and Roll" that he used as a ringtone. He dug it out of his float coat.

"This is James," he said.

He listened intently while Quinn scanned the hillside above them. Quinn switched on the dead contractor's radio and stuffed the earpiece in his ear. He was tempted to say something cavalier, but thought it better to keep the new crew guessing as to what had happened to their river-based compatriots.

Ukka's face went white and he ended the call.

"That was my neighbor," he said. "Two of those bastards are heading for my house."

# Chapter 5

*Langley, Virginia*
*George Bush Center for Intelligence*

Veronica "Ronnie" Garcia looked away from the image on her computer and rubbed her eyes with a thumb and forefinger. A leaning tower of manila folders that she should have been analyzing sat precariously close to the edge of her desk. Each was striped and marked according to their classification level. She nibbled on the lipstick-stained straw sticking out of her cup of Diet Dr Pepper, taking a moment from the tedium of scanning the monitor for the last three hours.

Sliding down to let thick, ebony hair fall over the back of her chair, Garcia looked around her cubicle. Apart from the purple stapler and a Far Side calendar, the only other decoration was a photo of her with Jericho tacked to the door of the overhead cabinet. It was early in their relationship, on a trip to Virginia Beach they somehow had been able to wedge between missions. Her canary yellow swimsuit accentuated long legs and a multitude of curves. The color was a perfect complement to her rich, coffee-and-cream complexion. Jericho wore blue bathing trunks and a rare smile, big enough to show his teeth.

Garcia's chair creaked as she leaned forward to touch the photo with the tip of a red fingernail, tracing the lines of Quinn's bare chest and the many scars that mapped his body. She thought of something her Russian father used to say—"The way a man fights is the way he does everything else"—and that made her miss Jericho all the more. She kissed her finger, and then pressed it to Quinn's bearded face. If they ever did have kids, the poor things were doomed to being hairy gorillas. Of course, you had to be in the same time zone to conceive a child, so even if they'd considered such a thing, the notion of it was as far as they would get.

For all practical purposes, she was alone in the bullpen. The girl that sat in the cubicle to her right had already gone home for the day, and Nathan, the tall, blond drink of water who occupied the stall to her left was off picking up copies at the communal printer, which happened to be next to the desk of the tiny brunette who was his latest conquest. He would be gone awhile.

Garcia took another quick sip of her Dr Pepper, and then turned back to the computer monitor. Resting an elbow on her desk, she began to scan the screen again while she pondered how odd it was that an intelligence agency that was so steeped in secrecy and compartmentalization would have a communal printer. Government cutbacks bordered on the bizarre. There were so many things about the present administration that were absurd. The new president had clamped down on everything and everyone with all the paranoid efficiency of communist East Germany. Garcia herself had been given the names of five people in the agency on whom she was to provide "vetting overwatch." She was certain *her* name was on at least two other agents' lists. Overzealous, even heavy-handed government employees were rewarded rather than constrained. Jericho Quinn and anyone else who'd ever stood in the way of the new administration were being hunted down, or, as in Ronnie Garcia's case, sidelined to a life of busywork.

Citizens followed like sheep because President Hartman Drake, a victim of a terrorist attack himself if you believed the papers, gave them what they wanted—free health care; snarky, populist sound bites; and the drumbeat of war with anyone who dared cross American policies.

But not everyone marched in lockstep. A sizable underground had sprung up in the aftermath of President Clark's death. Quinn, Garcia, and others who had worked directly for the former president's national security advisor, Win Palmer, knew the incoming administration was behind the assassination of Clark and the Vice President. There was just no way to prove it, yet.

Garcia clicked her mouse, switching screens. Her breath caught in her throat when the image loaded. She looked away, blinking to clear her eyes, then back to check again.

It was highly pixilated from being enlarged several times over, but it was definitely the needle in the digital haystack she'd been searching for. Dr. Naseer Badeeb, the mastermind of a plan to bomb the wedding of the former vice president's daughter, stood chatting with a man with a heavy black beard. But neither of these men were the most important find. Garcia clicked her mouse, enlarging the photo as much as she could without losing it completely. It was impossible to prove without enhancing the image, but Garcia was certain the young man standing behind Badeeb was Hartman

Drake—the President of the United States. He was younger, in his early teens, but there was no mistaking the condescending sneer and vaporous look in the boy's eyes.

"Way to go, Miyagi," she whispered, full lips trembling slightly as they formed the words. In the right hands, the photo could finally be something—something that could end this mess and bring Jericho home.

Lost in thought over how to proceed, Garcia nearly jumped out of her skin when her group supervisor walked up behind her and cleared his throat.

"Thought we agreed you wouldn't put that up until I went home for the night." Bobby Jeffery nodded toward the photo of Garcia and Quinn standing in the surf at Virginia Beach.

"So apparently," Ronnie sighed, "keeping a picture of one of America's most wanted fugitives is against CIA office policy."

"Apparently," Jeffery said. "Not to mention I have to keep all the straight guys in the office from trying to get a snapshot with their cell phone of you in your yellow string bikini."

"It's not a bikini," Garcia scoffed.

"Well, give the guys here five minutes with Photoshop and it'll be less than that."

Garcia put the photo in her lap drawer and spun in her chair to face her boss. She wanted to get rid of the image on her way around but decided it would look too guilty. She left it up, as if it was routine.

"I appreciate it," Jeffery said in his easy Georgia twang. If voices could grin, his did. As far as bosses went, he was likeable enough—a little aloof, but Garcia knew she shared that same quality.

He stood at the opening to her cubicle, his conservative striped tie hanging like a crooked noose around an unbuttoned collar. He was only a few years older than she was, but the way he kept his wireframe glasses low on his nose gave him the look of a favorite uncle.

"You okay?" he asked.

"I'm fine," Garcia said, gathering her wits. She forced herself not to shoot a look toward her computer screen. An image of the sitting president associating with a known terrorist was enough to put any good CIA agent on the guilty edge. "What's up?"

"I'm not sure," Jeffery said. "But something, that's for sure. I just got a priority call from our friends over at Fort Meade." He gave a noncommittal shrug, but his eyes stayed locked on her. "Some ID guy wants to have a chat with you."

Garcia forced a smile.

"They asked for me by name?"

Jeffery nodded. "Afraid so."

Stationed at Fort Meade in the offices of the National Security Agency, the Internal Defense Task Force was a government bureau formed by the new administration to root out moles and terrorists inside the government. Considering the assassination of the two top leaders in the nation under the very noses of the FBI and Homeland Security, this expansion of government was an easy sell to the American public.

Of course, Garcia could see the irony in the formation of such a unit by the President, who was now the highest-ranking mole in the government.

Other intelligence and enforcement agencies spoke of IDTF in hushed tones, if they spoke of them at all. Like the devil, if you admitted their existence, ID agents seemed to appear out of nowhere. Garcia wasn't alone in thinking of them as vicious Orwellian dogs from *Animal Farm*—with President Drake as Napoleon.

Much like Winfield Palmer had organized his team

using OGAs or Other Governmental Agents, the IDTF had handpicked its operatives from the NSA, CIA, and FBI, choosing, it seemed, those most bent on getting ahead in their careers at all cost.

Though rank-and-file citizens believed something with the innocuous name of Internal Defense Task Force was akin to a government Internal Affairs, that job fell to various OIGs or Offices of Inspector General. In reality, the IDTF was more like an American version of the Stasi, who had considered themselves the "Shield and Sword" of East Germany. Even agents within both the ultrasecret NSA and CIA saved a particular reverence toward those in the IDTF.

Ronnie remembered a CIA instructor at Camp Peary pointing out that in their heyday, the KGB had employed 1 agent for roughly every 5,800 Soviet citizens. The Nazis had 1 Gestapo operative for every 2,000 citizens in countries they controlled. But, using full and part-time operatives, the Stasi had 1 agent for every 6 East Germans.

The IDTF's organizational chart was classified, but they and the administration that created them were both in their infancy, so she assumed the new bureau was yet in the middle of empire building. It would not be long before they were up and running at full strength. There were plenty of people in government willing to stomp others to a bloody pulp in order to get ahead, as well as those who just enjoyed seeing other people squirm. Recruitment wouldn't be all that difficult.

Jeffery put a hand on the small of his back and arched, looked up at the ceiling to stretch. "Listen," he said, "these guys are as much about witch hunts as anything. You have to watch what you say. Understand."

She shrugged. "Okay."

"Anything you want to tell me about?"

"Nothing I can think of," Garcia lied. "Probably just another routine bunch of questions about my old boyfriend."

She nodded toward the lap drawer where she'd put Jericho's photo and then kicked back in her chair, trying to look relaxed. Inside, her gut was doing backflips. She'd taken an endless number of precautions, but obviously that was not enough. With offices at NSA and who knew how many agents on the CIA payroll, the IDTF had fingers in everyone's pie.

They might not yet be as well staffed as the dreaded East German Shield and Sword, but at least one of them had focused on Garcia. Considering what she was a part of, any sort of scrutiny would be a bad thing indeed.

# Chapter 6

Former Oregon governor Lee McKeon used the back of a slender hand to rub the skin of his furrowed brow. He ignored the quizzical looks from David Crosby, the President's disheveled chief of staff. The Veep was being vocal at yet another meeting in the Situation Room. No surprise there, considering nothing would ever get accomplished if it were otherwise. POTUS ran meetings in the Cement Mixer—but this particular POTUS had had a difficult first five months negotiating the pitfalls and intricacies of his new job.

President Hartman Drake was a fireplug of a man, barely five-seven, but broad shouldered and narrow hipped. He never missed an opportunity to take off his suit jacket to display thick arms that bulged against a starched white shirt. He had full hair and an easy smile that endeared him to voters of both genders, but especially the women. He'd used bow-tie bluster and sex appeal to bluff his way through Congress—but that was the bush league. McKeon saw he needed a considerable amount of help not to destroy everything they'd worked for now that a series of highly choreographed events had made him commander in chief.

The worst part was that Drake was completely numb to the fact that he was doing such a poor job.

McKeon hadn't thought being vice president would be so agonizingly difficult to stomach. He stood over six and a half feet tall with a gaunt face, narrow shoulders, and a bony, knock-kneed build. Though his name was Scottish in origin, his face held the dark complexion and East Indian features of someone from the subcontinent. Amber eyes narrowed with a hint of the almond shape of his Chinese birth mother. A self-proclaimed Chindian, he introduced himself as someone of Chinese and Indian descent. The world knew him to be adopted by a wealthy couple from Portland. According to his birth certificate, he'd been born in Salem, Oregon, in the good old US of A. His tall and gangly appearance brought a picture of Abraham Lincoln to the minds of the voters. He was willing to court wealthy donors and spout populist sentiment, but more than that, he possessed a certain magnetism, a soothing way that drew people to him and made them feel as if he had nothing but their best interest at heart. It had taken him to the governor's mansion the year of his fortieth birthday.

He'd needed a little more help to become the vice president—as had the new commander in chief. But his father—the real one, not Old Man McKeon—had paved the way for that to happen long before Lee McKeon was ever born—while he was still known as Raza Badeeb.

Dr. Naseer Badeeb had been placing children from his orphanage in the remote Wakhan Corridor of Afghanistan into American families for two decades. These children, well indoctrinated to hate America for the beast that it was, grew up in quiet suburban homes, went to school, got married, and moved up in society. The children always went to extraordinary families who saw to it they received outstanding educations. Many rose to the highest levels of government. The doctor was no longer around to enjoy the success of his labor, but he'd known intuitively how to prepare things so they would come to fruition later. McKeon had once heard his father say that the best time to plant a tree was twenty years ago. It broke his heart that he'd never really gotten to know the man. But that only doubled his resolve to carry on his father's legacy.

"What are my options?" the President asked, kicking back at the head of the long table and gazing at the myriad of television screens on the walls as if he was watching the Super Bowl instead of attending a high-level intelligence briefing from his National Security Council. Known as the NSC, these advisors included the Joint Chiefs, the secretaries of defense, state, and treasury, the director of national intelligence, and the national security advisor. All were men, all white, and all, but for the Secretary of Defense Andrew Filson, were brand-new appointees. A new man sat quietly in one of the royal blue high-back chairs along the wall. Only McKeon and the President even knew who he was.

Secretary Filson sat to the President's immediate left, across the oak table from McKeon. He was a pinch-faced man who glared at his cup as if he was angry at the coffee.

"You know my views, Mr. President," Filson said. Usually a man to bounce around the room when he spoke, the Secretary of Defense stayed glued to his seat, as if he was afraid someone might steal it if he got up. "I say we waterboard the shit out of them until they tell us what we want to know."

Drake nodded thoughtfully, like that might actually be something he'd consider with so many eyes and ears in the room. The depth of this man's stupidity made McKeon's head hurt. The Hell's Angels' adage "Two can keep a secret—if one of them is dead" held doubly true amid the vaporous political alliances of the White House. Security precautions only lasted as far as the door. In a place where leaked insider information was the coin of the realm that lead to multimillion-dollar book deals, the President's body language, let alone his spoken word, was a potential land mine.

"The Pakistanis want them back," Air Force three-star Greg Tolliver spoke up, stepping in front of Filson's proposal with one almost as outlandish.

"That would make trouble for me diplomatically," Tom Watchel, the Secretary of State, said. He rested the flat of his hands on a black leather desk blotter in front of him.

The President laughed out loud. "And that's why we're having this meeting, Tom," he said. "So we can all be certain and shield *you* from diplomatic damage."

The Sec State appeared to shrink in his chair. "Of course I meant us, Mr. President. We, I mean to say, the United States would be damaged. These men blew up a train in . . ." He shuffled thorough a file folder in front of him, hunting for a particular note.

"Urumqi." McKeon helped him, feeling impatience more than pity. For a Secretary of State, this man was sorely undereducated in world geography. "The train was leaving the northwestern Chinese city of Urumqi."

"Yes, of course." Watchel nodded. "Urumqi." He closed his folder. "Beijing demands to put them on trial for terrorism."

"What do I tell the Pakistanis?" Drake asked. "These

guys blew up a . . . what, some kind of a store there, right?"

McKeon blinked away the look of frustration on his face. "It was a café, Mr. President."

Drake gave a flip of his hand. "That's right. Anyway, the point is, Pakistan wants them for trial too. And their bombing was first."

"That's true," the Sec State said. "But the café was closed when it blew up so no one was killed."

"But the building was destroyed?" Drake said.

"Yes, sir."

"Well." Drake put both hands behind his head and leaned back in his chair, staring up at the acoustic ceiling. "Seems to me it would be a step in the right direction if Pakistan actually put a terrorist on trial."

Watchel nodded. "It would," he said. "But—"

Filson pounded his fist on the table, sending a little coffee tsunami over the lip of his mug. "We should not be in the habit of turning over terrorists to anyone. These men have a great deal of valuable information rolling around in their heads."

"Mr. President." Watchel made a last-ditch effort to bolster his case. "China is in a . . . how do I put this . . . in a bit of a spot at the moment. Chen Min is a very unique leader."

Drake cocked an eyebrow. "Don't forget," he said. "If you're one in a million in China, there are only three thousand more just like you."

McKeon groaned inside himself.

"Mr. President," General Tolliver said. "There is no doubt that the Chinese, specifically Chen Min, will view it as a slap in the face if we turn the prisoners over to Pakistan. But Pakistan will feel the same way if we give them to China. The question is, who do we need right now?"

"Let me see," Drake said, screwing up his face in thought. "Do I piss off a son of a bitch Chinaman who'd like to eat our guts, or the Pakistanis, who, at least in lip service, are our allies?"

"With all due respect, Mr. President," Secretary Watchel said. "Chen Min does not appear to be a rash man. He leads at a time when the Chinese are swollen with nationalistic tension. If we were to turn these men over to anyone other than China, Chen Min might have no other choice than to step up his rhetoric."

The President pushed back from the table and got to his feet, forcing everyone else in the room to stand out of protocol.

"Listen," he said, looking at the line of digital world clocks that ran along the far wall. "I have to shoehorn in a meeting in the Oval Office before I get my ass to the gym. It's leg day," he added. "And a guy can't miss leg day. I'll leave the rhetoric to you, Tom. I have to be honest, though, the Pakistanis seem to have more value in this fight than the Chinese. Work me up a brief of possible outcomes if I decide to hand the prisoners over to President Kassar."

McKeon smiled inside himself. Despite Drake's stupidity, things were working out just as his father had imagined.

# Chapter 7

*Alaska*

Knee-high beach grass rose up from the muddy bank. It grew quickly in the short Arctic summers and covered the hillside above the Yukon. Village women used the stuff to weave decorative baskets during the long winter nights and the sweet, wet-hay scent was prevalent in every home that had a basket maker. Quinn breathed in a lungful as he sprinted up the hill.

Rather than hiding, he had always found it more tactical to fight through the objective. Quinn's father was not much of a talker. The senior Quinn had expressed the notion most succinctly when he'd sat Jericho down at the kitchen table before his first deployment to the Middle East. "Attack back, son," his old man had said, dispensing serious counsel. "If you think you're going to be captured, fight your way through it. I'd rather you die in that initial assault than find yourself in the hands of this enemy."

Quinn knew then, and certainly learned later, that it was sound advice. And it still held true with men like the ones who'd come for him in Mountain Village. No badges, no agency authority, they had no intention of arresting him. These men had demonstrated that when they shot into a crowd of Eskimo families just to get him. These were contractors sent in with one mission, to kill Quinn and take back proof of his death.

Quinn tucked the MP7 he'd taken from the dead contractor tight against his side and dove into the willows, running for Ukka's house, nearly half a mile away.

Ken Proctor shoved the slender Eskimo woman across the room to his partner, a stocky little Italian pug everyone called Fico.

"Take care of Mama," Proctor snapped. He grabbed the woman's teenage daughter by her black hair and wound it around his fist, dragging her backwards to the front door.

The terrified girl's entire body shook so badly her teeth chattered. "Mom?" she whimpered.

"It's all right, Kaylee girl," James Perry's wife said. Her voice was tight, but under control. "Daddy and Jericho will be here soon. They'll take care of these guys, no problem."

Fico gave her a backhand across the face, splitting her lower lip. Blood poured down the front of her shirt.

She glared back at him.

"Oh, that's just precious," the broad-faced Italian said. "You're all angry at me now. Don't go giving your little girl hope." He leaned in and ran his tongue up the side of her cheek, then raised an eyebrow as if passing judgment on how she tasted. "Seems I read somewheres that your Eskimo men liked to loan out their women to visitors." His lips pulled back into a cruel snarl and he prodded her with the barrel of his pistol. "Well, I'm a visitor, ain't I? How about you show me a little of that northern hospitality I read about?"

"I don't really think you can read." Christina Perry wagged her head, eyes narrowed in defiance.

"Maybe you'd rather loan me your daughter."

She spat in his face, earning her another punch. This one broke her glasses, gashing her nose in the process. She didn't make a sound. Instead, she turned to wipe her face against her shoulder, leaving a bright swath of blood across the cloth of her *kuspuk*.

She sat perfectly still, panting, trying to make sense of what was happening around her—and then Proctor ran a hand down Kaylee's thigh. Eyes flying wild, Christina jerked away from Fico and sprang toward the door.

"You are a dead man!"

Proctor released the girl and smashed Christina in the side of her head with his pistol, knocking her back onto the couch. Fico gave her another cuff across the ear for good measure, but it was a useless blow. She was already unconscious.

"Someone needs to teach these bitches a lesson on how to treat a man," Fico said, rubbing the back of his hand where it had impacted with her jaw.

Proctor tossed his head in disgust at his partner's inability to control a prisoner. He was frankly not surprised. The Italian hothead was just the sort of man his boss was looking for—if they could only control him. He was recruited in Kosovo after he'd been fired from another security job, and found a new home with The Oryx Group. It was a private contractor firm specializing in gray-area heavy work in the rough edges of the world.

Ken Proctor's Special Forces training—if you left out the part about him getting booted for insubordination—made him a natural for Oryx. Fico's coarse demeanor and general distaste for anyone who didn't think exactly like he did made it seem like he would be a good attack dog—until his emotions got in the way. Proctor reported the erratic behavior to his superiors after Fico's hatred of all things female had nearly cost them their last mission in West Africa. The boss pointed out that Oryx was the perfect place for misogynistic killers, reminding Proctor that if they were all well-adjusted family men, they'd be fighting for God and country instead of the almighty dollar. The problem of Fico was shoved back to him as team leader.

Proctor gave the Eskimo girl's hair a cruel yank, taking out his frustration and trying to put Fico's ineptness out of his mind.

"You must be losing it," he said to his partner. "What do you think she weighs? A buck ten soaking wet? Just keep her quiet until we get Quinn, then you can teach her whatever lessons you want."

Fico ran a hand over the unconscious woman's knee.

"Get on with it then," he said. "We'll be just fine here. I'll see to this one."

Proctor got a better grasp on the quivering Kaylee's hair and dragged her backwards through the front door. Once outside, he stood on the raised porch and pulled the girl in close so she was in front of him. Quinn's dossier said he'd been a special operator, but that was with the Air Force so there was nothing to worry about. He'd probably get a call on the radio any minute that the guys down at the river had taken care of things. Still, Proctor took the precaution of using the quaking girl as a human shield.

There were two snowmobiles and two pickup trucks in front of the house, but anyone approaching would have to cross fifty meters of open ground before they made it to the vehicles.

Proctor switched on the voice-activated mike clipped

to his collar, then pressed the barrel of his pistol to the back of the girl's head. He hauled her neck back so she had to look up at the sky. Her sobs grew so violent her entire body shook and he found himself holding most of her weight just to keep her on her feet. Proctor groaned inside himself. He'd been a soldier once. How in the world had it come to pulling girls' hair?

"Shut up!" He yanked her head from side to side, taking his frustration out on her.

"Van, Perkins," he said, tilting his head enough the mike would pick him up over the stupid girl's bawling. "Haul ass down to the river and find out what happened. Watch yourselves. I'm sure every house in this shithole town has a gun in it."

"We're at the river now," Perkins came back. "It's—"

Someone else spoke, causing nothing but a garbled squelch to come across the radio.

"You two stop talking at the same time," Proctor said. "You're stepping on each other."

"Wasn't Van," Perkins came back. "He's standing right beside me."

"It was me," another voice carried across the radio, low and slow.

"Quinn?" Proctor pulled the girl closer as insurance. His head snapped around as he scanned the area in front of the house.

"I borrowed Lane's radio," the voice said. "He was finished with it."

"Van . . . Perkins . . ." Proctor clenched his teeth. "You two double-time it back here."

"Too late for that," the voice said. "I'm here . . . *now.*"

"Listen, you son of a bitch," Proctor spat. He yanked

the girl backwards so her entire body arched. "You show yourself or I'll—"

Kaylee threw her legs out from under her, letting her dead weight yank her out of Proctor's grasp, completely exposing him to Quinn's shots. The first round hit him just below the nose, the second, above his left ear as he began the corkscrewing fall peculiar to those who are already dead on their feet.

"I know," Quinn whispered to himself, mimicking Proctor's cadence. "'Show yourself or you'll kill the girl. . . .'" He surveyed the scene for a ten-count before rolling out from under the rusted pickup nearest the house.

Eyes on the front door, he bounded up the steps to put an arm around Kaylee and shoo her quickly off the front porch.

Like any good cop, Ukka was diligent about practicing hostage drills with his family. His wife and each of his children knew that when they heard the word *now*, they should do their best to drop out of the way and give any rescuer the best possible shot. Kaylee had been a little late on the uptake, but the training and role-play had paid off. When she did move, Quinn had been ready to carry out his part of the bargain.

"Your mom?" he whispered, squeezing the girl's shoulder, but watching the house.

"That guy hit her really hard." Great sobs wracked her chest, making it difficult for her to breathe.

"But she was still alive when you left?"

The girl nodded.

"How many in there with her?"

"Just one," Kaylee sniffed. "The guy who had me

called him Fico. He said he's going to . . ." She started to cry again. "He's going to do awful things. . . ."

"Run to your auntie's house," Quinn said. "There are more of these guys down at the river and they're probably coming this way. Work your way around behind the school. That'll keep you out of their way. I'll go take care of your mom."

"Okay." Kaylee sniffed. "Where's my dad?"

"He'll be with me," Quinn said, as a shattered scream tore from the windows of the Perry home.

# Chapter 8

*Langley*

Ronnie Garcia's group supervisor turned to go, and then spun at the last minute, Colombo-style.

"You know," Bobby Jeffrey said. "Why don't you just call it a night? Get out of here. Go home, go to a bar, go for a run or whatever it is you do when you're not guarding the nation's secrets."

Garcia's heart was in her throat, but she smiled broadly, trying to keep it light. "I'm always guarding the nation's secrets, Bobby," she said. "You know that."

"I'm serious." Jeffery looked over the top of his wire glasses. He tugged at his tie to loosen it even more than it already was. "They didn't order me to hold you, so I'm ordering you to haul ass. I'll talk to this ID guy. You and I can discuss what to do about it in the morning."

Ronnie took a deep breath. Jeffery had the face and demeanor of a man she could trust, with a reputation as a supervisor who took care of his people. A fifteen-year veteran of the Clandestine Service, he'd been yanked off what had to be a juicy counterterrorism assignment on the Pakistan Desk, and moved to be a group supervisor in Regional and Transnational Issues—Russia and Central Asia—just weeks after the new president took office. It was still important work, but pulling him off the major case was the equivalent of benching him.

A consummate spy, he kept his cards close, even among friends. He'd never say it out loud, but he seemed to know there was a movement against the new administration, and considering Ronnie's association with the former national security advisor, he was smart enough to know she would be a part of it.

"Okay," she said. "If you're going to order me." She logged out of her computer, then pulled the security ID card out of the slot in her keyboard and looped the lanyard around her neck. It was difficult to look nonchalant with her gut gurgling the way it was. Still, she didn't want to look as though she'd just been caught looking for evidence that could bring down the presidency. "I'm not going to argue with my boss when he's trying to get me to leave the office."

She threw on a thin linen jacket to cover the butt of a Kahr 9MM. The pistol rested in a flat inside-the-pants holster that peeked above her light wool gabardine slacks and pressed against the fabric of a silk blouse. It was small enough that she hardly knew it was there. The light jacket made sure no one else did either. Reaching under her credenza, she grabbed the leather backpack that contained her credentials, some makeup, and most important, her prepaid cell phones. Giving the dial on her desk safe one last spin, she turned to leave.

Jeffrey stepped to the door of her cubicle, blocking her exit. She gave him the most relaxed smile she could muster.

"So." She batted her eyelashes. "You'll let me know what's going on tomorrow?"

"Sure," he said, "if they don't cart me off to the gulag." Jeffrey sighed, stepping out of her way. The lines around his eyes said he was only half joking. "But I have a feeling you already know what they want."

He touched her shoulder as she slipped past. "Watch yourself, Garcia," he said.

She gave him a tight chuckle. "Relax, Bobby. You act like you're sending me on some suicide mission."

Jeffery opened his mouth to speak. Then, thinking better of it, he turned back to his office door.

Ronnie Garcia's cubicle was located in the OHB, or Old Headquarters Building, on the grounds of the George Bush Center for Intelligence. It was the iconic CIA building, made famous in movies and spy books with its huge seal of eagle, shield, and compass on the granite floor, portraits of past directors, and the memorial wall to fallen agents. Having patrolled these halls for years as a uniformed CIA security police officer, Garcia was intimately familiar with every inch of the entire campus. A relatively fast-rising star only months before, she was still low on the general pecking order when it came to seniority in the Clandestine Service and had to park in the hinterlands of the sprawling, mall-like parking lot to the north of the OHB. It was interesting to her that the closer spots were already vacant and the farther she walked—out to where the worker bees parked—the more cars were still in the lot.

She walked fast, low heels clicking on the warm pavement, but not so fast that she would look like she was fleeing the scene of a crime.

It was hot for June, not as humid as it would get later in the summer, but plenty uncomfortable for a girl who had to wear a jacket because of her firearm. Still, it was better than the uniform and ballistic vest she had to wear in her previous job. She pushed the auto-start button on her key fob. A half block away, wedged between a Lexus sedan and a beater Subaru, her black Impala flashed, and then roared to life.

"That's pretty smart," a male voice said from behind her. "Start it from a distance to check for an explosive device."

Ronnie turned to see a man she didn't recognize leaning against the hood of a dark blue Jeep Cherokee. He was tall, thick boned enough that he might have played college ball three decades before when he'd been in college.

"My mechanic told me it's good for the engine to let it run," she said, looking the man up and down. She didn't recognize him. And while she didn't know everyone at Langley, years in uniform at her previous job made her aware of most of faces that belonged.

"Still pretty smart," the man said. "Unless someone rigs a tremble switch or pressure device under your seat—or, heaven forbid, has a radio detonator—"

He looked tall, even lounging against the Jeep—Ronnie guessed around six-four. He wore a gray off-the-rack suit that was rumpled as if he'd lived in it for three days in a row, but his shoes were polished to a high, military gloss. Dark Oakley Half Jacket shades perched on top of dirty blond hair that was long enough to be tousled by the breeze.

Ronnie gave him a suit-yourself shrug and walked on toward her car. It was broad daylight and she had been through enough violent confrontations that it took more than some creepy guy in a bad suit to scare her. Still, she was realistic and felt happy to feel the tiny Kahr under her jacket. A violent encounter wasn't out of the question, even in the CIA parking lot.

"Miss Garcia," the man said when she'd made it two steps past, "I wonder if I could have a word."

Ronnie spun, staring him down.

"How do you know my name?"

He pushed away from the Jeep and held up a black leather credential case, open to reveal a frowning photo of him wearing what looked to be the same wrinkled suit.

"Glen Walter," he said. "Internal Defense." Ronnie caught the shadow of a sidearm on his right hip inside the suit jacket when he returned the credential case to his breast pocket. He smiled. "I actually came here to see you."

Ronnie checked her watch, swallowing back the surprise that this man had known exactly where she parked and when she would be walking to her car. He was IDTF all right. "Well, Mr. Walters, it's after five. You caught me on my way home."

"It's Walter," the man said. "No *s*."

"Whatever." Ronnie shrugged again. "Anyway, I'm on my way home. This is a weird time for a meeting."

"I suppose," Walter said, his face holding a crooked half smile. "But it's important to take care of some things right when they come up. Don't you think?"

There was a decided hint of the South in his voice. Maybe one of the Carolinas, Ronnie thought. He had an overly sweet way of talking that seemed calculated to put her off balance.

"Okay . . ." She half expected him to pull out a silenced pistol and try to assassinate her. "How about you get to the point then," she said, not one to dance around a matter for any length of time. "Because I've had a long crappy day."

"Sure." Walter shrugged, leaning sideways on the Jeep again and folding his hands. "I can appreciate that. How about I save us both a lot of time and tell you how this will go. I'm going to ask you a couple of very specific questions—for the record. I'm pretty sure you'll refuse to answer them, or, if you do, your answers will be a pack of lies. After you lie to my face, I'll read you a short statement from the Espionage Act, you know, 18 USC Title—"

"I'm familiar with the Espionage Act," Garcia said. Smugness was a quality she could not abide, even for a minute, from a man with the authority to arrest her on the spot.

"I'll just bet you are," Walter said. "Anywaaaay . . ." He drew the word out as if to chastise her for the interruption. "After I admonish you about your responsibility regarding the act, I'll ask you those same little questions one more time. You'll look me right in the eye and lie . . . again." He gave a halfhearted shrug, still leaning against the Jeep. "And we'll be right back to where we—"

"*Maldita sea!*" Ronnie cut him off with her go-to Cuban curse before she lost all semblance of self-control. "Look, Mr. Walters, if this is about Jericho Quinn, I've already told investigators from the US Marshals and the FBI everything I know."

"It's Walter, no *s*," he said. "And just like I predicted, there comes your first lie."

"We are done here." Ronnie turned to walk to her car.

"We may be done *here*, Miss Garcia," Walter said, again much too smugly for Ronnie. "But we're not done. I wouldn't be leaving town anytime soon."

Ronnie spun. "I don't know what it is you think you know—"

"That's true." Walter smiled his half smile, cutting her off. "You don't know what I know. Anyway, as you said, we're done here."

Agent Walter stood up from the Jeep. He gave a flip of his hand, as if he was bored with the conversation, and summoned a black Town Car that had been waiting down the aisle. A moment later, he was gone, leaving Garcia standing alone in the parking lot under a hot evening sun, wondering how much this guy did know about what she was doing for Jericho Quinn.

# Chapter 9

*Alaska*

Quinn was moving before the scream trailed away into a mournful, gurgling cough. He stepped over Proctor's lifeless body and shoved the front door open at the same instant Ukka charged in from the back hallway.

Both men stopped in their tracks at what they saw.

A squat contractor with dark curly hair lay on his back, glassy eyes staring up at the ceiling. The dead might leak, but they didn't bleed very long, and the growing pool of blood on the living room floor revealed he'd not been dead more than a few seconds. Ukka's wife, Christina, stood over him, a bloody skinning knife in her hand. A broken piece of what looked like ivory or bone, about the size of a child's baseball bat, lay on the ground beside the man's demolished skull. It was an *oosik*, the penis bone of a walrus, often found as decoration in Alaska homes. Christina had evidently used it to cave in the face of her attacker before grabbing a skinning knife off the table and virtually gutting him.

The mournful scream Quinn heard had been that of the dying man.

Ukka put a big arm around his wife and gently took the knife out of her hand.

"You okay?"

"I smacked him in the face with the *oosik*," Christina said, small shoulders trembling. She looked up at him weakly, fighting shock.

"I know you did, sweetheart," Ukka said, shooting a glance at Quinn. "He was a bad man. You did the right thing."

Fico's sidearm lay on the ground beside him. He was too far gone to lift it, but Quinn kicked it out of the way just in case.

A strained voice crackled over the radio. It was Perkins, one of the men who'd gone to scout the river.

"How about a SITREP up there?"

Quinn started to answer, but decided against it, listening instead.

"Proctor!" the voice called again. "What's going on? We heard shots."

There was a long pause, followed by another voice, presumably the pilot, letting them know he was coming to their location, down by the fishery plant. The man called Perkins cut him off, ordering radio silence.

Quinn sighed. It was too late for that. He had what he needed to know.

Ukka's cell phone began to ring. He listened for a few moments, a smile spreading over his wide face as he ended the call.

"Chantelle says there's nobody left to guard the plane."

Quinn checked the magazine on the MP7 while he

thought. "I don't think these guys are actually affiliated with any specific agency. None of them have badges or any kind of credential—but they still have the backing of the government. If any of them make it out of here, he'll come back with reinforcements and slaughter the whole village. It won't matter to them that I'm not here."

Ukka's daughter Kaylee had ignored the direction to go to her auntie's house. Unable to leave with the sound of the scream, she'd come in behind Quinn and now sat on the couch, helping to console her mother.

Ukka pulled Quinn to the side so his wife and youngest daughter couldn't hear. "It's all good, man," he said. "I had Chantelle do some work on the plane. If they try and make a run for it, they'll never get off the ground. If we take care of them somewhere else, she'll torch the plane at the end of the runway." He waved his hand as if saying good-bye. "No one's getting back to call in the cavalry."

"That might work," Quinn said, glancing at the couch. He nodded at the two women in the room. "Christina should probably see a doctor. And Kaylee might need a counselor after what these guys just put her through."

"All my girls are tundra tough." Ukka gave a solemn nod. "But you're right. This is a lot to process. I'm proud of Christina, though. Not a good idea to cross an Eskimo woman when she's protecting her home."

"Or any woman," Quinn said, thinking of his ex-wife and of Ronnie Garcia, wondering what they would do in such a situation.

"Maybe," Ukka said. "But most women don't know their way around a skinning knife like my wife does." He grinned. "Or a walrus pecker . . ."

"That's so wrong," Quinn sighed. He let the MP7 fall against the sling at his chest and lifted the curtain to peer out the window at the vacant dirt street in front of the Perry house. "We better get going," he said. "Maybe we'll get lucky and Alaska will kill these guys."

# Chapter 10

## *The White House*

The new president was a single man and, as such, had no one to push for the redecoration of the White House. Apart from a new leather desk chair and a couple of paintings staffers had spirited away from the National Gallery, the Oval Office was exactly as it had been under President Clark. Greens and whites ruled the day, as did paintings of Teddy Roosevelt and expansive Western scenes by the likes of George Catlin and John Mix Stanley. The former first lady had left everything behind, including the oppressive ghost of her dead husband that seemed to whisper in the halls to West Wing staffers that something was not quite right in the house.

Now, sprawling over the Oval Office furniture like the stain that he was, President Hartman Drake didn't help matters at all.

McKeon stood adjacent to the President against the wall, next to the Remington *Rough Rider* bronze. He used long, slender fingers to rub exhausted eyes as he tried to clear the image of this idiot out of his mind.

Drake sat with his feet propped up on the Resolute

Desk, leaning back in a plush button-leather chair. He cradled his head in his hands as if he owned the world—which, in fact, he did. His trademark bowtie, this one a conservative red-and-black stripe, hung open. His collar was still buttoned, as if everyone at the meeting had surprised him in the middle of changing clothes.

Across the room, Kurt Bodington, the director of the FBI, sat on one of the green sofas. He leaned forward with his elbows on both knees as if he was on the toilet rather than sitting in the Oval Office. Virginia Ross, the director of the CIA, sat beside him. Her ankles were crossed, her hands rested in her lap, like she was posing for a photo. More pear than hourglass, she'd recently lost a considerable amount of weight and wore clothes that were a size too large. The lacy cuffs of a white blouse hung from the sleeves of a voluminous blue suit that had once strained to keep her contained.

It had been obvious from the time McKeon and Drake took office that neither of these directors was particularly effective in their respective positions. And that was the only reason they were still in place.

A Japanese woman stood on the other side of the door from McKeon, hands folded at her lap. Her name was Ran. Japanese for *orchid*, it was pronounced to rhyme with the American name *Ron* but with a hard *r*, making it sound more like *Lon* or *Don*. In her early twenties, she had flawlessly smooth skin and a quiet presence that reached out into the room, touching anyone who dared look in her direction. She wore a cream-colored long sleeve blouse, unbuttoned enough to reveal the edge of a dark tattoo at her breast. McKeon knew firsthand that there were many more tattoos where that one came from. Director Bodington had unwisely attempted to shake her hand when he'd come in, but Ross had veered away from her as if she were poison—which was not far off. She worked as an aide—among other things—for McKeon and, to his wife's chagrin, rarely left his side.

"Chris Clark left me a real mess," Drake said, staring absentmindedly at his reflection in the windows that overlooked the Rose Garden. The man couldn't walk past a silver tea set without stopping to admire his physique. "I need to know what Winfield Palmer had going with him."

Bodington gave a concerned nod, as if he understood the gravity of the situation. He liked to paint himself as a big-picture man, but McKeon saw him as more of a paint-by-the-numbers stooge. The director of the most advanced law enforcement agency in the world was happy to do just what he was told and never dared to go outside the lines.

Virginia Ross spoke first.

"The national security advisor's communications to the president would be privileged," she said. "But I'm sure he left files. With the tragedy, it would be expected he'd turn them over to you for a seamless transition."

Nearly half a year after the assassination of both President Chris Clark and Vice President Bob Hughes during the last State of the Union address, people simply called it "the tragedy."

Unwilling to give his counterpart from the CIA too much floor time, Bodington spoke up before Ross could say more. "I have to be honest, Mr. President," he said. "I never did understand the absolute power President Clark gave to Winfield Palmer. Sure, they were friends from their days at West Point, but the man seemed to have carte blanche in the intelligence community. He could override anyone and everyone with his special projects. The President took virtually every matter of state to the man as if he were some oracle or something."

"They were friends, Kurt," Director Ross said. "Surely even you can understand what that would mean."

Bodington gave her a withering stare, then half turned in his seat, distancing himself.

"I know he had a pretty large network of agents working for him," he said. "Half the time, they did little but get in the way of my people."

"Right," Drake said. "And we know at least one member of that network tried to kill me in Las Vegas." He steepled his fingers under his chin, something McKeon had never seen him do until he'd become president. It looked asinine when someone like Drake did it, like he was trying to shoot himself under the chin—which, McKeon couldn't help but think, was not an entirely bad idea.

"We believe that to be correct," Bodington said, smugly like one child telling on another to his teacher. "Facial recognition from the Vegas security videos shows it was Jericho Quinn, an agent with Air Force OSI. He's also wanted for the brutal murder of a Fairfax County police officer. He ran with a big Marine named Thibeau or something."

"Thibodaux," McKeon interjected. "Your report says Jacques Thibodaux."

"Right." Bodington turned to Virginia Ross. "And some Mexican girl from your shop."

"She's from Cuba." Ross nodded. "I can't speak for Quinn or the Marine, but Veronica Garcia is a good one. I wasn't certain at first, but her heroism saved a lot of lives last year during the shooting at Langley."

Bodington steered the conversation back to Palmer.

"He had quite a few working for him that we wouldn't

know about, but it seemed to me he was grabbing people from other agencies and repurposing them for his missions. No doubt without any oversight from Congress. I've seen him with agents from the Secret Service, a couple besides Quinn from Air Force OSI, and several CIA types."

"But no one from the FBI?"

"Thankfully, no, Mr. President." Bodington nodded. "My agents have more sense than that."

Virginia Ross cleared her throat. "I have to say, Mr. President." She shook her head as if to try to hold back some comment that she couldn't quite contain. "I've already stated my opinion regarding Garcia. Though I have observed Winfield Palmer to be a steamroller with his programs—and often arrogant to the extreme—I have never known him to be anything less than a patriot. To think that he might be behind these attacks is, in my opinion, unthinkable." She scooted forward to the edge of her seat and leaned in toward the Resolute Desk. "Mr. President, I would suggest a small task force, perhaps some of my agents, and some from Kurt's shop. I am not privy to all the details regarding the shooting of the poor Fairfax County officer, but I am aware that it's not a forgone conclusion Agent Quinn is the shooter. There seem to be numerous mitigating—"

"We're not holding court here," McKeon cut her off. "I'm sure that, as with most issues, there are multiple layers to everything that has happened over the last few months. But what we must not forget is that there are yet moles within the government and it is imperative to the President that we root them out immediately."

"Thank you, Lee," Drake said, almost dismissively. McKeon would have to talk to him about that. "I'd like each of you prepare a list of everyone you've ever seen with Winfield Palmer." He raised an eyebrow at Virginia Ross. "And I'm not interested in your opinions. I just want names."

"That bitch has flown straight off the reservation," Drake said after the two directors had gone. "I thought she was one we could trust to toe the line—if only out of self-preservation."

"As did I." McKeon nodded. "But that does not appear to be the case. We should start thinking about a suitable replacement."

The Japanese woman stood stoically at her post along the wall.

"She seemed like such an empty suit," Drake went on. "What do you think prompted her little show of team spirit for Palmer?"

"Integrity, I'd imagine," McKeon said.

"Well," Drake said, "we can't have that screwing up our plans. What's your take on the Uyghur prisoners? Do you think turning them over to Pakistan will be enough to push Chen Min over the edge?"

"I do," McKeon said. He shot a glance at Ran, who rolled her eyes. She could not stand Hartman Drake and begged McKeon to let her kill the man every night when they went to bed. "We cannot be too brash."

McKeon knew his words were falling on deaf ears. Drake was the very picture of brash. Everything he did was flamboyant, from his colorful bowties to his firebrand speeches. McKeon's biological father had dreamed of the day when one of his children—or the children he'd placed in positions of power—made it to the White House. It had taken years of patience and planning to make it happen. But it would take much more patience

and planning to make it worthwhile. A sitting president, even one bent on the fall of the United States, had
to work slowly. He could not, for instance, just hand the
bomb to Iran, normalize relations with North Korea—
or declare war on China. Everything had to appear to
come from the outside. If he moved too quickly or
acted outside the apparent best interest of the nation,
there were still plenty of wary members of Congress
who would bring impeachment charges in a heartbeat.

No, there were better ways to bring down a government, insidious ways that would see the American public clamoring for—even demanding—the very actions
that would bring about their own destruction.

"Chen Min will rise to the bait. There is no doubt of
that." McKeon took a deep breath, too fatigued to re-
hash things they'd discussed ad nauseam. "Ranjhani's
plan will help us keep up the anti-China rhetoric with
the public."

"Another bomb." Drake snorted, his dismissive tone
rising to the surface again. His tone made McKeon
consider letting Ran have her way. But he needed the
imbecile for a while longer.

"A bomb, indeed," McKeon said. "But not just any
bomb. A simple explosion destroys only steel and bone.
My father was a brilliant man. He knew that America
was strong enough to fend off any outside encroachment of Islam. We have seen how good this country is
at stopping attack after attack. But my father knew, and
stated many times, when this country falls, it will be
because it rips itself to pieces from within."

Drake laughed to himself, as if he'd just thought of
something funny. His feet slid off the desk and fell to
the floor. Turning slightly, he took a moment to check
out the reflection of his shoulders in the Rose Garden

window. "I think my biceps might be shrinking. I have got to get down to the gym." He glanced up. "Anyway, good thing we're keeping an eye on Virginia Ross. We do have eyes on her, don't we?"

"Yes," McKeon said, suddenly more tired than he had ever been. With a partner like Drake, he might as well be doing this alone. "We have eyes on everyone we know of who had a relationship to Winfield Palmer. But the time for watching is over."

"Damn, Lee." Drake gave him a condescending grimace. "I'm surprised you ever got elected to public office. Didn't anyone ever tell you that you have a creepy way of saying things?" He grabbed a gym bag from under the desk and stopped to look at the Vice President. "Every time you talk about this thing we're doing, I expect you to follow up with an evil laugh. 'The time for watching is over. . . . Bwahahahahah.' I mean, shit, give me a break. . . ."

Ran tensed at the insult. She took a half step forward. Thick veins throbbed at the base of her neck. Drake was so caught up in his own joke that he didn't notice how close he was to dying. McKeon gave an almost imperceptible shake of his head, stopping her. He mouthed the word *soon* as the President continued his mock laughter and walked past the Secret Service agent posted outside the door.

# Chapter 11

Kim and Mattie Quinn made the perfect mother-daughter pair. Both wore blue ALASKA GROWN T-shirts and denim shorts. Their hair styled in classy, off-the-shoulder updos, the two were virtual twins but for the fact that Kim was a blonde and Mattie had coal-black curls like her father. Mattie also happened to have two working legs, where her mother sported a metal prosthetic limb where her left leg had been amputated above the knee. She was back to using a cane again for a few days while she grew accustomed to the newly fitted prosthetic.

Five months after a sniper's bullet that was meant for Mattie had torn through her thigh, Kim knew that she had more swagger with one leg than she'd ever had with two.

Of course, it hadn't started out that way. When she'd first come out of anesthesia after surgery, the look on Jericho's face had told her the leg was gone. She'd hated him in that moment, a difficult thing to do with Jericho, though she didn't let him know that. Considering the sort of work he did, it was not a hard case to make that her ex-husband was responsible for bringing the assassin's bullet ripping into their family. But Kim knew that life was much more complicated than that.

Despair and grief over the loss of her leg was compounded by the fact that she'd chased Jericho away with the lines she'd drawn and then dared him not to cross. Neither of them had ever been good with ultimatums—but she'd given them anyway. For a week after the surgery, she'd felt absolutely alone and feared that without two good legs, she'd never be attractive to any man, let alone Jericho. It didn't really matter. She'd kicked him out, driven him away with her wild fears about him getting killed. In her quiet, solitary moments, she told herself it would be better to have a little of him, than none at all—that Mattie deserved to have a father, and she deserved to have at least some semblance of a husband, even if he was gone more than half the time to godforsaken hellholes where everyone wanted to kill him. At least then, she had been able to call him hers. But then, he'd come around and her stubborn streak would rise up like some kind of bitchy dragon lady that she couldn't control—sending him retreating back into the arms of his new girlfriend. It didn't matter now.

Kim had just started to come to grips with that when the phantom pains began. They roared in like a river of molten lava, searing the bones of her missing limb and peeling back the toenails of the foot that was no longer even there. The docs had given her something to quiet the nerves and, in time, the phantom pain had retreated, but never quite disappeared.

Kim worked her butt off in rehab, learning how to walk on her new leg, enduring hours of painful stretching therapy. She walked for miles around the halls of the hospital, first with, then without the assistance of a cane.

Jericho was apparently good friends with the former national security advisor and Mr. Palmer saw to it that she had the finest in aftercare for an amputee. Sadly, years of war ensured that military hospitals received a great deal of experience in replacing lost limbs. At first, Kimberly Quinn had been welcomed at Walter Reed because she was a friend of the White House. Later, after the horrible accusations against Jericho, it seemed like the new administration wanted her there so they could keep an eye on her. She had to make this "new normal," as they called it, work for her before she could do anything.

Surrounded by servicewomen who'd had bits and pieces of themselves blown off in war, Kim had remained quiet about how she'd lost the leg. All the other patients in her ward had lost limbs as a result of roadside bombs or mortar attacks. She'd always felt a certain amount of pride at being married—at least for a time—to a member of the military. Now, for the first time in her life, Kim found herself truly embarrassed that she was not herself a veteran wounded in the service of her country. She'd been shot at a wedding, for crying out loud. For weeks, she didn't talk to anyone but her roommate, a female US Army corporal named Rochelle, who'd lost both legs in a helicopter crash in Afghanistan.

Then, a month after the shooting, Rochelle and four of her girlfriends, all amputees, cornered Kim in the gym with a dozen roses and a Wounded Warrior challenge coin. Kim had cried, protesting that she didn't deserve to be grouped with these brave women.

"Are you kidding me?" Rochelle had said, standing there on her twin prosthetic legs. "You took a bullet intended for your own kid. You're a wounded warrior if ever one wore a skirt. So strut that leg proudly. Wear shorts, go dancing, kick ass. I'm sure going to."

The love and companionship of those women was like nothing Kim had ever experienced. More even than the surgery, they had saved her life.

They'd given her the confidence to get out, to do things like go shopping with her daughter.

Mattie ran ahead, completely unbothered by the shiny stainless-steel "leg" that stuck out from the hem of her mother's denim shorts. She was happy to go to the mall, but happier still to be out with her mom. She darted back to hold Kim's hand and check on her every few seconds. They'd returned from Alaska so Kim could spend the last two weeks at Walter Reed, being fitted for her new, computerized prosthetic leg. This one adjusted to her changes in gait as many as fifty times per second. Kim had been so busy with doctors' appointments and physical therapy that this was their first day out together since coming back to DC.

"How about some supper at Johnny Rockets?" Kim asked, pointing Mattie toward the escalator around the corner from the Apple Store where they'd just spent the last hour picking out the perfect case for Mattie's iPod.

"That sounds great, Mom," Mattie said, skipping around the corner ahead. It did Kim's heart good that her daughter didn't try to coddle her—even if the extra exertion caused her to sweat through the armpits of her T-shirt. Her physical therapist had warned her that a prosthetic for an AK—above the knee—amputation would use far more energy than a normal leg. That, combined with the body's loss of all the pores on the missing limb, meant the rest of her was likely to perspire more in an effort to regulate her temperature. The other girls in her ward called it "glistening."

Mattie stopped in her tracks as soon as they'd rounded the corner.

"I forgot my new shirt at the Apple Store," she gasped. Stricken, she grabbed Kim's hand and spun her around, oblivious to how tricky such a move was on a prosthetic leg.

"Are you sure it was there?" Kim asked. "Maybe you left it somewhere else."

"No." Mattie shook her head. "I'm sure I had it there. We have to go and get it." She clutched Kim by the hand and led her back the way they'd come, rounding a square support pillar and nearly running headlong into a startled man walking directly toward them.

He was about Kim's age, in his mid-thirties, with a sullen flap of blond hair and an intense look she recognized from her ex-husband. He wore faded jeans and an unremarkable button-up shirt with short sleeves— loose, like the kind Jericho always wore to hide his gun. And this was the fifth time she'd seen him since they'd been in the mall. She felt a twinge of fear rising up in her stomach. Maybe living with Jericho for all those years had made her paranoid, but either this guy had the same taste in shopping as a seven-year-old girl, or he was following them.

# Chapter 12

*Alaska*

"Two of them are holed up in the Kwikpac building." Ukka did a quick peek around the corner of the weathered plywood fuel shed where he and Quinn were hidden.

Seventy-five meters away, the image of a weather-worn clapboard building ghosted through the curtains of drizzle and fog. It lay at the base of the village on a narrow spit of gravel that made it easier for boats to come up on the riverside and offload their commercial catch. The icy winds that shrieked off the frozen Yukon through the long winters made it impossible to keep paint on any of the buildings in Mountain Village. The blue splotches the fish buyers had slapped on their building the previous summer were now little more than a scoured memory.

According to Ukka's cousin, two of the contractors had grabbed a young schoolteacher named April John to use as a hostage when they'd come up from the river and dragged her into the fish plant.

While Ukka kept an eye on the Kwikpac building, Quinn lay on his belly, facing the opposite direction, making certain they weren't ambushed by the still un-accounted-for pilot.

Ukka wiped the rainwater off his round face. "I think I saw some movement through the front window. It's tough to tell in this fog."

"Okay," Quinn said. "Use those hunter's eyes of yours to watch our six for a minute. If there are only two accounted for in there, we still have a variable out here." He maneuvered around so he could get a look at the fish house while Ukka took up the job of rear guard.

"Tell me more about April John," Quinn said, watching the wide gray ribbon of the Yukon tumble along behind the Kwikpac building. He'd met her a couple of times over the last few months and knew she worked at the school. A sturdy-looking girl, she'd taken a moose during a late winter hunt that had filled the larders of a couple of village elders—but that didn't mean she was equipped to handle being a hostage.

"She's the kind of girl who'd beat a guy to death with a walrus pecker if he crossed her," Ukka said. "She'll not be one to boohoo to her captors, if that's what you mean. They'll have to tie her up or knock her out to keep her from fighting."

"Good." Quinn gritted his teeth, thinking through his options. "That gives her a chance—"

"Wait!" Ukka hissed, his voice a tense whisper. "I got movement five houses up from the fish plant. Looks like a boot sticking out from under Myrna Tomaganuk's house. I'll lay odds it's the pilot." State policy said village public safety officers were supposed to be unarmed, but he'd grabbed his favorite hunting rifle before leaving his house. It was a Winchester Model 70 chambered in 30.06. It was battered, and even a little rusty around the base of the Leopold

3X9 scope, but Quinn had seen the man use it to shoot a moose in the eye at over a hundred yards.

Quinn glanced down at the submachine gun in his hands. He had two extra magazines in his pocket and the Severance sheathed on his hip. These guys had obviously done their research and believed he'd come to the hostage. With two of the contractors barricaded with their backs to the river and the third hiding under Tomaganuk's home, ready to blow his brains out when he approached, a frontal assault was impractical.

The nearest armed backup were the Alaska State Troopers stationed in Saint Mary's, nearly an hour away by truck over a bumpy, pothole-filled road. It was more swamp than road this time of year. Even if they knew what was going on, the troopers would never get there in time to help. In some ways, the absence of law enforcement made Quinn's next moves that much less difficult.

"Okay," Quinn said a moment later, mulling through the specifics of his plan. "You know that cute Samoan girl from Mountain View you used to horse around with back in high school?"

Ukka looked at Quinn as if he'd lost his mind. "Yeah, but I don't see—"

"Remember how you had to sneak out of her bedroom window and tiptoe out the back alley to get past her father and two humongous brothers to keep them from killing you?"

Ukka groaned. "I sure do."

"Think you can pull off that same level of stealth and work your way over to Myrna's house? I need you to take care of the number three guy."

Ukka nodded. "I can shoot his nose hairs off if you want me to," he said.

"Outstanding." Quinn had seen the big Eskimo in enough sticky situations to know he could stalk up to a dozing grizzly if the situation warranted.

Quinn flicked open his ZT folding knife and reached for a length of water hose coiled around an old truck wheel that was bolted to the rear of the fuel shed. He cut a piece about a foot long, then returned the ZT to his pocket before blowing into the tube to make certain it was free of obstructions.

"What the hell kind of plan are you pondering here?" Ukka's cockeyed grimace was clear evidence of his doubts. "Looks like you've decided to attack them with a blowgun."

Quinn tucked the length of hose in his waistband behind his back. He tapped the magazines in his pocket, then the Severance in the sheath at his hip before taking up the MP7 again. "It's okay if you make a little noise when you take out the pilot," Quinn said. "In fact, I need those other two to be looking in that direction in five minutes. Can you do that?"

"Five minutes?" Ukka said, still shaking his head slowly. He peered down at Quinn through narrowed eyes.

Quinn pointed a knife hand toward a ratty copse of willows fifty meters upriver from the fish house. "River's moving fast," he said. "I should be able to drift down there in much less time than that, but you better give me five minutes to make sure I'm up on the back dock and ready to go."

Ukka's mouth hung open. "You're going to swim down the Yukon River breathing through a piece of garden hose?"

"Float would be more correct," Quinn said. "You don't swim in the Yukon."

"No shit." Ukka rolled his eyes.

"I'm open to better ideas," Quinn said, not relishing the thought of the frigid water.

Ukka sat completely still, just looking at him. Over the last five months in the village, Quinn had learned that Eskimos did a lot of talking using nothing but their eyes—and Ukka's eyes said Quinn had gone completely insane. Finally, the big man spoke.

"I'm getting cold standing out here in the rain," he said, "and I'm a damn Eskimo. You know that water was ice a couple of weeks ago, right?"

"I know," Quinn said.

"You'll be lucky if your muscles aren't too cramped to hold a gun after you been in the river two minutes— let alone fight those other guys. And that's if the current doesn't carry you all the way down to Alakanuk."

Quinn shrugged. "Like I said, I'm open to another suggestion. But it better be quick because these guys seem to be pretty rough on their hostages."

"Just go then," Ukka snapped.

"Outstanding." Quinn put a hand on his shoulder. "Start shooting in five minutes. I'll see you inside the Kwikpac in six."

Waves of heavy fog drifted in from the north, providing intermittent concealment as Quinn worked his way along the muddy road behind a row of gray wooden shacks, broken snow machines, and four-wheelers. Everyone had sought shelter inside when they'd realized what the government contractors were up to. Faces pressed against foggy glass windows, wide brown eyes flicking messages from stoic faces as they wished him luck. Village dogs, chained to plastic barrels or old vehicles, barked from the stress in the air, but stopped when they recognized Quinn as a regular.

Cresting a small hill on the road that led out to the airport, Quinn figured he'd made it far enough past Myrna Tomaganuk's house that the pilot hiding beneath it wouldn't be able to see him. Stooped at the waist, he moved quickly in a diagonal line down the gravel bank toward the churning water of the Yukon. The area on the upriver side of the willows was steep and he slid the last ten feet as if standing on ball bearings, landing with a splash in the sloppy gravel soup where current ate away at the bank. June in western Alaska was equivalent to spring in the lower forty-eight. A stiff breeze that had felt bracing while they'd been out fishing, now whipped the surface of the river into a frothy chocolate chop. Just three weeks before the area had been a sheet of solid ice. Shattered logs, some as long as a tractor-trailer, littered the river's edge. Great portions of land from upriver, complete with Medusa-like root-balls and moss-covered bank had been scoured away by slabs of ice during the recent breakup and bobbed in the eddies like small islands.

Quinn kicked off the rubber boots and stashed them in the willows, hoping he'd be alive to come back and get them later. Contrary to popular belief, he wasn't worried about the Xtra Tuffs dragging him to the bottom. In calm water, they would have merely filled and become neutrally buoyant. But the Yukon was anything but calm, so the boots would yank him around as they worked with the current like small parachutes around his feet—likely pulling him to the middle of the river and a watery grave.

The lower Yukon had seen three drowning deaths since breakup in this season alone. Two were men out getting logs and one was a little girl from Emmonak, another Eskimo village downriver. Like many of the children in bush Alaska, she'd lived all of her nine years surrounded by lakes and streams and one of the largest rivers in the world, but had never learned how to swim. The bodies of all three had been carried off by the current to be found hung up on some snag, miles away from where they'd drowned. It was foolish, he knew, but though Quinn didn't fear death, it filled him with a certain cold dread that his bloated corpse would be tossed around by a river, then impaled on a bunch of deadfall for days while the ravens pecked away. He shook off the thought. Picturing his own death was a bad start to any operation.

He wished he'd had on his hiking boots. The Lowas might have slowed down his kicking ability underwater, but he'd spent many hours swimming in boots during training and as a combat rescue officer, or CRO, in an earlier Air Force life. And when he reached the fish house, a fight in boots would certainly be more pleasant than one in bare feet—but it couldn't be helped.

His teeth already chattered from the effects of near constant adrenaline coupled with the chill of a nonstop drizzle. Barefoot and dressed only in his long merino wool sweater and khaki pants, he waded quickly into the water with the length of hose clutched in his hand. Employing the MP7 while navigating the Yukon's persistent current would be foolhardy, so he left it slung over his back to keep the sling from becoming tangled with any submerged deadfall and debris.

Frigid water lapped at his belly, driving the air from his lungs as surely as a hammer to his chest—but easing the ever-present ache in his kidney. He folded his arms tight and clenched his muscles, much like the grunt of the Hick maneuver fighter pilots used to counteract the effects of g-forces in flight. Compressing blood to the core of his body around his vital organs, he gave his system a quick five count to get over the initial shock of the cold.

With water temperatures just fifteen degrees above freezing, Quinn figured he had maybe ten minutes before his hands began to cramp into unusable claws. The fish house was a little over half a football field away. Ventilating with a couple of deep breaths, Quinn slipped noiselessly into the swirling currents, his body a toothpick in the jaws of the mighty Yukon.

He floated more than swam, navigating with just his head above the water, conserving energy as best he could, tensing to keep blood and vital warmth in his core. Rather than fighting the unyielding grip of the huge river, he used small strokes, adjusting his direction of travel instead of trying to make speed. The current was far faster than he could possibly swim and his puny efforts would do nothing but make him tired and colder than he already was. Quinn had learned as a small boy that, in the wilderness, a man is merely a hairless, clawless bear—weak and inconsequential without his wits. There was nothing like floating nearly naked in a river the size of the Yukon to drive that point home.

Roughly two minutes after entering the river, Quinn rounded the new barge docks and leaned toward the bank. Thirty seconds later, he grabbed the transom of an aluminum skiff that was tethered alongside the fish house.

Rain pattered on the surface of the river.

Arms shaking with cold, Quinn tucked the length of hose back into his belt in case he was discovered and needed it to slip away underwater. He grabbed the wooden rungs of the newly built two-by-four ladder on the wooden dock that ran the length of the Kwikpac building, adjacent to the skiff. Still half in, half out of the water, he waited, his head just below the bottom of the dock. Another minute of intense shivering and Quinn wondered if he'd even be able to haul himself up the ladder at all, let alone fight.

Water dripped from his eyes as he glanced down at the Tag Aquaracer on his wrist. Six minutes since he'd left the fuel shed. He felt sure the men in the building directly above him would be able to hear his chattering teeth, even over the constant slosh of the river. Clenching his jaws in an effort to stop the noise, he prayed for Ukka to start shooting soon.

# Chapter 13

*Las Vegas*

The humorless government machine that was TSA prodded Tang along as it had his wife, demanding he stand just so in order to scan his body for weapons. He had no doubt that the chemical sensors would scan his camera bag, but the portion of the device he carried was small and innocuous by itself—barely five ounces of material.

He made it through security with little more than a condescending nod from the harried TSA officers.

Ma Zhen called their plan the Honey Plot, pointing out that it took twelve bees, each bringing in a small droplet of nectar at a time, to produce one teaspoon of honey. Like Tang, Ma was Hui—Muslim Chinese. He was also a gifted bomb maker.

The five members of Tang's group would each pass through security with only a small portion of the device. That meant five chances for discovery, but the minuscule amount of contraband made the odds that any individual would be caught extremely low.

Tang and Ma Zhen and a half-Uyghur man named

Hu all carried PETN, a powerful, but low-vapor explosive secreted away in specialized Ni-Cad camcorder batteries. The batteries had been sealed by the man from Pakistan to Ma Zhen's specifications. Earlier that day, they had laid out all the components on the bed at the hotel. Tang had marveled at the workmanship of the batteries. They even had enough juice to power the camera for a few minutes if officials wanted to make certain they were operable. These were not batteries from some backroom workshop. The man from Pakistan had contacts in the manufacturing company or possibly even a government. They had now proven they could hide small quantities of PETN and were certainly good enough to conceal the powdered metal carried by Gao Jianguo, the fifth and final member of the team. He was a thuggish brute with a sloping forehead that hinted at the diminished capacity of his brain. He spoke of jihad in vague terms that made Tang wonder if he even knew what the word meant.

Tang stopped just past the screening checkpoint long enough to put on his belt and replace his wallet and wristwatch. A hundred feet from the gate, he could see the forlorn face of his wife as she sat facing the window, staring blankly at the plane that would see them out of their despair.

Ma Zhen sat alone on the row of black chairs behind Lin. He stooped forward, making notations in a small notebook. He was always writing something, as if he knew he should be in a university taking notes rather than masterminding the destruction of a commercial airliner.

Ma was a young man with thick, black-framed glasses and the large goiter of one who'd missed some vital element of his diet when he was a child. When he was just seventeen, Ma had seen his father and grandfather dragged into the street and executed by Chinese troops for the crime of nonviolent protest against majority Han Chinese encroachment in the traditionally Muslim Hui regions of Xinjiang. According to the man from Pakistan, both of the older men had been scholars, learned but quiet souls who espoused compromise and believed in a peaceful solution to all things.

After the murders, Ma's maternal grandfather—a man with only two fingers on his right hand and copious scarring on his neck and face had taken him aside and taught him the ways of bomb making. Ma had excelled at chemistry and physics and so was able to build on the concepts the old man taught him, making devices that were smaller and far easier to conceal. They were also much more powerful. His mother passed away from grief the following year, her dying wish that he would avenge his father.

The man from Pakistan had found him while he was still in mourning. Ma had seen the opportunity to be a dutiful son and followed without question on the path that had led him here, with Tang and the others.

Exhausted all the way to his bones, Tang dropped his camera bag on the floor and collapsed into a seat beside his wife. There was no consoling the poor woman, so he did not even try. He let his gaze wander down the wide terminal hallway past the shopping kiosks and milling crowds. The final member of their group, Hu Qi, would clear security soon and be along with his portion of the explosive for the device. Fifty meters away, the dimwitted Gao slouched in front of a slot machine. Tang watched as the muscular stub of a man dropped coin after coin into the machine, pressing buttons and spending money as fast as he could.

A strange sense of peace fell over Tang as he leaned back in his seat and closed his eyes. Soon, they would all board flight 224 for Los Angeles with all their portions of the device—and none of them would ever need money again.

# Chapter 14

*Alaska*

Trailing streams of frigid water, Quinn hauled himself up the ladder the moment the methodic flat cracks of Ukka's Winchester began to moan across the surface of the river. Feet shuffled on the plywood floor above, tromping to the uphill side of the fish house as the men inside moved to see what was happening, surely hoping their cohort had bagged their intended target.

Quinn took a moment to flex his hands open and shut in an effort to make certain they still worked before he moved at a crouch across the back receiving deck. Unfortunately for him, one of the contractors, a young man with sharp features and beard as dark as Quinn's, was savvy enough to periodically check over his shoulder during the sound of gunfire.

Quinn was far too cold to give up the ground he'd gained by jumping back into the water to escape. He was unlikely to survive it anyway. Instead, he raised his rifle and charged straight ahead, bent on attacking through the other man. The bearded contractor followed suit, firing his own weapon as he closed the distance.

Jericho's first two rounds went low, jerked downward by his still shivering muscles, but the third round caught the startled contractor on the point of his knee, tearing through muscle and bone.

It was possible to fight past any number of horrible wounds during the intense heat of battle, even one that would eventually prove fatal, but a shattered kneecap was difficult to ignore. The contractor stumbled forward, flailing out with his gun hand in an attempt to catch himself. His leg hinged the wrong way, folding backwards as if he'd been felled by an axe.

Quinn was vaguely aware of April John lying in an unconscious heap in the far corner of the room beside a stack of rubber fish tubs. He couldn't tell if she was alive or dead and, for the moment, it didn't really matter. He put the wounded contractor out of his misery with two rounds to the face as he turned to acquire the second man.

Apparently intent on the shooting outside, this tall brute of a guy had taken a moment to register that they were being attacked from the river. He was completely bald with deep lines in his forehead that made him look like he had two snarling mouths, one below and one above his deep-set eyes.

The big man's size belied his speed and agility. He bolted forward, drawing a pistol as he moved, intent on blowing Quinn's head off.

Still fighting the effects of hypothermia, Quinn was a fraction of a second late bringing his own weapon around from finishing off the first contractor. Again, he pressed forward, closing the short distance between them to the bald guy with his shoulder, reaching him just in time to shove the pistol out of the way. A volley of shots hammered into the roof. The rattling clap of gunfire was deafening in the small enclosure, making Quinn, who still had what felt like half the Yukon River in his ears, feel like he had a barrel over his head. He could tell the big guy was yelling something as he fought, but couldn't make out what it was.

He'd somehow managed to swat the pistol away, but the bald giant now had him trapped in a tight clinch. Struggling for breath, Quinn drove his knee repeatedly into the bald man's groin. It appeared to do little damage, but at least kept him from snapping Quinn's back.

The cold water had sapped Quinn of more of his strength than he'd realized. Reflexes and muscles that had served him so well in past conflicts refused to obey. The bald man's hand snaked up, snatching the barrel of the MP7 and attempting to twist it sideways. He couldn't quite bring it around to shoot Quinn, but drew the sling tight enough to restrict the blood flow in his neck.

Seeing stars, Quinn pummeled the man's ribs—to no effect. He abandoned thoughts of using the rifle, his hand flailing instead for the Severance at his side. The blade slid from the Kydex sheath with a satisfying click. Quinn lashed out, left-handed, across the man's thigh, slicing flesh, but missing anything that might have ended the fight.

The contractor howled in pain, shoving Quinn backwards as if he was on fire, but hanging on to the MP7's sling. Quinn stumbled back and down, allowing the sling to slide over his head. Grimacing at his stupidity for giving up the weapon, he swung the Severance's heavy blade in time to knock the rifle out of the big man's hands. It skittered across the plywood floor.

Ignoring the flashing blade, the contractor rushed forward with a furious roar, driving Quinn backwards against the unforgiving edge of a stainless-steel cleaning table. Quinn pushed upward at the last moment, catching the hard edge against his buttocks instead of his kidneys. He rolled backwards, lying on the table to plant his bare feet in the belly of his attacker, shoving him. It bought him the split second he needed to regain his balance. Razor-sharp fillet knives, abandoned on the table by the fish processers, clattered to the floor.

The contractor was on him again in a flash, swatting away the Severance before Quinn could bring it to bear. Quinn rolled out of the way, ducking under the other man's arm as it fell in a devastating blow that sent Quinn reeling backwards, past a wash rack and into a tub filled with a slurry of water, crushed ice, and gutted salmon. The snot-slick fish broke his fall but made it impossible to regain his feet with any speed. Swimming in dead fish, Quinn hooked a ten-pounder through the gills and flung it at the bald contractor.

The big man sneered, staring down at an apparently defeated target. His eyes darted around the room. The rifle was fifteen feet away in a grimy puddle. The pistol was lodged under the cleaning tables on the other side of his dead partner. Instead of going for either of the guns, the contractor scooped up one of the long fillet knives that cluttered the cleaning counters.

Chest heaving, sweat and fish slime dripping from his nose, the bald giant hovered over Quinn.

"Now I'm gonna hand you your ass," he growled.

Never much of a talker when he fought, Quinn answered by giving the man a face full of frigid water from the wash hose that hung down beside his tub of fish.

Startled by the sudden shock, the contractor stepped back, raising his hand to ward off the new threat. Steel flashed as he struck blindly with the fillet knife, lashing out to protect himself while he got his bearings.

As its name implied, the Severance was at its best when used as a hacking instrument. Its finely ground tip was, however, needle sharp and pierced the flesh between the contractor's wrist bones as surely as an axe through soft cheese.

With the thick spine of the blade facing backwards, toward the contractor's hand, Quinn yanked the man toward him, in the direction of his attack. Screaming in pain, the contractor's eyes flew open as he tumbled into the fish tub, while Quinn twisted the Severance's handle like a lever between the bones of his forearm. Even with nearly a foot of steel sticking out of his arm, the bald man was nowhere near finished. He lashed out with heavy boots, wrenching the Severance from Quinn's hand and sending him sliding backwards across the floor. Unfortunately for the contractor, Quinn stopped sliding beside the MP7.

A quick burp of six 4.6x30 rounds to his chest and the frown on the bald guy's forehead went slack. He collapsed back into the tub of dead salmon with a groan.

Quinn held the MP7 at high ready, giving the room a full scan for the first time since he'd charged through the door ninety seconds earlier. April John was unconscious in the corner, facedown on the plywood in a pool of grimy water and salmon blood. She had a bloody lip, and her hands and feet were bound with gray duct tape, but she was breathing.

Quinn checked both contractors to make certain they wouldn't cause any more problems, and then moved to cut April John's restraints. She drew back when he touched her shoulder, drawing her body into a tight ball.

"Get off me!" Her terrified scream was muffled in Quinn's ears.

"It's me, Jericho," Quinn said. He laid a hand gently

against her elbow to show he meant no harm. "They're dead."

She turned her head to look up at him, blinking terrified eyes. Blood and slime from the floor dripped from her round cheek. "Jericho? They . . ." She tried to sit up, but swayed in place. Quinn could now see the knot on her forehead from where she'd been hit, hard. "What happened? Where are they?"

"It's okay now," he said, still panting from exertion. "I'm going to cut you loose."

The door opened behind him and he looked up to see James Perry silhouetted against the gray fog. The big Eskimo took a quick look around the room, and then stepped up beside Quinn. His face was turned down in a somber frown.

"*Waqaa*, cousin." He gave the traditional Yup'ik greeting, voice drawn with pent-up worry. "You good?"

"Hey," Quinn nodded. "I'm fine. Looks like they knocked April around pretty good, though."

Kneeling, Quinn used a fillet knife to finish cutting away the duct tape on the girl's wrists and ankles. He helped her into a sitting position with her back against the tubs.

Swaying when he tried to stand, he reached out to Ukka for support. The adrenaline dump from his coldwater swim and subsequent fight behind him now, he began to shiver uncontrollably.

April John's two younger sisters poured in through the open door, scooping her up amid a shower of grateful tears and hugs for both her and Quinn. They whisked her away with a nod, getting her out of the place that had only moments before had been her prison.

"We got some bad news," Ukka said, as Lovita Aguthluk, his twenty-two-year-old niece, stepped through the door behind him. Dressed in a pink fleece sweater that was three sizes too big, she was a breath over five feet tall with long peroxide orange hair and a row of piercings festooning the top of each tiny ear. Her grandmother was from Kotzebue and she honored the older woman with a traditional Inupiat facial tattoo—three simple parallel lines, green and pencil thin, that ran from her lower lip to the bottom of her deeply tanned chin. On some women, such a marking might be considered a job stopper, but Lovita had the cultural background to make it attractive. Her fleece was grimy at the cuffs from fishing and gathering wood for the stove in her small shack in Saint Mary's. Any money she got was spent on airplane fuel and there were few clear days when she could not be seen drilling holes in the sky between Mountain Village and Saint Mary's in her ratty old Super Cub. She hauled whatever anyone would pay her to haul to support her flying habit and build time behind the stick.

"What is it?" Quinn asked, steadying himself on the cleaning counter. He wasn't sure he could handle much more at the moment.

Ukka looked at his niece. "Tell him what you saw."

"A plane full of these guys landed in Saint Mary's about half an hour ago," she said in a husky voice that sounded like she'd smoked two packs a day for twice her lifetime—which wasn't far from the truth. She was trying to quit and now had a wad of punk ash—leaf tobacco and a type of burned tree fungus—snuff beneath her lower lip. "They were going from house to house looking for you when I left, but I'm pretty sure they're getting ready to come this way."

She handed Quinn a tall plastic tumbler full of hot liquid, placing it carefully between his trembling hands to make sure he didn't spill it.

"How many?" he asked.

"I'm not sure," she said. "As soon as I saw them, I jumped in the Cub and headed this way to warn you."

Quinn nodded in thanks. He started to put the mug to his lips but raised a wary eye. He knew Lovita had a stomach of iron. She'd talked all spring about her favorite dish, called "stinkhead"—a concoction of fermented salmon heads that had been left in a grassy pit for a period of days. An ardent traditionalist, it was impossible to know what sort of ancient hunk of mystery meat she might throw into a soup or stew.

"It's coffee," she grunted. "We need to hurry."

Quinn took a tentative sip, grimacing at the syrupy sweetness.

Lovita gave a half smile. She wasn't much of a smiler, but when she did, it brightened the entire room. "I put lots of sugar in it to help your body warm itself." She handed Quinn a roll of dry clothes. "We gotta go now."

Nodding, Quinn handed the coffee to Ukka. Lovita turned her back while he slipped out of his sopping wet pants. She'd brought him a black wool sweater that zipped up the front and a fresh set of khakis.

"I didn't want to go rootin' around in your stuff for your tighty whities," she said. "I'm afraid you'll have to go commando."

Quinn shot a glance at Ukka, who shrugged.

"I don't know where they learn that stuff all the way out here," the Eskimo said.

"I got satellite," Lovita said, her voice even more gravelly than before. "Anyway, hurry up. I'll step outside while you change."

"I think she has a little crush on you," Ukka said.

Quinn steered the subject in a different direction. "If

they're leaving Saint Mary's now," he said, pulling the sweater over his head, "they'll be here in—"

"Ten minutes," Ukka cut him off. "We know. That's why we need to haul ass."

Once Quinn was decent, Ukka looked over his shoulder and flicked his hand to summon his daughter Chantelle, who stepped through the door carrying Quinn's Lowa boots and a rolled pair of wool socks.

"Lovita said she couldn't find his underwear," she said. "I could have brought his underwear if I woulda known."

"Will you girls forget about his underwear," Ukka bellowed. He looked at his watch. "It'll take us five minutes to get to the airport. That's cutting it pretty close."

Lovita poked her head in behind Ukka.

"I'm going," she said. "It'll take me a minute or two to get the plane ready."

Quinn dropped the boots on the floor and sat on an overturned fish tub to pull on the socks. He looked at the young pilot with a wary eye.

"The weather isn't too low to fly?"

"We got no choice." She shrugged, her neck disappearing down the oversize fleece like a turtle's.

"She's right," Ukka said. "We'll get rid of the bodies, then handle these new guys when they land. But who knows how many more are right behind them? It's been a great visit, but you gotta get outta here before someone gets hurt."

Quinn laced up his last boot and walked outside behind the others. Cold drizzle hit him in the face. Heavy curtains of fog obscured all but the base of the Azochorak Mountain to the west. The white crosses in the cemetery that had been visible when he'd entered the river were now gone.

Quinn took a lungful of air and let it out, able to see his breath. "You really plan to fly in this muck?"

Lovita nodded. "I can sneak out just off the deck and try to stay under the clouds."

"Try?"

Lovita ignored him. "Weather's better over past the Kilbucks." Her voice was matter-of-fact as if she flew in this kind of soupy fog every day. "It's not good, mind you—but it's a damn sight better than this."

# Chapter 15

*Pentagon City, Virginia*

Kim Quinn saw the man with the flap of blond hair again as they exited the mall. He was standing next to the Metro entrance between the taxi road and the main thoroughfare of Hayes Street. Worried over why someone might be following her, she'd talked Mattie out of dinner at Johnny Rockets and decided to go straight back to their hotel room. Jericho's parents were there—Pete Quinn would know what to do.

Kim tried to tell herself a life with Jericho had made her paranoid. But there was definitely something wrong. This guy had ignored her when she'd almost run into him. He hadn't given her a second look—which was virtually unthinkable. Kim had always been proud of her legs. The one that she had left was well worth gawking over—and the metal one drew even more stares, even from polite people who were usually more startled than anything. The fact that this man hadn't paid her any attention set off an alarm in her head.

Over the span of their marriage, Jericho had droned on and on about how she should trust her instincts. Go with her gut, he said. Her gut told her the man with the flap of blond hair was dangerous.

Pausing for just a moment outside the mall, she took Mattie's hand in hers.

"Stay with me," she said, leading her across the taxi and tour bus service road and weaving through the throng of summer vendors, lined up under umbrella carts, selling bottled water and WASHINGTON, DC T-shirts. The air was thick, but she didn't know if it was humidity or dread.

She cursed herself for not taking a closer parking spot. Her pride had made her want to show off to her daughter, so she'd parked across the street in the larger Costco lot, hoping to demonstrate that she was tough and resilient.

The blond man didn't move from his post by the Metro escalator, and made no secret of the fact that he was now staring directly at Kim. He must have taken the Metro tunnel out from the food court level of the mall and surfaced outside to wait.

Kim shot a quick glance up and down the street. She fought the urge to scream for help, realizing she was in the middle of a crowded sidewalk, and nothing had actually happened. The area around Washington, DC, was a busy place any time of year, but summer was the worst with visitors from all over the world pouring out of buses, taxis, and rental cars. Every ten feet she saw someone who looked like they might be working with the man by the Metro. There was a crosswalk to her right, halfway down the block at Fifteenth Street. It would be closer to where she'd parked the car across the street at the Costco lot. But the crowds thinned out down there. She made a decision to cross mid-block, staying with the herd for protection.

There were plenty of people here, she reasoned. No way anyone would try anything in the open in broad daylight.

Mattie kept quiet, sensitive to her mother's mood. With Jericho Quinn as her father, she was much more accustomed to sudden violence that any seven-year-old should have to be.

Kim was sure the pedestrian light was the longest in history of mankind. A middle-aged man in a loose Hawaiian shirt asked if she needed help crossing the street and she nearly punched him out of panic. Realizing he was just being kind, she thanked him instead and assured him she was fine. The last word had no sooner escaped her mouth than a tan minivan squealed up to the curb and stopped directly in front of her.

The door slid open and two men jumped out to the sidewalk. Both wore absurd-looking clown masks. One grabbed for Mattie while the other planted both palms in Kim's chest and gave her a rough shove, sending her sliding on her butt on the pavement.

The man in the Hawaiian shirt stepped in between the kidnapper and Mattie, shooing her behind him as he punched the other man in the jaw. He was strong, certainly no out-of-shape tourist, and the blow connected with a loud crack. He went to follow up, but the man who'd shoved Kim shot him twice for his trouble. He staggered, then slumped to the sidewalk.

"Mattie, run!" Kim screamed. She was on her feet in a moment, forgetting how difficult such a simple task had been in physical therapy. Swinging her cane like a baseball bat, she struck out at the gunman, impacting on the base of his skull. He squealed in pain and staggered into his companion. Kim swung again, but the aluminum cane was much too light to do any real damage and the kidnapper grabbed it in midair, yanking her to him and into his waiting fist.

Kim had never been hit so hard in her life and found it oddly liberating. She'd heard Jericho say punches didn't really hurt until later and was astonished to find out how right he was. Instead of wilting like a battered woman, she launched herself against her attackers with the renewed fury of a mother protecting her child. She tore at the gunman's eyes with her fingernails, screaming like a madwoman, intent on ripping his face off his body.

Nearly back to the doors of the mall, Mattie stopped in her tracks when she heard her mother's cries. She had her father's blood in her veins, so it was no surprise when she turned on her heels and ran back to help her mother.

The man with the blond flap of hair caught her as she came past and scooped her up in his arms.

"Let's get you out of here," he said, trapping her arms and legs so she could do the least damage with all her kicking and screaming.

"No!" Kim screamed, as the gunman hit her again, this time sending a shower of fireworks exploding behind her eyes. "Mattie!"

A distant roar seemed to fill the street, growing louder as Kim's vision cleared enough for her to make out what was happening.

A Harley-Davidson motorcycle roared up the mall service road, scattering tourists and vendors. At the same moment a black GMC pickup jumped the curb, ramming the minivan and raking the gunman with a running board. The biker rode straight for the blond kidnapper, striking him with the front tire before he could throw a squalling Mattie into the minivan. She scrambled out of the way, running back toward the mall.

Six feet, two inches of extremely angry grandfather boiled out of the black pickup. Pete Quinn sent a massive fist crashing into the temple of the stunned gunman, felling him like a tree. He bounced the second man's head off the hood of the minivan as the man on the motorcycle jumped off the bike and ran for the open door of the van. He was wearing a helmet, but moved with the same easy stride of Jericho. It had to be his brother, Bo.

The frantic driver threw the minivan in reverse, narrowly missing the downed Good Samaritan in the Hawaiian shirt, and then sped away down Hayes Street, fishtailing around the corner to disappear down Fifteenth.

Kim breathed a measured sigh of relief.

The sullen blond tried to push himself to his feet, but Jericho's father put the toe of his heavy leather boot to good use, nearly kicking the man's head off his body. As far as he was concerned, anyone stupid enough to grab his granddaughter would get no forgiveness in this world or the world to come.

The gunman's jaw hung oddly to the side, half out of its socket, courtesy of the punch from the man in the Hawaiian shirt. He jumped up and attempted to run, but Bo grabbed him by the collar, yanking him into a devastating left hook that reset his jaw and crumpled him into an unconscious heap.

Once she saw Mattie was okay, Kim half knelt, half fell to the pavement beside the wounded Good Samaritan. Her damaged prosthetic splayed awkwardly to one side, but there was nothing she could do about that now. She put a hand to his chest, pressing against the bullet wound. He was still breathing but losing a lot of blood.

"Thank you," Kim whispered. "For helping us."

The man smiled, but grimaced when he tried to speak.

A crowd of onlookers began to gather, happy to form a circle around the commotion now that the apparent danger had passed. Several people called 911 at the same time, arguing about what happened and their actual location. There was a firehouse just blocks away and sirens blared moments later. An ER nurse coming out of Fashion Center mall stepped in and relieved Kim to care for the man in the Hawaiian shirt. Pete Quinn, Jericho's father, helped her back to her feet.

"You okay?" He put a hand on her shoulder to steady her. His dark hair was mussed and the top button of his shirt had been torn off, but there was a glint in his eyes that said he'd enjoyed the scrap. He was broader than either of his sons, bigger boned, but he moved with the same purposeful intensity that Kim had always seen in Jericho. In all the years she'd known her former father-in-law, he'd always been in the shop or out working on the boat. They'd really never sat down to have a long conversation. To see him now, like this, was nothing short of mind-blowing.

Kim thanked him, panting so hard she could hardly speak. She fanned her face with an open hand. She'd just thought she'd been sweating before.

"I think my new bionic leg is toast," she said, glancing down at the bowed metal that no longer bent correctly at her knee. She dabbed her lip, tasting blood. "Where did you guys come from?"

The elder Quinn shrugged. "Bo thought someone ought to keep an eye on you." He'd never been one for much chitchat.

A shiver shook Kim's shoulders. The world around her began to blur and ooze.

Pete Quinn caught her as she swayed.

Three Arlington Police cruisers rolled onto the scene. Unsure of what was going on, the officers approached with weapons drawn, eyeing Pete and Bo Quinn as hard as they did the downed kidnappers.

Jericho's propensity to grow a heavy beard had come from his father. He'd surely shaved that morning, but already looked as though he'd gone a week. Bo, the younger and more wayward of his two sons, had bleached blond hair that was long enough to blow in the wind when he rode. He was more baby faced than his brother and father, but his life in a Texas motorcycle club that dabbled in the gray edges of the law had aged and hardened him.

Seven-year-old Mattie, clutching Kim's leg, appeared to calm the arriving officers a degree. Two of them handcuffed the downed kidnappers, while one checked on the status of the man in the Hawaiian shirt.

The responding sergeant, a tall, clean-shaven man named Oldham, approached Pete Quinn, nodding politely at Kim. He looked like a man with an easy smile, but for the circumstances. "They were trying to kidnap the little girl?"

"That's right," Kim said, still feeling shaky. "She's my daughter."

"And you guys stepped in to help?"

"Correct." Pete nodded. "I'm the grandfather."

Oldham collected their IDs, stopping to peer back over at them when he read the names.

"*Quinn*," he said, lips pursing in distaste. "You all related to the Jericho Quinn who's wanted for the murder of a Fairfax police officer?"

Bo began to speak, but Pete Quinn held up his calloused hand. "We are," he said. "But this has nothing to do with that."

"My experience," Sergeant Oldham muttered, still studying the two men, "is that this always has to do with that. And from where I'm standing, it looks like you have a lot in common with your son."

Pete Quinn took a deep breath, mulling his words carefully before he said them. "Sergeant," he said, his voice almost a whisper. "Haven't you ever had a relative that disappointed you?"

Oldham thought about that for a long moment. "Guess you can't choose your relatives," he said at length. "My bad. I'm going to need you to come down to the station and fill out some paperwork." He looked at Kim. "And I'm gonna get a paramedic to take a look at you."

Bo leaned in as Sergeant Oldham went to summon a paramedic. "The disappointing one—that's me you're talking about, right?"

"Pshh," Pete said. It was his way of dismissing any notion as so utterly inconceivable it didn't merit an answer. "I don't know about that guy, but I'm proud of my family. When he comes back, tell him I had to make a call."

Kim knew exactly who he was about to call—and she'd never wished for that man to be there as much as she did at that moment.

# Chapter 16

*Alaska*

Jericho's cell phone began to vibrate seconds after he'd fastened the shoulder harness in the cramped backseat of the tiny airplane. The little yellow Super Cub was a tandem-seat tail dragger. Lovita sat in the single seat directly in front of his. In her baggy pink fleece with the large green headphones over her orange hair, she looked like a child pretending to be a bush pilot.

The rain had started to fall in earnest on the way to the gravel strip and beat against the outside of the airplane as if someone was pelting them with a steady barrage of pebbles. Quinn used the forearm of his wool shirt to wipe away the condensation on his window, scanning what was left of the eastern horizon for the other plane as he pressed the phone to his ear.

Lovita applied the brakes to keep the Super Cub from rolling forward, and then slowly increased the throttle until it shook in place. The little airplane groaned, straining to leap off the gravel strip. Lovita watched the handful of simple engine gauges, checking oil pressure and both magnetos. She spun the dial to reset her altimeter and checked the fuel level in the clear plastic tubes above each window on either side of her seat. Satisfied, she worked the stick between her knees in all directions, and pumped the rudder pedals back and forth. An identical set of controls in front of Quinn moved in time with her as if operated by some ghost.

The rag and tube construction of the Super Cub did little to block the deafening roar of the Lycoming engine. Quinn wedged the phone under the earpiece of his headset and leaned down as best he could in the cramped confines behind Lovita's short seat.

He listened in horror as his father related the kidnapping attempt on Kim and Mattie. His stomach twisted tighter with each word. By the time he ended the call, he'd already reached a decision.

Lovita's husky voice crackled in his headset. It sounded much too mature to be coming from the little girl sitting in front of him.

"That other plane just overflew Pitka's Point," she said. "They're gonna be here any minute."

"Can we steer clear of them?" Quinn asked, looking out the window at the white sheets of rain marching along the river.

"Maybe so," Lovita said, releasing the brake. "But first we have to get in the air." The plane lurched forward. Fat tundra tires bounced toward the end of the gravel strip as they picked up speed. The tail lifted almost immediately, leveling the plane and giving little Lovita a better view out the windshield.

"I need to make a couple of quick calls before we

lose reception," Quinn said, punching buttons as he spoke.

"Go for it." Lovita added throttle and pulled back on the stick, causing the little plane to leap off the runway. One hand on the throttle, the other on the stick at her knees, Lovita worked the rudders at her feet, engaged in a sort of dance with the airplane as she committed it to the turbulent mixture of fog and driving rain.

Quinn felt his stomach fall away at the same moment Ronnie Garcia picked up on the other end of his call. He longed to talk to her more, but kept the conversation brief. There was still one more person he had to contact before he lost reception.

"We're going to need that babysitter," he yelled.

"The babysitter?" Garcia's voice came back amid a crackle of static. "You're certain about this?"

"Call my dad," Quinn said. "He'll explain."

"I love you," Ronnie said.

The phone went dead before he could answer.

Quinn punched in the second number as Lovita dipped a wing, banking the Super Cub to the right toward the razor-thin line of open sky between soggy tundra and trailing clouds. The plane lurched hard, buffeting as they flew through a band of turbulence where cooler air over the river gave way to warmer stuff over land. Rain splattered the windows, streaming backwards as they picked up speed. The Kilbuck Mountains lay ahead, and beyond them, the Alaska Range, and then the city of Anchorage—and somewhere in between, the other airplane.

Lovita cheated north, leaving the Yukon River and the sprawling settlement of Mountain Village. Breaking nearly every rule in the book, she nosed the little plane upward and into the clouds in an effort to avoid the other plane. The cell tower disappeared behind them in a shroud of gray mist. Quinn pressed the cell phone to his ear, knowing he didn't have long before he lost reception altogether.

"Come on," he said under his breath. "Pick up, Jacques."

# Chapter 17

Gunnery Sergeant Jacques Thibodaux dropped his carry-on roller bag on the chipped concrete porch and fished his house key from the pocket of his Marine Corps utilities. Two gallon jugs of milk and six flimsy plastic grocery bags hung from his massive left hand. The brim of his utility cover pulled low over his forehead, he clutched a stack of bills and credit card offers between his teeth. A black patch covered one eye, the wound courtesy of a gun battle in a Bolivian jungle alongside his friend Jericho Quinn. He was a big man with shoulders as wide as his own front porch and muscles that strained the seams of his MARPAT camo uniform. The black nylon rigger's belt with a single red stripe signified he was a certified instructor trainer of Marine Corps Martial Arts.

The door swung open before he could get the key.

"Hey, Boo," Thibodaux said to his wife. Her name was Camille, but he'd called her Cornmeal or Boo from the first time he'd met her when she was tending bar outside Camp Lejeune. She was a short thing, and at six-feet-four he had to lean down some to meet her.

Snatching the mail out of his mouth with the hand that held the grocery bags, he winked his good eye and tilted his head so she could give him their customary welcome-home kiss without bumping the brim of his cover.

Camille didn't move. Standing in the open door, she cocked her hip to one side—a hip that was nicely clad, to the gunny's way of thinking, in stretchy black yoga pants. Her deeply tanned arms ran up either side of the threshold, completely blocking his entry. Black hair brushed strong shoulders. The Eagle, Globe, and Anchor on the chest of her faded green USMC tank top swelled and dipped in all the right places.

He'd only been gone three nights—some training down in Georgia for his new job in logistics. Sheer torture for a man used to the rigors and adventure of the field, the hours of convoluted PowerPoints and bone-dry lectures felt like some new form of enhanced interrogation. Being able to lay eyes again on the mother of his seven boys took his breath away.

He leaned in again, trying once more for their customary hello.

Instead of kissing him, she folded her arms, obscuring his view of the Eagle, Globe, and Anchor, and threw him one of her patented pissed-off Italian looks. She was nearly a foot shorter than him, but standing inside the doorway made it easier to look him in the eye with him still out on the porch.

Thibodaux took a half step back.

"What?" he said. "Somebody die or somethin'?"

Eyes the color of black coffee narrowed under an even darker brow. "Don't pretend like you don't know." Her accent was a fricassee of the Deep South spiced with just a hint of her father's Mott Street Italian.

Thibodaux shook his head, rolling through his brain

for some anniversary or birthday he'd missed. They'd just talked the night before. She hadn't given him any indication then that she'd been mad.

"I really don't—"

"Yes, you do, Jacques," she whispered. "That's the problem."

"What?" He was begging now. "What is the problem?"

"I want to hear it from your own lips, Jacques Thibodaux," she said. "It'll be better for everyone that way."

*"Arette toi,"* he pleaded. *Stop, you.* "Baby, I got no earthly idea what you're talkin' about."

Her lips tightened into a terrifying line, the way they did when she banished him to sleep on the couch. "Jacques," she said, scolding. "You have got to tell me the truth."

"You're killin' me, here," Thibodaux said, his gumbo-thick Cajun drawl thickening even more. "I swear on my *mamere's* own grave . . ."

Camille's face melted into a wide smile

"Just checking," she said and leaned in to give him a peck on the nose. "Gotta keep what's mine, mine."

"Holy shit, girl," he moaned, throwing his head back. "You scared my mule there."

She raised a black eyebrow at his cursing.

"Come on," he said, walking in to set the bags on the dining room table. "You owe me that one."

"Maybe," she said, peeking out the mini-blinds that faced the street.

Camille Thibodaux, the churchgoing member of the marriage, allotted her gunnery sergeant husband a total of five non-Bible curse words each month in an effort to keep her boys from picking up potty mouths. As long as it was in the Bible, any word was fair game.

Which, Thibodaux discovered, actually gave him a pretty large lexicon to choose from.

"That van's back," she said.

Thibodaux shrugged. "I know," he said. "Just try and forget about it." He took the milk into the kitchen.

He knew what the van was all about—or had his suspicions at least. He even told Camille some of it. An OGA, or other governmental agent along with Quinn when Winfield Palmer had been in office, the change in the administration had forced him to return to his old unit. He returned from Japan as ordered and reported in to Quantico, but his command had been unsure of what to do with him. It seemed that anyone who'd had access to the former president was now damaged goods—even dangerous to be around. Gunny Thibodaux—the consummate warrior with more tours into forward operating areas in the hellholes of the Middle East than he had sons—which was saying a lot—had been relegated to desk duty.

Even there he didn't really have a job other than organizing paper files that seemed to be pretty damned organized already. It was the clerical equivalent of breaking big rocks into little rocks. Still, Thibodaux tried to make the best of it, biding his time until Palmer, and the few he had working with him, hatched a plan to deal with this current administration. Thibodaux had little contact with Quinn, but Garcia and Palmer reached out to him on occasion, using the old-school method of leaving a chalk mark on the bench at the ball field where his oldest sons played when they wanted a meeting. It was all basic tradecraft from the Cold War era, fascinating stuff in his early training with Quinn and the enigmatic Mrs. Miyagi, but certainly not something he'd thought he would ever put to use.

Camille's voice pulled him out of his thoughts. "Are you even listening to me, T?"

Thibodaux turned to see his wife had folded her arms again. After seven sons, her figure was still what his daddy would have called praline-scrumptious—a little curvier than she once was—but that was just fine with Jacques. The skin-and-bones things on TV looked about as appetizing as cuddling with a metal storm grate. Camille was, as Jacques liked to point out, built for comfort over speed.

"You know I'm listening, *mon cher*," Jacques said, flinging his Cajun charm at her. He ran the flat of his hand over the top of the bristles of his high and tight haircut. "What was it you were sayin'?"

"You big, stupid son of a bitch," Camille said, welling up with tears. Somehow, she could curse whenever she felt like it. She could have cursed him in her native Italian, but what was the good of cursing your husband if he didn't understand how mad you were? Some things just couldn't be picked up by context alone.

She threw her head back and stared at the ceiling, blinking away tears. "Sometimes you just make me want to scream."

Jacques grimaced. He truly hated it when his sweet bride was angry—on so many levels. "I'm sorry, Boo. I swear I didn't mean to hurt your feelings."

"I'm telling you that van is parked back across the street again. It was here for a week, then left when you did. You get back from training and now it's out there again. I can't help it if that scares me." She snatched a tissue from the table and blew her nose. "Sometimes I think you just don't give a damn."

Thibodaux took her gently by both shoulders, cocking his head to one side to try to make sense of what she meant rather than what she said.

"Of course, I give a damn," he said. "I give lots of damns. In fact, I give more damns than anyone I ever even heard of. You know that." He tilted her chin up with a crooked finger.

She put her arms around his neck and pulled him close. "I'm just tired," she whispered. "You being followed everywhere, creepy men watching us like this— it's a lot for a girl to take in. You know?"

Arms around her waist, he lifted her off her feet. "I hate it too," he whispered, pulling her body against his and giving her back a little crack the way she liked.

He put her down and gave her a peck on the forehead.

Camille sighed, semi-appeased. "I'm sorry for the hissy fit."

Thibodaux glanced at his watch. "I got an hour till I have to start making the rounds to go pick up the little *bougs*. We hardly ever get any time alone. What say you and me play a little game of Naked Twister?"

Camille took an elastic band off her wrist and looped it around her hair, pulling it up into a thick ponytail. "I guess I could pencil you in," she said. "If you help me put away these groceries."

"Sold." Thibodaux grinned, opening the refrigerator door to put in all his plastic shopping bags at once.

"I see where our boys get their behavior," Camille chided.

"I know," Thibodaux said. "I was just foolin' with you."

"Not until you unpack these groceries, you're not." Camille turned away, carrying a carton of Minute Rice to the pantry. He gave her a little swat on the butt as she walked away, keeping up the illusion that he was the one in charge.

\* \* \*

Five minutes later, Thibodaux followed his wife into the bedroom, hopping on one foot and then the other as he peeled off his socks.

Camille sat on the edge of the bed, swinging her legs and watching him undress. He rarely told her what he did when he was out of town, but she made it a habit of checking him over for new wounds and scars when he came home.

"When is the last time you heard anything from Jericho?" She asked.

Thibodaux shot a glance toward the window. He put a finger to his lips, and then leaned in closer, whispering. "There's a good chance the guys in that van have listening devices. They might able to pick up some of the things we say, even inside the house."

She raised an eyebrow, giving him a slow nod as she considered that information. "That being the case . . ." She looked down at the bed. "We should probably be careful then."

"Hang on, now." Thibodaux held up both hands, trying to salvage a few minutes with his wife before he had to pick up the boys. "I ain't saying they can really hear us. I'm just thinking we should be careful when we mention you know who."

"I see," she said, not moving.

"Does this mean . . . ?"

"Of course not." She peeled off her shirt and fell back on the bed, giving the mattress a playful bounce. "Remember that crap hole apartment we rented when we were stationed at Camp Pendleton?"

He nodded, dumbly. After seven boys, the sight of her body still took his breath away.

"Well, do you recall how the neighbor's TV was always so loud and how we could hear them talking about what to have for dinner?"

Thibodaux shrugged. "I suppose so."

"If I worried about people listening in on us, I'd never have gotten pregnant with our first two boys. I think the neighbors left their TV turned up all the time so they didn't have to listen to you jumpin' my bones every minute of the day." She patted the bed, talking out loud now. "Get your ass up here, Gunny Thib—"

The smaller of the two cell phones next to their bed began to chime. Jacques gave an exasperated sigh, but picked it up immediately. He rolled his hand in the air, motioning for Camille to make more noise to help camouflage his conversation.

Dressed in nothing but her grin, Camille began to jump up and down on the bed, squeaking the box springs and driving Thibodaux crazy in the process.

"Speak to me, *beb*," the Gunny said, eyes locked on his bouncing wife.

"It's happening," Jericho Quinn said. "They've found me."

"You okay, *l'ami*?" Thibodaux had to turn away so he could concentrate. The two men had known each other just over two years, but they'd bled and spilled blood together and were closer than brothers—even if Quinn happened to be a member of what he'd always considered the "pansy ass" Air Force.

The Cajun listened while Quinn ran down not only an attack on him, but on his wife and daughter.

"What can I do?"

"You know that thing we discussed?"

Thibodaux found himself shaking his head. "I remember," he said. "But you might want to rethink that, Chair Force."

"It's already in motion."

"You're serious about this?"

"Dead serious," Quinn said. "My dad and brother are with them now. Would you mind heading over and giving them a hand? You know, looking outbound. They need all the security they can get."

"No problem," Thibodaux said. "I just . . . I mean . . . Are you sure about this plan of yours?"

"I'm sure," Quinn said. "Listen, I have to go. Sonja will have the particulars."

"Okay," Thibodaux said, "I'll talk to *Sonja* then." He made a face when he said Ronnie Garcia's code name. He hated all the code names and beating around the bush. If something threatened him, he much preferred to walk up and shoot it in the face.

He ended the call and turned to catch his wife around the waist in mid bounce.

"What was that about?" She leaned forward off the edge of the bed to nuzzle his neck.

"It was Quinn," he whispered. "Sorry, Cornmeal, but I gotta run."

"Okay." She stuck out her bottom lip. That was the great thing about Camille. She might pout a time or two every year, but then she sucked it up and did the Marine wife thing, supporting her man when he went off to fight.

Thibodaux pulled on his socks and stepped into a pair of jeans, wondering how much of this he should tell his bride. He decided on anything that might make the evening news.

"Some guys tried to snatch Mattie," he said. "It was very likely an effort to lure our buddy out of the woods."

"That's awful." Camille knelt on the bed, hugging a pillow to her bare chest. "Is she okay?"

"She's scared," Thibodaux said, "but safe. Bo's there . . . and Quinn's dad."

Camille gave a low whistle. "I was just thinking . . ." Her voice trailed off.

"What's that, *cher*?" Thibodaux stretched a gray T-shirt over broad shoulders and monstrous arms.

"I was just thinking that if they really knew Jericho, they'd know it'd be better to let him stay on the run."

"You got that right," Thibodaux said. He left out the part about Quinn sending his daughter and ex-wife to Russia in order to keep them safe.

# Chapter 18

Ronnie Garcia set her leather backpack on the kitchen counter and activated the alarm on the panel inside the front door. She usually didn't do it until later, when she was about to go to bed, but things were getting weird. Standing at the kitchen counter again, she stared at the lone goldfish swimming in the bowl near the cordless telephone. A crusted soup pan sat nearby where Ronnie had spent last night's dinner watching, and sadly, chatting up the little bug-eyed fish while she ate on her feet.

Jericho had called the moment she'd walked in the door. She'd heard the urgency in his voice, but the fact that he was willing to send his ex-wife and daughter to communist Russia to keep them safe from the new administration said all she needed to know about his present state of mind.

Jacques had called seconds later, filling her in on the specifics of the attack on Kim and Mattie. He knew the plan and told Ronnie he'd brief them on what she was about to do.

She ran a hand through thick hair, rubbing her eyes with a thumb and forefinger as she thought through her course of action. A hot bath called her name, but there was no time for that. She had a call to make—and the sooner she made it the better. There was no way she could make it from her house—even on the burner phone. There was no way of knowing what someone might be able to pick up with infrared or laser listening technology.

Apart from letting her know how easy it was for someone from the Internal Defense Task Force to find out where she parked her car in the CIA parking lot, Garcia's conversation with Agent Walter had twisted her gut into a knot.

A long run would help quiet her nerves. More important, it would give her the perfect opportunity to make her call.

Stripping off her street clothes as she walked down the short hall to her bedroom, Garcia rummaged through the pile of laundry beside her dresser until she found a reasonably clean pair of running shorts and a loose T-shirt. Barefoot, she sat on the edge of the bed and rummaged through her wallet until she found a business card to a local pizzeria with a coded phone number written on the back.

The IDTF and NSA had become bosom bedfellows under the new administration—so much so that she'd had to purchase two prepaid cell phones. Not wanting to burn her communication link with Quinn in the event this international call was hacked, she dedicated one of these "burners" to Jericho and the other to calls like the one she was about to make. Monitoring was always likely, but tens of thousands of people made international calls from the US each day. As long as the conversation stayed plain vanilla and no names or trigger words were used, Garcia hoped she could melt into the digital background noise.

Falling back on the bed, she took a moment to decipher the safety code she'd written on the card. It was meant to slow down anyone who might have been snooping around her wallet. Once she figured it out, she picked up the phone and dialed 01 to exit the US, 7 for Russia and the Skylink prefix, which acted as an area code for the Russian cell service, before punching in all but the last digit of the number.

A member of the Russia's Federal Security Service or FSB, Aleksandra Kanatova was a spy Jericho Quinn had spent a considerable amount of time with, traipsing around South America while they looked for a missing Soviet-era nuke. Ronnie had seen her once, at a party near Miami where they had been hunting the same terrorist. They'd both been dressed in flimsy bathing suits so it had been easy to get a read on Kanatova, physically at least. Ronnie supposed the Russian was pretty if one had a thing for smallish redheaded assassins who were covered in freckles. Thankfully, Jericho Quinn seemed to prefer his killer girlfriends built a bit more on the robust side with a little more pigment to their complexions—and the hint of a Cuban accent.

Garcia laced up her running shoes and slipped the tiny Kahr 9mm pistol into a black leather fanny pack that blended in with her shorts. Skipping her usual stretch, she reset the alarm and headed out the door with the burner phone in her hand.

She put in a single earbud, letting the other one dangle. It was an unwise spy who cut herself off from the warning signs of outside noises when out on a run—or anywhere for that matter.

Garcia checked up and down the quiet residential street in front of her modest frame house. She was half surprised that she didn't find Agent Walter's black Lincoln Town Car parked half a block away. There were a couple of other runners out—the cute guy who worked at the Pentagon and a housewife from three doors down who was out jogging off the extra pounds her spandex shorts so prominently displayed. A small ganglet of three preteens rode by on their bicycles, heads ducked in an all-out race for the end of the block. She was a horrible neighbor and wouldn't have been able to give the names of a single individual who lived around her—even under threat of torture. But she was an excellent spy and recognized them as people who did in fact live on her street. It was a quiet neighborhood with quiet people who kept to themselves, just like Ronnie. The houses were modest things, some decades old, some built on subdivided lots within the last five years. None were very large. These were not the Great Falls or Vienna, Virginia, homes of three-star generals and undersecretaries to the presidential cabinet. They were the plain brick and stick homes of the worker bees, close enough to DC to be within commuting distance and far enough away to be affordable before you hit GS 14 on the government pay scale. The warm scent of new-mown grass and blossoming flowers hung on the humid air. The lawns were manicured and the shrubs well-trimmed, but there were no sidewalks, so Ronnie ran along the edge, next to the gutter.

She entered the last remaining number into the cell phone, and then pressed send before breaking into an easy trot. She'd just reached a comfortable stride when she heard a loud click on the line, as if the connection was a stodgy throwback to the Soviet Cold War days.

"*Allo.*" Aleksandra Kanatova smacked her lips as she spoke, as if groggy from a deep sleep.

Garcia kept up her pace, glancing at her watch. A quarter after six in Maryland. She winced. It was after two in the morning, Moscow time.

"*Zdravstvujtye,*" Garcia said. She used the more formal greeting. Speaking Russian always made her think of her father, which caused her to smile. She hoped the sentiment carried in her voice. She spoke slowly, allowing the woman on the other end to wake up and grasp the gravity of her call. "I am calling on behalf of your friend from Argentina."

Kanatova gave a heavy cough. Garcia thought she heard the scrape of a lighter. She envisioned the Russian in a drab flat with a weak, bare lightbulb hanging from the ceiling and flaking paint on the walls, smoke from the freshly lit cigarette swirling around her naked shoulders. Garcia didn't know why, but she imagined all Russian spies slept naked and smoked a cigarette each time they got up to pee during the night.

Kanatova coughed again. Her voice was coarse and whiskeyed. "We were better acquainted in Bolivia." She gave the preplanned phrase to assure her identity. "I trust he is well."

"For now," Garcia said, telling what little she knew. "He would like to visit."

"Ah. I see." Kanatova was smart enough to know Quinn would have called to make the arrangements himself if he could have, so she did not question the fact that he'd asked his girlfriend to do it for him. Paper rustled on the line as she turned the page of a notebook. "Will he be bringing any luggage?"

"Himself and two carry-ons," Garcia answered.

"A large and a small carry-on?"

"That is correct."

"I have been watching the news," Kanatova said. "This was to be expected. I will make the necessary arrangements on this end."

"I understand," Garcia said. "I will call again soon to get the details." She hung up, picturing Aleksandra Kanatova falling back in her rumpled sheets, blowing smoke rings in the darkness of her dingy flat.

Kanatova had already taken care of the visas for just such an eventuality—one for Jericho using the passport under the unofficial and, with any luck, untraceable alias, John Hackman, and two more for a Kim and Mattie Hackman. A softening of the rules and few hundred extra bucks made the visas good for multiple entries over a three-year period from the date of issue. But there were still things that needed to occur on the other end. Knowing someone like Kanatova would smooth the way for Quinn to travel quickly with his "carry-ons."

Ronnie pulled the bud out of her ear and slowed long enough to shove the phone in the fanny pack along with her pistol. It made her stomach hurt to think of Jericho going to Russia with his ex-wife, even if it was just a place to stash her and keep her safe. It would have been easier if the woman was a flaming bitch, but Kimberly Quinn was fragile—especially since the shooting. Beyond that, she was the mother of Quinn's child—and that frightened Garcia more than anything.

Ronnie decided a little tradecraft would help push the jealous thoughts out of her brain. She spun in her tracks halfway down the block to run back the way she'd come. A blue Ford Escape with heavily tinted windows had been matching her pace. It sped up when she turned, passing with both the driver and a passenger staring straight ahead as if she didn't exist. It was called "conspicuous ignoring." The nimrods may as well have had government surveillance written all over the vehicle.

Ronnie shook her head. It would have been funny if it hadn't been so sad. She turned back again, heading toward the nearby lake that was surrounded by jogging trails. This was going to be a long five miles.

# Chapter 19

*The White House*

Vice President Lee McKeon took the buzzing cell phone out of his pocket and looked at the caller ID. It was blocked, as he suspected it would be. Calls that came in on this particular phone were rarely from anyone who wished to be identified.

Drake was still in the gym on the second floor of the residence, foolishly working on his physique when he should have been attending to important matters of state, but McKeon didn't mind. It gave him some quiet time with Ran in the privacy of the President's study. Thin shafts of light filtered through the drawn curtains. He would have rather sat in the Oval Office, but there were too many gawkers walking back and forth along the colonnade. And, as he discovered when they had taken over, the door to the Oval Office had a peephole so staffers could look in and see when the President was about to finish a meeting.

McKeon sat at the end of a leather chaise longue across from Drake's desk. He'd kicked off his shoes and stretched out his long, somewhat bony legs to rest them on a Queen Anne chair he'd pulled around to use as a footrest. Though the West Wing staff, Secret Service, and Marine guards might not approve of the way the Vice President lounged around in the office while the commander in chief was away, there was nothing they could do about it as long as POTUS didn't put his foot down. And if POTUS put his foot down, that foot would not remain in the presidency very long. McKeon would make certain of that.

Ran, the Vice President's slender Japanese aide, lay stretched out on the couch beside him, asleep, with her head in his lap. He toyed with the collar of her silk blouse as he answered the phone, peeking at the dark green ink of a tattoo above her smallish breast. It hurt his heart to think that his wife would return from Oregon soon. He would have to do something about that. . . .

"Peace be unto you, my brother," the caller said, inhaling sharply to punctuate his words. It was Qasim Ranjhani, but neither man would ever speak the name aloud on the phone. Though their names and accents were miles apart, had the two men been standing side by side, people might believe Ranjhani was McKeon's shorter brother. They were in fact, distantly related.

"And to you," McKeon answered. "I assume you have important news to be calling me at this time of day."

"In point of fact I do," Ranjhani said, his voice clicking with Pakistani English. "Just moments ago, I received an interesting call from a friend with FSB."

"Is that so?" McKeon nodded in thought. FSB—*Federal'naya Sluzhba Bezopasnosti*—was the Russian Security Service, the modern offspring of the KGB. It made sense that Qasim would have a finger in that piece of Kremlin pie. "And what did this friend have to tell you?" McKeon asked. He ran his hand over the creamy skin on the nape of the sleeping Japanese girl's neck.

"It was regarding the fugitive," Qasim said. "The one from that business in Japan. It looks as though someone has booked him airline passage from Alaska to Moscow via Vladivostok."

"Interesting," McKeon said. That made sense, considering the sparse reports he was getting from the bumbling Oryx Group regarding their present mission. "When?"

"Tomorrow morning," Qasim said. "He's apparently going with his wife and daughter."

"His ex-wife," the Vice President corrected. "Priceless."

"I keep forgetting they aren't still married."

"So does he, apparently," McKeon said. "Do you know what I am thinking?"

"I believe I do," Qasim said. "I was thinking the same thing."

"Very well," McKeon said. "Is there time to make it happen?"

"Only just," Qasim said.

"I'll leave it to you to make it happen."

The Vice President used his thumb to end the call, and then sat staring at the phone for a moment.

The Japanese woman stirred in his lap. Taut muscles rippled under the sheer fabric of her blouse. She was curled into a fetal position, her wool skirt hiked up high on her thighs to reveal the heavy green-and-black shadows of the traditional tattoo that covered her legs like a pair of shorts. McKeon was certain she'd fallen asleep that way to tantalize him. She was a she-devil, of that there was no doubt. There was something about her that would surely drag him down to hell, singing all the way. The swell of a dagger was just visible at her waistline—a constant reminder of just how deadly she was.

She nuzzled his hip with her cheek, but didn't open her eyes.

"Why do you not just kill him?" she asked.

"Drake?"

"Quinn." She opened one eye, looking up at him.

McKeon shrugged. "To be honest, I thought we had—but the men I sent were not successful."

"I would sort him out for you," she said. "All you need do is ask." *Sorting out* was Ran's euphemism for killing. He's seen her work. It was always bloody, the bloodier the better for her, but she spoke of it as if she were alphabetizing files or folding socks.

Sometimes, in his dreams, he saw her as he had the first time they had met, completely naked, short sword in her hand, the gaudy art of her full-body tattoo bathed in the blood of her victim. It was a terrifying image. Thankfully, she was on his side.

"He'll be dead by noon tomorrow." McKeon put his hand on the swell of her hip, in the little hollow just below her waist. His fingers brushed the dagger. "But, if you need a throat to cut, my wife returns from Oregon at the end of the week."

Ran brightened at the notion of something to do. "I would have to sort out a couple of Secret Service agents to make it happen."

McKeon let his hand run down to the back of her knee. "Sacrifices must be made."

She grabbed his hand before he could move it any farther. "And what does Islam say about murdering your wife so you might take an infidel woman to your bed?"

McKeon let his head fall to one side, looking at this beautiful woman's face. "Make no mistake," he said. "My work here is not about my place in Islam. It is about my father's legacy. I have no delusions about the fact that you and I are both going to burn in hell."

# Chapter 20

*Las Vegas*

Tang Dalu stood in front of the floor-to-ceiling windows inside security, eyes locked on the plane he and his team would soon blow apart somewhere over the desert of eastern California.

He could see Lin's reflection in the glass. She leaned back in her chair, pallid face toward the ceiling, eyes closed as if she was asleep. Tang knew better. His wife rarely slept anymore. Many evenings he had returned home from his work as a Qingyang City policeman, to find her sitting in the same chair where he'd left her when he'd gone. The cup of tea he'd made her for breakfast, the cake, all untouched. At first he had pled with her, begged her to eat, to see a physician for something to help her sleep. Then, he'd screamed until frothy spittle had flown from his mouth. He'd even slapped her, knocking her from her chair, telling himself it was for her own good, to snap her out of her stupor. She'd merely knelt at his feet, soft hands clutching pitifully at the pistol on his belt, and begged him to put it to her head and end her misery. To his shame, he'd struck her again, harder this time—because he had not known what else to do.

He had locked his gun away in the box beneath their bed and gone to sleep, leaving her to climb back in her chair and stare at nothing.

Even when the man from Pakistan had come and given them purpose, that purpose had only given her blank eyes something on which to focus. It did not help her sleep.

Tang watched the last few passengers pull their roller bags off the plane, milling with the waiting crowd that would soon take their place. A man with a heavy suitcase stepped around him to take a seat by the window so he could get better phone reception. In his haste, the man kicked over the camera bag that sat at Tang's feet. Even through his misery Tang felt it deliciously ironic that a rude man would shove his way past the very object that would soon bring about his death.

Tang drew the bag closer with the toe of his shoe, holding it safely between his feet. Across the aisle from Lin, Hu Qi clutched his bag to his chest. They had decided against assembling the bomb in one of the airport restroom stalls. There was too great a chance that the hawkish TSA guards milling around in the gate area would decide to flex their inviolable muscles one last time during the boarding process.

Hu and Ma stood together, just outside the gate. Gao had put his last dollar bill into one of the slot machines in the middle of the terminal and now sat quietly, stooped over, head resting in his hands. Any talk was pointless. There were no more dreams to discuss, no more women to conquer, no more riches to seek—no more tomorrow.

Each man had long ago made peace with his decision. They waited quietly and thought about the things men think about when they stand on the bittersweet edge of death for a greater cause.

The gate agent called for their row, causing Lin to open her eyes. She did not smile, but looked at Tang and nodded, as if let him know that everything would now be all right. Tang hung his head, mired in a mixture of religious fervor and regret. He had never really made his wife happy, and now the only way to ease her misery was to watch her die.

The cell phone in his pocket rang as he bent to pick up the camera bag. He jumped a little when he felt the unexpected sensation. Other than the members of his team, only one person had the number.

"Yes?" Tang said, turning to face the window again. For some reason, it helped calm him to look at the skin of the plane he was about to destroy.

"There has been a change of plans," Qasim Ranjhani said, breathing deeply through his nose.

"We are boarding," Tang whispered.

"Well, stop boarding," Ranjhani said, calmly, not realizing that what he asked was akin to ordering a man not to kill himself once the blade was half into his belly.

"But, sir," Tang gasped. "We have prepared. We cannot abandon—"

"There will be no abandoning of anything," the Pakistani said, voice clicking away. "You will all accomplish the same mission, but it must be tomorrow—and with much greater effect."

"As you say." Tang felt as if he'd been kicked in the stomach. He glanced quickly at Ma Zhen, who was in the lead, just three away from the head of the line. Tang shook his head. He waved his hand, motioning for the young man to step aside. The others followed, heads bowed, eyes closed. Gao looked a little relieved, another problem Tang would have to deal with.

Ranjhani continued with his explanation. "The next flight to Alaska leaves in two hours. I have made arrangements for you and your people to be on it. I have booked you all on Global Airlines flight 105 from Anchorage to Vladivostok tomorrow morning. You will have to pass through Customs, but I have taken care of the necessary paperwork."

"Of course," Tang said.

"Believe me, my friend," the Pakistani said. "Nothing has changed but for the time and place. You will all make a great difference."

The others crowded around Tang by the time he ended the call. Lin slouched in a chair a few feet away. She had no stomach for petty details and wanted only for this to be over.

Tang explained their new orders.

"Tomorrow?" Gao said, his thick face twisting into a scowl. "I will need to borrow some money so I can eat."

Gao was chosen to be their muscle. He was a depressed psychopath whose mother would be well taken care of after his death. It was only right that he keep his strength up. Tang dug a twenty-dollar bill from his pocket and shoved it at the frowning man. It was all the money he had left, but that didn't matter, he had no appetite.

He was a bullet in a gun, with no will of his own— and bullets did not get hungry.

# Chapter 21

*Alaska*

Quinn had been so busy trying to connect with Ronnie and Jacques before he lost the cell tower that he hadn't had time to notice how cramped the interior of the little Super Cub actually was until they were well away from Mountain Village.

Rain streaked the Plexiglas, buzzing with the growl of the 150-horse Lycoming engine as the plane wallowed its way through guncotton clouds. Hundreds of silver lakes ghosted in and out of the heavy mist, pocking the tundra just five hundred feet below.

Not one to balk at any sort of danger, Quinn had never really been comfortable in small airplanes. He'd jumped out of a few to get his wings as an Air Force Academy cadet, then later, during training as a combat rescue officer or CRO—the commissioned rank of the Air Force PJs. It was an odd reality that he felt more comfortable dangling under the canopy of his chute, held aloft by only a few dozen lengths of skinny cord, than he did cooped up in a tiny winged box over which he had no control. He supposed that was the problem. If he'd ever taken the time to learn to fly, he might have

felt better about the whole notion. Placing his safety in
the hands of another had never been easy—and now
he'd turned his life over to a twentysomething girl
who was addicted to punk-ash tobacco and appeared to
be dancing to Queen behind the controls of the airplane.

Lovita's small shoulders and peroxide-orange hair
bounced in time to the music, just inches in front of
him. Her green David Clark earphones had a large
piece of sheepskin running along the top to cushion her
smallish head, making her look like an elf wearing a
ridiculous hat. Every so often, she gave in to the urge
and belted out the notes with Freddie, causing her
husky voice to buzz across the intercom into Quinn's
headset. She was amazingly good, though her voice
was an octave lower than any member of the Queen en-
semble.

Quinn shifted in his seat, trying to readjust in the
cramped quarters. He tried to imagine someone as big
as Jacques crammed into the tiny plane behind Lovita
and realized such a thing would have been impossible.
She was so close that it felt as though she was flying
with her shoulders between his knees. She would have
been wearing the big Cajun like a backpack.

The Piper was outfitted for search and rescue with
thirty-gallon tanks in each wing and bubble windows
that gave Quinn a better view than he really wanted out
of each side of the airplane.

Saint Mary's lay along the Yukon, nearly due east of
Mountain Village, so Lovita took them north at first,
avoiding the oncoming Cessna full of contract killers.
Twenty miles up, she cut back to the east, crossing the
squirming oxbows of the upper Andreafsky River. Low
clouds pressed her down, just a few hundred feet off
the deck. She had the heater cranked up to full, keep-

ing the interior of the little plane relatively warm, but Quinn's knees pressed against the outer walls, drawing in the moist chill through the thin skin of the airplane, and bringing back unpleasant memories of his recent swim in the Yukon.

His forehead against the bubble side window, Quinn was subjected to the dizzying view of thick willows and green swamps dotted with pairs of starkly white swans that had come north to breed. They were close enough he felt as if he could count their feathers. The plane passed over the occasional moose, lone bulls or cows with tawny twin calves. Traversing over the wider, meandering waters of the Chuilnak River, a monstrous brown bear that looked to be the size of a Volkswagen peered up from his fishing hole with a scolding, pig-eyed stare, reminding Quinn that he would not be at the top of the food chain should they have to set down out here.

Lovita's voice crackled over Quinn's headset, rough, like a mile of gravel road.

"Can I ask you something?"

"Sure," Quinn said, happy to take his mind off crashing in the wilderness.

"Are you some kind of secret government spy?"

Quinn chuckled, in spite of the situation. "No."

"What's it like?" Lovita asked.

"I said I wasn't one."

"Okay," she said. "But that's exactly what a spy would say." Though a rich purr, her voice bordered on a monotone and with nothing to judge by but the back of her head, it was difficult to read her emotions. "You came to us looking like you'd been mauled by a brown bear. I know you were in the military. You look at things different from other people, and nobody else I know would have been able to fight their way through all those guys like you did."

"I'm telling you the truth," Quinn said. "Spies are all about gathering information and reporting it back up the chain."

"But you are something else." Lovita banked the plane gently to the right, drifting between two low hills that rose up through the fog. "Some sort of secret government operative?"

"How do you know so much about government operatives?" Quinn mused, half to himself.

"I watch movies," Lovita said. "I told you, we got the Internet out here, and satellite TV, and books, and the mail, and everything."

Quinn didn't answer.

"My uncle said you're worried about guys like the ones that came to our village going after your daughter," Lovita said. "I thought government operatives were all single with no family ties."

"Some are," Quinn sighed. "But there are more with wives, husbands, and even big families."

"Looks like people with no ties would have less to worry about," Lovita said. The back of her head bobbed in time with her words.

"Or fight for," Quinn said, thinking of Mattie and Ronnie and Kim and his brother and parents and a dozen other people he held dear. "It's pretty difficult to go through life with no ties."

"Maybe," Lovita said. "Maybe so." She dropped another hundred feet, close enough that Quinn could see individual rivulets in the small streams and ponds that crossed and dotted the soggy tundra below. She checked the clear tubing that displayed the fuel level on each wall over her window. "We're golden on gas all the way to Anchortown," she said, using the slang for Alaska's largest city. "As long as we don't have to do too much pokin' around in these clouds. 'Course, I gotta warn you. I got five-hour fuel tanks and a three-hour bladder so we'll have to make a stop somewhere."

Two hours into the flight it became impossible to see the ground and, more important, the terrain ahead of the airplane, forcing Lovita to drop even lower. Quinn couldn't help but think they'd be driving across the tundra if she went much lower.

"I was trying for Ptarmigan Pass," she said, "but the weather looks bum up that way. I'm gonna cut south and take Lake Clark through the mountains. Lotsa glaciers so it might be a little bumpy." Lovita shimmied forward in her seat, her attention darting from the gray mass of nothingness in her windshield to the bracket-mounted GPS at the corner of her console. Quinn knew enough about the geography of western Alaska to know they were flying through the northern remnants of the Kilbuck Mountains. The terrain would flatten again somewhat after that, before the sharp, glacier-filled teeth of the Alaska Range rose up to block their way to Anchorage.

Quinn leaned forward, focused on the small blue triangle that signified their position on the GPS. "Everything okay?"

"For now," Lovita said, rolling her shoulders in a movement that reminded Quinn of a boxer preparing to step into the ring. "Those other guys are around here close," she said. "I can feel 'em. I've hid out below the clouds as long as I can, but we got some big hunks of rock coming up. I'm gonna have to punch through the tops to keep from drillin' a hole in some mountain. GPS says this is a good place."

She added throttle and pulled back on the stick, pitching the nose of the little plane upward so it began a gradual climb. The cockpit sounded like the inside of a tin barn during a hailstorm. The clouds darkened at first, and Quinn found himself calculating the odds of flying headlong into the other plane, or even a bird. He was so disoriented in the foggy gloom, he wouldn't have known otherwise until they augered into the tundra. Lovita appeared to be an excellent instrument pilot, but the Super Cub had no radar. No matter how skilled a pilot she was, not hitting something other than the mountains shown on the GPS was one hundred percent luck.

Quinn watched the hands on the altimeter climb through eight and then nine thousand feet before the clouds began to thin. Patches of hazy blue made more frequent appearances. Turbulence tossed the plane like a toy as it skidded through the top layer of weather at ten thousand feet.

When they finally popped through the clouds Quinn felt like a diver coming up for air.

Lovita kept climbing for a long moment, before diving back down into level flight. "This day is Super-Cubable," she said, the ear-to-ear grin audible in her voice.

A sea of clouds stretched for miles in all directions, silver white under a brilliant sun. Craggy black peaks rose like islands around them and made Quinn wonder how Lovita had managed to avoid smashing into one during their time down in the muck. Far to the east, the Alaska Range loomed in a hazy line. Below, hidden under a blanket of clouds, was a maze of passes and peaks that made up the Kilbuck Mountains—but above, the Cessna was nowhere in sight.

"Hear that?" Lovita said, an hour later. The GPS said they were flying over the foothills leading into the western entrance to Lake Clark Pass.

Quinn strained his ears. "Hear what?"

"There's nothing like flying a little airplane over mountains or ocean to make you hear all sorts of rattles and clangs in the—"

Her voice cut out. Quinn, who'd been scanning behind them, turned to see a blue-and-white Cessna Caravan cross their path from north to south, five hundred feet above and maybe a mile away.

A much larger and faster airplane than the Super Cub, the Caravan cruised the skies like a hunting shark, just waiting for the little Piper to show itself. It banked toward them immediately.

Lovita shot a glance over her shoulder. "What do you wanta do?"

"Not sure," Quinn said, watching the plane grow larger as it bore down on them. "Unless they're outfitted with jump doors, a Caravan's not set up to open up in flight and shoot at us."

With the closing speed of the two airplanes reaching nearly three hundred knots, the Cessna shot past seconds later, fifty feet off the little Piper's left wing. Quinn's head whipped around, watching it for as long as he could. At least three faces pressed to the Caravan's windows stared back at him.

Both Quinn and Lovita looked back and forth in an effort to see behind them. The Cessna made a tight banking turn, falling in easily on the Super Cub's tail.

"He doesn't have to shoot us down," Quinn said.

"He's got three times our range," Lovita finished his thought. "He can stay behind and wait until we land and then shoot us on the ground. I saw the way those guys were back in the village. They treat Natives like scum."

"They treat everybody like scum," Quinn said, mind racing through his meager options. "But you're right. They don't have to do anything but follow us and wait for reinforcements."

Lovita reached above her console and scrolled through several screens on the GPS, nodding to herself as she spoke. "It's a dead zone out here. No cell towers and radio traffic is no-go unless it's plane to plane. Satellites are so low on the horizon this far north a sat phone call is even iffy."

"Maybe," Quinn said, twisting around again to watch the plane behind them.

Lovita picked up her iPod and put on another Freddie Mercury song.

"Do you trust me, Jericho Quinn?" she said, shouting above a throbbing engine and the loud music that now streamed across the intercom.

Quinn turned from where he'd been watching the plane behind them to stare at the back of her head.

"Yes," he said. "I trust you."

"Good." She pulled back the throttle, slowing the plane a hair and allowing the Caravan to close the distance behind them. Freddie Mercury still wailed over the headphones. "Because we need to get them really, really close for this to work."

Lovita waited until the other plane was almost on top of them, and then dropped the Piper's nose, plowing back into the weather.

The brilliant sun winked out as clouds enveloped them again. Quinn's stomach rose into his chest. His back pressed against the seat. He didn't know if he should worry more about the planeful of contract killers behind them, or the hungry black rocks that lurked in the fog below.

# Chapter 22

*Las Vegas*

Tang boarded the underground train that would take them to the Alaska Airline gates on the other side of the airport. They had plenty of time, but he could not bear the thought of missing the flight and prolonging their agony even more than the Pakistani already had.

"Why would they do this?" Hu stood clutching a stainless-steel handrail as the train started to move. "At the last possible moment . . ." Oblivious to the other passengers now, he whispered what everyone else on the team was thinking.

Tang shook his head. He spoke in Mandarin, but kept his words broad. The number of Americans who spoke Chinese—or any other language—was small, but it was prudent to be careful. "I do not know," he said. "But his reasons are surely important."

Hu grabbed the rail with both hands and leaned a distraught face against his arms. His eyes glistened with tears. For a time, Tang thought the man might cry. He certainly deserved to.

Hu Qi had been a champion gymnast and still found time to study law at Zhejiang University. His coaches said he had a chance at the Olympics and his professors spoke often of his future in government. But those dreams were crushed when his father had been arrested for trafficking heroin. The man was a devout Muslim and never touched alcohol, let alone something as evil as heroin. The entire family knew the drugs belonged to Qi's older brother, but the authorities had found them at his parents' home. Any mitigating circumstances had been swept away when a routine blood test at the time of arrest revealed old man Hu had AB-negative blood, the same type as a deputy minister in need of a liver transplant. Both Qi and his elder brother had been tested as well. Qi was A-positive, but his brother, the real owner of the heroin, shared his father's blood type. He was summarily arrested as an accessory.

A speedy trial found both men guilty of the capital offense of trafficking dangerous narcotics. In keeping with *Yanda*, China's policy to *strike hard* against drug traffickers, both men were sentenced to death. With many such cases, the court might hand down a death sentence with a two-year probationary period—showing the seriousness of the crime, but demonstrating the mercy of the state if the condemned did not commit another crime during the two-year period. In the case of the Hus, all appeals were carried out with lightning speed, in order to ensure the deputy minister received his vital organ transplant before it was too late. Both men were executed four days after the original verdict was pronounced.

Hu Qi, little more than a boy, had waited in the shadows across from the prison and watched the nondescript white bus roll through the iron gates. This mobile execution van parked in front of the administration building, behind the prison walls, but in plain sight of the road. Qi was able to witness a chain gang of five men, including his father and brother, as they were ushered at gunpoint into the open back doors of this kill house to have their organs harvested for party officials and Chinese businessmen rich enough to afford them. A short time later, uniformed guards carried coolers of what were surely kidneys, hearts, and even eyes out the back, while the van exited the gate and turned up the quiet road toward the crematorium with what was left.

Hu Qi had withdrawn from the university at once to take care of his mother, getting a job digging graves at the cemetery where the ashes of his mutilated father and brother were buried. Somehow, the man from Pakistan had found him as well. He'd plucked the bitter young student from the life of misery with the promise of a chance to fire a killing shot at the regime that had destroyed his family.

Tang gathered his bag as the train came to a stop and the passengers poured out. The crowd clumped together as they waited for the escalator that would take them up to their gates. He turned to make sure Lin was still with him. She shuffled along behind, barely more than a shell anymore. She looked so much like their daughter, a fact that added even more anguish to Tang and surely pierced Lin's heart each time she looked in the mirror.

# Chapter 23

*Alaska*

Quinn twisted in his seat, face pressed against the window, doing his best to keep an eye on the other plane. The Caravan drifted back and forth in the clouds behind them as if towed by an invisible rope. It was close enough he could almost see the sneer on the pilot's face.

"Okay," Lovita said. "This is where it's gonna get a little hairy."

Quinn looked forward to see nothing but gray fog. The instruments on her console said they were flying straight and level, but there was absolutely nothing to reference outside but mist and rain.

Lovita checked her GPS again and then reached down long enough to bring up another song on the iPhone connected to her headset. There was a flurry of drums and electric guitar as "Crazy Little Thing Called Love" started to play.

"Hang on to your lunch!" Lovita said as she added steady power. Hauling back on the stick, she began to sing along with Freddie.

The Super Cub nosed up into a near vertical climb

as a rock face loomed up through the fog, less than a hundred meters in front of them.

Quinn leaned back in his seat, hands in his lap—helpless to do anything but sit there. He'd never been a screamer, and in any case, there was little he could do.

Lovita kept adding power until the throttle was all the way to the wall, putting the plane as nearly straight up and down as she could. The rock face grew darker as they closed in. Quinn could see the deep blue of a glacier and the black cracks and jagged teeth of its crevasses spilling over the peaks like froth running down the side of a glass.

There was no way to see what was going on with the plane behind them. He was only aware of the scream of the Piper's engine, and then weightlessness as the little airplane reached the apex of its ability to climb. It hung in the air for a brief moment, before breaking to the right.

Black rock and blue ice flashed through the clouds as they fell, close enough to reach out and touch. Quinn hung from his seat belt, above Lovita now as she pointed the nose straight down, gaining back the speed she'd lost in the climb.

The sharp concussion of an explosion somewhere behind them caused the little Super Cub to shudder as Lovita leveled her out going away from the mountain, less than two hundred feet off the valley floor.

Quinn breathed for the first time in two minutes.

"That big Cessna may have had more range and speed than my little bird," Lovita said over the blaring music, her husky voice an octave higher than normal. "But it couldn't do what we can do at slow speeds."

Quinn worked to slow his heart rate. He didn't know many professional jet jockeys that would have tried such a maneuver in a plane like this. But Lovita knew bush Alaska. She'd probably made the trip through this particular pass a hundred times and knew each side canyon as well as the gravel streets of her own village. The hammerhead stall had taken them straight up the face of the mountain, leaving her just enough room to pull out and go the other direction while the larger, less limber Caravan had simply flown into the face.

Lovita banked to the left and back into the main pass. Raindrops streamed along the windows again and the world seemed to close in around them.

They were back on the deck again in no time, skimming the turquoise waters of Lake Clark, ghosting in and out of clouds.

"How are we for fuel?" Quinn asked, checking the indicator tubes on each wing. He could tell they were fine, but wanted to make sure Lovita's head was still in the game after such a huge adrenaline dump.

Lovita's shoulders rose and fell as she took a deep breath. She craned her head around to look back at Quinn. "We're fine," she said, eyes narrowed in a tight smile. It was the happiest face he'd ever seen her put on.

"Good," he smiled back. "Because I really need to pee."

"That's funny." Lovita's tiny body shook with a nervous laugh. "I already did that a couple minutes ago."

# Chapter 24

*The White House*

Vice President McKeon had not moved from the lounge in the presidential study. Long brown fingers still stroked the Japanese woman's hair as she rested her head in his lap. Her shoes lay on the plush cream-colored carpet. Her skirt had crawled farther up, revealing the dark images of a mountain demon tattooed on the smooth flesh of her thigh. Small toes curled and clenched, like a cat moving just the tip of its tail. McKeon thought it both incredible and frightening that such a skillful killer could have such beautiful toes.

Drake was still in the gym so they had the room to themselves.

Ran shifted her weight slightly, rolling on her back. She made none of the grunts and groans normal people made when they moved after long periods of being stationary, calling such sounds "victim noises." All her motions—all of them—were done in silence.

"I do not see how you continue with this ignorant man," she said. Her chest heaved in pent-up frustration.

"Drake?" McKeon continued to stroke her hair.

"I had a dream that you were in that chair," she said, arching her neck to look toward the small passageway that led to the Oval Office and the Resolute Desk. "It would be a simple matter to sort him out and put you there."

"In time, my dear," McKeon said. "But not quite yet. I have too much to do without a new vice president to contend with, one who might not work together with me as he should."

Ran looked up at him, her eyes, it seemed, penetrating to the back of his skull. "Drake is unpredictable," she said, the hint of a Japanese accent in her flat voice. "He is much too soft and comfortable in his new position. I think it will be difficult to give up his seat of power now that he has it."

"Ah." McKeon smiled. "He does not know it, but that is all part of the plan."

"What if he has plans of his own?" Ran asked.

"I am counting on it." McKeon smiled again.

"And what of me?" Ran closed her eyes, as if she knew he needed some respite. "I will never cover myself with a veil."

"It would be a crime to cover you," McKeon said, wondering if he would go to hell for saying such a thing.

"But you believe all women should," Ran said. "Is that not your ultimate goal?"

"I fear you would kill me if I tried to cover you."

"Without question," she said. "And so I ask again. What of me?"

"What of either of us?" McKeon said.

Ran closed her eyes again. "That is the only answer I would have accepted." Her breathing slowed and for a moment, McKeon thought she might be asleep. She spoke again, changing the subject. "Do you trust this band of misfits Ranjhani has tasked with sorting out Jericho Quinn?"

"They are all more than willing to die," McKeon said. "If that's what you mean."

Ran shook her head, half dozing. "I am Japanese, so I am intimate with death for an honorable cause. My father spoke with great reverence of *Tokubetsu Kōgekitai*—the Special Attack Squadrons—suicide pilots of kamikaze planes and *kaiten* submarines. I know full well that there are many besides the followers of Islam willing to give their lives in battle—or as you would call it, jihad. But from the descriptions given by Qasim, this group seems to be merely deranged."

"Deranged or not, they are useful to our cause," McKeon mused. "They share a common hatred of China, and that is enough."

"Maybe." Ran gave a soft sigh, thinking this over. "But the will to die is as fragile as life itself. I often wonder how many samurai who chose to commit seppuku changed their minds when the blade was a few inches in their belly. . . ."

McKeon nodded. "That is why they had a second present to finish the job with a quick blow to the neck."

"That is so. . . ." Ran sat up suddenly, causing McKeon to flinch. He made a small victim noise, earning him a sidelong glare. "In any case, I am a patient woman, but I grow tired of endless meetings and the parade of politicians. A diversion would be good. Perhaps I should take care of your wife while she is yet in Oregon?"

"I need you here." McKeon's phone rang. "You will have the chance to do plenty of sorting out, in the near future. I promise." He fished the phone from his pocket and pressed it to his ear. "Yes . . ." he said. "She will be a good place to start."

He patted the back of Ran's hand as he listened to

the caller. It was small and delicate for one who spoke so often of blood and death.

"No, I agree," he said, drawing the hand to his lips to give it a silent kiss. "Pick her up right away. I'm keenly interested to hear how much she will tell you. . . . By all means . . . Whatever methods you deem appropriate. You have the full support of the office of the President."

# Chapter 25

*Maryland*

"She's just coming back from her run now." The man in black BDUs and a matching ballistic vest spoke into the voice-activated microphone pinned to his collar. He was on the heavy side, with a jowly face and wavy hair that had been slicked back with half a jar of pomade. "She'll be rounding the corner toward you in less than two minutes."

"Copy that, Joey," Agent Glen Walter said, giving one last piece of advice before his team made contact. "Okay, boys. This is sure to make the ten o'clock news. Make it look professional."

Her code name was *Fable*—and she had zero doubt that any of the five men and women jogging around her in the loose diamond formation would take a bullet on her behalf. The same went for the agent on the twelve-speed race bike ten yards ahead and the young man in the armored Suburban that crunched slowly along the road behind them. It was getting dark, and though CIA Director Virginia Ross's Rockville neighborhood was upscale to the point of old-money snobbishness, the protective agent in charge of her detail hated it when she ran so late in the evening.

Adam Knight had been with her for the past three years and he was still as doting and overprotective as a young father with a first baby. Rarely letting her out of his line of sight, even at state functions, he often looked as if he wanted to taste her food before she ate it, just to be on the safe side. The tragic assassination of both President Clark and the Vice President had, she supposed, taken its toll on every agent charged with the protection of government officials.

Still, Ross had to live her life. She had an agency to run—and a body that wasn't getting any younger.

She'd never been a skinny woman, but eight months earlier her doctor had pointed out that she was lugging around the equivalent of a bushel of corn in extra body weight. To get rid of that burden had meant lots of walking at first. Later, when half that bushel had gone the way of the dodo, her fifty-four-year-old knees had been able to take her on long and glorious—if ploddingly slow—runs. She'd always been bottom heavy. Thankfully, her deceased math-professor husband hadn't minded what he called her "butt to boobs ratio." One could not put in what God had seen fit to leave out and she would forever be built like a pear, no matter how much she exercised. But the good Lord didn't say that numbers in her husband's ratio had to be quite so large.

Ross wasn't oblivious to the stress living her life caused her protective detail. As a sort of moral trade, she made it a habit to get to know them all personally, along with the names of their spouses and significant others. She couldn't keep their kids straight, but forgave herself for that since she had trouble keeping up with the names of her own nine grandchildren.

Three blocks from home, Ross picked up the pace, catching a smile from the tawny woman jogging next to her. Wiki was her name, a broad-shouldered Maori woman of twenty-nine. She'd spent time as an MP in the Army before joining the CIA's Protective Division. Most of the men and women on Ross's detail had military service—and while some clandestine agents thought of the protective folks as the knuckle-draggers of the agency, she'd come to respect their dedication and that no-BS swagger that earned them the reputation of knuckle-draggers in the first place.

More academic than spy, Ross had grown up on an Iowa farm seeing the value of hard work and the good in her neighbors. In college, she talked her way out of trouble and into a political circle of friends that got her plucked from a career as an economics professor at Dartmouth to become the US ambassador to Chile before she was forty years old. A knack for being in the right place at the right time had put her in line to be director of the CIA under the president prior to Chris Clark's administration. She'd done well her first few years, putting her mark on the agency and, to her way of thinking, making it better. Then, both her husband and her youngest daughter had passed away without any warning, sending her into a nosedive that surely bled into her professional life. It had taken her the better part of two years to dig her way out of that one, never quite having the energy to resign, but believing Clark would name a replacement at any moment. The fall of a very bright star was a notable, and often celebrated, event in DC. When otherwise brilliant people stumbled, the difference was drastic. The press and others who wanted the job circled like sharks.

Things looked as though they might be getting better. Cogent thoughts began to work their way back into

Ross's head. She took an active interest in life again, and dreaded the thought of being replaced. She knew Winfield Palmer had President Clark's ear and had spoken to him several times about it. He seemed happy enough with her performance to let things remain status quo long enough that if she did leave, it would be on a positive note.

Then Hartman Drake had taken over. Ross didn't quite know what to think about him. It would take some time, she thought, time to learn exactly what he was all about. In the interim, she'd keep running, climbing out of her personal funk, and leading the agency as best she could until he fired her.

Just off her right shoulder, she saw Adam Knight lift a small microphone to his lips, calling ahead to the residence no doubt, to let them know that "Fable's arrival was imminent." She'd not chosen the code name herself, but Ross liked it. She was a woman in a business traditionally dominated by men with code names like Renegade, Lancer, and Rawhide. *Fable* let her pretend an air of femininity in the testosterone-infused world.

Panting now, sweat soaking the front of her green Dartmouth T-shirt, Ross glanced over at Wiki, who loped along easily beside her. Ross's feet, carried by somewhat stubby legs, hit the ground twice for each one of the young agent's lengthy strides. Long, graceful arms seemed always ready to reach out and catch her or stop some oncoming threat. It was impossible not to notice the black fanny pack cinched tightly round the young woman's waist and the beige radio wire that led to her flesh-colored earpiece.

"Race you the last block," Ross said as they rounded the corner on the homestretch to her house.

"Feeling energetic are we today, ma'am?" Wiki said,

saying "energetic" in the particularly pinched nasal New Zealander accent Ross found endearing.

She had bowed her head to pick up the pace when the agent on the bicycle slid to an abrupt halt and began to shout,

"Gun front! Gun front!"

Adam Knight bolted into the lead, yelling, "Ambush! Ambush! Ambush!" into his lapel mike.

Ross caught a fleeting glimpse of men standing in front of her house half a block away. She couldn't see any guns, but trusted her detail. An instant later, Wiki enveloped her. The protective agent used her own arm as a fulcrum, jamming it into Ross's solar plexus while at the same time grabbing her by the back of her collar and bending her forward at the waist. They ran together toward the Suburban.

Ross's driver screeched in next to the curb. The forward agent had already thrown his bike to the street and stood with pistol drawn beside the open door, scanning for threats beyond the obvious. Wiki shoved Ross in the backseat—nearly ripping her T-shirt off in the process—and then piled in beside her. Adam Knight jumped in the front passenger seat and slammed the heavy armored door. He beat on the dash with the flat of his hand.

"Go, go, go!"

Once Ross was in the relative safety of the armored Suburban, the driver threw the vehicle in reverse, accelerating backwards away from the threat. Per protocol, he abandoned the agents on the ground to fight their own way out.

Still on her belly, Ross was thrown forward, smacking the front seats. She slid into the armrest with Wiki piling up behind her as the driver suddenly let off the gas and cranked the wheel, spinning the SUV in a quick 180 to head toward the safe site, the Rockville Police Station less than three miles away.

Ross tried to raise her head to get a peek at what was going on, but Wiki leaned on top of her, pressing her down.

"The truck's armored," the agent said, her Kiwi accent stronger from the stress of battle, "but I don't know what sort of weapons they have, ma'am. Let's keep our coconuts down, shall we for now?"

Knight snatched up the microphone clipped to the console. "Rockville PD, Rockville PD, Fable Limo," he said, his voice much calmer than the sweat on his upper lip made him look. He shot a backward glance at Ross while he waited for a response. "You okay, ma'am?"

"I'm fine," Ross said. "What—"

The dispatcher cut her off.

"Fable Limo, Fable Limo, go ahead for Rockville PD."

"Possible compromise at Fable residence," Knight said. "We're four minutes out, en route to your location."

"Ten-four, Fable Limo," the dispatcher came back. "You are clear on this end."

As detail supervisor, Knight would have made it a point to liaise with nearby police departments and hospitals in the event their assistance was ever needed. The detail often ran drills, but they were dry runs that Ross only read about. She'd never taken the time to participate in one.

"What did you see, Adam?" she asked, still pressed down against the seat.

Knight held up his hand and continued his radio conversation. "Fable CP, Fable CP, Limo," he said, trying to raise the command post at the residence. He cursed when there was no answer.

Brian Shumway, the agent who'd been on the bicycle, came across on the radio. His voice was breathless, but in control. "No idea what's going on, boss," he said. "I'm not getting the CP either—by radio or cell."

"Tell me what you do see," Knight said, still tapping the dashboard with his open palm, willing the Suburban to go faster.

"I count three white males," Shumway said. "All with MP5s standing in the front yard. Barb and I have good positions about half a block out, but these guys aren't doing a damn thing. They know we're here, but they don't seem to care."

"Okay, sit tight," Knight said. "PD will have SWAT heading your way."


The CIA had footed the bill for a series of heavy concrete bollards to reinforce the fenced parking area behind the Rockville Police Department. They'd also paid for the steel-wedge barrier that had to be lowered to enter or exit the lot in a vehicle. Knight used a remote that looked like a garage door opener to lower the barrier when they were fifty yards away.

"PD, PD, Fable Limo," Knight said as they spend into the parking lot, the barrier coming up behind them. "Arrival. Arrival."

"Ten-four, Fable," the dispatcher said. "Chief's at the back door to bring you in."

Ross adjusted her sweaty T-shirt and tugged at the legs of the shorts. They were fine for running, but seemed much too immodest to be wearing during an attack. She often ran in public, but wasn't accustomed to being thought of as the director of the CIA dressed only in gym gear. Stress made her chuckle at the thought.

Knight got out of the car first, checking the surroundings to make certain they were clear before opening Ross's door.

Disheveled or not, Ross was a professional. She put on a pleasant face for the chief as they hurried toward the open back door to the PD where the lanky man waited to greet her. He was not smiling, a fact that made both Adam Knight and Wiki stop in their tracks.

A second man Ross did not recognize, with dirty blond hair and a high forehead, stepped out from behind the chief. Rumpled as if from an all-night drinking binge, he held up both hands to say he came in peace. A cadre of three other agents, all stodgy and overfed-looking things, piled up behind the man in the wrinkled suit.

"Glen Walter," he said. "ID Task Force."

Ross cringed at the mention of the IDTF. She shrugged the protesting Wiki off her arm and stepped around Adam Knight. If someone had taken over the police department to ambush her, there was little any of them could do about it at this point. The fact that this was an IDTF man made her think things were even worse than that.

"Virginia Ross," she said. "What can I do for you, Mr. Walters?"

The man's face pulled into a half smile as he extended his hand. "It's Walter," he said. "There's no 's.' Madam Director, I'm going to have to ask you to come with me."

Knight drew his weapon and pointed it at Walter. "You step back until I figure out exactly who you are."

Walter raised his hands again, giving a nod to Knight's pistol as if this sort of thing happened to him all the time.

"It's a touchy thing to serve an arrest warrant on some-one when they have the luxury of a protective detail."

"You don't arrest a sitting director of the CIA," Knight snapped. "Not without the President getting in-volved."

"Believe me," Walter said, still smiling a sort of smirky half grin that made Ross's stomach sink with dread. "I wouldn't get within ten miles of something like this without making sure all the piddly work was done up front. I've already taken the liberty of provid-ing a copy of the warrant to the PD."

Ross looked at the chief, who gave her a solemn nod. "It's legitimate, ma'am," he said.

"I assume those are your men back at my house," Ross said.

"They are," Walter said.

"Well, call them off right now," she said. "Before we have a blue-on-blue shooting."

"Good idea," Walter said. Ross thought he might be from Florida or maybe Louisiana. Walter nodded to a shorter man with thinning blond hair. "Go ahead and call Benavidez." He let his eyes play up and down Ross's body, shaking his head. "Forgive me for saying so, but you've lost a heck of a lot of weight from your photographs."

Knight, who was on the phone with CIA general counsel, stopped talking and turned to Walter. "I don't care if you're the President's favorite nephew. Talk to the director like that again and I'll kick your ass across this parking lot." He wasn't pointing his pistol, but he'd not gone so far as to return it to the holster in his fanny pack.

"It's fine, Adam," Ross said, knowing he was a half a breath away from shooting the ID agent. "Stand down."

"A courtesy call wouldn't have worked?" the protective agent snapped. "You're a presidential appointee, ma'am."

Walter gave an insolent shrug. "The United States government isn't really comfortable giving courtesy calls to suspected spies."

Knight held the phone away from his face a bit so the general counsel rep could hear the conversation.

"You're arresting her for spying?"

"Violation of the Espionage Act," Walter said, almost as an afterthought. "I'm not at liberty to get into specifics. I will say it's a pretty serious charge, considering you're the director of what is arguably the world's most powerful intelligence agency. I don't understand how a woman of your standing could—"

"Shut your mouth," Knight said, stepping in between them again, daring the ID agent to make a move.

Ross put an arm around his shoulder. "Calm down, Adam," she said. "There's no doubt that this is a bizarre situation, but if he's got a warrant, we don't have a choice." She turned to Walter. "I'll go with you," she said, "but I'll have to call the President first."

"Oh, Virginia," the gloating agent said. He shook his head like she was a small child that just didn't understand the reality of the situation. "Do you really think I'd be here if he didn't already know?"

# Chapter 26

*Maryland*

Garcia felt the phone buzz in the pocket of her running shorts and replaced the tiny bud back in her ear. She'd only planned to do five miles, but being followed gave her the extra adrenaline to run the entire ten-K loop through the park. Besides, her ex had often reminded her that running would keep what he called her "ghetto booty" from getting any larger than it already was. She preferred to think of herself as having breeder's hips, but deadbeat son of a bitch or not, her ex happened to be right—at least on that aspect of her booty.

"Hello," she said, slowing her pace some so she could hear over her own breathing.

"Garcia?" Winfield Palmer said.

"Yes, sir." Ronnie slowed to a walk, confident there was an unmarked car a block or so away that she was driving crazy with her changes in pace. She owed Palmer her job—and more. As national security advisor to President Clark, he'd seen her for what she was, and plucked her from the obscurity of being a CIA uniformed officer and thrown her in to work with people like Quinn and Thibodaux. It was dangerous work, but, as Jacques often pointed out: What was the fun of livin' if someone wasn't tryin' to kill you?

"Can you talk?" Palmer asked. Not one to check in and chat with subordinates, he didn't really care if she was busy. He wanted to know if the line was secure.

"We're okay," Ronnie said. "I do have a tail, but the phone is good and I'm out on a run."

"Outstanding," he said, deadpan as if his news was anything but good. "An ID team just arrested Virginia Ross."

Ronnie stopped altogether, leaning forward with her hands on both knees as if she was catching her breath. "The director?"

"Afraid so," Palmer said.

"When?"

"Five minutes ago."

Garcia put a hand on her head, walking in a slow circle while she gathered her thoughts. She wondered how he'd found out about it so fast, but then remembered she was talking to Win Palmer, the man who had contacts inside virtually every agency in the government.

"What did they charge her with?"

"Spying," Palmer said. "Listen, I'm doing some research of my own, but I'm under a pretty fine microscope here. Is there any way you can use some of your contacts to dig into this? Find out where they're holding her."

"Why Ross?" Ronnie mused out loud. She didn't voice it, but she wondered why Palmer was suddenly so interested in the director of the CIA.

"I had to talk the President out of replacing her a couple of times after her daughter died. But she's a good woman. I'm thinking the new administration asked around and heard she was the same old stuffed-shirt bureaucrat. That's why they kept her on. Look at what the taxpayers are getting for their buck. He's kept Andrew Filson in place as Secretary of Defense because he's a warmonger, but replaced the Sec State with Tom Watchel, one of the most self-serving dilettantes I've ever met in Washington. Last time he was on *Meet the Press* he kept calling North Korea North Dakota. Every other cabinet member and high-level position is being replaced with empire-building yes-men who care more about their careers than running the government."

"From my lowly viewpoint," Ronnie said, "that's not much of a change in the status quo."

"Touché," Palmer scoffed. "I'm still trying to figure out their endgame. There are too many checks and balances in place to allow them to do anything drastic right away. Congress, the courts . . . and even the military would nip any overt action in the bud. But, they're moving slowly to keep public opinion on their side. They've had nearly six months to lay the groundwork for whatever it is they plan to do."

"What about the commission?" Garcia asked, referring to the bipartisan Rand Commission, chaired by Chief Justice William Rand of the Supreme Court.

"Don't even get me started on that," Palmer said. "Not on the phone at least. Can you get rid of your tail long enough to do some checking on Ross?"

"Of course," Garcia said, jogging again. "Any word on Miyagi?"

"Just find Ross for me," he said, avoiding the question. Anyone who knew Palmer well knew he had a soft spot for the Japanese woman.

"Will do, sir."

"Ronnie," Palmer said before she could end the call.

He always called her Garcia and the personal touch caught her off guard. There was a catch in his voice she'd not heard before. "You watch yourself."

"I'll do some checking and get back with you," Garcia said. She'd be careful, but if the IDTF had killed a woman as tough as Emiko Miyagi and carted the director of the CIA off to jail, there wasn't a whole lot for her to depend on but dumb luck.

# Chapter 27

Ronnie bumped her front door shut with a hip and twisted the dead-bolt lock. She reset her alarm on the panel just inside, next to a framed photograph of her Russian father and smiling Cuban mother. She kicked off her shoes and peeled away her sweaty shirt and sports bra, grateful for air-conditioning and the chance to have a shower. Her confrontation with Agent Walter had made her feel dirty and being followed all day by people who surely worked for him made it even worse.

She set the fanny pack with her gun and phone on top of her bedroom dresser and stepped out of her running shorts. Naked, she caught a glimpse of herself in the closet mirror and laughed out loud at the bruises that mapped her body. Her defensive tactics instructor at Langley was no Emiko Miyagi, but he was a skilled practitioner of Krav Maga and jujitsu. The daily sessions allowed her to work off some aggression, but turned her forearms, ribs, and thighs into mottled purple punching bags—with bruises dark enough to show through even on her dark complexion. She'd inherited her father's long sprinter's thighs along with his broad shoulders and keen eye for his surroundings. From her mother she'd gotten a bawdy sense of humor, the full-figured curves that required a sports bra a small man could use as a two-room tent, and her tendency toward the ghetto booty. Garcia had always thought she had the sort of body that teetered between female boxer and hooker, depending on what she wore. Jericho seemed to appreciate it—and she was comfortable with that.

Garcia leaned in closer to the mirror on her dresser and pulled her hair back. The tiny lines around her eyes showed in horrifying detail that she was on a collision course with her thirtieth birthday. Her chosen career had a way of smiling on attractive and intelligent women in the early days—and then sneaking up when they weren't looking to turn them into old and spent intelligent women well before their time. She let her hair fall and sighed. There was nothing she could do about it now.

Unwilling to be far from her pistol under the circumstances, she carried it into the bathroom and put in on the counter, within reach from the shower. Over the past year and a half she'd killed half a dozen people, been blown off the side of a mountain in Afghanistan, stabbed in the back by a psychotic little kid, and shot at more times than she could count. Keeping a gun next to her shower curtain was a far cry from needless paranoia.

Ronnie liked her showers hot enough to pink her skin. She stood for a long time with her hands on the wall, letting the water scald her back and chase the stiffness of defensive tactics class out of her joints. The pinpricks of pain were her way of relaxing and doing penance at the same time.

She washed her hair before the hot water ran out,

never knowing when she might have the chance again, using the laurel conditioner Jericho said he liked. She turned off the shower and stood dripping in the tub for a long moment, thinking about Jericho and wondering how he was. Wrapping a towel around her head like a turban, she spread another towel along the edge of the tub and sat on it, still soaking wet. She took her time shaving her legs—another task she might normally put off for a week or more since Jericho was out of town—and hummed *"Drume Negrita"*—"Sleep My Little Black Baby"—a Cuban song her mother used to sing to her at bedtime.

The handprint on the mirror didn't catch Ronnie's eye until she was standing at the sink brushing her teeth. Spitting, she glanced up, thinking at first that she had to be imagining things. Out of instinct, she forced herself not to stare directly at the thing, instead scrubbing her teeth as if she wanted to start a fire by friction.

High in the right corner of her bathroom mirror, not far from the ceiling, the perfect imprint of a man's palm stood out clearly against the condensation from her hot shower. Jericho had sometimes left little notes for her with his fingertip on the glass so the words would show up in the steam—but as far as she knew, he'd never climbed up on her counter. Whoever had left this handprint had likely caught himself while accessing the air vent above the medicine cabinet on the wall adjacent to the vanity.

Fighting the urge to throw on a robe—which would broadcast the fact that she knew she was being watched—Ronnie replaced her toothbrush in the holder beside the sink and reached for a tube of face cream from the cabinet. Piles of laundry and dirty dishes testified to the fact that she was a horrible housekeeper, but even that didn't explain the tiny chips of paint on the counter. They had to have been knocked loose when someone had reattached the vent to the ceiling.

In general, Garcia was not a prudish sort of girl. She was perfectly content with her body and had never been uncomfortable on a clothing-optional beach. CIA operatives had to go through several iterations of training designed to snuff out as much of the natural embarrassment reflex as possible. Long surveillances often called for the use of a soda cup urinal while another agent sat just a few feet away. There was nothing quite as embarrassing as strip-searching a fellow classmate to look for contraband, and ordering them to lift and separate the various folds and crevices of the human body. But all that said, the thought of some sleazebag peering at her through a hidden camera in her own bathroom added a whole new level to the term "creepy."

She did her best to ignore the air vent, taking the towel off her head and wrapping it around her torso, tucking it under her armpit. Agent Walter had likely sent in a black bag team while she was away on her run. They wouldn't know that her normal routine was to walk around naked until she was completely dry, so covering herself now with the towel wouldn't raise any alarms. Ronnie seethed inside at the thought that these pervs had actually put a camera in her bathroom. There was not a lot of useful intelligence to be gained from watching someone shave her legs and pee.

It took just a moment for the shock of finding the camera to wear off and Ronnie's sense of self-preservation to kick in. Fighting the urge to flip the bird at the vent, she decided to use the camera to her advantage. She let the towel fall to the floor, thinking, *"Get a load of them apples, you sick bastards."*

She spent the next five minutes standing in front of the mirror and putting on makeup as if to go out for a night on the town. She went so far as to hike up one foot at a time, resting it on the vanity counter so she could touch up the paint on her toenails. That would give them the show they were looking for. The more radical hormones they had flowing through their brains, the less likely they would be thinking straight when she did what she planned to do next.

# Chapter 28

A block away from Ronnie Garcia's house, backed into the driveway of a vacant house, IDTF agent Gene Lindale hit the button on the driver's seat of his forest green Ford Expedition to lay it back as far as it would go. He shot a glance at his partner, a bruiser named Kevin Maloney.

"This ain't bad duty," Lindale said, peering at the open laptop computer on the console between them.

"This is dope!" Maloney grinned. "I hope we get to arrest her ass before this is over."

"Yeah," Lindale said. "I could give that a thorough pat down. . . ."

Before being tapped for work in the Internal Defense Task Force, both men had been agents for Homeland Security. Both their files had noted severe Giglio issues. That is, they were both known to be liars. In *Giglio v. the United States*, the Supreme Court had decided that defense counsels and juries in any trial where such liars testified had to be made aware of that fact. Such a record made it virtually impossible for a federal law enforcement agent to do his or her job. When they'd come aboard, the supervising agent, a guy named Walter, had told them not to worry about it. He didn't expect them to spend much time on a witness stand.

"Looks like she's going out for a drink or something," Lindale said, rubbing his eyes. The dim light from the computer screen gave the men's faces an eerie, other-worldly glow in the darkness of the vehicle. Dark tint on the side windows made them invisible to nosey neighbors.

"Look at that," Maloney said, leaning forward so he could get a better look. "She carries that little pistol in a holster that hangs from her bra. I've heard about those."

"I'll make a note of that," Lindale chuckled. "Don't want to get my fingers shot . . ." His voice trailed off. "What the hell is she doing?"

The men watched as Ronnie Garcia walked to her kitchen wearing only jeans, a black sports bra, and a pistol. She knelt in front of her oven, screwdriver in hand, and opened the oven door to remove both metal racks so she could lean inside.

"You think she's going to gas herself?" Lindale mused.

"It's an electric oven, dipshit," Maloney said. "So I'm thinking no."

A moment later, Garcia backed out of the oven and set a metal plate on the linoleum beside her. She went in again and, after a moment wrestling with something at the back of the oven, brought out a desert tan duffel bag.

"You need to put the panel back on, sweetheart," Lindale said to the computer screen.

"You just want to see her bend over one more time." Maloney rubbed his eyes again. "How do you suppose that bag keeps from burning up in there?"

Lindale scoffed. "Does this bitch really look like a Suzy Homemaker to you? Even if that plate isn't some sort of heat shield, I'm betting she doesn't do a hell of a lot of baking—"

"I've lost her," Maloney said a few moments later. He moved the computer mouse so he could click through a screen menu. "Did we put cameras in the garage?"

The garage door rumbled open in answer to his question, throwing a shaft of light onto her driveway. Garcia's black Impala backed out a moment later. She turned west, thankfully moving away from the green Ford.

Maloney punched a speed dial number in his cell phone. "Mr. Walters . . . Sorry, I mean Walter," he said when the other end picked up. "You wanted us to tell you if she moved."

# Chapter 29

Ronnie took a meandering route through the neighborhood to make the guys following her earn their money. If they knew her at all, they'd know it was a normal habit for her to throw in an alternate route or two when she went anywhere. If she didn't, they might smell a trap. She headed south on I-270 meandering back and forth across all six lanes, again making the guys in the green SUV behind her work for their pay. Slowing at every exit, she kept them guessing as she scanned the businesses along the service roads, looking for the specifics she would need for her plan to work.

She found exactly what she was looking for on the outskirts of Bethesda and took the exit for a little convenience store that Jericho would have called a "stop-and-rob." Ronnie pulled her Impala under the bright lights of the awning beside the gas pumps. Ahead of her, a kid who looked like he might still be in high school fueled up a Kawasaki Ninja sport bike. She couldn't help but smile at him. Every motorcycle she saw reminded her of Quinn. She'd known how to ride before she met him, but she'd never loved it the way she did since that first time riding with him on a rented Enfield Bullet high in the Pamir Mountains of Afghanistan.

She swiped her credit card at the pump and topped off the fuel in the Impala. Might as well make the guys in the green Expedition believe she was about to go for a long drive.

# Chapter 30

*Alaska*

Blue sky, marred by only a thin line of halfhearted clouds over the distant Chugach Mountains, greeted them when Lovita brought her little Super Cub out of Lake Clark Pass. CAVU, they called it—Ceiling and Visibility Unlimited. She turned back to the north, skirting the mudflats on the western edge of Cook Inlet, staying low to avoid notice by other aircraft the contractors in the Caravan might have been able to contact. The city of Anchorage lay like a pile of reflective glass blocks on the flat delta below green mountains on the other side of the inlet. A steady line of commercial jets, both passenger and cargo, lumbered over the silver-brown water toward Ted Stevens Anchorage International Airport at the end of the point. Like any other day in Alaska, it was impossible to look any direction for long and not see some kind of airplane. Small aircraft were the station wagons, taxis, and cargo vans of the wilderness—which started just a few minutes from the city of Anchorage.

Quinn's phone chirped as soon he had a signal. He

stuffed it under the seal of his headset, pressing it down as best he could to avoid the engine noise.

"Jer?" It was Kim. Everyone else knew not to use names on the phone, but he couldn't blame her. She'd not signed up for this kind of work

"Hey," Quinn said, half yelling. The fact that she was able to talk to him gave him more than a tinge of worry. "I thought you'd be on a plane by now."

Silence.

"Hello?" Quinn said.

"I'm still here," Kim said. "Are you okay? Jacques said there was some trouble out there."

"I'm fine," Quinn said, making a mental note to talk to Jacques about the information that was passed on to his ex-wife. "Everything's fine." Saying it twice had always been necessary with Kim.

"I don't want you to worry," she said, "but my leg was reinjured during the attack this afternoon."

"Reinjured?" Quinn pressed the phone tighter to his ear.

"I feel okay. It's just a big bruise really, but the doctor is worried about blood clots if I fly."

"Okay," Quinn said. "What about Mattie?"

"She's with your parents," Kim said. "They are on the way to you now."

Quinn gave an audible sigh of relief. "We'll get you over as soon as you're able to fly," he said. "I'm not happy leaving you here with all that's going on."

"Yeah," Kim said, her voice faltering, the way it did when she was about to get mad. "And I have to tell you, it scares the shit out of me to send Mattie over with someone I've never met. Promise me she'll be all right."

"Of course," Quinn said. He fought the urge to snap back.

Kim laughed, changing the subject. "I never saw your dad fight before. I can see where you get it."

Quinn smiled at that. "Nope," he said. "I get that from my mom. She's way meaner than he is."

He promised to check in as soon as they got to Vladivostok—if they got to Vladivostok—then ended the call.

From the air, Cook Inlet resembled a giant beetle jutting up from the Gulf of Alaska with the Knik and Turnagain Arms forming two antennae that pointed north and east respectively. Lovita cut across the muddy tidal waters of the Knik Arm, losing altitude as they neared Birchwood, a small public-use airport. As its name implied, it was nestled among thick stands of white birch that blanketed the lower elevations between water and mountains north of Anchorage.

Quinn asked her to circle twice before entering the pattern, unsure if there would be a welcome party bristling with weapons to mow them down as soon as they climbed out of the plane. Quinn still had the MP7, as well as a .45 Ukka had tucked in his hand before they departed Mountain Village, but they would be sitting ducks as soon as they were on the ground.

Judging everything as clear as it would ever be, Lovita touched down on 1 Right, the gravel strip that her balloon-like tundra tires preferred to the adjacent asphalt runway.

Once the Super Cub came to a bouncy stop, Quinn grabbed his small duffel, including the MP7, out of the back and squirmed his way out of the tiny cockpit after Lovita.

No one shot them so he relaxed a notch.

He reached to shake her hand. "I owe you," he said.

She pushed her way past his hand and threw her arms around his neck, giving him a trembling hug, all the tension and emotion of the flight bleeding out of her now that they were relatively safe. When she finally let go, she stepped back and looked at him, but said nothing, communicating in the way of her Yup'ik people with her eyes.

"You're an incredible girl, Lovita," he said. "A friend for life."

She nodded, as if that was the most obvious thing in the world, and then took a few steps away from the airplane so she could light a cigarette.

"I got a friend who lets me use the apartment in her hangar when I come to the big village." She pointed with her cigarette toward the line of metal buildings across the taxiway. "She's got a dusty old bed and pretty comfortable couch. We can stay there tonight."

"When are you going back?"

"I gotta make a Costco run tomorrow morning. My friend has an old car she lets me use too. I can take you to the airport."

She took another drag off her cigarette and let it dangle in her lips while she checked her cell phone. "I need to call Ukka and tell him we made it in."

Quinn couldn't help but think of how small she was, like one of Mattie's seven-year-old friends pretending to smoke.

"Good deal," he said. "I need to make a couple of calls as well. Tell Ukka I'll get with him in a few minutes."

Quinn walked to the rusty hulk of an old fuel truck, still scanning for an ambush as he walked. When none came, he dropped his duffel on the asphalt and dialed Ronnie Garcia. He hadn't spoken to her since he'd asked her to make the call to Aleksandra Kanatova and wanted to be certain everything was in motion.

He got nothing but voice mail. Two calls in quick succession was his signal that it was important, so he tried again. He got her voice mail again. He listened to the entire thing this time, happy, at least, to hear the familiar hint of a Cuban lilt in her voice. Exhausted, Quinn shoved the phone back in his pocket and walked toward the hangar. He couldn't help but worry that his plan was coming unraveled right before his eyes. If Ronnie wasn't answering, she was in trouble—and if Ronnie was in trouble, they were all in trouble.

# Chapter 31

*Maryland*

Gene Lindale found a discreet place to park one lot over from the convenience store and backed into the shadows against a graffiti-covered fence. He and Maloney watched as Garcia chatted up a guy fueling his motorcycle at the pump ahead of her.

"What do you suppose she's saying to him?" Lindale muttered, half to himself. The dash lights cast a green, otherworldly glow on his face.

"I don't really give a shit," Maloney said. "I just wish she'd go home and take another shower."

"You got that right," Lindale said, watching through binoculars now. "She paid at the pump. Wonder why she's going inside."

Lindale panned the binoculars, watching Garcia through the window as she browsed up and down the aisles. The shop was well lit and the shelving was low, so it was easy to keep track of her. She paused at the magazine rack long enough to flip through a couple. Instead of buying anything, she made her way to the counter, where she waved at the clerk like she knew her, then picked up a key chained to a toilet plunger, presumably to the restroom, before walking out of view toward the back of the store. A moment later, the kid with the bike went inside as well. Like Garcia, he loitered up and down the aisles until he apparently found what he was looking for.

"That's no coincidence," Lindale said. "That kid just went for the same magazine. She just passed him something." He looked at his watch. "And anyway, where the hell is she at? How long does it take a girl to take a piss?"

Maloney cracked open his door. "I'll go around and check to make sure she didn't slip out the back."

"You do that," Lindale said, his voice muffled by his hands holding the binoculars. "Watch yourself. Big-ass girls like that can fight. Take my word for it."

Five minutes later, Lindale began to worry. Maloney was MIA and Garcia had yet to show her face. The stupid kid was still inside the store, buying cigarettes and killing time talking to the clerk, who was old enough to be his grandma.

Lindale tried to shake off the worry. Maloney was probably taking a leak himself. But even if that was the case, he should have been back by now. Something just wasn't right. Lindale unbuckled his seat belt, deciding to go inside and talk to the kid—and if Garcia came out and saw him, so be it. It would be a lot better to get burned than to lose her. Lindale pitched the binoculars on the passenger seat and opened his door. His left shoe had just touched the pavement when he heard a faint scrape of gravel in the darkness behind him.

\* \* \*

Ronnie padded up, quickly reaching the driver of the green Expedition before he had time to turn around. Putting her full weight against the door, she slammed it hard against his exposed shin, letting it bounce before she slammed it again. She heard the satisfying crunch of bone a millisecond before his scream rose from the space between the door and the SUV's interior. In the middle of turning when she'd come up behind him, the man fell toward the vehicle. Ronnie helped him along, using the heel of her hand to slam his head sideways, bouncing it hard against the doorpost. She leaned in, lifting the sidearm from his belt as he slid to the ground, writhing in pain from the shattered leg.

Squatting beside him, she snapped her fingers in front of his face. "Cell phone!"

Eyes clenched, he threw his head back, wailing, "You broke my leg, you bit—"

In his agony, he'd forgotten he was still clammed between the open door and the Expedition. She gave it another slam to get his attention, catching him across the ribs and pinching his right arm above the elbow. He retched. Spittle dangled from his chin as if he might throw up.

"You need to talk nice, *postalita*," Garcia spat. "Now, where's your cell phone?"

He shoved it to her, his head lolling in the direction of the stop-and-rob. "Maloney?"

"Is that your little girlfriend's name?" Garcia said. She leaned inside the Expedition and yanked the wires out of the radio. "He'll live . . . but he'll be singing with the soprano section of the choir for a while." She looked down at the laptop on the center console. "I assume this is what you were using to spy on me." She shook her head in disgust. Standing, she snatched the man's credential case from his jacket and flipped it open. "Seriously, Agent Gene Lindale, what's with all this following me around shit? I'm a federal agent too, you know. Sneaking around like this is a good way to get yourself killed."

"I . . . I'm with ID," he groaned.

"Yes." She nodded. "I can smell that."

He retched again, head hanging toward the pavement. "You got no idea how much trouble you're in now. . . ."

"Oh, I know." Ronnie gave him the sweetest smile she could muster. "I'm royally screwed." Garcia squatted low on her haunches so she could look Lindale square in the face. "But you know what, Gene? I got no patience for guys who hide a camera in a girl's bathroom. I mean seriously, my computer, my phone, even my kitchen table. I do a lot of work there so that I can understand. But what kind of valuable intelligence did you think you were going to get from spying on my toilet?"

She threw his keys over the privacy fence and crushed his cell phone under her heel. Spitting in disgust, she gave the door one last slam for good measure. At this point, breaking another bone or two wouldn't dig her in any deeper.

Back at her Impala, she grabbed the duffel and two bungee cords from inside and dropped the keys in the front seat, leaving them for the kid. She'd left an envelope inside the store with the signed title to the car and ten one-hundred-dollar bills in exchange for the keys to the Kawasaki. Using the bungees to fasten the duffel to the back of the bike, she threw a long leg over the seat and hit the ignition.

The green Ninja gave off a bright metallic glow under the stark lights of the fuel bay. It felt incredibly powerful beneath her, just a little bit out of control—which, under the circumstances, was just what she wanted.

# Chapter 32

Garcia peeled out of the parking lot, half from nerves, half from jubilation at doing something that made her feel closer to Jericho. She took the bike around the block, cutting behind the stop-and-rob to get back to the highway. The ID agents wouldn't be able to do much but lick their own wounds for the moment, but it wouldn't be wise to take any chances and let them see which way she'd gone. She'd not only hurt them physically, but she'd damaged their pride. The sort of men who would put cameras in her bathroom would take that personally—and she'd seen firsthand how the emotions associated with revenge could give a man strength to stand on a broken limb as surely as any crutch. There was no doubt that she'd made a couple of enemies for life. *Get in line*, she thought. Seemed like that list grew longer every day.

Ronnie hadn't ridden without a helmet in years, preferring to keep her head more or less round and brains in place. It couldn't be helped for now. And, whatever the ID agents' endgame had been, it was likely just as bad as—or worse than—getting her face smeared on the asphalt. Virginia didn't require a helmet, but they did require eye protection and the kid had given her a pair of Wiley X goggles to go with the bike. Unfortunately for Garcia, the state of Maryland had strict helmet laws and she wouldn't hit Virginia until she crossed the Potomac.

Wind whipped at her hair, taking her breath away and buffeting her chest as she hit the southbound entrance ramp back onto I-270. Leaning forward, she tucked herself in behind a semitruck, far enough back to avoid most of the turbulence that would flip the bike around like a toy. She prayed she wouldn't run into any state troopers until she hit Virginia. Any officer who stopped her would call in the stop and Lindale had surely dragged himself inside the store to call in the cavalry by now. The IDTF would cast a wide net enlisting every sworn officer and informant to help them find the dangerous Hispanic woman riding a green motorcycle.

Traffic was creeping along at its normal glacial pace when she hit the Beltway, causing her to do a lot of stopping and starting. Every driver who caught her eye seemed to be scolding her for being a scofflaw.

Garcia felt like an enormous stone had been lifted off her chest when she crossed the river and entered Virginia without being stopped. She took the exit just before Highway 193 and meandered through the back streets until she found an Embassy Suites in Tysons Corner.

A false ID and credit card from her go-bag got her past the desk clerk with no problem. Palmer had always stressed the necessity of having identification her agency didn't have on record. Too many agents had lost their lives over the years because some moles gave up a list of cover identities. Thankfully, Palmer had been in a position to have documents made that were completely real but for the names associated with them.

Garcia began to feel the aftereffects of conflict and the fatigue brought on from her ten-K run as soon as the desk clerk slid the room key across the counter. Her stomach growled, demanding to be fed. She grabbed a bowl of instant ramen and a Diet Dr Pepper from the snack store. She debated on an ice cream bar, but decided she'd best stay at her fighting weight.

The room was freakishly clean compared to how she normally lived. There were no piles of clothing on the floor or dishes in the tiny stainless-steel sink.

"Give me time," she muttered under her breath. "I'll wreck it."

She tossed the go-bag on the bed and went through the contents while she waited for a coffee cup full of water for the ramen to heat up in the microwave.

Jericho had taught her never to step out her door without at least four things—her sidearm, a knife, a light, and something to start a fire. EDC, he called it—*Every Day Carry*. With those four items you could get any of the other bullets, beans, and Band-aids that might become a necessity.

Ronnie reached under her blouse and pulled the Flashbang holster and Kahr PM9 from where they hung suspended comfortably from her bra. She put the gun on the wooden nightstand beside the bed, and then took out her wallet, folding knife, LED flashlight, and Zippo lighter and set them beside the pistol.

Inside the go-bag, there was a Browning Hi-Power, because if she needed the bag, things were floating south in a hurry and a second gun was always faster than reloading. The Browning ate the same 9mm ammo as her diminutive Khar, but carried thirteen rounds in the magazine and one in the tube—a real plus when things got sticky. Jacques Thibodaux, whose mantra was "Don't go to a gunfight with a handgun in a caliber that doesn't start with at least a four," turned up his nose at the puny 9mm. But her hands were on the smallish side for being such a big girl in other places. She reasoned that it was better for her to hit with a 9mm than miss with a .45. Besides, the Browning just felt good and the inside-the-waistband holster made it possible for her to carry it concealed as long as she had on a loose blouse—two of which were also included in the go-bag. Jericho had insisted she include a fixed blade in her kit, so there was a wicked little two-finger thing his knife-maker friends in Anchorage had given him called the Scorn—along with extra magazines for both pistols. In addition to the weapons, she had a wound kit, two more flashlights—you could never have too many of those—a small pair of binoculars, a pair of jeans, comfortable running shoes, a baseball cap, a pair of polarized Oakley sunglasses, a Windbreaker, extra socks, and two pairs of underwear. Four thousand dollars in rolls of twenties and hundreds and another burner phone rounded out the contents of the bag. There had been five, but a thousand had gone to the kid with the motorcycle.

Satisfied she had what she'd need for the short term, she mixed the ramen and sat back on the bed to drink her diet Dr Pepper. She'd lost count of how many nights she'd spent in business hotel rooms just like this one—during training, on missions, interviews, polygraphs, and clandestine meetings with contacts. It was easy to wake up and have no idea where you were. Cookie-cutter designed, they were all virtually the same—with nice furniture, heavy blinds, and the lingering odor of someone else's cologne.

The ramen did little to take the edge off her adrenaline-stoked hunger. She pulled back the sheets and fell back on the bed. Hands behind her head, she closed her eyes and thought about ordering room service.

Her eyes flicked open at a sudden thought. What if the IDTF had somehow installed cameras in this room? She knew the notion was absurd. It had been a last-minute decision. She hadn't even known where she was going to stay until she rode into the parking lot. But the feeling of being watched was a hard one to shake. The flashing green light on the smoke alarm in the center of the ceiling caught her eye. Smoke alarms had a built-in power source. They were the perfect place to hide cameras and listening devices.

She stood up and double-checked the latch over the door, hoping that would make her feel better. It didn't. Jericho had often accused her of having a panic button on her back that made her agonize over little things whenever her head hit the pillow.

She considered another shower, but shoved the thought out of her mind. Getting naked again today was not an option. In the end, she leaned a chair against the door and then climbed into bed wearing all her clothes. Worrying over Jericho, she glanced at both pistols in the dim glow of the nightstand clock as she fell into a fitful sleep. Her panic button was working overtime.

# Chapter 33

Virginia Ross found herself shoved unceremoniously into the backseat of a black Suburban. It was nearly identical to the armored one her protective detail used but for the fact that instead of tinted bulletproof glass, this one had blackout material fixed to the windows.

"Curtains," the director mused, as Walter slid in the backseat beside her. "I half expected to have a black bag pulled over my head."

Agent Walter chuckled. "We're not heathens, Director Ross."

"Well," Ross said, crossing her hands in the lap of her gym shorts. "Would you mind telling me what this is all about?"

"In due time," Walter said. "In due time."

He sat in silence throughout the rest of the trip, looking at his phone and ignoring her completely.

It took them the better part of an hour to get wherever they were going. The driver kept the air conditioner on its coldest setting for the entire trip. Ross folded her arms across her chest in an effort to keep from shivering. Wearing nothing but her damp T-shirt and thin running shorts, she was freezing by the time they came to a stop.

Walter didn't even look up.

"Are we just going to sit here all night?" Ross asked, looking forward to even a brief moment of warm outside air.

Walter groaned, stowing his phone back in the inside pocket of his wrinkled gray suit.

"All right," he said. "But if I were you, I wouldn't be too excited."


Ross had been inside prisons before, but her knees nearly buckled at the sound of the heavy metal door slamming shut behind her. She'd been witness to several . . . intense interrogations, the memory of which only added to the fear roiling in her chest. A second door, identical to the first one, formed a small mantrap prior to the main receiving area visible through a tall, slender window. It began to rumble open as soon as the first door slid closed.

Walter and another man, younger and blond with bad acne, flanked her, each holding an elbow as if there was anywhere else she could go. A shadow behind the dark tint of a huge window—presumably the control center—buzzed them through another door. A long, polished hallway with tiny windowed cells running the length of both sides stretched out in front of her. She recognized Brigadier General Tim Crutchfield in one of the cells. An Army advisor to the Secretary of Defense, he'd given an interview with *Rolling Stone* magazine about his views on the new administration—and disappeared shortly after. She slowed to look, but his head ducked away from the window when he saw Walter.

They picked up the pace and Ross was ushered through another door along the far end of the hall and into a sprawling interrogation room. At least twenty by twenty feet in size, it was surely designed to make the prisoner feel insignificant. It worked. Ross had to concentrate to keep her feet when they led her into the room. Along with being big, it was blindingly bright with glaring light that made it difficult to tell where polished white tile ended and painted walls began. This door had no window, but it was impossible not to notice the cameras at each corner of the ceiling. A stainless-steel table sat in the center of the room, with brushed metal chairs on either side. There was no bunk and the only other furnishing was an institutional combination sink, water fountain, and toilet sitting in the open along the back wall.

The stark lighting and clinical lack of privacy sent a wave of cramps through Ross's gut.

"Have a seat, Virginia," Walter said, dismissing the acne-covered man with a nod.

"I prefer to stand," she said. The door slammed shut and she jumped in spite of herself. Folding her arms across her chest, she paced back and forth, wishing she had the skills to beat the hell out of the man on the other side of the table. She was at least five years his senior and had always been a writer over a fighter, even in her prime.

"Please sit," Walter said again. He dropped a thick manila folder on the table between them. "It will make this so much easier."

"I expected you to take me to some black-site ship out at sea," she said, mustering the cool that had gotten her the job of CIA director in the first place.

Walter gave a smug nod. "Why's that? Is that what you order your agents to do with spies?"

"You and I both know I haven't violated the Espionage Act," Ross said. "Why don't you tell me what this is all about?"

Walter picked up the file again, flipping through it. He glanced up now and again to study her, and then went back to the file. After a full five minutes, he tossed the folder aside as if it didn't matter anyway.

"Well, I'm tired." He flopped black in the chair. "So I'm going to sit even if you won't." He folded his hands on the table in front of him. "You've made some pretty bold statements in favor of enhanced interrogation."

"Desperate times," she said. "The nation is under attack."

"So it is." Walter nodded.

Ross put both hands flat on the table, leaning over it. The sureness in her voice belied the turmoil inside her.

"Is that your plan with me?" she asked. "Enhanced interrogation?"

Agent Walter leaned back, resting his hands on his stomach, eyeing her. "That depends," he said. "Please sit down."

Ross sighed, deflated. Her fingers trembled as she pulled back the chair and sat. She was a professor, an expert in foreign affairs and world economies. In the past decade she'd become an expert on espionage. While she'd approved the use of harsh interrogation methods and even sent her agents into missions that put them at risk of enduring such treatment, she was in no way wired to withstand such abuse herself. But then, she remembered, if torture was administered correctly, no one was.

"Depends on what?" she whispered.

"On you." Walter leaned forward, elbows on the table. He rested a smug face in his hands and smiled that horrible half smile. It made her, a grandmother, want to kick his teeth out. "Tell me what you know."

Ross's mouth fell open. "I'm the director of the Central Intelligence Agency," she said. "I *know* virtually everything."

"Fair enough," Walter said. "We'll narrow it down some. Tell me what you know about Winfield Palmer."

Ross nodded. So that was it. She'd seen the way both the President and Vice President had glared at her when she'd taken up for him.

"I'd imagine he's looking for a job," she said, forcing a smile.

"You know," Walter said, "you guys took ugly interrogation techniques to all kinds of exotic levels—drugs, light, noise. . . ." His eyes narrowed, peering right through her. "In my experience, you don't need a bunch of fancy things to convince someone to talk. A wet washcloth and a can of Sprite work as good as any fancy waterboard."

"I suppose," Ross said.

"Tell me more about Palmer."

Ross shrugged, seeing where this was going. "There's nothing to tell. He was President's Clark's closest advisor and confidante."

"But you were aware of his little stable of private agents?" Walter prodded. "His side work, so to speak."

"I knew he borrowed assets from me on occasion, with the approval of the President."

"Like Veronica Garcia?"

"She worked for him from time to time, yes," Ross said.

"And now?"

"What do you mean?" Ross said.

"I mean does Veronica Garcia still report to Palmer?"

"She works for me," Ross said.

"Who else works for Palmer?"

"I don't know."

"What are his plans as of now?"

"I told you"—Ross turned up her palms on the table—"I do not know."

Walter toyed at the corner of the folder in front of him.

"Have you ever been punched in the mouth?" he asked.

"I . . ." Ross shook her head. What sort of question was this? "No, I can't say that I have."

Agent Walter took a long breath through his nose, as if considering her words.

"Ms. Ross," he said. "I want you to take a minute and consider a couple of things. Chiefly, I want you to think of what kind of power I must have to arrest the director of the Central Intelligence Agency." He chuckled. "I knew you would make this harder than it has to be. . . ."

"I'm not trying—"

"You're the nation's top spy," he cut her off. "You must know what comes next in this process."

Ross felt as if her tongue were made of cotton. "I can assure you, I do not—"

"I'll tell you anyway." Walter held up an open palm to stop her. "We strip you of everything—clothing, sleep . . . and, most important for our process, we take away your hope. In time, you will tell us everything we need to know."

Ross clenched her jaw, arms folded across her chest, clutching herself. She would not cry in front of this man.

"I'll let you keep your clothing for a little longer," he

said, the crooked lips barely concealing a smirk. "As a courtesy to your position. We have to ease into these things. . . ."

Fear gave way to anger and her head snapped up defiantly.

Walter cut her off before she could speak. "Director Ross," he sighed. "You've signed orders for humiliation treatment dozens of times. Don't pretend this is something that flies in the face of some newfound moral code."

"I'm not a terrorist," she spat. Her shoulders shook with rage.

"Well." Walter shrugged. "We're not a hundred percent sure on that." He moved to the end of the table as if to pick up the folder. Without warning, he punched her square in the face.

The blow knocked Ross out of her chair and she landed butt first on the polished tile floor. A bolt of pain shot from her tailbone to her shoulders. Blood poured from her nose, running through the fingers of her cupped hand and covering the front of her T-shirt.

Agent Walter brushed the hair out of his eyes. He stared at her for a long moment, and then flicked his fingers toward the camera above the door, signifying that he was ready to be let out.

There was a mechanical buzz as the lock actuated. He pulled the door open.

"Now, you can," he said without turning around.

Ross lowered her bloody hand, seething. Her lip was already beginning to swell. "Now I can what?"

"Say you've been hit in the mouth." He shut the door behind him.

Virginia Ross used the chair to pull herself up. Once on her feet she began to tremble so violently she had to use the table to keep her balance. She'd been put in charge of the CIA because she was also an intuitive genius—and of one thing, she was certain. The IDTF hadn't spirited her away to some black site where the rules of law could be thought of as gray at best. They had put her in a prison on American soil—and one of their agents had just struck her in the face. They never intended to let her leave there alive.

# DAY TWO

*'Twould be an ill world for weaponless dreamers*
*if evil men were not now and then slain.*
—RUDYARD KIPLING

# Chapter 34

By six-thirty a.m., Garcia sat cross-legged with her back against the headboard of the hotel bed. Five hours of fitful sleep had chased away enough of her panic that she'd been able to take a shower. A white towel now sat piled around her wet hair like a turban. She wore a clean pair of faded jeans and a white T-shirt that was loose at the waist to conceal her Browning Hi Power and tight enough at the chest to ensure no one looked down there anyway. Barefoot, she wiggled her toes, tapping a pen against her teeth while she considered the list in the spiral notebook that lay in her lap.

Empty dishes from her breakfast of steel-cut oats, three slices of bacon, and toast covered in orange marmalade cluttered the room service tray next to her knee. The first cup of coffee from the little hotel-room coffeemaker had revived her just enough to stumble into the shower. The stuff that came with her meal was much better and actually made her feel something close to human again.

The notebook held two dozen names and their associated contact information. The problem with ditching a cell phone so it couldn't be used to track her location was that all the phone numbers and e-mail addresses got ditched as well. She hated committing sensitive information like this to paper, and would eventually drop the entire notebook in a burn bag, but for now, she had to decide where to start.

The volume on the television was low, but the willowy brunette on FOX News seemed to shout every word that roamed across her teleprompter, from barked sound bites about the national debt to some slutty pop star's latest vacation to rehab. Ronnie had picked up the remote to turn it off when the news anchor called in a hunky *GQ* model with "leaked" news about the arrest of the CIA director.

". . . Ross's capture comes amid a massive series of intergovernmental probes," the reporter said from his vantage point outside the US Capitol. "The Justice Department would make no statement regarding the investigation, but sources confirm that Director Ross is suspected of leaking sensitive, even top-secret, material to foreign agents."

"This is just incredible, Steve," the shouting brunette said. "Do we know yet when she'll appear in court?"

"As I said, Leslie, the government has not commented officially," *GQ* said. "We can only assume that some of the hearings will be held in camera or, in other words, closed to the public due to the extremely sensitive matters that are certain to come out. That said, we can confirm that Virginia Ross, director of the Central Intelligence Agency, has been arrested and is being held in federal custody at an undisclosed location. . . ."

Garcia picked up the notebook and ran her finger down the back page, looking for a particular number.

"Undisclosed federal custody," she said to herself. She found who she was looking for, then picked up the burner phone.

He would either be the perfect guy to call . . . or he'd throw her in jail.

# Chapter 35

Above all the other aspects of protective work, Deputy US Marshal August Bowen enjoyed the chance to explore. A Montana native and former US Army scout, he was a tracker and hunter by nature. He liked the conquest of things that others might consider mundane. The back hallways, restaurant kitchens, laundry rooms, and basements of five-star Washington, DC, hotels—all proved to be new frontiers as far as Bowen was concerned.

He had a pleasant face with deep dimples on either side of a well-trimmed goatee. At thirty-six, his beard was still dark, as his hair had been when he'd deployed to Afghanistan two years before. That trip had changed many things about him, the most noticeable being that his hair had turned gunmetal gray.

Broad shoulders and a trim waist made his off-the-rack suit look more expensive than it really was. A clear pigtail ran from his ear to the flesh-tone wire clipped to his shirt collar, disappearing beneath his jacket and running down to the brick-sized radio on the left side of his belt. A second and third wire from the radio ran respectively up the back of the coat and down his sleeve to a small beige microphone pinned to his lapel and an activation button held in place on his left wrist with a rubber band. This "surveillance kit" allowed him to use his radio without going all Hollywood and putting his finger to his ear or raising his hand to his mouth every time he spoke. The suit coat also covered a pair of handcuffs, a X26 Taser, and a .40 caliber Glock 22 with two extra magazines.

A voice came over the radio, crackling in his ear. "He wants to head to the courthouse in thirty minutes."

"Advance copies," Bowen said. As the deputy out front of all movement, he'd need to go check with the deputy assigned to sit with the vehicles and make sure the exits were clear. After that, he'd scout the route to the courthouse ahead of the detail.

Deputy US marshals worked with so many different agencies that they generally dispensed with cumbersome codes and signals on the radio, instead using plain talk that was understood by all, no matter the jurisdiction.

Picking up his pace, Bowen moved down the bright hall that ran below the main lobby of the hotel. Absent the fancy carpets and mood lighting of the guest areas, these subterranean passageways were steaming hives of activity with thriving cultures that were far more interesting than the stuffy cigar bars upstairs.

They also made excellent entry points for threats to the protectee, providing plenty of places to explore.

The principal, US District Judge R. Felix Knudson, was new to the bench. His chambers were in Norfolk, but he was in town training with some of the more experienced judges. One of his first cases had seen him rule against a group of white separatists who had a compound near the North Carolina border. The ruling had garnered enough death threats that the Marshals

Service was still in the middle of trying to discern if the letters were sent by genuine "hunters" who planned to make good on their threats, or "howlers" who talked a loud and bothersome game but were basically harmless.

Of all the judges Bowen had protected, Knudsen had to be the easiest. He warned his detail well in advance of any movement and acted as though he realized they were genuinely concerned for his safety. He'd not been on the bench long enough to "turn purple" or "royal," as often occurred to powerful judges and senators. It was a difficult thing, hearing nothing but yes to every question and hearty laughs at all your jokes, no matter how lame.

Bowen wouldn't know. Few people ever told him yes.

Making his way down the hallway past the kitchen toward the alley exit where the vehicles were staged, he passed a smiling Hispanic woman wearing blue hospital scrubs. She stood beside a train of canvas laundry carts working at a huge blue-and-white sheet-pressing machine that was called a mangler—a little factoid Bowen would never have known had he not explored the back hallways of the hotel.

"Augusto." The woman smiled, raising dark eyebrows up, then down to flirt. "I take a break in five minutes. Why don't we sail away on that boat you are always talking about? My husband, he would never be able to track us down."

"Ah, Josephina," Bowen chuckled. "*Mi Corazon es perdido en ti.*" He used six of the dozen Spanish words he knew—and those from a Brooks and Dunn song. *My heart is lost in you.* "But I think I could not keep up with a woman like you."

Josephina was old enough to be his mother, but she

gave him a sly wink that would have scared a lesser man. It was all innocent flirtation.

As advance deputy, Bowen made it his job to know the backstairs staff by name. It took a little extra time, but gave him two dozen more sets of eyes and ears to help protect the judge.

Saying good-bye to Josephina, Bowen worked his way down the hall, past industrial driers that hummed and thumped and filled the air with the pleasant smell of warm cotton. The hotel was built on a hill, so he exited the steel delivery doors at ground level, across the street from a Panera Bakery and a Starbucks. The Suburban and Lincoln Town Car they used for the protective detail were parked around the corner, but they would come this way en route to the courthouse in Alexandria. It was Bowen's job to let them know the area was clear of any possible threats.

It was still early and crowds of commuters ducked in and out of the bakery and Starbucks, getting their morning bagel and coffee fixes before heading off to work. A group of three youths in their early twenties hung out near the doorway to the coffee shop. Their swaggering demeanor caught Bowen's attention as he crossed the street. They wore baggy jeans, loose NFL jerseys, and colorful tennis shoes. One, the tallest of the three, wore a ball cap turned sideways. But their clothing, their race, or the fact that there were three of them was not what aroused his suspicions. It was the way they looked at the people walking by.

They were predators looking for someone to catch unawares. A hunter himself, Bowen watched a young woman just a few feet away from the boys, and recognized her as just the kind they would target. She had a messenger bag over her shoulder and a rolled copy of the morning paper under her arm. Her eyes were glued to the screen of a smartphone and her ears plugged with buds that piped in music to block out the noises— and threats—of the world around her.

Bowen picked up his pace, watching the kid with the ball cap step out as the girl walked by. She was too close for Bowen to reach her in time so he shouted, trying to get her or, at the very least, Ball Cap's attention before he sucker punched her in another senseless game of "knockout"—just to watch her fall.

"Hey!" Bowen yelled as loud as he could, running now.

Even wearing earbuds, the girl heard something and looked up in time to see the kid swinging at her with a doubled fist. The blow still came in hard, but it hit her shoulder instead of her head. She staggered sideways.

His knockout sucker punch foiled, the kid turned to run, and came face-to-face with Deputy August Bowen.

His two buddies just stood there, waiting to see how their friend handled a full-grown man.

Realizing he didn't have time to get away, Ball Cap bladed his body, bringing his right arm back as if to chamber it for a punch.

Bowen had been a boxer since junior high school, and sent in a left jab before the kid even had a chance to make a good fist. The jab put him in perfect line for a right cross, which in turn set him up for Bowen's left hook—a powerful blow that nearly took the kid's head off. With punks like this a simple combination was all it took. Bowen didn't even have to get clever. Reeling, Ball Cap's main problem seemed to be trying to figure out which way to fall. Bowen helped him with a wicked uppercut that snapped his teeth shut like a gunshot and shut out his lights.

The deputy turned to look at the other two, but they'd wisely decided to vanish somewhere between the cross and the left hook.

Bowen flipped the kid over on his belly and handcuffed him, patting him down for weapons as a gathering crowd cheered and applauded. He got on his radio and briefed the protective detail supervisor, letting her know what had happened. She advised they would take the alternate route away from the hotel, and told him to hang back with his collar and fill in Arlington PD when they arrived.

Bowen showed his badge to the victim, who seemed more shaken up than anything. She was anxious to stay and give her statement to the police. Scribbling something on a piece of her newspaper, she shoved it toward Bowen with a shaky hand.

"Here's my number," she said, smiling. "You know, in case you need it for your report . . . or just want to call me. . . ."

Bowen's cell phone began to buzz in the pocket of his suit, but an Arlington squad car rolled up so he ignored it for the moment.

He made his excuses to the girl and turned to hold up his credentials.

"Knockout game?" the officer said.

"Yep." Bowen grinned. "And you can maybe add assault on a federal officer because his chin sort of hurt my fist." He'd been known to cross three lanes of traffic and pull his car over just to right the smallest of wrongs, but he'd prayed for the day he was around when some delinquent turd decided to play the knockout game

Bowen winked at the girl as his phone began to buzz again. He looked at the officer, holding up the phone. "Sorry," he said. "I need to take this."

"Hello," he said, pressing the phone to the ear without the pigtail radio wire hanging out of it. He walked down the street a few steps.

"Deputy Bowen." The caller was female and spoke in the snapped speech of someone on a mission. "Do not say my name out loud, but do you recognize who this is?"

"I do now," Bowen said. Even when she was rushed, there was no mistaking the sultry tones of Ronnie Garcia, peppered with just a hint of Cuban spice. Hers was one of the few voices that, like the voluptuous Jessica Rabbit from the cartoon, actually belonged to the lips that made the noise. "Who else besides you and that boyfriend of yours would get all spy games on me?"

"True," Garcia said. "How are you?"

"I'm well," he said, chuckling at the pleasantries. "What can I do for you?"

"I need to ask you a favor," she said. "But I have to warn you that it could get you into serious trouble."

Bowen groaned inside. Just being assigned the Jericho Quinn fugitive case had nearly gotten him relegated across the river to work the DC Superior Court cellblock—otherwise known as "Marshals Service Hell." Still, dismissing the fact that Quinn had beaten the snot out of him when they were both still in the military, he was a good man and there were damn too few of those.

"What's the favor?" Bowen asked when he was well away from the Arlington PD officer and the growing crowd.

"I can't talk about it on the phone," Garcia said. "We need to meet."

"Okay," he said. "Come by the courthouse. I'll be there most of the day after I finish up here."

"That won't be possible," Garcia said. "I'll explain it all when we meet. Someplace public."

"Public?"

"Look," she said. "I'm not sure who I can trust right now."

"You called me," he said. "Remember?"

"I guess I did," she said. "Listen, there's a water park near Manassas. Can you meet me there?"

"Well," Bowen said, "I was assigned to a protective detail, but as it happens I just got relieved to deal with a local police matter. I can meet with you tonight, no problem."

"That's too far off," Garcia said, sounding as if she about to loose a flood of Cuban curses. "This is life or death. I wouldn't bug you if it wasn't."

Bowen took a deep breath. "Okay. A water park in Manassas."

"Eleven o'clock."

"I'll be there." He looked at his watch. "But I'm not wearing a swimming suit."

"Up to you," Ronnie said. "But this is a family place. They won't be too happy with you lounging around in the water without one."

# Chapter 36

*Alaska*

Quinn hung his head out the window of Lovita's borrowed Pontiac, thinking of how many times he'd ridden this road on a motorcycle. Die-hard riders often called other vehicles cages. The little Pontiac was a perfect example of why. Thankfully, the passenger window was completely gone, allowing some escape from the stale odor of fast food trash—and some creature that had crawled up inside the air vents and died.

It was not quite seven in the morning but the sun had already been up for three hours and the Chugach Mountains glowed with the brilliant golden-green of summer. Joggers and bicyclists moved steadily through the crisp Alaska morning down the paved pathway between the Glenn Highway and Joint Base Elmendorf Richardson. There was a time Quinn had thought of becoming the OSI detachment commander here at JBER. His parents pushed for it. Kim certainly wanted it. Heaven knew he owed Mattie a little more of his time. But for some reason, that normal, move-up-the-ranks-and-become-the-boss portion of his career just wasn't meant to be so the det co thing never materialized. He was an Air Force Academy alumnus, a Fulbright Scholar, and spoke five languages. Out in the world he could have been described as a renaissance man. But he was just rough enough around the edges that he always felt like a bit of a thug compared to the other Air Force officers in garrison. He supposed he just wasn't cut out for it. Lately, it had been difficult to comprehend what he was cut out for except for slitting the odd throat now and then. It sure wasn't being a father—no matter what patriotic platitudes he spouted to Lovita about having something to fight for.

His mind had covered a dozen different scenarios for his arrival at the airport by the time they passed the National Guard Armory—known as the "Green Banana"—between Eagle River and Anchorage. He had never been the nervous sort. When he made a decision, he followed through, leaving the outcome to God or fate or whatever great cosmic dice game was in control of his destiny. But that was him. When it came to his daughter, he was capable of worrying a hole in his gut.

Quinn's greatest worry was that his parents had been followed out of DC and a crowd of IDTF agents or contract killers would swoop down on them as soon as he set foot in the airport. If by some miracle his parents were able to get Mattie to Alaska unimpeded, there was the high likelihood that some other passenger, a TSA officer, or even a US Customs agent might recognize Jericho from having grown up with him. Nearly 300,000 people called Anchorage home, but the small-town feel made it difficult to go to a store or restaurant without running into someone who knew him.

Five months of heavy black beard had made him look like a pirate. He'd trimmed it back to a more city-acceptable length before leaving the hangar that morning. Lovita said it gave him "ambiguous ethnicity." He wore a ball cap pulled down low and black Wiley X shades that he hoped were all enough to camouflage his identity.

Traffic was heavy with morning commuters along the Glenn, but Lovita took C Street through midtown and hung a right on International Airport Road across from Baily's Furniture Store. He'd met plenty of pilots who scared him to death when they got behind the wheel of a car, but Lovita, a village child who rarely drove anything larger than a four-wheeler, handled the car as if she'd grown up driving in a city much larger than Anchorage.

His head still out the window, Quinn caught the flowery sweet scents of birch and balsam poplar as they neared the airport. The air was still crisp enough that no one questioned the fact that Quinn was wearing a black motorcycle jacket. A Vanson Enfield, the jacket was heavy leather but old and worn enough to fit like a comfortable baseball glove. It wasn't armored like his customary Aerostich Transit Leather, but that one had been cut to ribbons back in Japan.

Lovita pulled up next to the curb at the North Terminal and put the car in park. She turned to look at him, smiling softly.

"I think I would make a good government operative," she said, out of the blue.

Quinn cocked his head to one side, studying her face. The traditional tattoo notwithstanding, she was probably right.

"I think so too," he said. "Give me a call after this is over. I can introduce you to some people."

"Be careful, Jericho Quinn," she said, as if his name was all one word. "I need to keep you as a contact."

Her voice was even huskier than usual, her eyes red as if she'd stayed awake much of the night. She was an incredibly tough human being, but coming within inches of crashing into a mountainside was enough to work on anyone's emotions.

She leaned across the seat to give him a hug. The smell of cigarettes and some sort of musky perfume she'd found back at the hangar was a welcome cover for the odor of the Pontiac.

"Thanks for flying Air Lovita," she said.

"Yeah, well, thanks for saving my life." Quinn turned to grab his duffel from the backseat. "You flying back tonight?"

She nodded. "Got a Costco run, then fish to cut when I get back," she said simply. Good-byes over, she waited for him to shut the door, then pulled away without another word.

The North Terminal was the older portion of Ted Stevens Airport. It wasn't quite as swank as the newer, main terminal across the way, but it did have a huge stuffed polar bear in the waiting area outside security—the part of the airport Quinn most remembered as a child. It was also the terminal for US Customs and international flights arriving and departing Alaska.

The Alaska flight from DC had arrived an hour earlier at the South Terminal, but Quinn was already inside by the time his parents had retrieved their bags and hopped a shuttle to the north side of the airport. Quinn didn't see any tail, but if there was one, it wouldn't matter at this point anyway. He'd known Kim wasn't coming, but his heart sank a little when she didn't get off the shuttle with everyone else.

Mattie bolted to him as soon as she came through the door. It had been half a year since she'd seen him last, beside her mother's hospital bed. It was a lot for an adult to handle, let alone a seven-year-old girl.

She buried her face in his chest, squeezing him until her arms shook.

"I missed you too, Sweet Pea," Quinn said, glancing up at his father. He mouthed the words "How's Kim?" so Mattie couldn't hear him.

Pete Quinn took a deep breath, putting a hand on the little girl's shoulder. "Can you help Grandma with the luggage, sweetheart?" he said. "I need to talk to your dad a minute before y'all go."

Mattie looked up, arms still locked around her daddy's neck.

"We'll just be a minute." Jericho hugged her one more time before peeling her away.

Mattie nodded and dutifully went to stand with her grandmother, a tall woman with deep brown eyes and silver-gray hair she liked to call "Arctic Blonde."

Pete Quinn's large gray eyes held the same look they had one winter when Jericho and Bo were boys and he'd told them their favorite dog had been eaten by a pack of wolves.

"What is it?" Jericho said, bracing himself for the worst.

"She banged her leg pretty bad when those guys tried to get her and Mattie in the van," he said. "I think she'll be fine, but doctors are worried about blood clots. She's in the hospital at Bethesda. I know you're worried, son, but Bo is with her night and day. Your friend Jacques is pulling security and helping out more than seems humanly possible. He's a good man. I like him."

"Me too," Quinn said. "But he's got his own family to worry about."

\* \* \*

Quinn's mother handed him the folder with Mattie's passport and the visas Thibodaux had given her. Quinn gave her a hug at the base of the escalators leading to the second level and through security, apologizing for turning her into a mule for forged documents. She gave him a tense smile, tears welling in her eyes.

"Don't cry, Mom," he said. "Dad always said God counts a woman's tears and blames them on us guys."

The matriarch of the Quinn family smoothed the front of her light Windbreaker. "Well," she sniffed, "if that's the case, you boys are going to have a lot of explaining to do someday." She gave him a kiss on the cheek before gathering Mattie in for one last hug. "Now remember," she said. "Your name is Mattie Hackman. Don't forget that."

"Ten-four, Nana." Mattie grinned, giving a little mock salute.

Jericho shook his father's hand. "I wish you'd let me make some calls. I've kind of turned you into a target over here."

The elder Quinn shook his head. "Have you seen the fish runs this year? I have a boat to tend and a crew who depends on me. We'll be so far out in the ocean, nobody's going to bother with us."

"Don't you fret over us." Quinn's mother waved off any thought of worry. She seemed soft, but Quinn knew she was tough as barbed wire underneath the façade. She had to be to be married to his dad and raise the two boys she'd been given. "We'll be fine."

"All right." Jericho sighed. "I don't like it, but there's nothing I can do about it now."

His mother gave him a half grin. "Those are the exact words I used when you told me you were taking up boxing."

*   *   *

Since they were taking an international flight, Quinn produced a notarized letter at the security checkpoint, signed by Kimberly Hackman, giving him permission to leave the country with their child. Kim had signed it, and Bo had used his charm to get one of his girlfriends to notarize it. The heavyset TSA officer, who was all of twenty-four, had still quizzed Mattie with some half-hearted questions and consulted with his most recent Amber Alerts and NCMEC Missing Children photos to make sure Quinn wasn't stealing his own child. Thankfully, he worried more over that than checking out their false identification. The ID was plenty real. It was, in fact, manufactured by the government and presumably off the books. But allegiances changed and unless Miyagi or Palmer had printed the passports themselves, someone else knew of their existence. Quinn had never worried about it before, but Mattie's presence added an entire new level of tension.

When they finally made it past security and were sitting at the gate, Quinn found himself mildly surprised that he wasn't dog piled by law enforcement. Still half an hour away from boarding, passengers crowded around the podium so they could be the absolute first to board. Quinn suppressed a smile in spite of his nerves. It was easy to see why airline personnel called such impatient passengers "gate lice."

Mattie had calmed down quickly, as she always did, and now sat listening to music on her iPod. A multitasker at seven, she swung her legs off the edge of her chair while she flipped through the pages of her Lemony Snicket book. Her mother had been shot, her father was a fugitive, and armed men had tried to shove her in a van just hours before, but she appeared to share Quinn's ability to compartmentalize and carry on in the face of events that would cause other people immobilizing stress. She'd not skipped a beat in giving the TSA agents her fake name, jabbering away with just enough details about their long-planned vacation to Russia. Quinn couldn't help but wonder how many other traits she'd inherited from him—and worried over how much of a problem this special talent at lying would be when she hit her teens.

He took a deep breath and willed himself to be as calm as his daughter. The next big hurdle would be clearing Immigration and Customs once they reached their destination. If anything, Russians were known for their convoluted bureaucracy. He'd been through plenty with Aleksandra Kanatova and he knew she was trustworthy enough to keep up her end of the plan. But even with her help, the odds were overwhelming that they would run into all manner of problems entering the country—even on clean passports.

Quinn consoled himself with the idea that the twelve-hour flight would give him time to rest and make plans. The plane would stop in Petropavlovsk on the Kamchatka Peninsula first, then Vladivostok, before continuing on to Moscow, where he'd have to make first contact with Russian immigration officials. He hoped Kanatova would be there and waiting.

Quinn looked at the information board above the Global gate, and then checked the Tag Aquaracer on his wrist. If nothing happened for the next half an hour he'd be able to relax—at least while they were in the air.

# Chapter 37

***Near Manassas, Virginia***

August Bowen located Garcia with little trouble amid the crowd of families, flirting teenagers, and screaming children at the outdoor water park. It was ironic that a woman who seemed bent on playing spy games should possess oh so many traits that made her do everything but blend in. She lounged up to her shoulders in a raised tile hot tub that was tucked in behind a gigantic, spaghetti-like yellow waterslide. Deeply bronzed and well-muscled, she was still supremely feminine. The parts of her that lay above the surface shouted for everyone in the park to guess what lay beneath the water.

Bowen walked barefoot across the concrete, smiling, happy to feel the heat against his toes. He'd changed into a pair of blue board shorts in the locker room and shut his clothes up with a combination lock that reminded him of his days back in junior-high gym class. Even a halfhearted thief would be able to defeat such a basic padlock in a manner of seconds, so he kept the dive watch on his wrist and submitted his wallet to fate. He congratulated himself for having the forethought to leave his gun locked in the center console of his Charger.

A blinding sun reflected and refracted off the rippling blue surface of the many small pools and rivers that made up the park. The warm Virginia air, heavy with the odor of chlorine and Coppertone, mingled with the must of oaks from the greenbelt that ran between Manassas and Centerville before sliding like a leafy delta into Battlefield Park.

Bowen worked his way through scattered deck chairs and gangs of barely dressed teenagers. Screaming toddlers ran by on stubby legs or washed back and forth with their mothers in the nearby wave pool.

With so many big-armed, khaki-clad federal lawdogs wearing all the latest gadgets, August Bowen strove for practical over *practi-cool,* both in gear and physique. Blue jeans and a T-shirt beat out khakis and polo shirts when the marshal didn't force his hand at work. Like many boxers, he rarely lifted weights, feeling they slowed him down and gave him mirror-muscles instead of true, usable power. He worked hard to keep the body of a fighter, hardened by hours of skipping rope, long runs, and years of pounding the heavy bag.

Such a level of fitness brought with it a certain don't-screw-with-me vibe that stopped most fights before they started—and garnered him stacks upon stacks of cocktail napkins with women's phone numbers.

A bright scar, the size and shape of a football, stood out against the tan skin of the ribs on his right side. His blue board shorts covered a corresponding scar on his buttock and thigh, all from a long-forgotten Russian land mine near Mazar-i-Sharif. The mine put him in the hospital, but it had turned his interpreter into a red mist. Bowen thought about that good man each time he saw the scar in the mirror. Few people ever even noticed the scar at first, focusing instead on the full head of silver hair on a seemingly healthy man in his early thirties.

Garcia looked up when he approached and nodded him over with a wide smile that could have stopped a charging buffalo in its tracks. Bowen imagined she'd hooked Jericho Quinn with much the same look.

"Hey there," she said, as he stepped into the cool water. "Thanks for meeting me."

Though the water park was relatively crowded, the moms and kids that made up the bulk of the patrons were much more interested in the high-octane slides and wave pools than a simple whirlpool tub. Ronnie shared the ten-by-fifteen pool with only a couple of pimple-faced teenage boys who lounged along the wall opposite her, willing themselves to look ten years older. They cast expectant glances every few moments, just waiting for her to stand up so they could get a better look at her. The boys stared at Bowen with dagger eyes when he encroached on their territory, but cowered when he came closer—small dogs, brave only when safely behind their screen doors.

Bowen gave the boys a polite nod. He remembered all too well the mind-numbing rush of hormones he would have felt at their age in the pool with someone with the curves of Veronica Garcia. Pushing through the waist-deep water until he was beside her, he slid down the cool tile wall with his shoulders against the concrete lip of the pool.

Garcia rolled solid shoulders as if she was trying to relax. Bowen, whose army shrink had told him after the nonsense in Afghanistan that he should use his artistic talent to work though his issues, watched this woman and told himself he was thinking only of what fine art the lines of her body would produce. His artist's eye picked up the slight unevenness in her collar-bones—a car wreck, maybe. She had a tiny mole on the lobe of her left ear—something he would certainly high-light if he were drawing her face.

He blinked to clear his thoughts, covering with a smile. "How have you been?" he asked.

She glanced back and forth, dark eyes scanning the crowds. The last six inches of her black hair pooled in the water around her neck, mopping bronze shoulders when she moved.

"I'm good," she said, her voice detached, distant. She scooted closer so her thigh brushed his under the water.

Bowen knew it was just so their conversation would be more private, but it still made him catch his breath. He hid it with a cough, he hoped.

"Did anyone try to follow you?" she asked.

"I don't think so," he said honestly. It hadn't really occurred to him to look for a tail, but he was pretty sure he would have noticed one had it existed.

"Okay," Garcia said, lips pursed as if mulling over one last time how much she wanted to tell him. "I need your help," she finally said, "but I have to warn you again. It could get you in a lot of trouble."

"Trouble is my middle name." Bowen smiled, hop-ing to tamp down the drama.

"It's 'danger,' Mango." She smiled. "*Danger* is your middle name."

"Are you sure?" Bowen said. "Because I get in a hell of a lot of trouble." He leaned back, draping his arms along the pool deck. They were close enough it was impossible to avoid touching one another and his fin-gers brushed the moist skin of her shoulders. "Anyway, I'm used to it. Trouble, I mean." He coughed, clearing his thoughts. "So, what can I help you with?"

Garcia leaned in close and let her head tilt sideways. Her damp hair slid across his arm. "Are you familiar with the IDTF?"

Bowen gave a thoughtful nod. "Who isn't?" he said. Mention of that agency alone was enough to sour anything positive about sitting in a hot tub with a beautiful woman. "President Drake's new department of Internal Defense. Rooting out the bad apples in government and safeguarding the freedoms of all Americans . . . if you believe their press." He turned to look her in the eye. "Which, as far as I can see, no one in the government does."

"Well," Garcia said, eyes still flicking nervously around the crowded water park. "A couple of their goons did a black bag job on my house. The bastards even put a camera in my bathroom."

"Yeah," Bowen chuckled. "I saw that. It's already up on the Internet at Ronnieshowers.com."

She slammed a sharp elbow into his ribs. "Shut up."

"I apologize," he said. "I shouldn't joke. That's a bad deal."

"Anyway . . ." Garcia's chastening glare faded slowly. "They followed me to a gas station, so I knocked one of them out with a two-by-four and broke the other guy's leg with his car door—"

Bowen sat up straighter. Grimacing, he showed her the flat of his open hand. "I don't think you should tell me stuff like that."

"If you're going to help me, there are things you need to know."

"My drill sergeant used to tell us that some things are *nice to know* and some are *nuts to know*. Any alleged assaults against federal agents . . ." Bowen shook his head. "That's just nuts for us to talk about."

"Gus." She ignored him, big eyes blinking as she

gazed across the water. "If you knew half the things I've done, you wouldn't even bother to read me my rights before you carted me off to the electric chair. Jericho trusts you, so I trust you. I may as well come clean and confess. If you have to arrest me, so be it." She glanced at him from downcast lashes, watching for a reaction. "Did you hear they got Virginia Ross last night?"

Bowen gave her a slow nod as if he was still making up his mind on what to do. "It was all over the news," he said.

"I'll bet." Garcia quit talking as a blond man in his late twenties walked down the steps to enter the whirlpool. He was alone, in good shape, with a couple of scars on his right shoulder that looked like shrapnel wounds. Conventional wisdom said that if an IDTF agent had war wounds, they were likely to be in the back from running away or getting shot by his own guys.

Garcia stood up, unwilling to take any chances. "Let's swim," she said.

Water ran in silver rivulets down her body, following the swells and dips of her skin. Bowen had drawn dozens of different women and wasn't the type to be easily overwhelmed by a girl in a bathing suit, but Veronica Garcia's purple one-piece made it hard for him to swallow. It was as modest as humanly possible on a body like hers, but no wet fabric capable of being sewn into clothing was truly able to contain the parts of her that needed containing.

Rather than walk to the steps at the other end of the whirlpool, Garcia put both hands on the concrete and pressed herself up, bringing one knee and then her entire body onto the pool deck in one smooth motion. It would have been easy for her to look like a wallowing seal, but she pulled it off like a dancer. Standing, she reached back to adjust the seat of her swimming suit, and then tilted her head to wring the water from her hair. Her movements carried an innocent allure that Bowen suspected she wasn't even aware she possessed.

The new guy in the pool followed her with his eyes, but that was likely a function of watching her curves try to escape the bathing suit rather than any thought of seeing her arrested. Bowen's Montana-born grandfather would have described her body as a litter of puppies trying to squirm their way out of a gunnysack.

Never turning to see if he was behind her, Ronnie stopped long enough to rent a yellow tube from a kid under a big umbrella. Oblivious to the other teenage boys with gaping mouths, she told the kid at the register to keep his change. Bowen found himself wondering where she'd gotten the money from to pay him in the first place.

A moment later, Garcia tossed the tube into the water and slipped smoothly into the long ribbon pool that wound its way through the entire water park. Known as the "Lazy River," there was just enough current that swimmers could hang on to their big tubes and drift along without expending any energy.

Apparently satisfied it was safe to talk again, Garcia draped her arms over the tube, breasts mashed against the yellow plastic, and waited for Bowen to join her, which he did.

He pulled himself up across from her, legs trailing in the cool water, steering them so they moved sideways and neither had to drift backwards. If gunfighters swam in lazy rivers, this was the way they did it.

"Nice necklace." She nodded at the black pearl hanging from the chain around his neck. "Looks real."

"Hmmm," Bowen grunted. "It is."

"Doesn't really fit the rest of your profile," Ronnie said, half to herself. "There must be a story behind it."

"So, what is it you need from me?" He repeated his question from the whirlpool, changing the subject. The last thing he was going to do was talk to this spy chick about his past.

She nodded and got down to business, obviously realizing they weren't that close.

"Marshals usually end up with federal prisoners once they see a judge, right?"

"That's right," Bowen said. "But things are a little muddy on that front lately with the IDTF sticking their noses in everything. I'm assuming Director Ross will have some kind of in-camera hearing with only the ID agents and the judge in attendance. And that's if they have a hearing at all. The stories about these guys would give you chills."

"I'm sure," Garcia said. She waved a hand under the water, toying, watching the trailing whirlpool as she spoke. "But you could find out where she's being held, right?"

"I can try," Bowen said. "For all the good it will do. I'm guessing you've lost your friends in high places if you've gone outlaw like Quinn."

"That's an understatement," Ronnie said. "My friends in high places don't have even have friends anymore. But you let me handle that end when the time comes. I'd appreciate it if you can just find out where she is. I'll take it after that."

"Of course, I'll help you." Bowen smiled. "If only for the chance to go swimming with you again." Bowen had never been very good with gray areas. If someone needed their ass kicked, he kicked it. If they needed arresting, he arrested them and let the courts figure out the rest. But something was different here. He'd sensed a sea change the moment he'd set foot in Japan when he'd first been assigned the fugitive warrant for Quinn. Washington had always been full of powerful forces that could rip a person to pieces if they took a wrong turn. Bowen couldn't put his finger on it, but sometimes, he wondered if he was still working for the good guys.

Ronnie looked back at him across the tube, seeming to realize he was coming to grips with the situation. He rubbed a wet hand across his face, resolving to march forward at full speed if he was going to march. "Who do you think is behind all this?" he said.

"The President," Ronnie said without a moment's hesitation. "And I don't just think. I'm sure of it."

"That's a pretty bizarre thing to be sure of." Bowen watched her eyes for any sign of doubt.

She stared back at him, lips trembling with the heat of pure conviction. "Doesn't it strike you as odd that the Speaker of the House came within an inch of stepping into the presidency once before because of a bomb a year ago, and then both the President and VP are assassinated a short time later so he gets another chance? There has never in our history been another assassination of both a sitting president and VP—and now we have one near miss and a bull's-eye during the same administration with exactly the same players."

Bowen shrugged. "It wasn't the Speaker's fault someone killed the President and VP on the same day."

"I'm positive it was," Garcia said. "And look at what he's doing with the country. Do you think Clark would have put so many thugs in high-level government positions?"

"Washington is full of thugs," Bowen said. "People like that are drawn to money and power."

"I can't argue that," Garcia said. "But you have to agree that there are more in place now than ever before. The Secretary of Labor has known contacts with organized crime in Chicago. The Chairman of the Joint Chiefs was twice accused of sexual harassment of female subordinates. The Secretary of State is a moron and the Secretary of Defense is an avowed isolationist who can hardly order pizza without threatening to kick the delivery boy's ass. Does that sound like the kind of people that should be running a government?"

"Look," Bowen said, "if the President is leading some secret cabal, it seems impossible that he'd have so many co-conspirators with his same ideology. From what I've read, the Taliban, al Qaeda, and even the Baader-Meinhof gang may have been highly organized, but in the end, they couldn't even agree on what to have for lunch, let alone find enough like-minded guys to run an operation as large and unwieldy as a presidential administration within the United States."

"That's the beauty part." Ronnie brushed a lock of damp hair out of her face. "They wouldn't have to share the same ideology. Have you ever had a bad boss?"

"Of course."

"What happened to him?"

"Well," Bowen said, "it was a she, and the people above her in rank eventually tuned her up."

"Exactly my point," Ronnie said.

They floated under a series of metal teapots raining water down on their heads. Elbows hooking the tube, Ronnie wiped her face with both hands and looked at him. "Think about it. What if the man at the very top turned a blind eye to bad behavior? Imagine the worst bully in your office, and then imagine him with all authority of a Nazi SS officer or East German secret policeman. He wouldn't have to share the President's ideology—because he has one of his own that is equally rotten. It really doesn't matter what that ideology is. It still benefits Drake's plan."

Bowen sighed. All this talk about ousting a sitting president made him wonder how he'd do in prison.

"And exactly what do you believe that plan to be?" he asked.

"I don't know," Garcia said. "But it's not good. Just imagine all the things you could do to bring down the nation if you were the president of the United States."

"I'm not that much of an imaginer," Bowen said, though the entire story made more sense than he'd like to admit. "I am going to help you though. Those Internal Defense guys are the kind of people I cannot abide."

"Thank you." Ronnie smiled. Her eyes fluttered, half shut as if she was on the verge of drifting off to sleep. "You have no idea how much I appreciate it."

"Listen," Bowen said, "I'm sorry for being so flip about those guys putting a camera in your bathroom. That's pretty twisted. I shouldn't have made light of it."

"No big deal." Garcia gave him another killer smile. "Anyhow, it's a conscience like that will keep you from getting recruited by the IDTF."

She shoved Bowen backwards as they approached a large waterfall that fell in a roaring curtain from a fake stone arch across the Lazy River. Garcia was on her back now, and strong legs propelled her toward the falls. Her feet cleared the surface so he caught delicious glimpses of her painted toes. Just before she disappeared behind the falls, she flipped onto her belly. Her butt arched out of the water as she dove below the surface to vanish under the silver curtain.

Bowen kicked the tube through the falls, just seconds behind her. His mind worked double-time, pondering ways he could prolong this conversation, thinking of when they might meet again.

But when he pushed the yellow tube into the calm water, Ronnie Garcia was gone.

# Chapter 38

DTF agent Roy Gant bounced on his feet behind a scrawny oak, a hundred meters to the west of the water park. He was a heavy guy with a big belly that the tree did little to hide—but he had bigger problems than that now. He'd been assigned to follow the deputy marshal, didn't know why, didn't care—especially once he'd had the happy accident of stumbling on this meeting with the girl. Every ID agent within two hundred miles of the Beltway knew what she'd done to Lindale and Maloney. They all wanted to get her in their crosshairs. Gant had literally jumped up and down like a kid on his birthday when he'd realized he had Garcia in his sights. He'd called it in right away so he could bask in the praise of his superiors, giving none of the credit to his partner, a former FBI agent named Miller.

And now the girl had disappeared.

"Tell me you have eyes on," Gant said into the small mike attached to his iPhone.

"That's a negative," Miller said, from his vantage point fifty meters away, nearer the parking lot. "I never did have a clear view. You get all the credit for this one."

Gant stomped his foot. They should have been closer, but how was he supposed to know he'd need a pair of swimming trunks in order to blend in? Besides, he was not a small man and if he'd stripped down to his shorts, some wise guy might have harpooned him as the great white whale.

"Keep watching the parking lot," Gant said. "She'll have to leave the area sometime."

"What about the deputy?" Miller said. "He's a hard one to miss with that head full of gray."

"You're tryin' to tell me Veronica Garcia is easy to miss?" Gant snapped.

"No," Miller said. "I'm telling you that I have a visual on Bowen. If we can't find the girl, I say we stay with him. She met him once. She'll meet him again. Looks to me like they may have a little thing for each other."

Gant leaned against the rough bark of the tree, steadying his arms as he played the binoculars back and forth among the crowd. He searched frantically for any sign of the curvaceous Latina. His heart rose for a moment when he saw a girl in a dark swimsuit and large white hat—until she scooped up a little kid and took him to the wading pool.

"I am so screwed," Gant muttered to himself. She couldn't have just vanished—but that is exactly what she had done. Backup teams were speeding in his direction at that very moment, ready to make him a hero when they swept in and arrested Garcia. "Forget the deputy," he said to his partner. "Keep looking for the girl. She has to be here. She's the priority."

"Roger that," Miller said, the shrug evident in his tone. He'd received none of the credit, so he wasn't about to share any of the blame. "Just sayin', the deputy is walking to his car right now."

"Is he by himself?"

"Affirmative."

"Then forget him," Gant said, fighting back the rising panic. "Keep looking for her."

"You want me to slam a car door on your leg?" Miller said. "It worked to get Lindale out of hot water when he lost her."

Gant chewed on the inside of his cheek as he kept up his search with the binoculars—and seriously considered Miller's offer.

# Chapter 39

*Alaska*

A faulty gear indicator on the Alaska Airlines plane carrying Tang Dalu and his team from Las Vegas to Anchorage kept them on the ground in Seattle an hour longer than planned. His entire team was sweating by the time they made it to the North Terminal. They reached security with less than fifteen minutes until boarding, which, Tang supposed, helped their cause. The Anchorage TSA officers, though watchful as ever, showed a modicum of compassion and hurried them along so they would not miss their flight.

The last-minute change in plans had set everyone on edge, but their rushed demeanor had masked their nervousness. Ma Zhen, the most pious among then, attributed the delay to the will of Allah. Tang wondered why this same Allah that would reach down with his merciful finger to break a tiny gear light had not chosen to save his daughter. The others might be doing this as part of some personal jihad. Tang had other reasons.

Anchorage International's North Terminal was minuscule compared to the Las Vegas airport, with only eight gates—and the massive Airbus A380 took up two of them. All two stories of her loomed outside the windows like a great white whale with her nose to the glass. At once bloated and sleek, the "super jumbo" was the largest plane in the sky. The Global CEO's wife was French, giving him the impetus to stray from their usual fleet of American-made Boeing 747s, making this Airbus an even richer target in the eyes of the man from Pakistan. Bringing it down would not only destroy the company that had gambled on something European, but enrage American nationalism.

Tang had read the statistics on the airplane while he'd waited for their connection in Vegas. Seven stories tall at the tail, the Airbus was three quarters of a football field in length and had an interior almost seven meters wide. Most airports placed an eighty-meter wingspan limit in order for a plane to use their runways. The A380 made it under that with just inches to spare. Promotional literature said the wings were so large that seventy passenger cars could be parked on each one. Each of the four Rolls-Royce turbofan engines weighed more than six tons, providing a combined total of over a quarter million pounds of thrust.

Tang had never read the Christian Bible, but he knew enough of the stories to recognize this airplane as a potential Goliath that would, despite its enormous size, be brought down by something extremely small.

With the plane's capacity at nearly 600 people, the boarding area was packed with passengers and carry-on baggage. Lin found one of the only empty seats along the windows looking out at the runway and fell into it, shutting her eyes. Her boarding pass slipped out of her jacket pocket and fluttered to the carpet. Tang moved to pick it up, but a small girl with dark hair and a broad smile rushed forward, beating him to it.

"*Ni chi fan le ma?*" The little girl asked, handing the

ticket back to Lin. It literally meant *have you eaten?*, but was colloquial for *hello*.

Lin opened her eyes. She took the boarding pass and shoved it back in her pocket. Even Tang was dumbfounded by the child's grasp of Chinese.

"*Wo chi le*." Lin nodded. *I have eaten.*

"*Ni okay ma?*" The little girl said. "*Nide lianse weishenme bu gaoxing?*" *Are you okay? You seem sad—* literally, *Why is your face color not excited?*

Lin sat up straighter in the chair. Tang was horrified when he saw a smile perk the corners of his wife's lips.

"You are a cute little thing," Lin said in heavily accented English. "How did you learn to speak Mandarin so well?"

"My school," the little girl said, beaming at having been understood. "We can start in kindergarten."

Ma Zhen began to glare over the top of his glasses. A dark man with a thick beard stood behind the girl, close enough that he was obviously her father—or some kind of protector. The man smiled at the little girl's skill but his eyes challenged everyone around him. Tang had been a police officer himself for eleven years. Either this man was a policeman or something very close to it. He tried to shrug off the worry. It would not matter. A policeman could do nothing to stop them once they were in the air. Tang touched his wife on the shoulder. "Come," he said. "We should prepare to board."

Lin ignored him. She smiled openly now—something he hadn't seen her do in a very long time.

The little girl put a hand to her chest, introducing herself. "*Wo jiao* Mattie," she said.

"We need to get in line." Tang mustered a tight smile of his own. It felt like he was squinting at the sun.

"It is so nice to meet you, Mattie," his wife cooed.

She grudgingly got to her feet, and then turned back to the child. "My name is Lin. Maybe I will see you on the plane."

The dark man with the beard called the little girl to him, praising her Mandarin. He acted as though he spoke the language himself, which made sense considering his daughter was so fluent. Tang made a mental note to remember that when speaking around him.

Ma Zhen came up to stand beside them when they got to the other side of the room. Arms folded, he looked sternly at Lin, then back at Tang, frowning. He'd been close enough to hear the exchange.

"It would be best if you avoided conversations with other passengers," he whispered so they could both hear. "It will only complicate matters at this stage of the affair."

"The child spoke to her," Tang said through clenched teeth. He was put out with Lin, but furious that this boy would doubt their commitment. "Everything will be fine." But when he looked at Lin, the remnants of a smile on the corners of her mouth told everyone he was a liar.

Ma Zhen stalked away and flopped down next to Gao, sulking like an angry teenager. When he wasn't making bombs, he rarely did anything but sulk. Fate had dealt him that sort of life. Tang supposed such a look was to be expected from a man who had resolved to kill himself—even for a greater good.

Any evidence of Lin's smile vanished by the time the gate agent called for them to board. Tang calmed some as they walked down the Jetway, considering what lay ahead.

British Airways, Lufthansa, Emirates, and several

other airlines had Airbus A380s in their fleets, but Global was the first American carrier brave enough to snub venerable US-made Boeing. Most of these passengers had never flown on this type of aircraft and they stood in nothing short of awe when they first boarded, clogging the aisles when Tang and his wife finally made it down the Jetway. It took time to find their seats and get their carry-on luggage situated. Tang inched ahead slowly, memorizing the surroundings in case he needed them later. Years as a policeman had taught him nothing ever went as planned.

The interior was double the size of any plane he'd ever seen. Highly polished walls of marbled teak rose up on bulkheads at either side of the boarding door to form a wide and welcoming foyer. Three well-groomed flight attendants, wearing Global Airline's red pencil skirts and white blouses, stood under an ornate glass light fixture that hung down like a palace chandelier. Rather than the musty smells of old carpet and recirculated sweat common to commercial aircraft, the pleasant odor of fresh espresso wafted up from a plush galley. Leather stools ran along a rolled leather bar just inside the entrance. It looked more like a fancy nightclub than something found on a commercial airliner.

Tang could picture the diagrams he'd seen on the Internet and knew the exact location of their seats. Still, it wasn't good to appear too self-assured, so he showed his ticket to an overly helpful bald man wearing a red vest. The man directed him to his left, forward and through the luxurious first-class cabin and up a flight of teak stairs located across from the cockpit door, which for the moment was open, revealing a crew of at least three as they prepped the plane for takeoff. Tang knew the crew could be completely self-contained once in the air, with their own rest quarters and lavatory facilities. He sighed to himself. It wouldn't matter. Hiding behind a reinforced door would do little to keep their precious airplane in the sky.

Once at the top of the stairs, Tang worked his way back, through the forward business-class seats, past another galley with yet another coffee bar, this one only slightly smaller and no less elegant than the one in first class. A Global flight attendant with brunette hair piled on top of her head like an urn approached as he helped Lin get situated next to the window. She was wearing a barista's apron and offered freshly ground espressos and scones before takeoff.

Tang thanked her and stuffed their camera bags into the cubbies under each footrest so they'd be able to access them without having to drag everything out of an overhead bin when the time came. Each seat sank down inside its surrounding plastic walls when it reclined to meet its footrest, forming a plush bed and a good semblance of privacy. Lin's seat was located one row back from the forward emergency exit door, closest to the wall. On the flight from Las Vegas to LA, she'd planned to wedge the bomb between her armrest and the skin of the airplane. Business class on the A380 provided a small storage bin along the outer wall, next to her armrest, much like a lazarette on a boat—a perfect place for the device.

The flight attendant brought two cups of espresso for them before their flight. Lin waved hers away, but Tang accepted his in order to appear compliant.

"That little girl was amazing, don't you think?" Lin said, once the attendant had moved on with her tray.

Tang gave a thoughtful nod. His stomach began to knot again. Now? After a nearly two years, Lin had chosen this moment to display some hint of emotion—all because a filthy *guizi* child had picked up her boarding pass? His hand shook when he tried to sip the espresso. He took a deep breath, screwing his face into a calm smile.

"She spoke passable Chinese," he said. "In any case, her father looks dangerous. We will have to be careful of him."

Lin ignored the last, thinking only of the child. "She was so . . . I cannot even say it . . . so alive." She turned away, the refection of another smile clearly visible in the aircraft window.

She didn't say the words, but Tang knew what she was thinking. The child named Mattie made her think of their daughter—happy thoughts of better times that threatened to ruin everything.

# Chapter 40

Not ready to relax until the plane was in the air, Quinn herded Mattie down the aisle in front of him. Their seats were on the main deck, in the far back section of the aircraft that Thibodaux would have called "steerage." Out of habit, Quinn studied the faces and moods of the other passengers as he passed, watching for people who seemed out of place or more interested in him than they should have been. So far, no one seemed to care about anything but grabbing the overhead bin space before it was all gone.

They walked nearly the full length of the plane to get to their seats so Quinn got a pretty good look at the passengers who'd boarded before him. Of course, there were still plenty who came in later, and an entire second floor of potential threats that Quinn knew he had to consider. This "unseen threat" way of thinking had driven Kim crazy during the years they'd been married. Stupidly, he'd tried to explain to her that just because she wasn't paranoid didn't mean someone wasn't out to get her. They'd shared all too many silent dinners, with her staring daggers across her Greek salad, because he'd observed someone who looked suspicious in the restaurant.

One thing they had always been able to agree on was the need to be overprotective of their daughter. Mattie negotiated her way down the aisle with her bagful of books and electronics like a miniature adult. It killed Quinn inside that he had to cart her off to Russia in order to ensure her safety. Once she was seated, he made a mental note to go for a short walk upstairs after they got airborne, just to ease his mind. The thought of over five thousand square feet of floor space was a little overwhelming.

An Alaska girl from birth, Mattie had been used to flying from the time she was still in diapers, but even she'd stared open-mouthed at the luxury of the upper-crust seating when they'd walked through first class. The rest of the main, or lower deck, was coach, with three-four-three seating and an aisle down either side. The forward two-thirds of the second deck was reserved for business class, not quite as fancy as first, but still relatively spacious—and expensive at around eight grand a seat. The rear of the upper deck contained more economy seating, cramped and ordinary like the seats Quinn had been able to afford.

Mattie stopped in mid row and compared her ticket to the number above the seat. They were about as far from the ritzy real estate up front as they could get.

"Here they are, Dad," Mattie said. Quinn was amazed at how much the tone and lilt of her voice sounded like Kim's.

Seats were scarce with their last-minute booking, but Quinn was able to get theirs on the left side of the plane. Years of flying armed had ingrained the habit of choosing a seat where his gun hand could be next to the aisle—as much to keep from having to explain the bulge between himself and another passenger as to get access to any problem that sprang up during flight.

The guy in the window seat, on the other side of Mattie, looked to be in his late forties. His graying hair was buzzed short over a high forehead. Slightly built, he had a perpetual squint and a prominent chin that reminded Quinn of Popeye the Sailor. Slouching back with the big chin against his chest, the man's head bobbed to the tune on his headphones. A sweater and a paperback spy novel lay beside him in Mattie's seat.

She stood politely, waiting for him to move his belongings while Quinn stowed their bags in the overhead. The guy looked up, still nodding to his music, and grudgingly picked up his stuff.

Mattie flopped down beside him, exploring what was to be her new home for the next twelve hours. She brushed the man's arm when she fished her seat belt out from the space in between their seats. He recoiled as if she'd slapped him, yanking off the headphones.

"Lucky me," he groaned. "An entire day of flying and I get stuck by some kid who's all elbows."

"I'm sorry." Mattie flinched, shooting a glance at her dad. "I was just trying to get my seat belt."

"How about that." He mocked her high voice. "Let's just try and keep our bony little selves in our own seats. Okay?"

Quinn gave Mattie a wink, nodding her back out into the aisle.

"I think you're in my seat, Sweet Pea," he said. "I'll take the middle."

The guy groaned again when Quinn moved in beside him.

It was amazing how quickly the airline got so many people to board and buckle up. A few minutes later, the screens on the back of each seat in front of them flickered to life and the Global safety video began to play as the gigantic aircraft began the lumbering taxi toward the runway.

Quinn settled in, letting his arm and shoulders spill over into Popeye's space, forcing him to readjust with a sidelong glare. He started to say something, but the pilot came over the intercom, introducing the crew.

"*Dobroye utro,*" the pilot said, showing off his Russian *good morning*. "I'm Captain Rob Szymanski. Captain Rob, to make it easier on everybody. Welcome aboard Global Airlines Flight 105 from Anchorage to Petropavlovsk, Vladivostok, and continuing on to Moscow. They want to get us out of here quickly this morning so they'll have room for three more normal-size airplanes. They didn't quite take the size of our bird into account, so they need to move some things before we can push back and get in line for departure. We'll be underway shortly, so sit back and let our capable flight attendants see to your comfort—but more importantly, your safety. . . ."

An attendant named Carly stopped her walkthrough beside Mattie. She was tall with broad shoulders and thick curls of bourbon blond hair that was heavy enough to stay put over one shoulder where it played peekaboo with her eye like a 1940s starlet. The ID card hanging around her neck said her last name was Shakhov and Quinn wondered if she might speak Russian. Smiling, she leaned in to remind the man with the Popeye chin to take his headphones off during the safety briefing.

The man threw his head back, like a teenager who was angry at being told to clean his room, and stared up at the attendant. He left the headphones in place, forcing her to ask him again.

She did, smiling as she'd been trained to do when dealing with turds.

"As you wish, my queen," Popeye said. He gave a flourish of his hand, mocking her with a theatrical bow.

Carly chuckled as if she'd seen it all before. She was dressed in Global's trim red skirt and white blouse. Quinn guessed her to be in her early thirties, but she carried herself like she'd been in the business for some time.

She caught Quinn's eye, shaking her head as if to apologize, before looking back to the passenger with the Popeye chin. "You can put them back on as soon as the briefing is over," she said. "Believe me, if anything were to happen, you'll be glad you paid attention."

Satisfied her orders were being obeyed, Carly gave Quinn one more nod—identifying him as an ally—and continued down the aisle.

Mattie leaned forward looking up and down the aisle. "Four back, three forward, Dad—in case the lights go out."

"Good deal, Sweet Pea." Quinn gave her a thumbs-up for remembering. When she was only three years old, he'd taught her to count the number of seats between her and the exits in case she had to find her way out in the dark.

Her eyes sparkled as she focused on the safety video playing in front of her, sucking in the information the way Quinn took in languages.

She glanced up at her dad. "My teacher told us why they have you bend forward in case of a crash," she said, putting herself in brace position. "This way you're only thrown backward into your seat if the pilot has to land hard and won't get whipped forward and then back, like this." She demonstrated the movement in her seat.

"That's exactly right," Quinn said, genuinely proud.

Popeye threw up his hands. "Seriously," he said. "Do I have to listen to two safety briefings at once?"

Quinn turned to look the man in the eye. That prominent chin was an awfully tempting target.

"What is it that you do?" Quinn said. He kept his voice low, just above a whisper.

"What?" Popeye sneered, leaning backwards as far as he could, creating as much distance as possible before the window stopped him. "What do you mean?"

"For a living?" Quinn nodded slowly. "What is it you do for your job?"

"Not that it's any of your business," he said, "but I'm in the crab industry."

"A crab fisherman?" Quinn mused. This guy was far too flighty to survive on board any crab boat he'd ever been around. Quinn's father would have thrown him out for chum ten minutes after his shoes hit the deck.

"No, not a fisherman," the guy said, pursing his lips as if the very word was distasteful. "Fishermen are shit for brains stupid. I'm a buyer. I buy Russian crab for the US market."

"My dad's a crab fisherman," Quinn said. "He fishes Alaska crab for the US market."

"Yeah, well, too bad for your dad." The man shrugged.

Quinn folded his arms across his chest and then leaned sideways so his face was close to Popeye's ear. His head was almost on the other man's shoulder. "I want you to consider something." Quinn's voice was coarse, a quiet growl. "As a buyer of crab, I want you to think of all the things you would do to protect someone you cared about."

"What the hell are you talking about?"

Quinn ignored the question and continued his thought.

"So, now that you're thinking of all the things you,

as a man who buys crab, might do to protect his wife, or girlfriend or even, say . . . his daughter, you might be interested to know what it is I do for a living."

The man's eyes flicked toward Quinn, and then looked quickly away as if they couldn't abide the pressure.

"What is it you do?" he asked, trying in vain to hide the tremor that had crept into his voice.

"I'm a butcher," Quinn said.

"A butcher?" The man gulped.

Quinn nestled back in his seat and closed his eyes, knowing he'd gotten his point across. "In a manner of speaking."

# Chapter 41

Popeye kept to himself during takeoff. The puny crab buyer was a far cry from any real threat and Quinn knew he should have left him alone. If Quinn was anything he was tactical, but when it came to the protective envelope around his little girl, he rarely thought long before he acted—even at the risk of getting himself kicked off the plane. He didn't like putting Mattie on the aisle seat and planned to move her back as soon as he was sure Popeye was going to behave himself.

Until then, he leaned his seat back and stared up at the ceiling. The Airbus A380 was incredibly quiet, absent the gushing whir prevalent in other commercial airliners. If not for the pressing urgency Quinn felt to get out of the country, it would have been easy to forget he was seven miles above the earth.

According to his frequent flier programs, Quinn had flown nearly a million commercial miles over the course of his career—back and forth across the US, down to South America, all over Asia, and too many deployments to the Middle East.

From the time he'd received his Bs and Cs—badges and credentials—at the Federal Law Enforcement Training Center, he'd carried a sidearm every time he'd flown domestically. Most international flights made that impractical since the Status of Forces Agreements with countries not immediately involved in a conflict precluded him from carrying a weapon as an agent. Now, as a fugitive, he often found himself without a sidearm—and flying with one was out of the question. Still, on the ground or in an airplane, Quinn could usually find something that he could use as a field-expedient weapon if things happened to go south. He looked for them without conscious thought, cataloging their location for later use.

A ballpoint pen, a pencil, the spine of a hardback book could all come in handy in a pinch. A metal fork from first class could be bent at a right angle at the base of the tines to form a workable push dagger. The wooden cane placed in the overhead compartment by the elderly man who'd boarded just ahead of him made a convenient striking weapon, while a rolled magazine made a fairly efficient club. The magazine was especially painful when shoved end-first into someone's face. Unopened soda cans could be thrown, as could beer and wine bottles from first class. Neckties made for quick garrotes—as Quinn felt they did every time he wore one—and the crooked metal side support of a folding tray table could be accessed with the removal of a couple of metal pins and wielded like the jawbone of an ass that Samson used to smite his thousand Philistines.

Quinn was a gun guy and freely admitted it. He'd have carried every chance he got, even if he hadn't taken up the badge. But even in his line of work, he'd used his intellect and powers of observation exponentially more often than he'd ever drawn a pistol. He often thought that the mind was the only real weapon, everything else—be it gun or blade or blunt instrument—was merely an element of strategy.

More than just looking for weapons, Quinn made certain to study the other passengers. Most fell asleep quickly. A few watched movies on their seat back screens and some unrolled sandwiches or other snacks they'd bought at the North Terminal shops. Not a soul on board seemed to care about him or why he happened to be heading to Russia with his daughter. Everyone was the star in his own little show, and thankfully, no one was interested in his.

Even so, Quinn located the pins in the metal arm of his tray table and began to work them loose—just in case the need arose for the jawbone of an ass.

# Chapter 42

*Washington, DC*

August Bowen started making calls as soon as he left the water park in Manassas. There was an endless list of crappy things about living and working as a deputy US marshal in the DC area. The flagpole, or HQ, for instance, was much too close for Bowen's blood. Even as an Army officer, he'd never been the spit-and-polish sort, preferring the ragtag, grimy life in the field to the relative comforts of being a garrison soldier. The upside of working in the seat of government power was a fat Rolodex full of contacts.

Ronnie Garcia's questions about a tail made him jumpy and he found himself looking in the mirror more than usual. He didn't see anyone, but decided it was worth the time and trouble to drive around a little while he made his calls. He took random turns, cutting back to cover the same road he'd just been down before taking a different side street. He stopped at green lights, waiting for them to turn red before speeding through at the last possible moment, and circled an entire block three times. He could almost hear the Pac-Man music inside his head.

Feeling reasonably certain he'd lost anyone who happened to be following him, Bowen worked his way south and east, generally pointing himself toward Lorton, Virginia, where he jumped on I-95 going south. He took the next exit to circle back north toward Alexandria.

Though well-educated and worldly-wise if he was to believe his mother, Bowen was self-aware enough to know he was little more than a knuckle-dragger in the eyes of Washington elite. To the bad guys on the street, deputy US marshals came down from Mount Olympus on special occasions to rub shoulders with the normal folk, flash a silver star, and snatch a fugitive from their life of crime. But to the established gentry, a GS 12 deputy was like a major in the Pentagon. Their rank might garner respect in the field, but they still fetched coffee for the generals.

When asked what branch of law enforcement they wanted to pursue, high school students often listed the Marshals, FBI, and CIA as high on their list. The truth was law enforcement and intelligence were miles apart in scope and duty. Even much of the protective work he did as a deputy marshal was far removed from the mission of a beat cop or detective. To him, intel was something you used to find the bad guy or keep your protectee alive. The term had nothing to do with bringing down or propping up governments—and Bowen preferred it that way.

Apart from Veronica Garcia—who made his stomach hurt when he thought about her too long—Bowen didn't know anyone in the intelligence community. But he knew someone better—the ranking staffers on Senate Appropriations who held the purse strings for Intelligence and Justice. It had come as a surprise to him, a natural cynic, that the true bastions of power in Washington were these staffers. Most of them were in their early thirties—drafting bills, shaping policy, and controlling the money for their powerful senators and congressmen.

A call to a staffer named Jennifer at the Hart Senate Office Building provided Bowen with the name of Director Ross's CIA protective team leader—an agent named Adam Knight. Jennifer assured him that Knight was "one of the good guys."

Knight answered on the first ring. He apparently had little to do since Director Ross was now behind bars. Bowen told the agent he was working on a congressional inquiry. Knight was hungry for answers himself so he swallowed the story without a hitch.

The poor guy was still spitting blood from losing his protectee. Bowen could hear his teeth cracking from tension as they spoke over the phone. He wanted to investigate matters himself, but had been ordered to stand down by his deputy director, who was now at the helm of the agency. Knight had little to offer, but was able to give Bowen a name.

Joey Benavides had been hired by the IDTF just before being fired from the Clandestine Service. According to Knight, a long-distance affair with an Internet porn star on his government computer had earned Joey B a suspension. Lying about the continuation of the affair and the use of a government computer had cost him his job. Benavides had been one of the men next to Director Ross's house just before they'd evacuated to the safe site.

The consummate protector, Knight was itching to have a long face-to-face with the guy, but he'd been threatened with violations of any number of laws if he so much as sent a text.

Bowen promised he'd do enough talking for both of them.

"He's a smarmy son of a bitch," the agent said. "It wouldn't hurt my feelings if you put the boot to him a few extra times for me."

"I only plan to talk to him," Bowen said. He gave the Charger some gas, speeding up to take the Beltway exit toward Alexandria.

"Whatever," Knight said. "But when you listen to that slick bastard for two minutes, you'll be ready to mop the floor with his ass. From what I understand, he's mooching off a woman who owns an empanada shop somewhere north of Dupont Circle." The line went silent while Knight checked his watch. "If he's not on shift yanking the fingernails out of some poor schmuck the IDTF has in custody, you'll find him at a blues bar called Madam's Organ about now having a liquid lunch. It's on Eighteenth Street. Big mural on the side of the building of a redheaded saloon girl with writing all over her chest. You can't miss it."

"Got it," Bowen said.

"Don't forget to give the bastard a little good feeling for me."

"You have no idea where Director Ross is being held?" Bowen asked. "No guesses?"

"None," Knight said. "But Joey will know."

"Like I said," Bowen reminded him, "I only plan to talk to him."

"Look," Knight said, "Bowen, or whatever your name is, let's get one thing crystal clear. I'm smart enough to know deputy marshals don't do congressional inquiries. Do you think I'd be talking to you over the phone about this if Jennifer hadn't called me after she talked to you? There's a war going on. Hell, I'm sure my boss is tied up in it somehow. That's why they carted her off to a secret cell somewhere in Mugambu or wherever the hell she is. But anyone interested in finding her is on the same side of that war as I am, so more power to you. Just cut the bullshit and knock out a couple of Joey's teeth."

Bowen ended the call and made a U-turn to get back on the GW Parkway. He took the 14th Street Bridge across the Potomac into DC, and then headed north, cutting through the National Mall and past Ford's Theatre. It took him another fifteen minutes to zigzag his way through DC's never-ending road construction and end up in front of the bawdy mural on the side of Madam's Organ. There was no missing it. Nothing like a redhead with breasts the size of boulders to welcome a guy to an establishment.

Bowen backed into an open parking spot a half a block down from the bar. It was a little past one and the sidewalk in front of the blues bar was still buzzing with patrons. The darkness inside pulsed the tones of a tenor saxophone with mournful notes that could have made Pollyanna weep.

Adam Knight texted an Agency file photo of Benavides. The buttons on his white shirt strained against their stitching, ready at any moment to pop off and zing around the room like so many stray bullets. It was difficult to say if the oil that slathered Joey B's black curls simply oozed from his body, or if he applied it in the form of a gel. Dark chest hair that looked like a dead animal pelt provided a tangled nest for the gold chain that draped above his open collar. They weren't visible in the photograph, but Bowen was sure this guy would have rings, lots of them, gold and dripping off his fat fingers.

It took all of five seconds to spot him once Bowen's

eyes adjusted to the dark interior of the Madam's
Organ. He was sitting in a side booth like a cockroach
in the shadows, chatting with another guy. The protégé
looked to be in his early twenties—probably a newbie
whom Joey thought he could train up in the finer points
of greasiness.

The big-bosomed mural outside of the bar had nothing on the waitress who met Bowen at the counter.
Everything about the woman oozed pissiness. Even her
double-D chest frowned at being stuffed into a C-cup
T-shirt. Bowen gave her ten bucks to seat him in the
booth where he could watch the door and still have his
back to Joey Benavides. She didn't actually smile, but
the ten bought him a dab more attentiveness than he'd
expected. He told her he was waiting on someone who
might join him, so she brought two glasses of water
just in case.

Bowen ordered a burger and sweet potato fries at the
recommendation of the waitress, and then sipped his
water while he listened to Benavides crow in the ad-
joining booth. The little turd could not seem to shut up
about his recent escapades with some housekeeper at a
hotel in Colombia. Bowen's mother called such talk
"singing your own mighty songs." She had assured August when he was still in grade school that others
would be much more impressed when you sang mighty
songs about them.

Benavides's story about his prowess with the Co-
lombian maid dragged into disgusting minutiae. Bowen
thought his plan to eavesdrop was going be a bust, but
the kid sitting with Benavides finally got a question in
at about the time Bowen got his food. His waitress wrote
her phone number on a bar napkin and slid it over next
to his water. He gave her a wink, trying not to imagine
what might come exploding out of the tight T-shirt if he

got too near the woman. He stuffed the napkin in his shirt pocket with a conspiratorial nod.

She walked away to growl at another customer.

". . . I heard it got pretty rough," the kid next door said. His voice was wobbly with excitement.

"Rough, hell." Benavides laughed around a mouthful of hot wings. Bowen could hear the pop as he sucked the dressing off his fingers. "It was epic. You should have seen her. Oh, she sat there all high powered and dictatorial when we brought her in. . . ."

Bowen pushed the voice memo button on his cell phone, and slid it along the rail to his left so it rested between the wall and the high wooden partition that separated him from Benavides.

"Did she give anything up?" the kid asked. "I mean, you know, anything useful?" He spoke in a fearful hush and Bowen wasn't sure his phone would pick it up. It didn't matter. Joey B spoke in the sotto whisper of someone who'd had too many beers.

"Not yet," Joey said, slurping on his fingers again. "At least not while I was there." He laughed, snorting. "She's on the older side, but she's lost a shitload of weight. Not half bad to look at . . . if you're into the whole mom sort of thing. That dude, Walter, really has his eyes on her though, because I thought he was going to throw her down on the table right there."

"I called him Walters once," the kid mumbled. "I thought he was going to shoot me for adding an 's.'"

"Yeah, he's a real bastard," Joey said. "But he's good at what he does. Probably because he enjoys it so much. The guy's ready to go all medieval on anybody's ass to get them to talk. I'll tell you this though: He gets results. That's for sure." Benavides laughed, snorting through his nose as if he couldn't quite contain himself. "Ross was out running when we arrested her. Wal-

ter sent us in to take her little shorts and T-shirt away
from her." Benavides's voice grew quieter as if he was
confiding a secret. But he'd drunk enough beer that it
was still plenty loud for Bowen's phone to pick it up.
"He made her think we were going to rape her." Joey
paused to take a drink of his beer. "The poor bitch was
so scared she pissed herself."

"Geez!" the kid whispered. "I'm not cut out for that.
I'll stick with surveillance."

"It's part of the job." Joey laughed. "You get used to
it. Sometimes you have to close your eyes and do the
hard things for your country. I'll tell you this though, if
she doesn't talk, Walter has some things planned for
her that will make sittin' naked in a cold cell seem like
a cakewalk."

Bowen took a long, deliberate breath through his
nose. He slowly opened and closed his fist, feeling the
knuckles pop. It took every ounce of self-control to
keep from reaching around the partition and turning
the greasy excuse for a human being into fry sauce. Instead, Bowen watched the bouncing needle on his phone
and took some measure of solace in knowing that he
was recording every vile word that spewed from Joey
Benavides's mouth.


Deputy August Bowen paused the recording long
enough to ask the waitress with grumpy boobs if he
could borrow the phone behind the bar.

"What's wrong with your cell?" she asked, bending
a painted eyebrow.

"Almost out of juice," he said. "It's a local call.
Those sweet potato fries are awesome, by the way. Just
like you said they would be."

The corners of her mouth perked into what was not

quite a frown. For all Bowen knew it was her version of giddy.

"Sure." She nodded at the second glass of water. "You still waiting for your girlfriend?"

"Not my girlfriend," Bowen said. "A work associate. That's who I'm calling."

"That so?" She blew him a pouty kiss. It gave him chills—and not the good kind.

Before he asked to use the phone, Bowen had checked contacts in his cell and found the number for Jacques Thibodaux.

The big Cajun picked up after the first ring.

"Hallo."

"This is Deputy Bowen with the US Mar—"

"I remember you," Thibodaux cut him off.

"I'm helping out a mutual friend," he said. "I could use some assistance."

"Where and when, *cher*?" Thibodaux said. "You call it and I come runnin'."

Bowen expected he'd have to provide a long explanation. "Okay then," he said. "I'm at a place called Madam's Organ in—"

"I know that place." The Cajun laughed like they were old friends. "Been booted out a time or two. I'm downtown now, but I can be there in twenty minutes if traffic cooperates."

"You don't want to know why?"

"I surely do not," Thibodaux said. "Not on the phone anyhow."

"Watch your back trail," Bowen said, almost as an afterthought.

"Always, *cher*," Thibodaux said, then hung up.

Bowen barely knew the big Marine. They'd met during the initial interviews when Bowen was assigned the fugitive warrant for Jericho Quinn. They'd crossed paths again in Japan. Quinn, Garcia, Thibodaux, and their badass friend, Emiko Miyagi, had all been involved in some deadly spy games that were miles above his pay grade.

Bowen had been around long enough to know that the big world was really a very small place. Whatever it was that was going on in the highest levels of government, it was very likely related to that group's bloody adventures in Japan.

Bowen needed backup, but he wanted someone who wasn't committed to the wrong side. He had no doubt Ronnie could handle herself in a confrontation, but his chivalrous bones couldn't bear the thought of exposing any woman, even one as tough as Garcia, to the likes of Joey Benavides—or what he planned to do to him.

# Chapter 43

*Global Flight 105*

Tang clutched the end of his armrest in a death grip, turning his knuckles white. He closed his eyes and worked to slow his breathing. There was little else he could do.

Intermittent turbulence and an overly cautious pilot kept everyone in their seats for nearly an hour after the aircraft reached its cruising altitude. Unable to keep still, Tang snatched the phone from the cubby beside his seat and checked the clock, like he'd done every two minutes for the last half hour. The window of opportunity was slamming shut before his eyes and he was powerless to fight it.

It was imperative that the plane be brought down over the Bering Sea. Apart from the fact that the icy waters would ensure there were no survivors, an investigation over international waters made it much more likely that the Americans would find the necessary clues regarding the cause of the plane's destruction. The Russians were far too cozy with Beijing to let the US find out Chinese operatives were behind the crash if Global 105 went down over Russian soil. There was too great a risk the investigation would be mired in the black hole of Kremlin bureaucracy and the whole thing would simply be written off as another unexplained aviation disaster. That was all good food for conspiracy theorists, but useless for Tang's purposes—or the purposes of the man from Pakistan.

If the death of his daughter was to matter, the device had to be deployed within the next ninety minutes. It would take half of that to assemble—leaving very little room for error.

Virtually chained in place by his seat belt, Tang turned to check on his wife. Her seat nearly all the way back, she hummed softly to herself, facing the window. For months, through all his begging and pleading, she'd been silent as a stone—and she chose now to show her emotions. He recognized the song immediately as one they used to sing to Mei Li, their little girl.

Over the last hour he'd watched her come undone before his eyes, thawing from her two-year emotional freeze. It would not last, he was certain of that. The American girl had touched a delicate nerve. That was all. All too soon, Lin would slip back into her miserable trance. Their daughter was dead and no saccharine-sweet words of clumsy Chinese from a *guizi* child would do anything to bring her back.

Lin's humming grew louder until it threatened to fill the quiet cabin of the aircraft. Tang watched in horror as a smile crept across the reflection of her face. This newfound flash of happiness, this . . . counterfeit joy, made him want to slam her head against the wall.

Oblivious to his inner turmoil, she turned on her side, looking at him as she used to when they talked together in bed. "I worry for that little one if we continue," she whispered.

Tang's mouth fell open, dumbfounded. "What do

you mean *if* we continue?" he hissed. "We have no choice but to continue." He'd thought she might feel pity for the American child, but he never dreamed she would consider not following through with the plan.

Lin studied him without blinking for a long moment. Wispy lengths of hair, thin and dull from her two-year diet of little but tea and crackers, fell across gaunt cheeks.

Heavy turbulence continued to creak the giant aircraft, reminding Tang that he was trapped. It felt as if they were riding over a badly maintained road.

"Mei Li is dead," Tang said, as though he were telling her for the first time. Tears welled in his eyes, running down his face. Rage and despair clutched at his throat, threatening to strangle him. He leaned closer so the other passengers could not hear their exchange. "Do you hear yourself? She is dead. Are you ready to forget so quickly?"

"How dare you ask me that?" Lin's nostrils flared. "I have done nothing but think of her since she died."

Tang took a deep breath, speaking the unthinkable.

"And what of our other child?" He knew the mention of their son was akin to stabbing his dear wife in the belly. But it had to be done. "Do you grieve for him as well?"

She shook her head, begging him not to continue.

"Do you remember how you assured me that it was foolish to pay the fee that would have allowed us to have a second child? You and your gaggle of friends . . ." He spat the words. "Those leftover women who were not smart enough to find a husband, but plenty wise enough to be absolutely certain the government had moved beyond such barbaric notions as the One Child Policy. So you used the life of my unborn son to make a stand and show the world that Chinese women are free to choose—"

"Stop it," she mouthed the word on a quiet breath.

"Do you not remember the two army hags who dragged you in the back room during your doctor's office visit and forced you to endure an abortion and sterilization—to make an example out of us? And then influenza took Mei Li, leaving us childless—all because you were much too progressive to pay the small government fee."

"You are not human. . . ." Tears pressed through her lashes. "I know I am to blame."

A porcelain chime pinged over the intercom. Finally, the seat belt sign above winked out. Tang wiped his nose with the back of his forearm and took a ragged breath. He looked up to see other passengers reading books or watching movies—ignoring what they thought was a marital spat.

"No," he said. "The blame lies with government thugs who trample the weak." He gave his wife a reassuring pat on the arm. She was better now, he could tell. Back to her old self, ready to do what she knew needed to be done. "Do you still believe it is time to pull down the powerful who have caused this great harm?"

Lin swallowed back a sob, giving a halting nod, like a child submitting to some horrible medicine. "What do we know of America and all the people on this plane?"

"I could not care any less about America," Tang whispered through clenched teeth. "You know that. But I will see China's government punished."

"Even if that means killing me?"

"Without question," Tang said, too quickly.

Lin rolled thin lips inward until they turned white, biting her words. He may as well have slapped her. When she finally did speak, she sounded weary, laden with the weight of abject grief.

"Then I am your wife and I support you. There is nothing else to say."

Tang took a quick breath through his nose, composing himself.

"Very well," he said. "I will go meet the others." He touched her arm again, more tenderly this time. He knew he'd been much too harsh, but it had to be done. Soon, their misery would be over and the great and powerful would begin to pay for their sins.

# Chapter 44

Quinn glanced up from his motorcycle magazine to find Mattie hunched forward over her tray table. Her tongue stuck out of the gap where her front tooth should have been. Her red marker moved across the paper in rapt concentration. It had been forever since he'd been able to sit back and watch her play or draw.

Most parents were prejudiced when it came to the talents and intellect of their children—but Quinn was absolutely certain Mattie was a prodigy. She could already suss math problems Quinn would have found difficult in junior high. Quinn was a linguist himself, fluent in four languages besides his native tongue. The fact that his little girl's Chinese was already better than any of her nonnative teachers flushed him with pride. She'd inherited his ear for languages, but her gift for music came from Kim. Mattie had played the violin with the Anchorage Youth Symphony when she was only six. She'd been working on Vivaldi recently and now hummed the bouncing "Spring" concerto from *The Four Seasons* as she put the finishing touches on the art project. Finished, she held it up for her dad to see.

She grinned, showing off her picture and her missing front tooth.

Quinn shook his head in disbelief. It was one thing to speak passable Chinese at seven years old, but Mattie already knew many of the intricate symbols that comprised Chinese writing. In bright red marker, she'd drawn a good luck symbol comprised of two identical characters side by side, known as "double happiness." Common in China, it was not something many little girls in America would be familiar with.

"This is incredible, Sweet Pea," Quinn said, genuinely impressed.

Mattie beamed. "I drew it for that lady." She unbuckled her seat belt and slid off the edge of her seat. "I'm going to go give it to her."

"Hang on now." Quinn put a hand on her arm. "I don't want you running all over the plane by yourself."

"But, Daddy." She threw her head back and groaned. Yep, there was a lot of Kim in this girl. "She was so sad."

"We'll give it to her when we land," Quinn said. The idea of letting his daughter out of his sight so soon after getting her back made his stomach ache.

"But it's still hours until we land," she said. "You don't want her to be sad for hours when I could make her happy now."

"Mattie—"

"This airplane is one big adventure." She stopped the whining and turned on the charm, batting her blue eyes—another Kim maneuver. "You would have wanted to explore a little bit when you were younger."

Quinn thought of how he and Bo would have had every bin and bulkhead mapped out by now if they'd been able to travel on such an airplane when they were boys. Still, the last behaviors he wanted his daughter to emulate were those set by him and his brother.

"There are some bad people in the world, sweetie." She'd been through enough to know it, but he reminded her anyway. That's what fathers did.

She nodded but came back with a counterargument of someone twice her age. "Dad, all the people on this plane had to go through the X-ray thing already. Don't worry so much." She looked back and forth, and then leaned in closer, whispering. "Besides, you already trusted me with the big fat lie about our names."

Quinn couldn't help but wonder what she was going to be like at fifteen.

Carly, the blond flight attendant, came by with a cup of coffee for a woman across the aisle. Mattie tugged on her apron before she could walk away.

"It's safe for me to walk up front and give a present to someone, isn't it?" she asked, again with the eye batting.

To her credit, Carly shot a glance at Quinn before answering. "Whatever your dad thinks." She looked down at the book on the tray next to Mattie's drawing. "Lemony Snicket! I just love those books."

Mattie smiled, proud to be reading a chapter book. "I'm almost finished with it."

The flight attendant's eyes opened wider when she noticed the drawing. "Is that Chinese?"

"A card for my friend," Mattie said. "*Shuāngxǐ*. It means 'double happiness.'"

"How old are you?" Carly gasped, genuinely impressed.

"Seven," Mattie said.

"That's amazing." Carly gave her a conspiratorial look that said she thought a little girl this intelligent should probably be given a tiny bit of latitude.

"Okay," Quinn said. "But I'm coming with you."

Mattie stuck out her hand like she was going to push him back in his seat. "No!" she said. "You scared her last time. Just let me give her the card and I'll come right back."

Quinn sighed, anxiety over his little girl's safety wrestling with the fact that he just might be a little overprotective.

"She'll be fine," Carly mouthed so Mattie couldn't see her.

"All right," Quinn said. "But don't stay too—"

Mattie was up and gone before he could finish his sentence.

"She's precious," Carly said, gazing toward the front of the aircraft.

"Thanks." Quinn nodded. "You have kids?"

"My husband and I are trying," she said. "But with his schedule and mine, it's hard to get together long enough to . . ." She blushed and her voice trailed off. "Sorry, definitely TMI. Can I get you anything?"

"I'm fine," Quinn said, eyes boring holes in the curtain where his daughter had just disappeared. Mattie was right. There was very little to fear on board a commercial aircraft, but that didn't matter. Quinn was what he was, and that wasn't likely to change. He felt sorry for her dates when she got to be a teenager. Lucky for them, he probably wouldn't live that long.

# Chapter 45

The others met Tang at the forward lavatories on the upper deck as soon as they were free to move around. Each carried two spare camcorder batteries in their pockets. Seen as normal Ni-Cad batteries under X-ray examination, they were able to power a camcorder for a short time if TSA had asked to turn the thing on. The bulk of their interiors was dedicated to the storage.

Apart from the detonator, which was still in Lin's possession, the device would be comprised of two ingredients. When mixed together and stuffed into Ma Zhen's ingeniously shaped carrier, these ingredients would become exponentially greater in power than the sum of their parts.

The men disappeared one by one into the lavatories, carrying out a surreal ballet as they retrieved their portion of the bomb components, and then passed it over to Ma. Each face had the silent resolve Tang had seen in the countenance of Tibetan monks who had set themselves on fire to protest Chinese policies. They knew what they were doing and were determined to do it right. Even Gao, the piggish tough, who'd become the de facto security man for the group, had a sweet earnestness about him as he stepped into the lavatory for his turn in the process.

The stress of waiting wore heavily on everyone. Hu's hands shook, Gao's eye twitched, and Ma snapped angrily at the slightest question or suggestion. Tang had to force himself to calm after the panic brought on by Lin's recent bouts of faux happiness. This was no time to lose focus.

The device was relatively small, capable of bringing down the plane only if placed in the correct location. If it went off early, while it was being assembled, Tang and the other ran the risk of doing little damage but to themselves. If they lived through the explosion, they would be badly maimed prisoners of the United States government for the rest of their miserable lives—if they weren't beaten to death first by angry passengers.

Hu, Ma Zhen, and Tang carried the primary explosive, a compound known as PETN. Experts sometimes pronounced it "*petin*." It was an acronym for pentaerythritol tetranitrate, in the same chemical family as nitroglycerin. An ingredient of the commercial plastic explosive Semtex, PETN had been around since before World War I. It was more stable than some of its sister compounds and its quality of giving off a very low vapor trail made it a favorite for terrorists to try to tuck into all sorts of interesting places like Richard Reid's shoe or Umar Farouk Abdulmutallab's underwear.

Gao's batteries carried the second component, the powdered metal that would add heat to the PETN's explosive power. Altogether there was a scant twelve ounces of material—just enough to fill a soda can. According to Ma Zhen, twelve ounces would be plenty.

Ma had chosen PETN for its shattering force—known as *brisance*. And unlike the Shoe or Underwear bombers, who had tried to use conventional fuses or liquid igniters, Ma had designed an actual electric shock detonator, utilizing the flash attachment from a large DSLR camera.

Once assembled, the device would be marginally larger than the shoe bomb Reid had tried to use on the Paris to Boston flight. In theory, the pressure differential outside the aircraft would help rip a hole in the fuselage—but the man from Pakistan did not want to depend on theory. Ma Zhen had added another component to his device that would double its effective power—something they wouldn't have to smuggle because they could easily get what they needed once on board the plane: water.

Once it was well mixed, Ma would pour the PETN and powdered metal into a flat, plastic case that resembled a mini tablet computer. This slightly malleable explosive tile would be nested between two plastic hip-pocket water flasks, one concave and one flat, each roughly the same dimensions as the tablet.

The resulting shape charge would turn the water in the concave flask into a liquid blade, slicing like butter through the thin metal fuselage of the Airbus. Pressure differential would do the rest, sucking loose objects and people out the gaping hole. Tang wanted his wife sitting as close as possible to the initial explosion, mercifully sparing her from the long minutes of terror and panic as the plane fell from the sky.


Eyes closed, with her seat almost fully reclined, Lin heard a rustling beside her. She thought Tang had returned and ignored the sound until she heard a different voice, higher and more tentative. For a fleeting moment she thought it was her daughter, Mei Li. Her heart swelled, but when she turned, it was the little girl with blue eyes from the airport.

"Mattie, right?" Lin pushed the button on her armrest so her seat slid upright.

The child nodded, smiling wide enough to show her missing front tooth. Her face glowed because Lin had remembered her name.

"You should not be here." Lin craned her head to look up the aisle, terrified of what her husband would do if he came back to find her speaking with this little one. "Where is your father?"

"Reading a motorcycle magazine and worrying about me," Mattie said, still grinning. "I made you something to cheer you up." She handed her a piece of carefully folded notebook paper.

Lin opened it up to find the symbol *Shuāngxǐ– double happiness*—drawn in Mattie's youthful hand and colored with a red marker. She held it to her chest.

"This is . . ." The words stuck in her throat. She swallowed back a sob. "This . . . is much . . . too kind."

Lin started to say more, but the little girl leaned across her armrest and wrapped both arms around her neck. She held on the way Mei Li had once done.

"I hope you can be happy," Mattie said, her face pressed against Lin's neck.

The plane gave a sudden shudder. Lin clutched at the girl to keep her upright. For a moment, she feared her husband had detonated the bomb in another part of the plane. When she realized they'd only hit more turbulence, her heart sank even more. Tang would soon return with the device. If she did not detonate it as planned, he would only do it himself. This little angel reminded her so much of Mei Li. It was unthinkable to kill her.

The plane gave another violent lurch. An overhead bin fell open, dumping a leather briefcase into the aisle. The seat belt chime rang, seeming even more urgent amid the commotion.

"My dad will be worried about me," Mattie said. She didn't seem afraid, only aware of her father's concern. "I should go back to my seat now, but I'll come see you again."

"No!" Lin shook her head, horrified at the thought of putting little Mattie near the bomb. "We will talk more when we land," she lied. "Too many bumps for now."

"Okay," Mattie said, reaching to give her one last hug. "I hope you can cheer up."

Lin watched the precious child run toward the stairs that would take her to the lower level and back to her father, a man who surely would do anything to protect her. The journey would take her past Tang and the others. She groaned within herself, hoping he would be too focused on his task to notice a child.

Lin wracked her brain for a way out. If she spoke up, they would still detonate the bomb. That was far too dangerous. Her husband would return any moment. He was a good man. She knew that. Perhaps she could talk to him, explain the way she felt and buy this child some more time. Lin cared little for the other faces on the airplane, and nothing for her own life. Her sorrow was a stone against her soul that could not simply be removed by a hug or a piece of paper with a childish symbol—but she would not stand by and watch this sweet little girl die.

Gao was still in the lavatory when the plane began to pitch violently. Waiting outside by the bulkhead, the bucking knocked Tang sideways, shoving him into a wide-eyed blonde as she stumbled out of the adjacent lavatory. The woman gave him a cold glare and muttered some invective oath in Russian. The rumbling continued, as if the pilot had decided to drive over a field of large stones. Hu and Ma had to lean against the wall to keep their feet.

"This will pass," Tang said. "Go back to your seats before someone sees us loitering together."

A bony man wearing the red vest of a flight attendant made his way toward them, eyebrows raised, chiding them for disregarding the seat belt sign.

"Go now," Tang whispered.

Ma checked his watch. His face was pinched into an angry wedge, but he turned to go before the attendant could tell him to. Hu ducked down the front stairs, back to his seat on the lower deck.

Tang wasn't sure what Gao would do if everyone left him alone. He waited as long as he could, smiling politely to the advancing flight attendant. Behind the lavatory door, Gao banged around as if he was in a fight, letting loose a string of vehement curses.

The seat belt sign chimed again as if to emphasize the need to be seated. The plane continued to rattle and shake. The flight attendant hustled up the aisle.

"Sir, the captain has ordered everyone back to their seats." The attendant looked at him with raised eyebrows and the half smirk of a little man who thought he had unfettered power over another.

Tang gave a polite nod toward the lavatory. "My friend is sick." He spoke in halting English, acting as if he'd not fully understood.

Gao's cursing was easy to hear, even over the rattling airplane.

"We'll look after your friend," the flight attendant said. "But you have to return to your seat."

The restroom door levered open and Gao poked his head out like a camel nosing its way into a tent. His face was pale and slack as if he might actually be ill.

"Your seats, gentlemen." The attendant shooed them both on their way, then turned his attention to other passengers now that they were moving in the direction he wanted them to go.

"I dropped it," Gao groaned, grabbing seat backs to steady himself as he shuffled down the aisle.

Tang stopped dead in the aisle, blocking his way. His voice was deadpan, deflated. "What do you mean, dropped it?"

"The powder," Gao said. The squat man was on the verge of tears. "It was very cramped in there. I removed the lid carefully, just like you showed me, but the plane began to jump around. It's cramped in there. . . . Anyway, I dropped it."

"Wait." Tang's chest tightened. The walls of the plane seemed to close in around him. "You lost the powder?"

Gao nodded, hanging his head. "Most of it spilled out when the batteries hit the floor."

Tang found it difficult to see. He could hardly think. "Could we sweep it up?"

"I tried," Gao said, stricken by guilt. Nervous blotches mottled his skin from his neck to the top of his head, visible under the short stubble of his haircut. "The rubber tile on the floor is porous, made with tiny lines and cracks for drainage. The powder sifted away before I could retrieve it."

Tang could do nothing but shake his head. Gao, who

barely understood the gravity of what had happened, was already beside himself with guilt.

Another flight attendant in a red sweater stalked up the aisle from the galley, herding them back to their seats.

Tang nodded meekly, belying the turmoil in his gut. He shuffled forward like a condemned man, not even trying to dodge the knees and elbows that blocked his path, ignoring the protesting grunts of other passengers.

His brain was racing by the time he made it back to his seat. "Let me think," he said to Gao. "We will speak with Ma Zhen when this stops. There is always a way."

Gao gave a somber nod. "I am sorry, my friend," he said. "Truly."

Tang shooed him away with a tight smile, the best he could muster under the circumstances. "We will speak to Ma," he said again, because he did not know what else to say.

Back in his seat, Tang buried his face in his hands. He pressed against his eyes until he saw shooting lights and felt the welcome, calming pain.

Could it all be lost so easily? They had all left letters implicating the Chinese government in the attack. If left alive, they would all look like fools, until they were hunted down and killed for their parts in the useless conspiracy. He sighed, resigning himself to living his remaining days in shame. It made sense. This was the fickle Allah who had taken his daughter.

Lin glanced at him from her seat next to the window, perfectly silhouetted against the beam of light pouring in from the thin air outside. She'd become animated again—like she was on some kind of happiness drug. She tilted her head, and then reached to touch his arm.

Her tray table was open and on it was a card drawn in the hand of a child—it said "double happiness."

Tang almost screamed when he saw it.

"What is this?" he said in rapid Mandarin. It didn't matter if they could understand him or not, the other passengers recognized a man chiding his wife in any language. They looked away in embarrassment.

The stupid little *guizi* had come to bother Lin once again, stirring up old thoughts and pain. *Double Happiness,* indeed. Tang ground his teeth with the anger of a helpless man. If he could not bring down the plane, he would strap what was left of the explosive to the little girl's back. That would punish her for the pain her antics were causing his wife.

Lin sat quietly, waiting for him to calm down.

He decided to keep Gao's clumsiness to himself. In her present condition, Lin would see it as a sign. Instead, he ignored his wife's new mood and stared forward, toward the stairs. There had to be another way.

The cockpit doors lay on the level below, at the bottom of the stairwell. Surely the PETN alone would be enough explosive by itself to breach the flight deck. But even if they were to get through the reinforced door, there was the strong possibility that at least one of the crew had a pistol.

Tang was not afraid to die. He was, in fact, resigned to it. But he did not want to waste his life by giving it prematurely—without bringing down the aircraft.

By the time the turbulence settled to a low rumble, Tang felt as if a bleeding ulcer might kill him. He was just about to resign himself to failure when the two business-class flight attendants began move back and forth in the galley two rows ahead. The smell of beef and pasta began to drift down the aisle. Dressed in bright red aprons, one woman prepared silver and glassware, while the other pulled tray after tray out of the warming oven. Machinelike, she removed the aluminum foil cover from each meal and threw it in a plastic recycle bag before passing the tray to her partner.

The tiniest crystal of an idea began to form in Tang's brain.

He checked the time on his phone. The monstrous Airbus traveled at nearly 600 miles an hour. They would cross into Russian airspace in a little over an hour; a few minutes after that and they would be over land.

He needed more time—but to get it, he would somehow have to make the airplane turn around.

There was another chime and the captain's voice blared over the speaker.

"Ladies and gentlemen," he said. "This is Captain Rob. I apologize for that choppy air. Sometimes that happens out here over the Pacific. We've done a little checking with a couple of other flights ahead of us. It looks like we'll have smooth flying for the next few hours.

*No*, Tang thought, *the next few hours will be anything but smooth*.

# Chapter 46

Jacques Thibodaux rumbled up on a big BMW motorcycle twenty-five minutes later. He backed the bike into a parking spot in front of the used bookstore down the block from the bar. Joey Benavides and his young protégé were still inside finishing up what looked to be their last beer.

The streets were beginning to hop as government workers, congressional aides, and lobbyists poured out of the Adams Morgan district to return to work after lunch. Many were likely to return for happy hour, then be back in their offices again by seven or eight that evening—continuing to work for another three or four hours. It was a sobering thought that many of those running the government relied on so much liquid inspiration.

The hulking Marine swung a leg off his motorcycle and ripped an enormous and unashamed fart.

"Speak to me, oh, Toothless One," he sighed to himself.

Bowen chuckled. It was impossible not to like this guy.

The Cajun's black leather jacket hung open to reveal a tattered AC/DC BACK IN BLACK T-shirt. His jeans were faded and frayed at the cuffs from being just a little too long at the heels. The patch over his eye seemed to add inches to his already enormous bulk.

He took Bowen's hand in a giant paw and drew him to his chest to give him a hearty pat on the back—the brotherhood hug. Bowen was no small fry but he felt like a toy in the Marine's grasp.

As a deputy marshal he'd made a habit of sizing people up. There were those he could control by swagger alone. Some he knew he would have to lay hands on, while others might turn violent and needed a two-by-four to the head in order to bring them into line. Some were too dangerous even for that, and required a high-power rifle from very far away.

Jacques Thibodaux, a man who surely tossed around small cars and yanked trees up by their roots for sport, fell squarely into the last. Bowen noticed a dark red raspberry on the big man's forehead over his good eye—and found himself wondering about the "other guy."

Thibodaux saw the concern on his face and touched the wound with his fingertip. "Bedroom accident." He grinned.

Fearing Benavides might come out at any moment, Bowen briefed the Marine quickly, highlighting the fact that Ronnie Garcia had asked for his help.

Thibodaux rubbed a hand over his square jaw, taking it all in.

"You want to get him off somewhere by hisself and ask him a few questions?"

"He's with another guy, but there were two sets of keys on the table so I'm thinking they came in separate cars." Bowen nodded across the street. "There's a Metro police substation over there, so it's not optimum."

"That don't matter." Thibodaux smirked. "We'll just watch which way your guy goes and follow him. You kick him in the nuts and I'll drag him into the alley so we can chat."

"Or," Bowen said, "I can play back a little of the recording where he implicates his boss in the torture of a high-ranking US official."

"Your call," Thibodaux mused. "But he'd probably rather get kicked in the nuts."


Benavides said good-bye to his young friend and then began to jostle his way through the crowds that mingled in front of Madam's Organ. The kid turned right and, thankfully, Joey B turned left, away from the police station. He wasn't drunk, but chose his steps carefully like someone who knew he had a pretty good buzz. He carried his keys in his hand, moving toward a silver Audi A8, wagging his head as he walked as if still singing his own mighty songs.

Bowen fell in behind him as soon as he left the restaurant. Thibodaux hung back a few steps.

"Joey," Bowen said, stepping in before Benavides could unlock the Audi. "Got a minute?"

The ID agent turned a little too fast at the intrusion, teetering so he had to catch himself on the roof of the car. The tail of his white shirt hung half out of navy Sansabelt slacks. He held a chubby hand up to his face as if to ward off a blow or shield his eyes from a bright light. Three gold rings adorned stubby sausage fingers.

"Do I know you?" he said. He rubbed his waist with the other hand, obviously trying to remember what he'd done with his pistol. Bowen had seen it earlier, sagging in a loose sheepskin holster on the man's left ankle. When caught unawares, having a gun in an ankle rig was akin to not having a gun at all.

Thibodaux moved up behind Bowen. "Afraid you've never had the pleasure, *cher*," the Marine said. "But we know you. How about we all have a seat in your car and, you know, get to know each other?"

"I know one thing," Benavides said. "You're not getting in my car."

"*Au contraire*, my brother," Thibodaux said. He nodded at Bowen. "My friend here happens to be in possession of a recording you're gonna want to hear."

"How do I know you're not going to kill me?" Benavides said.

"I can't speak for my friend," Thibodaux said, "but if I aimed to kill you, you'd be a greasy dot on the sidewalk already."

Bowen stepped in closer and held up his phone. A quick replay of Joey B's own words convinced him to unlock all the doors and slump behind the wheel. Bowen sat in the passenger seat. The big Marine folded himself into the back, behind Benavides.

"What now?" Joey asked, hands rubbing the sides of his head like he was getting a migraine.

Bowen half turned, his left arm running along the back of the seat between Benavides and his headrest. He held the phone in his right, between them. The recording played on, describing the treatment of a defenseless older woman at the hands of common thugs. Benavides closed his eyes when he heard his own voice connecting Agent Walter with the incident.

Bowen turned off the recording and returned the phone to his jacket pocket.

"Do you know why most people aren't very good at boxing, Joey?" Bowen said.

"No," Benavides scoffed. "What the hell difference does that make?"

"Because they worry too much about their teeth."

Bowen grabbed a handful of Joey B's greasy curls, yanking back just enough to make the moron pull against his grasp. As soon as he felt the tug, Bowen went with it, changing directions and slamming Benavides's face into the top of the steering wheel again and again. Teeth shattered against the hard plastic wheel. At least two fell in a series of tiny thumps against the rubber floor mat, like coins slipping out of a pocket.

"Sthopppp it!" Benavides screamed. Blood poured from his burst lips. "What do you want from me?" He held up both hands, showing that he didn't intend to fight back.

Bowen shoved him sideways. He wiped the hair gel from his hand on the back of the calfskin seat. "Come on, Joey," he said. "I just helped out your boxing career. Now you don't have to worry about so many teeth."

"Whath the hell?" Benavides said. He sounded like he had a mouthful of marbles. "Do you know who I work for?"

"Wait," Thibodaux said, grimacing. "Don't tell me you're with ID." He shot a fearful glance at Bowen. "We're done, brother. They'll arrest us for sure now, steal our clothes, and send this jackass in to rape us. . . ." He cuffed Benavides on the back of the head with a hand the size of a pie pan. "What the hell's the matter with you? Of course, we know who you work for, *cochon*."

"Why are you doing this?" Benavides whimpered.

"I . . . I . . . don't even know you guys. . . ." Each breath brought a wincing gasp as he sucked air over the freshly broken teeth.

"Waaa," Thibodaux mocked. "*I don't even know you guys.*" He looked at Bowen, telling him it was his turn.

"Where is she?" Bowen said. The "tell me or I'll kick your ass" was implied.

Benavides gulped. "Look, guys. I—"

Thibodaux cuffed him again. "I swear, Joey . . ." A slap from the big man was the equivalent of being hit in the head with a baseball.

"Where?" Bowen repeated.

"Bethesda," Joey said. "A secure wing of the psychiatric hospital."

Bowen shot a glance at Thibodaux, who raised the brow on his good eye.

"Makes sense," the Cajun said.

"Are they going to take her in front of a judge?" Bowen asked.

Benavides braced himself for another blow from Thibodaux. A smear of bloody drool dripped from the corner of his mouth. "I don't know." He choked back a sob. "I'm just a grunt. I do what Walter tells me to. He's the one running the show."

"I guess your boss wouldn't be too happy to hear you're blabbing your head off in a bar," Bowen mused.

Benavides slumped even farther in his seat, defeated. "He'd kill me."

"Okay," Bowen said, "Walter doesn't need to know anything. As long as you keep me informed about Director Ross."

"That's all?"

Thibodaux loomed over the backseat. "Hell no, that ain't all," he said. "Both hands on the wheel and hum quietly to yourself while I make a call. Don't be listen-in' in. That'll get you killed."

Benavides looked as though he'd been shot. "I can't help but hear if you talk sitting back there. Can't . . . can't you just step out of the car if it's a secret call?"

Bowen stifled a chuckle as Thibodaux pressed the phone to his ear and swatted Benavides in the back of the head. "I told you to hum."

Joey B began to hum something unrecognizable—far from the mighty songs of himself he'd been croon-ing earlier.

Thibodaux hit him again. "Would you shut up," he snapped. "I'm on the phone."

Bowen had to look away to keep from laughing.

Dazed and confused, Benavides leaned his forehead on the steering wheel, bloody lips emitting something in between a sob and a hum.

"It's me, sir," Thibodaux said in the backseat. "Yes . . ."

Bowen wasn't sure who the Cajun was talking to, but it was someone he trusted. Thibodaux ran down the specifics of the conversation with Joey Benavides—who hummed louder every time his name was men-tioned.

"Yes, sir," Thibodaux said after he finished his re-port. He listened intently, nodding and making just enough noise so the other party knew he was still on the line. "I understand, sir," he said at length. "No, I agree. It has to be done. We'll take care of it."

"What *has* to be done?" Benavides sobbed, unable to contain himself. "You don't *have* to do anything. . . ."

"Ahhh." Thibodaux tilted his head to the side and leaned over the seat. "Somebody's been listenin' when I told them not to. . . ."

Benavides deflated like an empty balloon.

"Here's the deal, Joey B," Thibodaux said. "Turns out Director Ross will be moved today. You're gonna call me and tell me where they're takin' her."

Benavides groaned. "I'm not approved to know that kind of thing before it happens."

"Well go and get your ass approved," Thibodaux whispered. "Because if you screw me around, I'm gonna come to your house and mess up your shit." He leaned in so his eye patch was almost touching Joey B's cheek. "And I don't mean your stuff. I mean your actual shit. Your house will be covered in little tiny bits of what was once you. Understand?"

Benavides nodded quickly, forehead wrinkled like his head was about to explode. Unintelligible whimpers gurgled from his throat.

"I'm done here," Thibodaux said. "Being near this guy makes me feel like I might catch PMS."

Bowen looked at him.

"Puny Man Syndrome," Thibodaux said.

Bowen gave a slow nod. "Yeah," he said. "Me too." He raised a brow at Joey B. "Not a word to your bosses about our meeting."

Benavides dabbed at his split lip. "What do I tell them about what happened to my face?"

"Not our problem," Thibodaux said. He flung open the rear door.

"Run your car into a tree on the way home," Bowen offered on his way out. "Tell them you fell asleep at the wheel. I got a feeling they'd buy that."

Thibodaux leaned down, looking in the window with his hand to his face, thumb and little finger extended to look like a telephone. He grinned like they were old friends. "Call me," he said.

# Chapter 47

*Flight 105*

Quinn had only meant to close his eyes for a moment, but the massive adrenaline dump from the day before had taken a heavy toll. More even than the physical stress, hours of worry over Mattie and Kim had eaten away at Quinn's reserves. Once on the plane, he felt relatively safe, and allowed himself to relax before his body shut down entirely. He'd all but passed out after Mattie had returned from visiting her new friend, leaving her to watch over him while she read Lemony Snicket.

Quinn had always been athletic, climbing mountains, running track, and boxing from the time he was a boy. He'd learned, even then, that when in peak condition, the mind and body could do amazing things. In China and Japan, he'd witnessed feats of skill and stamina that seemed superhuman. The Air Force Special Operations pipeline taught him that human limits went far beyond the wildest imagination of most—but there was always a price. Reaching those limits required huge expenditures of energy—and with that came the eventual need to recharge. No matter how tough and well-trained a person was, at some point, body and brain needed a break.

Roughly an hour after Quinn had closed his eyes, he became aware of someone in the aisle beside his seat.

Willing himself back to consciousness, he sat up to find Carly the flight attendant standing above him. Her hand resting on the back of his seat, lips tight, she looked down as if she was afraid to disturb him. Her blond hair had lost the perfection of before, more disheveled, as if she'd been on a run or just gotten up from a nap.

Quinn coughed, rubbing the grit of sleep from his eyes. His head ached and he felt as if he'd swallowed a cup of sand. He wondered how long she'd been standing there and chided himself for allowing her to hover over him at all. That kind of lapse could get a man in his line of work very dead.

Carly forced a smile, probably for Mattie's sake. She cast a quick glance toward the rear of the plane. "May I speak with you a moment?"

Quinn was instantly awake. Flight attendants didn't summon passengers out of their seats for no reason. He half turned in his seat, expecting to find a couple of ham-fisted government agents waiting for him at the bulkhead, ready to slap the cuffs on him. There was no one there but an elderly woman who disappeared into one of the lavatories.

He looked at Mattie. Her nose was still buried in her book. "Hey, kiddo, you be okay for a minute?"

She shook her head without looking up, the way Kim did when she was exasperated about something— which was usually him. "We're on an airplane, Dad," she said. "Where am I going to go?"

Quinn looked at Popeye, who was snoring soundly next to the window. Malleable wax plugs stuffed his ears. "Okay." He smiled, mussing her hair. "I hear you. But do me a favor and lose the attitude."

Mattie gave him a thumbs-up to go with her snaggle-toothed grin. "I hear you," she said.

The seat belt sign came on with another porcelain chime. Captain Rob's firm voice warned everyone of bumpy air.

Quinn looked up at the attendant, nodding to the light on the console above him. "Shouldn't I . . . ?"

She gave a slow shake of her head, the kind of shake a doctor uses when he's telling someone their loved one didn't make it out of surgery. "The captain knows I need to speak to you."

Quinn flicked the latch on his seat belt and stood to follow the attendant down the aisle. Rather than stopping to talk when they reached the open area behind the bulkhead lavatories, she kept walking, moving with a purpose toward the galley and lounge area at far end of the aircraft below the curving stairwell that led to the upper deck. Carly didn't just want to talk. She wanted to show him something.

The Airbus A380 was designed for long voyages of relative luxury, where passengers could get up and move around. As such, the aft section of the plane was furnished as a comfortable lounge, complete with mood lighting, a magazine rack, and leather couches along both sides of the airplane. A row of vending machines with everything from electronics to perfumes was situated at the rear bulkhead—in the event someone couldn't do without a new iPhone or bottle of eau de toilette before they landed.

Carly turned abruptly when she reached the curved wall at the base of the stairwell. A thick velvet rope, maroon, like those used in theaters and banks, cordoned off the bottom step.

A second flight attendant with silver hair in an elegant updo had parked herself immediately around the corner with her back to the bulkhead. She faced the stairs, blue eyes locked forward, as if on a target. Quinn recognized someone standing guard when he saw her. He gave this new attendant a polite nod, which she returned mechanically, saying nothing.

Carly clasped her hands in front of her, bringing them up to her mouth, as if she meant to pray.

"I need to ask you something." She spoke around her hands. "Are you a cop? Because you look like a cop, and you handle yourself like a cop. I've been doing this job for twelve years, and I think I can tell if someone's a cop. You have one of those faces, you know?" She finally took a breath.

"I am," Quinn sighed. "In a manner of speaking."

"I knew it." Carly chewed on her knuckle. Opal-pink nails dug into the back of her fists. She glanced at the other attendant. "I told you, didn't I, Natalie?"

"Yes," Natalie said, deadpan, eyes still aimed on the stairs. "You said he was a cop." If she was impressed by Carly's insight, she didn't show it.

Before she could get to her point, a stern-eyed woman wearing lumpy black yoga pants that were several sizes too small pushed her way through the curtains at the bulkhead. She had a boy of four or five in tow and they were headed for the stairs.

Natalie perked up at the sound of her approach, turning to intercept her. "I'm sorry. The stairs are closed," the attendant said. "And the captain has turned on the seat belt sign. I'm going to have to ask you to return—"

"I don't feel any bumps." The woman in yoga pants crossed her arms over her chest and glared. "And besides, how can the stairs be closed? It's not like you can break a flight of stairs."

"Ma'am," Natalie said, through a tight smile. "Return to your seat."

"Well." The woman gave a sarcastic wag of her head as she spoke. "That is exactly what we are trying to do. My son wanted to look around your fancy airplane. We came this way so he could use the restroom."

"You'll have to use the front stairs," Natalie said.

"I don't see why—"

"Go the other way," Quinn said. His voice was barbed with the pointed ambivalence of a man who'd ended people's lives. He had never hurt a woman just for being rude, but Yoga Pants didn't know that.

"This is going in my TripAdvisor review!" the woman said. "I can assure you of that." She drew her son to her like a shield, thankfully, Quinn thought, covering the most offending portions of her yoga pants.

Once the woman had stomped away, Carly turned her attention back to Quinn. "See what I mean," she said. "You sounded like you would have slammed her on the floor if she'd refused your order."

"I should have slammed her because of those hideous tights," Natalie said, still deadpan.

"Okay," Quinn said. "Before someone else comes back and challenges any authority I don't actually possess, tell me what is it you need."

Carly let her hands fall to her sides. "You held that rolled motorcycle magazine like a club when you were boarding. And you handled your idiot seatmate like someone who's used to tough situations." Her eyes played up and down, studying him, as if she was still trying to convince herself she'd made the right decision. "And the way you interact with your daughter . . . I told the captain you were a man we could trust." She lifted a beige handset off the rear bulkhead and extended it toward Quinn. "He wants to speak with you."

Quinn sighed, taking the phone. This couldn't be good.

Rob Szymanski's voice came across the line. He didn't sound nearly as upbeat as he did over the intercom. "Mr. . . . Hackman, is it?" the captain said, using the name on Quinn's passport.

"Yes, sir," Quinn said.

"Carly thinks you're some kind of police officer. Is she correct?"

"She is," Quinn said. "Air Force OSI." There was no point in lying. There was obviously something going on that made the crew think they needed someone with law enforcement experience.

"Very good," the captain said. "An old ROTC buddy of mine is the OSI detachment commander in New York. Maybe you know him."

"Dave Fullmer," Quinn said. "He was one of my instructors at FLETC. He's a good man." FLETC was the Federal Law Enforcement Training Center.

"Yes, he is," the captain said, apparently convinced now that Quinn was actually an OSI agent. "Listen, I'll just cut to the chase. Carly brought you back there because we've had a murder on board."

Quinn's breath caught like a stone in his throat. He'd expected that they might want his help with an unruly passenger. "You mean an unattended death?"

"No," the captain sighed. "Well, yes. SOP says I'm not allowed to open the cockpit door under these circumstances, but from the way they describe it to me, we're pretty sure it's a murder, throat cut, the whole nine—"

"Just a minute." Quinn cut him off. "Do you have the killer in custody?"

"No, I—"

Quinn dropped the handset, letting it fall against its cord without another word. He shouldered his way past a dumbfounded Carly, and ran back up the aisle, scanning for threats as he went.

Mattie was too short to be visible over the back of her seat, but he sensed something was wrong when he was still five rows back. The guy with the Popeye chin was gone. Quinn picked up his pace, shoving aside errant knees and elbows as he rushed down the aisle. He couldn't believe he'd been so stupid as to leave her alone.

He nearly collapsed when he reached their row and saw her kneeling beside her backpack at the foot of her seat. She'd finished one Lemony Snicket book and, being too small to reach her bag, she'd unbuckled her seat belt and climbed down on the floor to get another from her backpack. It had been impossible for Quinn to see her until he was right on top of their row.

He ignored the glares of surrounding passengers when he not only snubbed his own nose at the seat belt sign, but told his daughter to get up and accompany him to the back of the plane.

"Bring your book," he snapped, a little more harshly than he should have.

Mattie followed without a word.

Though Quinn had been deployed or absent on assignment through fully half of Mattie's short life, she was smart enough to know when the time for joking was over. She walked obediently behind him, sensing somehow, even at this tender age, that there were things more important than seat belt signs.

Quinn got her situated on the couch along the wall nearest Natalie the guard. Carly was still on the phone with the cockpit. She passed the handset to Quinn.

"What was that all about?" the captain snapped.
"I'm in the middle of telling you about a murder and
you walk away?"

"Captain . . ." Quinn took a slow breath. "I'm not
willing to leave my daughter unattended when there's a
killer free on the plane."

"Right," the captain said. "I understand. Look, I have
to be honest with you. The FBI will be pretty upset that
I'm breaking protocol and having someone else investigate this murder before we get back. But, as you said,
I'm not happy about a killer running around on my airplane. If you don't mind, I'd appreciate a professional
pair of eyes on the body. Maybe there's some clue that
will lead us to the killer right away. I'd come out and
give it a look myself, but after something like this, I
can't even crack the door until we land."

"OSI doesn't pull lead on homicide investigations,"
Quinn said. "But I'll see what I can do."

"Very well," Captain Rob said. "I'm not too keen on
landing in Russia with a dead body on board. Take a
look and get back with me quickly. I've got some deci-
sions to make and I got about fifteen minutes to make
them."

"Roger that," Quinn said. He was at once worried
over Mattie's safety and excited at the prospect of the
hunt.

"It . . . I mean he's around the corner," Carly said.
She nodded at the stairwell that curved upward in a
slow arc to the second level. A pool of yellow light
washed down the polished teak, spilling onto the maroon Berber carpet of the lounge. "Your daughter can
sit right here at the bottom without seeing too much.
You should be able to keep an eye on her and still see
what you need to see. I'll help you watch her."

"Thank you." Quinn nodded. "That will work."

"I'm sorry I didn't think about the danger before," Carly said. "It was pretty stupid of me to leave her sitting there by herself, considering."

"No worries," Quinn said, pausing as Carly moved the rope barrier to one side. "Tell me, what was it really that made you think I was a cop?"

"You remind me of my dad," she said, holding out her hand to motion him in.

"Your dad was in law enforcement?"

"No," she laughed. "He was a news correspondent for the wire services. We lived all over the world. Anyway, he had a laminated saying on his computer that was something like: 'Every man is sometimes tempted to cut throats,' or something like that."

Quinn smiled in spite of the dead body ten feet away. "It's a Mencken quote," he said. "He was a journalist like your father. 'Every normal man must be tempted, at times, to spit on his hands, hoist the black flag, and begin slitting throats.'"

"Yeah, that's the one," Carly said. "When I first saw you, that's what came to mind."

# Chapter 48

*The White House*

President Hartman Drake leaned back in his chair with a phone pressed to one ear. His bowtie was crooked. His face was still flushed from his recent workout, which, McKeon knew, included a certain amount of exertion with Barbara Wong. The attractive Navy ensign was the only female in the room and now stood at the end of the desk with a second handset, acting as interpreter. President Chen spoke excellent English and she was only there in the event the conversation reached a more nuanced level. Both countries, after all, had the means, and lately the will, to see each other reduced to glowing piles of ash.

The President nibbled White House M&Ms as he spoke, snatching little handfuls from the bowl on his desk and dropping them into his mouth during the conversation. McKeon could not help but think that for someone who was so concerned about his physique, the man ate a great many M&Ms. President Chen Min of the People's Republic of China was on the other end of the line and must have heard the crunching.

McKeon stood behind the President, arms folded,

looking out the window. David Crosby, Drake's chief of staff, stood by the main door, his body obscuring the view of the peephole the President's secretary—and anyone else who happened to be standing beside her desk—used to check on the status of meetings in the Oval Office. Two admirals and five generals—with more stars among them than two colonial flags—crowded onto the small spot of carpet between the sofas and the President's desk. Secretaries Watchel and Filson were on opposite sides of the situation and the room. Apart from the President, no one sat.

". . . I'm sure you do, Mr. President," Drake said around a mouthful of red, white, and blue M&Ms. "But it would be helpful to take a little more of a worldview on this. I . . . No, I completely understand. . . . It saddens me that you feel that way. . . . No, I have made my decision."

Drake hung up the phone and grabbed another handful of candy.

"He's pretty pissed," Drake said. "Gave me a rant about our relationship with what he called the 'illegal government of Taiwan' and our treaties with Japan over the Senkaku Islands. A lot of saber rattling, but that's it so far."

A buzz ran between the military leaders. Filson gave a bellicose nod and Watchel bit his tongue to keep from saying "I told you so." McKeon had hoped, but not expected this would push China over the edge. The more independent leaders who'd taken over after Mao might have fired a missile directly after hanging up the phone. They had been able to command, where the current leader had to consult. McKeon understood the realities and planned for them.

"Andrew," the President said to Secretary of Defense Filson. "Have your guys monitor the situations in the South China Sea as well as Japan. . . . Hell, just keep an eye on China." He turned to the Secretary of State. "Tom, get in touch with our embassy in Islamabad and let's get these Uyghur sons a bitches back in a Pakistani prison where they belong."

Crosby stepped up and whispered something in the president's ear. He was a pasty man who looked as though the pressures of the job were eating him alive—but he'd been the keeper of Drake's dirty laundry since his time in the House. There was really no one else who could do it.

Drake took a deep breath. "Seems I am needed in the Roosevelt Room."

Wong's eyes flashed momentarily toward the president, looking, no doubt, for some sign of appreciation for their earlier time in the gym. When he gave her none, she tucked the white dress cap under her arm and squared her shoulders. "Thank you, Mr. President."

"Thank you . . ." Drake consulted the name tag on her uniform. "Ensign Wong."

She addressed the rest of the heavy brass in the room, and then excused herself before she started crying. Drake had that effect on women—a fact that kept his chief of staff perpetually busy fending off civil suits and blackmail threats. At least Crosby thought he was fending them off. Ran, McKeon's Japanese friend, had done the heavy lifting, sorting out many of Drake's women before they even hit Crosby's radar.

JFK and Bill Clinton were his heroes, but the Warren G. Harding White House made their liaisons seem like college indiscretions. Drake had outdone them all in his first six months in office. If things continued as planned, Drake would have a great deal in common with the twenty-ninth president.

\* \* \*

The baby-faced Marine Corps sentry posted outside the West Wing did not acknowledge Ran when she walked by, but three uniformed Secret Service officers and two plainclothes agents nodded in turn as she walked down the colonnade toward the Rose Garden. Armed with pistols and expandable batons and radios on their belts, these agents stood by with a twitchy hyper-awareness that made them jump at the click of a cicada. Counter-snipers patrolled the roof and some of the agents carried small submachine guns on hanging harnesses under their jackets. It had been nearly half a year since the assassinations, but security personnel, from the president's bodyguards to the uniformed mounted DC Park Police who patrolled the Capitol on horseback, still operated as if they were under immediate attack. Staffing in and around the White House had tripled. Ran had to stifle a laugh at all the precautions since the greatest threat to their way of life was sitting inside the Oval Office. If these men and women knew what their precious POTUS was up to, they would kill him themselves. Ran had certainly thought about it.

Ran viewed everyone she met as a possible opponent whom she would eventually have to crush. She had vague recollections of a mother who was pretty, but essentially soft and flawed. From the time she was old enough to walk, her father had drilled into her an exactness of spirit, a focus that cut through weaker souls and saw them for what they were—nothing. She'd killed her first human being before she was six—a boy two years older than her. He had sneered when he saw he was fighting a girl—and then vomited up his own blood when her dagger had pierced his belly. One of her father's counselors, a lusty wrestler with rippling muscles and an ego the size of the sea, made advances on her when she was thirteen. He fell to her sword like rice stalks before a fire. She'd counted at first, seen the faces in her dreams, but by the time she was twenty, there were too many.

The fact that she wore no ID badge hanging around her neck was a sign of her importance. Virtually everyone working or visiting the West Wing wore a color-coded badge identifying their work status and clearance level. Only four people were exempt: POTUS, VPOTUS, David Crosby, and the Vice President's special advisor, Ran Kimura. The fact that she was included in that list caused no small amount of jealousy among staffers.

Ran stopped at the east door off the Rose Garden. Through the rippled glass, she watched several generals from the Joint Chiefs spill out of the Oval Office into the main corridor. The Vice President stood at the threshold with the President's chief of staff, having a heated discussion about something. She watched as Crosby's posture softened. He nodded, as if caught in some hypnotic spell. The man didn't like McKeon— no, Ran thought, that wasn't strong enough. Crosby despised McKeon, seeing him as usurping the power of the presidency. But those feelings melted when the two men were together. That's the way it worked with Lee McKeon. He had a way. An inexplicable force that twined its way into your good sense, into your strategy and will, and made you think you were the most important thing in the world.

At first glance, it was impossible to see how a tall, gawky skeleton of a man with dark skin and deep-set eyes ever got elected to public office. His Pakistani blood gave him the features many Americans saw as a personification of the enemy—and yet, each speech saw hundreds more followers jumping on board his political machine, writing checks and donating time, because Lee McKeon, the Chindian underdog with the Scottish name, looked like a very tan Abraham Lincoln and entranced others as surely as the mad monk Rasputin.

Ran had seen the power of his presence firsthand, two years before, when he'd talked her out of killing him.

# Chapter 49

*Flight 105*

Quinn turned to check on Mattie one last time before venturing closer to the body.

She peered over the top of her new book, craning her head in order to sneak a look up the stairs. She had inherited his curiosity for anything that smelled of adventure and danger—even if she was only seven.

"Stay put, you," Quinn said. "There are some things you just can't un-see. Got it?"

"I know, Daddy," Mattie said, sounding decades beyond her years. "I've seen them."

Her directness took Quinn's breath away. She was definitely his daughter—and he was pretty sure that was not something she'd put on the plus side of her résumé in the future.

Quinn was nearly fourteen when he'd stumbled upon his first body—a hunter who'd frozen to death in the Talkeetna Mountains north of Anchorage. The bears were in hibernation and he'd found him before the wolves did. But pine martens and weasels had begun to nibble away at the man's hands, leaving nothing but finger bones hanging from the frozen cuffs of a wool shirt that was oddly clean. They radioed the troopers and watched when a ski plane landed in a snowy clearing among the gnarled black spruce. The plane looked barely large enough for the pilot, a tall man with a blue uniform and thin mustache. The Quinn brothers and their father helped the trooper stuff and cram the body into the airplane, frozen in a seated position, where it sat, staring blankly at the back of the trooper pilot's head as he took off for Anchorage. There was no blood, no guts, nothing but emptiness—and bones where fingers should have been. Quinn's conscious mind found the experience more reverent than traumatic, but the skeletal hands of that first dead man had shaken him awake from his dreams many times over the decades since.

Violent brushes with evil men already gave Mattie plenty of cause for nightmares. Quinn knew from hard experience that these things had a way of adding up. "Stack-tolerance," they called it. At some point, the mind couldn't handle any more. The last thing he wanted to do was put her near another grisly murder scene while she was still young enough to be reading Lemony Snicket.

"That's how we found him." Carly's voice pulled him back to the present.

Quinn moved slowly, searching step by step for any clue before he put his foot down. Apart from a cascading pool of blood and the lifeless body draped across the stairs, the polished teak was remarkably clean.

Early in his OSI career, before he found a natural home in counterintelligence, Quinn put in some time in Criminal Investigations—known as "Crim." He helped local authorities and the FBI with several homicides where Air Force personnel were involved, both on and off base. Two cases had been robberies gone bad, but most were crimes of passion. In all cases, clutter and chaos ruled the day. The scenes were in shambles.

Even at first glance, Quinn could tell this was no crime of passion. The killing had been quick and precise, by someone who knew exactly what they were doing. It all had to have happened in seconds, while the victim was alone on the stairs, without alerting the other passengers above or below. When done by an expert, assassinations—something with which Quinn had a certain amount of experience—very often appeared as sterile as an operating room.

Still four steps below the body, Quinn squatted to get a better look. The dead man lay facedown, legs trailing, arms above his head, as if he'd been trying to climb the stairs on all fours before he died. He was white and looked to be in his early forties, with a receding hairline and a sizeable spare tire around his waist. A well-worn leather penny loafer hung from the toe of one foot. A gray polo shirt, the back of which was oddly clean for the amount of blood on the stairs, bunched up around his armpits, exposing his back and belly—as if the killer had attempted to lift him off his feet during a struggle.

Quinn looked over his shoulder, checking in on Carly. "You okay?"

She nodded quickly, mouth clenched tightly as if she was trying not to throw up. "I've just never seen anything this gruesome before."

Quinn took a deep breath, wishing he could say the same.

There was a bizarre obscenity in looking at someone who'd died a violent death—especially when that death had come at the hands of another. The dead could not turn away or cover their own nakedness. Investigators, for a time at least, were forced to leave the bodies exposed and twisted, frozen in their final moment of terror. Worse than that, the sight of such a scene drew in the unprepared, making them ponder too long and too hard on the short distance between life and death.

Carly stood behind him, hands at her sides. Her twitchiness disappeared now that she was certain Quinn was going to help.

Still squatting, Quinn studied the curvature of the wall above the body, where the victim would have been standing when he was killed. A swath of blood spatter, four feet wide, flecked the white plastic in tiny specks of red. There was a notable vacancy in the pattern, where someone or something else had blocked the path of the spray.

Quinn glanced back at Carly. "Don't you carry some nitrile gloves for cleanup in case someone gets airsick?"

"I'll get you some." She ducked back down the stairs, apparently happy for the chance to step away from the gore.

"And a camera," Quinn added. "Something better than a phone if you can find it, with a good flash."

Quinn stepped up next to the void in the blood spatter and found, as he suspected he would, that it was roughly the shape of his shoulder. He bent at the knees to make the comparison, which put the person who'd been standing there when the victim's throat was cut at around five-seven or five-eight.

Carly returned a few moments later with a pair of blue gloves. Quinn hung the camera around his neck, and then slipped the gloves on with a snap. He took photos from every angle, noting the way the man was positioned, the spatter and the blood that pooled on the polished wood beneath the body, before overflowing and dripping down the riser to the next step.

Moving up beside the victim, Quinn stooped to take close-ups of the wound in the man's neck before he moved him. Whatever it had been, the weapon was sharp, maybe a piece of glass. A deep gash began under the dead man's left ear, severing both the carotid and jugular before continuing around to open his windpipe.

"So," Quinn muttered to himself. "You're right-handed."

"Pardon?" Carly took a tentative step forward, watching where she put her foot to avoid stepping in blood.

"Our killer is probably right-handed." Quinn pantomimed grabbing someone from behind and drawing a blade from left to right, as much to get the movement in his own mind as to demonstrate to the flight attendant.

The wound was deep enough to expose the grotesque white of vertebrae and glistening cartilage. Quinn knew from experience that it took someone with a substantial amount of upper-body strength to hold even a small victim still while inflicting this much damage.

After he'd taken far more pictures than he'd ever need, Quinn passed the camera back to Carly. He fished the wallet out of the dead man's back pocket and flipped it open.

"Aaron Foulger," he said, reading the man's driver's license. "From south Anchorage . . . There's about five hundred bucks cash US and roughly . . ." He thumbed through the bills and did some quick math in his head. "About two grand worth of 5,000-ruble notes."

Quinn found a faculty ID for the University of Alaska and passed it back to Carly, along with the wallet. "Have Natalie get somebody to check and see if he's traveling with anyone. Don't make contact if he is. Just let me know one way or the other."

Carly ducked away long enough to use the interphone and find out Foulger was traveling alone. She studied the ID and looked up at the body from her vantage point on the gentle arc of the staircase below Quinn. "Why would anyone want to kill a UAA professor?"

"We're looking for opportunity, means, and motive," Quinn said. "Our killer had opportunity when he caught Foulger alone on the stairwell." Quinn nodded toward the gash in the dead man's neck. "He had access to some sort of sharp blade, which should theoretically be difficult to come by on a commercial aircraft. I'm guessing it was a piece of glass—maybe a broken wine bottle or something. Anyway, the blade, along with the strength to employ it, gave him means."

Quinn scanned the body again to see what he'd missed. "What I'm not seeing is motive." He bent to study the dead man's hands. "There's a good chance the professor was a target of opportunity. If this was preplanned, I can think of a dozen better places to kill somebody than in the stairwell of a crowded airplane."

Carly gave him a weak smile. "You know it doesn't calm a girl to know you can think of a dozen better places to commit a murder."

Quinn ignored her, instead working through the odds that someone would risk committing a murder at this exact spot with five hundred potential witnesses.

"Too big a chance that you'd get caught here," he mused. "Why not wait for him in his house, wire his car to explode, slip something in his coffee? If it just had to be up close and personal, you could even cut him like this when he's walking past a blind alley in downtown Anchorage." Quinn paced back and forth on the stairs. "He lives up on the Hillside, not five hundred feet from Chugach State Park. It would be nothing to set up a sniper nest and pop him while he was out walking his dog. . . ."

"Again with the creepy stuff," Carly said. "You just rattled five ways to kill a man right off the top of your head."

"Yeah." Quinn shrugged. "I guess that is a little scary." He resisted the urge to explain himself further.

Carly cocked her head to one side, pondering. Her long hair hung down, away from her shoulder. She wrestled with her thoughts for a moment before looking up at Quinn.

"What kind of sick person murders a random passenger on board an airplane?" she said.

Quinn took a deep breath, thinking through the ramifications of his theory.

"Somebody who wants a diversion," he said.

Carly's eyes narrowed. "A diversion from what?"

"I'm not sure yet," he said. "It's still only a theory."

Quinn stepped down to the base of the stairs so he could talk to both Carly and Natalie and do a quick check on Mattie.

"How many people in the crew?" Quinn asked.

"Twenty-two flight attendants," Carly said. "And the two up front in the cockpit. We don't pick up the relief pilots until Vladivostok."

"Twenty-one," Natalie corrected. "Stacy Damico called in sick."

"Okay," Quinn said. "From this time forward, every attendant needs to find a buddy and stick with them. A murder is too big an incident to keep buttoned up. Word will spread quickly, if it hasn't already. There'll be a lot of uncomfortable questions that no one will be able to answer. My advice is to keep up service."

"To keep people calm." Carly nodded.

"That, and to give us eyes moving around the air-craft," Quinn said. "Let the others know right away. Everyone moves in twos."

He picked up the phone on the bulkhead, reporting his findings to the captain. He spoke in whispered tones so as not to reach Mattie's straining ears and give her more than she should have to handle.

Ninety seconds after he hung up, the massive Airbus dipped her wing, and began a slow bank to the right. The pilot was taking the plane back to Anchorage.

Quinn felt the white-hot gush of anticipation that came before a conflict. Someone on this plane had cut the throat of a complete stranger to divert attention from something else—a bomb, a hijacking. Quinn didn't know what, but it was something bigger than murder.

# Chapter 50

*Fifteen minutes earlier*

The actual act of killing happened more quickly than Tang had anticipated. One moment he stood at the top of the stairs, ensuring no one interrupted Gao while he did his work—and the next Gao was there, tiny droplets of blood on his face and neck. There had been no thump, no groan, no scream. Tang didn't know what he'd expected, but it seemed to him that bloody death should come with some sound. He was still processing when he returned to his seat. Lin knew nothing about the murder and, though they had planned to kill everyone on the plane from the moment they boarded, he kept this death to himself. He would keep the entire secret, until the last possible moment.

Still, many years of marriage made it impossible to hide the concern in his face.

"What has happened?" she asked.

"We are going to try something different," Tang said. He could see the corner of the recycle bag sitting on the floor of the galley just two rows ahead. There were ninety-six seats in business class, ninety-six meals, ninety-six sheets of aluminum foil. He hoped that would be enough.

"Different?" Lin stared at him, head tilted to one side, trying to make sense of what he was saying. "I find it difficult to believe you would change your mind so easily."

"I love you," he said, voice tight and plastic—surely she noticed that. "I am ready to make necessary sacrifices."

Tang looked away under the heavy burden of her gaze. He checked his watch for something to do. "I must go," he said.

She took his arm, leaning in close so as not to be heard by other passengers.

"I will not detonate the device," she said.

"You will not have to," he said softly. "I told you, I am making some sacrifices because of my feelings for you."

Red-and-white uniforms seemed to be everywhere—but any minute there would be even more. He waited for the business-class flight attendant to move down the aisle on her rounds, then grabbed the recycle bag and whisked it into the lavatory. Once behind the safety of the locked door, Tang spread the foil dinner covers out flat, then worked feverishly to rip each sheet into smaller pieces until he had a pile of silver confetti that filled the small sink. The entire process was simple, but it took time, time Tang knew he did not have.

Word of Gao's bloody handiwork spread among the cabin crew like a grass fire. Those that didn't go all the way to the back went as least as far as mid cabin, to see for themselves if the rumors were true. While they were looking aft, Tang used the opportunity to slip down the front stairwell with his shirt stuffed full of foil strips. He ducked around the corner to the espresso bar, which was now empty but for the single attendant.

The seat belt chime sounded and the slender man in a crisp red vest nodded politely when he saw Tang. "Can I get you something, sir?" he said. "I'd be happy to bring it back to your seat." The tag on his vest said his name was Paxton. He had the youthful eyes of a man with lofty dreams, who was only here serving coffee for a time while he worked out his road to somewhere bigger and better.

Tang nodded toward the bulkhead separating the espresso bar from the front of the aircraft. "I cannot be certain," he said, "but I believe I saw a child go through that door." Tang stepped closer to the edge of the semicircular bar, resting a hand on the rich leather edge as if to steady himself.

"What door are you talking about?" Paxton said.

"That door around the corner." Tang pointed toward the cockpit. "By the stairs. It looks as though someone must have left it open. I'm not sure where it leads. . . ."

"Dammit," the attendant said. He wiped his hands with a bar towel.

"What is it?" Tang asked, though he already knew what it was. "Some kind of coat closet?"

Paxton shook his head. "It's a rest area for the crew," he said. "A little girl, you said?"

"A boy." Tang made up the story as he went. He wouldn't need it long. "He had a teddy bear."

"Thank you for letting us know, sir," the attendant said, coming around the bar. "But I need you to sit down."

Tang followed on the attendant's heels. "I heard

someone was killed," he said, grimacing as if the very words were distasteful.

Paxton looked over his shoulder as he punched the code into the cipher lock. "Sir," he finally said, "do me a favor and sit down."

All the seats were aft of the espresso station, so Tang had the attendant alone as soon as they made it to the corner.

When Paxton turned around to descend the ladder into the crew rest area, Tang kicked him in the face.

Tang jumped into the darkness. He assumed all personnel had reported topside as soon as they'd learned of the murder, but there would surely be an intercom. He moved quickly before Paxton could cry out for help.

The only light came from an orange strip of ribbon that ran along the ceiling of the small cabin and gave off little more than a faint glow. The rest area was hardly more than a narrow aisle with three sets of bunks on either side, and the two men had little room to fight. Tang didn't need much. He'd undergone months of physical training during police academy—and though he was far from the strongest or quickest in his class, he was certainly more experienced than the hapless flight attendant.

Paxton outweighed him by at least thirty pounds and had a much greater reach—but Tang doubted the young attendant had ever seen real violence. Rather than fight back, the young man tried to get away, fleeing toward the ladder and the brighter light above.

Tang pushed him the way he was already trying to go, but redirecting his head into the hard plastic upright of one of the bunks. It was a stunning blow that sent Paxton reeling. Tang grabbed a handful of hair and slammed the dazed man's head again and again into the sharp plastic edge. The flight attendant went limp at the first blow, but Tang took him with both hands and bashed his forehead against the upright until the man's eyes rolled upward, glassy and lifeless. A trickle of blood ran from his ear.

Tang wrestled the body into the bunk farthest from the hatch and covered it with a blanket. By the time anyone had a chance to look for him, the plan would either have worked or failed miserably. Either way, it wouldn't matter.

Tang climbed back up the ladder and opened the door a crack to find Ma Zhen standing outside. Lin was behind him, just as he planned, though she knew nothing of the dead man below. Ma's intensity frightened her from the first time she'd met him. Her face was creased with worry until she saw Tang on the other side of the door.

"What is happening?" she whispered. "The other passengers are saying a man has died."

"I have heard the same thing," Tang said. "Hurry, I will explain." He turned to descend the ladder, knowing that she would follow, but half hoping she would not.

Ma came down behind her, carrying the coffee grinder he'd stolen from the espresso stand. He reached around Lin when they were at the bottom of the ladder, crowding her as he handed the grinder to Tang.

"What are you doing?" She looked over her shoulder at Ma, then back at her husband. "Dalu?"

"I am sorry, my love," Tang said. "But you must understand . . ."

Lin's jaw dropped when she realized what was happening. Ma Zhen looped a charging cord from his computer around her throat, hauling her backwards. He was taller by six inches and easily lifted her tiny body off the floor. The intensity of the attack pulled her blouse to one side, exposing the tender flesh of her collarbone. Ropelike veins on her slender neck swelled above the biting electrical cord as if ready to burst. Her eyes flew wide. Tiny hands clawed the air. Hands that once caressed him reached out, trembling, pleading for help.

When it was done, Ma let her body slide to the ground. Even in the shadows, his face was bright from the frenzy of killing. He dropped the cord and wiped his hands on a pillowcase from one of the bunks.

"I did my best to make it quick," he said.

Tang's eye began to twitch. It was impossible to erase Lin's final look of betrayal from his memory. But that could not be helped. Ma did what had to be done. Lin had agreed to die. That was the plan since they had met the man from Pakistan. She had even embraced the idea. Tang told himself that this was quicker, perhaps, he thought, even less cruel since she would not have to pull the trigger. Death had freed her from the awful state of confusion brought on by the little *guizi* bitch. The child would pay for forcing him to take such drastic measures.

Ma put a hand on his shoulder.

"Are you all right, my brother?"

"We have to hurry," Tang snapped. The killing had to be done, but that did not keep him from hating the man who did it. "Go and see to the others."

Ma paused, dark eyes still frenzied. "She . . . she was to detonate the device."

"I am aware of our plan." Tang draped a flimsy airline blanket over his wife's body. "Go and tell the others we are back on track."

Eager to move toward his own end, he found an outlet for the coffee grinder and some pillows to muffle the noise. He dropped a handful of the aluminum foil strips into the grinder and turned it on.

Ma Zhen steadied himself on the edge of a bunk as the plane dipped suddenly, beginning a slow 180-degree turn back toward the United States.

"Will you take her place?" the young man asked. His hands shook from the aftermath of killing.

"You will have that honor," Tang said, staring at his dead wife. "This is a large aircraft. There is always a chance that there will be a few survivors. I will make certain the *guizi* child is not among them."

# Chapter 51

*Maryland*

Bowen drummed his fingers on the armrest of a stolen concrete truck and tried to get his head wrapped around the situation. Thibodaux had commandeered the thing from a construction site in Silver Spring, reaching under the chassis to disable the GPS as if he swiped concrete trucks several times a week.

Bowen had followed in his Charger to a strip mall north of the Beltway, next to some new construction so they wouldn't seem so out of place. The government car, or G-ride, was parked in front of a beauty salon a few spots away where Bowen could keep an eye on it while Thibodaux filled him in.

"Well, *cher*," the Cajun said. "I guess now is when you decide if you're in or out."

"What the hell?" Bowen shook his head. "I think we're up to three felonies apiece already."

"And the night is young," Thibodaux said.

"Whatever," Bowen said. "I'm in."

"Fair enough," Thibodaux said. "I've been given approval to bring you into the fold, so to speak."

Bowen said nothing, so the Cajun continued.

"Here's the way this'll go down," he said. "An army three-star named Lucas Hewn is about to conduct a surprise inspection of the mental health ward at Walter Reed Hospital. It's well known that certain high-value prisoners are being held there. General Hewn wants to make certain everyone is watching their P's and Q's, so to speak, and ensure we don't have ourselves another Abu Ghraib. Anyhow, he's loyal to us and understands the urgency. One of his staffers is a known IDTF snitch. He'll leak it that there is about to be an inspection. If they're keeping the director naked and threatening her with rape, Walter is bound to want her moved before the general can talk to her. If Joey B does his job, we'll have enough time to set up and grab her when they move."

Bowen thought for a moment before he spoke. "You're talking about grabbing a federal prisoner during transport?"

"That's exactly what I'm talking about, *cher*," Thibodaux said.

"Look," Bowen said, "that could be some of my friends conducting this move. What if there are guys involved in the transport that aren't a part of this whole secret government takeover thing?"

Thibodaux shook his head. "You ever move an ID agent's prisoners before?"

"No," Bowen said.

"There ain't no clean end on a turd," Thibodaux said, looking like he wanted to spit. "I understand the need for secrecy and all, but these guys are beyond dirty. You heard what they did to Garcia."

"Okay," Bowen said, convinced, but easing into it. The cab of the concrete truck seemed to be closing in around him. He'd done a lot of iffy things in his life, but nothing close to this. "I understand Ross is the director of the CIA, and there's no doubt she's being treated badly. But if what you say is true, so are a lot of other high-level people. There's got to be something else about her you're not telling me."

"Now you're trackin'." Thibodaux smiled as if he was happy Bowen had figured out some clue. "How much do you know about our new president?"

"Garcia gave me her thoughts on the matter," Bowen said. "I hate to say it, but it sounds reasonable."

"Good," Thibodaux said. "Because you've just been inducted into a secret group committed to bringing them down. General Hewn, Palmer, Garcia, me, and a shitload of others are in it up to our necks right along with you."

"Wait, wait, wait . . ." Bowen shook his head. "You're telling me you guys are planning a coup?"

"What we're planning to do," Thibodaux said, "is cut their damn heads off."

"You mean figuratively," Bowen said.

The Cajun shrugged. "Remains to be seen," he said. "And don't go all flabbergasted on me. Joey B laid out exactly what's going on. You want men like him and his pal Walter running the show? Because there's a hell of a lot more where they came from. This ain't the America I know."

"And Director Ross?" Bowen asked again. "Where does she fit into this?"

"She's part of us," Thibodaux said. "It's not like we have group meetings or anything, but she and Palmer were working through several scenarios, so she's pretty much up to speed on everything—names, plans, you know, shit that will get us all killed if she gives it up."

# Chapter 52

*Flight 105*

"So," Carly said when the captain finished his 180-degree turn and the airplane was pointing back out over the Bering Sea. "Just under four hours until we're back in Alaska. You think we can find the killer by then?"

"We're going to try." Quinn bit his bottom lip, his mind racing.

There was no way this killer was working alone. He would need accomplices to make sure other passengers were kept away from both the upper and lower decks in the moments while he murdered Foulger. Anything else would have relied too heavily on luck. No, there was more than one actor out there. It was the only thing that made sense.

*See one, think two*, he said to himself. The philosophy had kept him alive on more than one occasion when others wanted him DRT: Dead Right There.

"I'm a doer, Mr. Hackman," Carly said, momentarily startling Quinn with his alias. "Looking for clues on a dead body is a good start, but tell me what we have to do next."

"First, we're going to look for blood." Quinn kept his voice low so Mattie couldn't hear the gory details. "Whoever killed Foulger took a big hit of spray."

"You don't think he would have wiped it off by now?"

"I'm sure he would have tried," Quinn said. "No offense, but it's hard to wash all the soap off your hands in those little airplane sinks. The human heart pumps a lot of blood under substantial pressure. It has a tendency to go in unintended directions when something gets cut."

"Something else in which you're an expert?" Carly said, looking a little sick to her stomach.

"You might say that." He nodded. "Anyway, we're looking for a guy with blood on his left shoulder."

Carly leaned around the bulkhead so she could look up the aisle. "So we just walk up and down trying to find someone with stained clothes."

"I'd have the other flight attendants keep an eye out," Quinn said. "But chances are our killer is wearing dark colors or someone would have pointed him out by now. Blood might be impossible to see with the naked eye. There are, however, devices that can pick it up, even on dark fabric."

Carly gave an exasperated sigh. "We're seven miles up in the sky," she said. "You have one in your carry-on?"

"Not exactly," Quinn said. "But I've been looking for a reason to show off for my daughter."

It took ten minutes for Quinn to gather the materials he needed and bring them back to the couch below the stairwell.

As with any operation, his first priority was security. He posted Natalie at the bulkhead, facing forward so she could keep an eye on both aisles. There was a calmness to her demeanor that he supposed came from having seen it all over her years of flying. Quinn put two more flight attendants in the passenger lounge above, to make sure no one could sneak up on him while he worked. He left the body where it was.

Both Carly and Mattie stood beside him watching intently as he knelt in front of the couch and spread everything out on the tan leather cushions. Natalie sacrificed her small digital camera to the cause. Carly commandeered a DVD of the movie *Titanic* from a passenger. There was a roll of clear packing tape from the first-class galley, two malleable wax earplugs from his Popeye-chinned seatmate, and a set of tiny screwdrivers another flight attendant used for repairing her eyeglasses. The most difficult thing to find had been a blade—an item Quinn was rarely without on the ground. He ended up making do with a case knife from the first-class galley that was at least sharp enough to carve the filet mignon.

He pressed the power button on the camera, saw the battery was fully charged, and then turned it off again. Using the minuscule screwdriver, he removed the six screws that held the back in place and passed them to Mattie so they wouldn't get lost—and so she would feel useful. The lens assembly was easy to find, but before he touched it, he located a blue insulated cylinder that resembled a stubby double-A battery. Two wires protruding from the base were soldered to a circuit board.

Careful not to touch the wires, Quinn pried the top of the cylinder upward with the point of his screwdriver. He bent it back and forth against the solder until it broke free, leaving two quarter-inch leads attached. He took one of the wax earplugs and used it to cover the wires before handing it to Carly.

"Careful," he said. "That's the flash capacitor."

She smiled. "Like *Back to the Future*?"

"That's a flux capacitor," Mattie said, grinning that she'd gotten the joke.

"No kidding," Quinn said. "Be careful with it. It powers the camera's flash. There's enough electricity stored in there to knock you off your feet if you make contact with the wires. You now have what we call a field expedient stun gun."

Carly pinched the small metal cylinder by the insulated sides and held it away from her body. "What am I supposed to do with it?"

"You don't have to be that careful." Quinn took it back and held it in the palm of his hand. "It won't bite you unless you give it a shove and push the wires through the wax. Put it in your vest pocket. You might be glad you have a weapon if things get hairy."

Quinn checked his watch and then turned his attention back to the camera. Four more tiny screws allowed him to access the CCD, or charged coupled device, that was the brains of a digital camera. He lifted it out carefully to find what he was looking for.

"Wow," Mattie whispered as if she was in church.

Quinn used the tip of the smallest screwdriver to lift the tiny square of glass far enough so he could get his fingers around it. He held it up to the light, turning it back and forth so it changed from green to shimmering purple, the colors of an oil slick on water.

"What is that?" Mattie leaned in, peering at the jewel-like treasure.

"It's an infrared light filter," Quinn said. He was never one to dumb down a conversation for his daughter's sake. "It keeps the regular pictures from getting all hazy. When we take it out, the camera will let in light that we can't see with our eyes."

He used the tip of his thumb to measure the size of the interior lens assembly, and then set the camera aside. Ripping a piece of the clear packing tape, he stuck it to the media side of the DVD and smoothed it with a tissue from the lavatory. He was careful to keep his fingerprints off it as best he could. Once he'd burnished the tape enough that he was satisfied there were no air bubbles underneath, he began to peel it back, a millimeter at a time. A metallic layer of gold-colored film from the back of the disk came up fixed to the sticky side of the tape. It took a few minutes with the case knife, but he was finally able to saw out a square of the material the size of the little IR filter.

He used his thumbnail to rub off just enough of the foil backing along the edge of the tape that it stayed in place when he pressed it to the lens assembly.

Natalie's curiosity got the best of her and she craned her head to get a better look from her security post by the bulkhead. "How can you take a picture now?" she asked. She frowned as if she disapproved of this science project when there was a murderer on the plane. "Won't the foil get in the way?"

Quinn took the screws one at a time from Mattie and began to replace them as he explained. "With the filter gone, it will be too bright inside the plane to get a good image," he said. "We need something to block out as much of the visible light as we can. They make special filters for this sort of thing, but we have to use what we have on board. The black ends of developed photographic film, the inside of an old computer floppy disk—"

"That's a funny word," Mattie said. "What's a 'floppy disk'?"

"Never mind," Quinn said, tightening the last screw on the back of the camera. "You've heard of infrared light, but you don't know what a floppy disk is. . . . It makes me feel old, but I guess they were before your time." He held up the camera. "Okay," he said. "I've got to get back to work. How about you go on and read some more of your book?"

Mattie skulked to her seat. She stared out the window, thinking, no doubt, of building her own infrared camera. She was like that.

Quinn walked back to the stairwell and turned on the camera. Thankfully, he hadn't damaged the fragile lens mechanism during the process of his hack. The focal length had changed when he'd removed the glass IR filter so the focus was slightly off. But other than that, the device worked perfectly. The dark teakwood stairs showed up a ghostly gray in the LCD screen while the blood looked like pools of black ink around the body.

Carly's mouth hung open in amazement when he showed it to her.

"That's incredible," she said. "How do you learn stuff like that?"

"A misspent youth." Quinn shrugged. "I learned the stun gun thing with my brother during a break from college."

Carly started to laugh, but her eyes locked on the dead body. The success with the camera had taken her mind off it for a moment, but the stark reality of death came flooding back.

"What now?" she whispered.

"Now?" Quinn said, holding up the camera. "Now we go hunting."

# Chapter 53

*Maryland*

Virginia Ross stood naked and very much alone in the corner of the empty concrete room. She'd always envisioned cells as being smaller, but this one was cavernous—big enough to add to the heavy weight of insignificance brought with it. The echoing expanse of the place only made her feel more naked than she was. Closer walls would have been welcome friends.

Apart from the institutional stainless-steel toilet with a water fountain and small sink at the top, there was nothing else in the room, not even a privacy screen that was common in modern prisons. No bed, no chair— even the table where Agent Walter had questioned her had been taken away, presumably because it gave her something to hide behind.

Until she'd been dragged off to this secret hellhole, no man had seen Virginia Ross out of her clothes since her husband had died. She'd never been svelte, even in college, but the very thought of intimacy after her husband was nothing short of gruesome. She found it sobering how much emotional safety the thin layers of cloth had offered. Even the scant running shorts and clammy

T-shirt had allowed her some sense of humanity. Now, even that was gone and the lily-white object of her self-doubt now glared at the cameras in full, uncovered glory.

Of course, she'd read reports of the resistance training agents endured as part of specialized units. She was well aware of how instructors systematically broke them down by taking away anything that made them human. But reports could not come close to the abject terror of a fifty-four-year old woman when the three men marched into her freezing cell and ordered her to hand over the last few scraps that covered her body.

Ross was a highly educated woman who held her own in debates with world leaders from some of the most misogynistic countries on the planet—but when those three men, hardly older than college frat boys, backed her against the concrete wall and sneered at her nakedness, she'd babbled like an infant. A slap would have stunned her less.

Ross read somewhere that the more civilized a person was, the harder they took certain forms of interrogation. It made logical sense, but logic flew out the window when dimpled nakedness was exposed to the stares of leering men. She'd lost control of her bladder, setting her captors to cackle at her predicament.

She'd wanted to ask for a towel but, she, who just hours before had commanded the most powerful intelligence organization on earth, found it impossible to open her mouth and speak.

The men had fanned out like wolves, ready to rush in and grab her. Ross could hear blood rushing in her ears. Tears poured down her cheeks. Her throat was so tight she was certain she might choke to death at any moment.

The apparent leader of her tormentors, a pasty thing with greasy black curls and a gold chain on his neck, took a half step forward. He towered over her, using his bulk for intimidation.

"Boo!" he said, his face just inches from hers.

Ross recoiled as if she'd been punched. The men all shook their heads as if they were disgusted. They left her alone—shaking, naked, and vulnerable, but untouched.

She was standing with a shoulder tucked in the corner, forehead leaning against the wall, when she heard the metallic click and whir of the cell door. Agent Walter walked in carrying a thick file folder tucked under his arm. He was wearing a different suit, brown but just as wrinkled as the gray one. Two men in gray coveralls followed him, carrying a rusted set of bedsprings. They set the springs inside the door and then ducked out for a moment, to return with two stainless-steel chairs. One chair had a padded seat. One did not. Both shone like mirrors under the bright light of the cell.

Agent Walter said nothing of the rusty springs, leaving Ross's imagination to run wild about their purpose. After checking to make sure there were no more instructions, the two helpers left Walter to his work.

Ross tried to squeeze deeper into the corner when the heavy steel door slammed shut.

"Looks like you found the only hidey-hole you could." Walter chuckled, nodding toward her corner. His voice rattled around the room like a pebble in a tin can, grating on Virginia Ross's nerves and making her want to scream. She bit her tongue, resolving not to give him that satisfaction.

He shook his head when she didn't answer, still laughing under his breath. "I'll have to suggest we move to circular rooms. That way you people won't have anywhere to run." He flipped the padded chair around so he could sit looking across the back, staring at her as if she were an animal in a zoo.

"I assume you've taken a polygraph before," he said.

Ross held her breath. She wanted to act indignant, but when one's appendectomy scars were showing, haughtiness was a difficult thing to muster.

Walter's chin rested on his hands along the back of the chair, muffling his voice. "It's a simple question, Virginia."

"Of course, I have," she said. "Many times. I want to know why I can't have my clothes."

"You'll have to earn them back," Walter said. He reached in his suit pocket and pulled out a small wad of white cloth. "But, as a sign of good faith, I brought you this." He pitched the cloth on the ground like it was a treat and she was a dog he was trying to lure closer.

She took a tentative step toward him, stooping quickly to snatch up the gauzy scrap. It turned out to be a robe like some women wore over their swimsuits on the beach. Several sizes too small and made of thin, nearly transparent cotton, it barely reached the middle of her thighs. She had to hold it closed in the front, but it was still a welcome gift.

"Thank you," she said, angry with herself the moment she'd uttered the words.

All business, he nodded to the other chair, five feet in front of him. "Go ahead and sit," he said.

"I'd prefer to stand."

"It wasn't a request," Walter said, his voice dripping with contempt.

Clutching the robe shut with both hands, one at her breasts, the other just below her bellybutton, Ross maneuvered herself into the chair so she didn't have to face him directly. She shivered as her skin touched the cold metal.

"Anyway," he said, once she was seated. "About the polygraph. I have some questions we need to go over beforehand, you know, to make certain you are aware of what we'll be asking you."

Agent Walter opened his manila folder. He began with a series of rapid-fire questions about her education, where she'd lived, her family, the date and cause of death for both her husband and her daughter. He touched on, but never delved deeply into, CIA operational issues. Everything he mentioned was already widely known and a matter of open source. The questions went on and on, more like some sort of word-association test than any quest for information.

Ross sat with her legs crossed. The flimsy robe covered her as long as she held it shut, but added little to her modesty. Movement meant exposure and exposure meant Walter would win. So, she remained frozen in the same position, eyes locked on the agent's dowdy flap of hair. Ten minutes into the conversation, her lower back screamed for relief. Five minutes later, her legs were numb from lack of circulation. It was hard to judge time in the windowless cell, but she'd always had a fairly accurate internal clock. As best she could tell, she'd been without sleep for at least a day and a half.

Dizzy with fatigue, she burned a great deal of energy just trying to control her terror. It took Ross half an hour to realize she was sitting in a specially designed interrogation chair. Though nearly impossible to tell from looking at it, the front two legs were almost an inch shorter than the back ones. Unlike Agent Walter's chair, this one had no padding and the seat had been polished to a high gloss. Even in the chilly cell, stress and fear induced great droplets of sweat to roll down Ross's back and buttocks, adding to her embarrassment and slicking the stainless-steel chair. With her legs crossed, all her weight was on one foot against the floor in order to keep from sliding out of the seat.

Forty minutes into the questioning, she couldn't help herself and planted both feet on the ground. Hiding behind clenched eyes, she arched her back to relieve the pain. She jumped when she heard the door buzz open.

The two men in coveralls had returned. Flanking the door, they stood at parade rest and waited for instructions.

Agent Walter bent his neck from side to side, groaning as if he was the one in pain. He closed the folder and dropped it in his lap.

"Are you hungry?" he asked.

She stared at him, fearing he was only going to toy with her again.

"You've lost a considerable amount of weight, but I assume you still enjoy food."

"My stomach couldn't handle anything right now," she whispered, staring at the tiny hairs on her thighs. She, who would have tugged the hem of her skirt down if even an inch of her knees peeked out, was talking to this man while looking at the hair on her thighs. The world was a very strange place.

The faint click of shoe leather on tile caused her to look up as the two men took up positions on either side of her.

She followed Walter's gaze to the rusty bedsprings against the wall. She'd wondered when he'd get around to them.

"Are you familiar with the word *parrilla*?" he asked. He gave a cursory nod to the men, but they seemed to know already what to do.

Ross began to hyperventilate as they grabbed her cruelly by each arm and dragged her on her heels to the springs. She'd never seen one in action, but could only imagine what the man had in mind for the metal frame. Time seemed to unhinge in her head. Oddly, she was more concerned that her robe had fallen open than she was about the rusted metal. She watched in horror as Walter rose from his chair and walked toward her. The men held her arms, but her legs were free. She wanted to kick out, to smash her heel into Walter's smirking teeth, but her feet felt anchored to the concrete floor.

"*Parrilla* is Spanish for *grill*," Walter said. Methodically, he handcuffed her wrists to the rough corners of the bed as it leaned against the wall. Stepping back, he waited while the men did the same to her ankles. She turned her face away and shut her eyes, fighting the urge to scream.

"Pinochet found grilling with electricity on a *parrilla* such as this to be quite effective in getting his point across," Walter explained as though they were walking through a museum. "I believe agents of your own black ops department employ something similar from time to time—unofficially of course. Crude but very effective."

Ross caught her breath. "You haven't asked me anything important."

Her eyes darted around the room, looking for an electrical outlet. The cell spun as she tried to make sense of what was about to happen.

"I have a small generator when the time comes," Agent Walter said, reading her mind. He reached inside the pocket of his suit jacket and produced a small syringe. It was white, with an orange cap like the ones used by diabetics for insulin. Ross turned her head as he brought it to wave under her nose. A tiny bit of amber fluid formed a drop at the end of the needle. She caught a whiff of vinegar.

Heroin.

Agent Walter sighed. "I made a little stop on Fourteenth Street on the way in to work today," he said. His face was close enough now that she could smell the odor of cheese on his breath. "Did you know dealers give their product brand names?"

Ross gagged.

"The stuff I brought you is called White House, as a matter of fact. Funny, eh? Amazing what ten dollars buys you these days. They say it's five percent pure. . . ."

Ross struggled in vain against the metal cuffs, wrenching a knee and jerking at her arms until she thought they would rip out of their sockets. The men stood back and let her thrash, faces impassive as if they were waiting for a car to finish filling up with fuel.

She sank against her restraints, her body sagging on the metal frame. "We both work for the same government. . . ."

Walter reached to touch her neck, stroking it tenderly, and then pressing a thumb against her flesh to get the vein to bulge.

"What do you want?" Ross sobbed, though she knew the answer all too well. It was only a matter of time before she gave in. Everyone did.

She felt a sharp prick of pain as Walter slid the needle into her neck.

He released his thumb. "It's time to relax, Virginia. You will find this part more pleasant than anything you could possibly imagine."

White-hot liquid coursed into her bloodstream, pooling, it seemed, behind her eyeballs. Tremors of euphoria flowed down her shoulders, shooting through her arms and pulsing in her hands. She was keenly aware of each individual toe, ringing like tiny bells. Her knees, her elbows, her ears, and even her hair crackled with static warmth.

There was a muffled sound of the cell door opening, then footsteps slapping the tile. Ross was vaguely aware of a new voice speaking in hushed tones.

"When?" she heard Walter say.

"They'll be here within the hour," the new voice said.

Ross gave a fleeting thought to opening her eyes, but decided it was just too much effort.

Agent Walter erupted in a flurry of violent curses, roaring at the newcomer.

"How long have you known about this?" he screamed. "Would it have killed you to get off your ass and tell me before I shot her up?"

Virginia Ross took a deep breath, feeling the cozy warmth course through her body, causing her belly to pulse as if she was in the passionate embrace of a lover. She realized she was naked and rough men stood over her, one of them screaming about something. She couldn't remember who he was, and found she no longer cared.

# Chapter 54

*Flight 105*

Quinn had no conventional weapons since he was on a commercial aircraft—but he didn't intend to work empty-handed. He'd watched an older gentleman a few rows ahead of him stow a wooden cane in the bin over his seat and asked Carly to take Natalie with her and borrow the cane. Waiting for them to return, he sat down on the leather sofa by Mattie and thought about what he'd do with her. It set his nerves on edge to even think of letting her out of his sight again, but bringing her with him while he walked up and down the aisles looking for a killer was not an option.

She'd seen him fight before, so that wouldn't be the worst of it. Fights rarely went as planned. He was fairly certain he'd be able to take gain control quickly, but in the close confines of the cabin, there were simply too many variables—especially if Mattie was just a few feet away.

Even if the digital-camera hack worked perfectly and he was able to find the killer splattered in blood, an accomplice could be seated nearby watching and waiting, unidentifiable until he started killing people. A little girl made for a ripe hostage. The killer might have a weapon. He'd certainly had one earlier and used it to great effect on the stairs. The entire plane was a lit fuse, with all the passengers on edge and unpredictable.

Grabbing someone in the tight quarters of an airplane added an enhanced level of danger. Movements were subtle in close-quarters battle and often could not be seen with the natural eye. They had to be felt. When it came to joining a fight, Quinn very literally went with the flow. There was no way of knowing what he'd have to do to win the fight and the thought of his little girl seeing that side of him again chilled him to the core.

"Got it," Carly said, bringing Quinn out of his thoughts when she and Natalie returned to the rear of the plane. She handed him the cane and three white plastic restraints airlines used on unruly passengers.

He passed the cane to Mattie while he fed one end through the other on each of the thick plastic cuffs so they formed large loops that he'd be able to zip tight quickly around a prisoner's wrists. He tucked the "loaded" restraints into his waistband.

Taking the cane back from Mattie, he held it in both hands and flexed it against his knee, testing it for strength. A simple wooden design with a shepherd's crook, it seemed plenty strong for his intentions. He removed the rubber grip on the bottom and picked up the digital camera.

He turned to Carly. "Do you still have that capacitor?"

"I do." She took it out of her pocket and passed it to him quickly, happy to get rid of it.

Quinn held it out toward Natalie on his open palm.

"I'd appreciate it if you'd look after my little girl for a few minutes. Anyone gets near her, scream your head off and jab them with the wax end of this. The wires will push through and give them a good shock. I'll be here before they're back on their feet."

Natalie took the improvised stun gun. Her eyes narrowed. Her lips pursed. "I'm a grandmother, Mr. Hackman. If anything happens to your daughter, it'll be because I'm already dead."

"Thank you," Quinn said, a measure calmer knowing that he was leaving Mattie with an honest human being. She'd made the only promise she was capable of keeping—not that she'd absolutely be able to keep Mattie safe, but that she would die trying.

The economy-class beverage carts were stored in the aft section of the second level, so Quinn decided they should start there. Carly pushed the cart ahead, moving up the right aisle as if to start the service in front. This drew the passengers' attention forward while giving Quinn a reason to move slowly, scanning as he walked. He held the improvised IR camera in his left hand, dragging his leg to feign a need for the cane, which he carried in his right.

Global had advertised this new seasonal flight from Anchorage to Moscow for months, so there were few vacant seats in any of the cabins. In another time, under less bloody circumstances, Quinn would have enjoyed the cosmopolitan makeup of the flight. Japanese, Korean, and Chinese made up a good portion of the passengers. Many of them would get off in Vladivostok to catch flights to their various countries that were just short hops away. There were Siberian Yupiks, cousins of the Eskimos of western Alaska; dark-faced Turkic peoples from central Asia; and of course, Americans visiting Russia and Russians returning home.

Quinn scanned with the camera as he walked, looking for evidence of the murder, but not allowing himself to get stuck on any particular stereotype of race or ethnicity. He could be looking at a Middle Eastern man reading a copy of the *Economist* in the seat to his left, while someone like the blue-eyed brunette to his right stabbed him in the neck with her pen. He'd earned several scars before he'd figured out that though there were certain indicators, all threats didn't present an evil image.

Danger did, however, have a feel—an aura that could be felt low in the gut. To the Chinese it was *zhijue—straight sense.* The Japanese called it *haragei* or the *art of the belly.* Quinn felt it before he'd reached mid cabin. He slowed his breathing, which, in turn, did the same to his heart rate. He popped his neck from side to side.

Even on a wide-body aircraft like the A380, economy seats were cramped. Elbows and arms spilled into the aisle, forcing Carly to plod along behind her cart, warning passengers to pull in their appendages as she went. Many of the passengers eyed Quinn as he limped by. An Eskimo man in the collar, beard, and long black robes of a Russian Orthodox priest gave him a quiet smile from his window seat. An attractive redhead to his left turned at his approach, eyeing him warily as if she didn't believe he needed the cane. If Quinn had had a sister, he was fairly certain she would have the same look in her eye. The redhead wore jeans and a sleeveless, blue wrap-around kimono top that exposed her well-muscled shoulders. The deep color of the blouse showed almost white in the camera viewfinder and was absent of any blood. Quinn continued to scan, feeling the woman stare at him as he passed.

A stocky man in the aisle seat on the right side of the plane stretched his arms just as Carly passed with her cart. Quinn could only see a portion of his head and one shoulder, but he had closely buzzed black hair and Asian features. Thick arms filled out the black leather sleeves of a designer jacket. White in the IR camera, the left shoulder was spotted with a spray of dark spots.

Moving forward, Quinn abandoned the limp and shoved the camera in the pocket of his jeans. He studied the passengers seated around the man in the leather jacket. An older woman sat in the window seat on the same row. Members of a girls' college volleyball team with matching jerseys took up the two rows behind him and most of the seats in the center rows to his left.

When he reached the row directly behind his target, Quinn saw the faint hint of a blood smear on the side of the man's neck—where he would have cradled Foulger's head while he cut his throat.

Carly was three rows ahead with the beverage cart, nearly to the center galley and bank of lavatories that divided the aft economy and mid-cabin business class. Though he'd warned her about it, Carly's curiosity got the better of her and she looked over her shoulder to check on Quinn's progress. Backward looks were contagious, and every passenger who happened to be watching—including the Asian man in the blood-spattered jacket—turned in their seats. What they saw was Quinn, holding the wooden cane like a club.

Quinn jumped forward, shoving the smooth crook of the cane between the man's forearm and seat back as he came up alongside. By lowering his center and pushing the cane upward, Quinn was able to graft the polished wood up past the man's elbow and against the armpit so it stuck toward the ceiling behind his neck. Using the stick as a lever and the armpit as a fulcrum, Quinn slapped the crook end forward with his right hand while he hauled back on the base, torqueing the killer's head down and sideways, slamming it against the back of the armrest on the seat in front of him with a dull thud. Quinn kept the man tied up as he rebounded off the seat, torqueing the man again as soon as he had room. He pulled up hard on the end of the cane, wanting to end the fight quickly, inflicting maximum damage to the shoulder that would tenderize the killer, but leave him well enough to question. Tied up with the cane and Quinn's arcing movement, the man was twisted out of his seat and onto the floor so his shoulders and chest were in the aisle and his legs trailed behind him, trapped between the seat rows.

The entire process took less than three seconds. By the time the killer's nose collided with the in-floor lighting tape, the panicked passengers surrounding him sprang, jumped, and stampeded out of their seats. They got away by any means they could, putting as much distance between themselves and the crazy man with the cane as possible.

Trapped next to the window, the elderly woman on the other side of the killer merely stomped over the top of his body, stepping on his back and head as she pushed her way into the aisle. The girls' volleyball team cleared out in all directions, screaming and shoving other passengers out of their way. Quinn looked up to see Carly being pushed over the top of her beverage cart in the panic. Juice cartons spilled. An ice bucket poured its contents onto the floor. Carly slid along on her belly, to disappear into the aisle on the other side, out of his view.

The killer struggled, but Quinn heaved up on the cane. He gambled that the man was Chinese and barked at him in Mandarin to stop moving. Chinese people were often startled to hear their language pouring so fluently from the mouth of a Caucasian, and he froze for a moment, trying to make sense of the situation.

Quinn kept steady pressure the cane while he pulled one of the plastic restraints from his waistband. Before he could get it cinched, something heavy crashed into the back of his head.

Quinn reeled at the impact, springing to his feet. He drove himself backwards into whoever had hit him as he fought off a wave of nausea. Fully upright now, he spun in mid aisle, the point of his elbow extended and looking for a target. It found one in the jaw of the redhead who'd been watching him earlier when he'd walked by.

Quinn was still stunned and his delivery was slow, allowing the woman to step back enough that his elbow slid off with little more damage than a slap. The woman's hands came up to cover her face like a boxer. Rather than regroup, Quinn stayed committed to his original spin, stepping into a furious left hook that caught the redhead in the temple, dropping her like a stone. She fell sideways across the now vacant seats in the middle rows. A hard plastic water bottle rolled up the aisle between them, water pouring from a crack that had very likely been caused when it had smashed into Quinn's skull.

Behind him, a shout rose up from Carly. The man in the leather jacket had regained his senses and now held the cane in both hands, high above his head like a sword. Before Quinn could move to close the distance, the attacker was slammed forward, struck hard in the back by Carly's rolling beverage cart.

The harried flight attendant blinked at Quinn, wide-eyed. Her face was wet with spilled coffee and juice. Once perfect blond hair was plastered to flushed cheeks.

Her shoulders shook so violently she had to hold on to the cart to keep her feet.

"You good?" she asked.

"I'm fine," Quinn said, zipping restraints around the wrists of the Chinese man and then the redhead. His vision was still hazy. Waves of nausea lingered in his gut. He wondered how many more blows to the head he could take before he started seeing double—or not seeing at all.

Pulling himself to his feet with a low groan, Quinn scanned the cowering passengers. They blinked up at him from their various hiding spots around the cabin. Some looked like they were deciding whether or not to rush him. Others turned half away, eyes down, hoping not to be noticed. While those around the fight had dispersed at the first signs of the trouble, many passengers from business class now crowded together at the bulkhead to see what the fuss was all about.

Quinn could see no one else that presented an immediate threat—for the moment anyway. The dozens of other Asian passengers, many of them families with young children, took a particular interest that Quinn had beaten up one of their own, but that was easy to understand.

He held up open hands to reassure them.

"You have probably heard," he said, catching his breath, "but there has been a murder on this airplane. I am a police officer. The captain has asked me to assist in arresting this man who we believe to be the killer."

Hearing Quinn's voice appeared to bring Carly's pulse down to a manageable level. "Please, ladies and gentlemen," she said. "Take your seats. We have everything under control now. Everything is fine."

She broke into a string of fluent Russian. Quinn assumed she was repeating herself for the Russian passengers. She switched back to English again as the passengers began to comply. "That's right," she said. "Go ahead and take your seats. Mr. Hackman is a law enforcement officer."

The redhead lifted her head and moaned. A white paper napkin from the floor was stuck to her forehead. "Wait a minute," she groaned. "You're a cop?"

She winced when Quinn took her upper arm and hauled her to her feet alongside the Chinese man in the leather jacket.

"I only ask," the redhead continued, "because I happen to be a cop too."

Quinn stopped. "Then why did you hit me?"

"Because, genius, you were beating the shit out of a passenger." She squinted trying to clear her vision. "Madonna Foss, federal air marshal. Reach into the front pocket of my jeans and you'll find my creds."

Quinn knew she was likely the real deal when she used the word *creds* instead of saying "identification." A city or state officer might say "My badge is in my pocket"; an NYPD cop would simply tell you he was "on the job"; but a fed would show you his or her creds.

The redhead bent at the waist a little to give Quinn space to retrieve the credentials from the pocket of her tight jeans. "Go ahead," she said. "Nothing in there that will cut you."

The Chinese man tried to yank away. Quinn gave him a hammer fist to the groin to calm him down. He sank to the armrest of the nearest seat, wheezing in pain. Quinn let him fall.

"These igmos," Madonna Foss said. "Always forgetting they're on an airplane with nowhere to run." She batted green eyes at Quinn. "You going to look at my creds or not? A girl can't wait all day for a man to dive into her pockets."

Quinn ran a hand over the outside of her jeans. A couple of near-death experiences had taught him to treat males and females the same way when it came to security pat-downs. Professor Foulger's throat had been cut, so he wasn't about to take any chances. Feeling nothing but the outline of a flat wallet, he reached in and retrieved it.

Her name was Madonna Foss and she was indeed a federal air marshal. Fire-red hair was cut just above the shoulders of her wraparound blouse. Though not a big woman, she was fit enough Quinn's head still pounded from the blow she'd given him with the water bottle.

Hands behind her back, she nodded at the credential case in Quinn's hands. "I'm not on duty," she said. "That's why the flight attendants didn't know I was on board. My fiancé is a Diplomatic Security agent at the US embassy in Moscow. I'm on my way over to see him."

"Yeah," Quinn said, smoothing the hair on the back of his head. "I wasn't on duty either."

"Listen," Foss said, raising an eyebrow. "I'm just as kinky as the next girl, but we're going to need some kind of safe word if you plan to leave me trussed up like this much longer."

"Not sure we're set up to cut them off," Quinn said, only half joking. "But we'll see what they have in their kit. Come on, let's get this guy to the back so I can ask him a few questions."

He grabbed the Asian thug by the collar of his leather jacket and hauled him to his feet again. Barking in dismissive Chinese, Quinn shoved him toward the rear of the airplane.

Agent Foss peered at Quinn through narrow eyes. "What kind of cop did you say you are?"

"The kind who's pretty good at getting answers from guys like this."

# Chapter 55

Quinn yanked the curtain shut as he dragged his prisoner past the bulkhead that separated the aft section of the aircraft from the view of the rearmost row of seats. The passengers would be able to hear, but that could not be helped. Once at the base of the stairs, he shoved the man in the black jacket on the floor, facedown, and slipped another set of plastic restraints around his ankles. Even metal cuffs were temporary restraints at best. Quinn had escaped from enough of the plastic ones never to trust a single set of any kind.

A quick pat-down revealed a passport with the name Gao Jianguo of the People's Republic of China. He was clean-shaven, with black hair that was buzzed short. Not a tall man, he had thick muscles, with the scarred hands of someone accustomed to physical labor.

Quinn asked a series of rudimentary questions about where he was from, his destination, and if he had any confederates on board. The twitches of Gao's face showed he understood the questions. He would not speak a word.

Carly came back with a small set of clippers from the emergency supplies closet. The plastic cutters had hidden blades that weren't exposed so they were worthless for anything but cutting plastic cuffs.

Mattie stood on the other side of the plane with Natalie, giving her some distance if not actual separation from the events that were unfolding.

Quinn checked the Aquaracer on his wrist. It had been nearly forty-five minutes since the pilot had turned the plane around. Whatever this guy was up to, it would be happening soon.

Free from the restraints, Madonna Foss rubbed her wrists and worked her jaw back and forth.

Quinn noticed her left shoulder drooped like a broken wing.

"Is it bad?"

She shook her head. "Not sure. I hit the armrest pretty hard when you popped me." She opened and closed her hand, but grimaced when she tried to raise her arm. "Yeah," she said. "That makes me want to puke. It's broken, but I'll be fine until we land."

"Good to hear," Quinn said. "Because I'm going to need your help. There is no way this is the only bad guy on board. The killing was random, but so professional it has to be some sort of diversion."

"Makes sense." Foss nodded. "A murder on board would make the pilot divert to the nearest US airport that was safe and secure. In this case that means turning around and heading back to Alaska."

"Keeping us over water," Quinn said, finishing her thought.

"You think it's a bomb," Foss said.

"Good possibility," Quinn said. "But I'd keep that to myself."

"No kidding," Foss said, her air marshal training kicking in. "I need to discuss this with the captain."

"Phone's on the wall," Quinn said. "But I'm about to

start questioning this guy. If, as we suspect, he has compatriots on the plane, I need someone to keep eyes on my daughter while I'm otherwise engaged."

"Look," Foss said, "I can help with the interrogation, but I'm not a babysitter."

"You're hurt," Quinn said. "But you seem to be good at what you do. I don't count protecting my daughter as babysitting."

"I'm not too hurt to help you," Foss said.

Quinn lowered his voice so Mattie and the others couldn't hear. "We don't have much time," he said. "Who knows how many others there are out there or what they plan to do. I don't want my daughter out there with some unknown killer—but I can't have her watching me work either."

Foss took a deep breath. "Okay," she said. "But I'm pretty sure you broke my arm so you'd have someone to watch your kid."

"I wish I could think that far ahead," Quinn said. He turned to Carly. "I need you and Natalie to go get me the EMK."

"My arm isn't that bad," Foss said. "Certainly nothing in the enhanced medical kit that would do me any good."

"It's not for you," Quinn said. He shot a look at the prisoner.

Carly's eyes fell on Mattie. Her face suddenly went slack. Quinn felt her tense beside him. "Can I talk to you and your daughter a second?" she said.

"You okay?" Natalie said, noticing her friend's sudden change in mood.

"I'm fine," Carly said, still looking down. "I just need to talk to Mr. Hackman about something. Would you mind grabbing the kit?"

Quinn followed her gaze down to the book in Mattie's lap. It was open to the title page where she'd written her name in beautiful cursive.

*Madeline Irene Quinn.*

Natalie shrugged and went to retrieve the EMK while Carly followed Quinn to the other side of the plane, away from Foss and Mattie.

Carly looked him straight in the eye. "I can't handle being lied to right now," she said. "Any other time and I'd think, oh, you and her mom are divorced, and that's why her name is different . . . but something awful is happening on this airplane and I need to know who I can trust."

"You can trust me," Quinn said—bold words, he thought, for a man living a lie.

Carly folded her arms across her chest and set her jaw. One part *I'm-fragile*, nine parts *don't-screw-with-me*, it was a particular look he'd seen on Kim too many times. "Is her name Mattie Hackman?"

"No."

"Really?" Carly let her arms drop, looking surprised at his lack of denial. "What is it then?"

"Mattie Quinn."

"But you *are* John Hackman?"

"Jericho Quinn," he said.

"But wha—"

Mattie padded up behind them. She looked back and forth to make sure no one else, including Madonna Foss could hear. "Remember when Mom was in the hospital after she got shot and we were all in her room?" she said.

Quinn nodded, looking at an astonished Carly, and then back at his little girl. He had no idea what she was about to say.

"She told me a secret," Mattie said. She had tears in her eyes, but was remarkably composed.

"I remember," Quinn said.

Mattie rolled her lips, rocking back and forth on her heels. She looked so much like Kim. "She said we should give you a break. You're doing the best that you can."

"Oh, sweetie," he said.

She hugged his leg.

Carly closed her eyes. "Are you even a cop?"

"I'm exactly what I said I am," Quinn said. He ran a hand over the top of Mattie's hair, and then gathered her up in his arms. She put her arms around his neck and hugged him until she shook. "Just traveling under an assumed name."

"With your daughter?"

"Long story," Quinn said.

"When this is all over," Carly said, "will you tell it to me?"

"Honestly . . ." Quinn gave her a tight smile. "Probably not." He carried Mattie back over to Foss and buckled her in with her book, giving her another kiss on top of the head.

"I never should have gotten into this," Carly said when they'd walked back to the other side of the plane.

"Asking me to help?" Quinn said, feeling a twinge of guilt for the lies.

Carly shook her head. "No, being a flight attendant. I'm scared to death of flying."

"That is a thing," Quinn said.

"Do you remember the shoe picture?" Carly asked, gazing into space in a thousand-yard stare.

Quinn shook his head. "The what?"

She took a ragged breath, trying to gain control of herself. "From the first time I saw it in training, I've had nightmares about the picture of all the shoes from KAL 007."

Quinn put a hand on her shoulder. Now he knew what she was talking about. He'd been a small boy in 1983 when a Korean Air 747 from New York via Anchorage had mistakenly wandered into prohibited Soviet airspace while en route to Seoul. A Soviet SU 15 "Flagon" fighter was dispatched when the aircraft crossed the Kamchatka Peninsula, shooting it down over the Sea of Japan. All 269 passengers were lost. The Soviets denied involvement at first, but eventually turned over items that were found floating at the crash site. A photograph of dozens of shoes—sneakers, loafers, and pumps of all different sizes, piled on top of a plastic bag—had appeared in *LIFE Magazine*. Several of the victims' families recognized them as belonging to their loved ones. Quinn had a distinct memory of his mother holding the magazine and crying—and his father's angry words at the Russians over the incident.

Carly looked at her feet. "I don't want my husband to find a photograph of my red Danskos in some magazine. . . ."

"We're going to get through this," he said, but wondered if it was just another lie. He couldn't help himself and looked across at Mattie's shoes.


Every commercial airliner is required to carry not only a first aid kit containing bandages, aspirin, and other basic supplies, but an enhanced medical kit as well. These EMKs contained the equipment that trained medical personnel from EMTs to thoracic surgeons would be able to use to treat an emergency while at altitude. There was nitroglycerin for heart issues, scopolamine patches and Zofran for acute nausea, epinephrine for shock, and several medications for pain. Quinn opened the soft duffel case and looked through the items inside until he found the diazepam.

It was common knowledge that a physician on American Flight 63 had dosed Richard Reid with a shot of Valium from just such a kit after Reid attempted to ignite a bomb in his shoe on the Paris to Miami flight. His attorneys argued that the drug was what caused him to confess to the FBI when they'd landed in Boston.

Quinn was counting on it. He peeled the backing off two scopolamine patches and stuck them under each of Gao's ears for good measure, leaving him facedown on the carpet.

"Can you watch him for a minute?" he said to Foss.

"Happy to," she said, moving to take a position at the prisoner's head so she'd be able to stop him if the need arose.

Quinn took Mattie aside, and knelt down beside her next to the curtain on the opposite aisle. He was grateful to be on an aircraft large enough to get her away from his interrogation.

"Daddy," she said. "Have you ever been really scared and really excited at the same time?"

He kissed her on top of the head. "Many, many times, Sweet Pea."

"That's how I feel right now," she said. "I don't think Mom would like this very much."

"I expect not," Quinn said.

"Did he murder the man on the stairs?" Mattie asked.

"It looks that way."

"Okay." She nodded, mulling this over. Since she'd been old enough to talk, Mattie had been one to ruminate deeply on things. "I wish I could help you."

"Someday," Quinn said, thinking of how Kim would kill him if she knew about this conversation. "You're a tough kid. I'm going to have you sit with Agent Foss. This is important. Okay?"

Quinn gave his little girl another quick kiss and left her in the care of a woman he'd punched in the face exactly nine minutes before. The only thing that had kept him alive over the last few years was his ability to compartmentalize thoughts about his family when things heated up on a mission. That was going to be doubly difficult with Mattie sitting behind a curtain fifteen feet away. Well-adjusted as she was, it could not be healthy for a seven-year-old to hear her father do what Quinn was about to do.

Quinn drew twenty CCs of Valium into a syringe, and then held it sideways in his teeth while he hauled Gao to his feet and slammed him back on the bottom steps of the stairs. A few feet above, Professor Foulger's body lay ghostly pale in the pool of drying blood.

Gao groaned in pain as his tailbone impacted the hard wooden step. Quinn used the opportunity to jab the needle into the man's belly and inject him with all twenty CCs.

"What was that?" Gao said, eyes wide now. It was the first time he'd spoken.

"Something to make you feel a little better," Quinn said in Mandarin. "Let's get started."

"Your Chinese is remarkable," Gao said, honestly impressed.

"What is your name?" Quinn asked, peering over the top of Gao's open passport.

"You know my name," Gao said. His speech began to slur just moments after the injection. The fire of contempt bled from drooping eyes as the powerful sedative took control of his body.

Quinn had used scopolamine combined with other drugs before during interrogations. He wasn't sure how it would react with Valium in the long term—but the mutilated body of Foulger and the fear in his daughter's eyes made it hard for him to care.

"To be honest with you," Quinn said, sitting beside Gao on the stairs, as if they were old friends, "I'm accustomed to hurting people to get information. But I thought we might try something different here."

Gao's head lolled. He caught himself, as if startled out of a dream. He gazed at Quinn, trying to focus.

"Who are you?"

Quinn patted him on the knee. "I'm wondering that about you," he said. "Where are you from, Gao Jianguo?"

"Shanghai," Gao said, nodding off again.

Quinn gave the tender flesh on the inside of the man's thigh a sharp pinch to get his attention.

"I am familiar with Shanghai," Quinn said. "What part?"

Gao glared at him, blinking stupidly. Drool poured from the corner of his mouth.

"You know what I think?" Quinn chuckled like they were compatriots talking over a drink. "I think your accent tells me you're from the northwest. Xinjiang maybe."

Gao gave a silly smile, but held his tongue.

"They have good food in Xinjiang," Quinn said. "*Plov, suoman, pamirdin* . . . I miss good *pamirdin*. . . ." His voice trailed off. *Pamirdin* were baked meat pies with lamb, carrot, and onion—a popular halal dish. "I would walk across the desert to Kashgar if I could get good *pamirdin*."

Gao licked his lips. *"Pamirdin,"* he said.

Quinn rested his hands on his knees, letting his gaze slide over the prisoner.

"So," he said, "you're not from Shanghai after all?"

Gao shook his head. "Not really."

"I notice a little tan line on your forehead," Quinn said. "Like you might have if you wore a Hui hat. . . ."

"So what if I do?" Gao frowned. "Do you have something against Islam?"

"Not at all," Quinn said. "There are plenty of Hui Chinese who have contributed much to the world." He stooped lower to look Gao in the eye. "But you are not one of those Hui."

"I think you pick on me because I am a Muslim," he said.

"I'm picking on you because you're covered in the blood of the man whose throat you cut," Quinn spat. He softened immediately, keeping the drug-addled man off balance. "Anyway, it doesn't matter." There was no time for a lengthy interrogation—so he guessed. "We have located the bomb. You may go ahead and have a rest."

"You joke," Gao said. His eyes shifted to the base of the stairs, trying to lean out so he could see what might be happening. Facial tics, the dilation of his pupils— known as micro expressions—told Quinn he was on to something real. The Valium suppressed his emotions, but it did not yet mask them. Gao chewed on his tongue as if trying to hold back the words. "You have found nothing."

"Yes," Quinn said, giving a satisfied nod. "We have. We have your partners who helped you kill the man on the stairs. It is over, my friend."

"It is my fault we have failed," Gao sighed. He threw back his head. A tear ran down his cheek. "May Allah forgive my clumsy hands. . . ."

Quinn pinched the man's thigh again, harder this

time, pulling a chunk of skin and giving it a sharp twist before letting it snap back into place. It brought on a yowl of pain, but focused the man a little too much.

He looked up suddenly, regaining what sense he had. "You know nothing."

"I know you are not from Shanghai." Quinn shrugged.

The key to a successful interrogation often lay as much in the things that were not said as much as the things that were. One moment Gao's shoulders slumped in defeat, the next they began to shake. Turning his head slowly so he could look Quinn in the eye, he loosed a cackling laugh.

Quinn stood up, thinking through what to do next. He considered administering one of the epinephrine pens to bring Gao out of his stupor and question him under the added anxiety. The truth was there was no time to do this the right way—especially with Mattie sitting so close.

Carly and Natalie appeared at the bottom of the stairs. Carly's neck was blotchy and red from nerves. Even the normally unflappable Natalie was mussed as if she'd been in a scuffle, her face drawn and stricken as if she'd seen a ghost.

Quinn stepped away just enough to keep an eye on Gao and spare them another sight of the dead body.

"What is it?" Quinn's first thought was of Mattie's safety.

"We found something you need to see," Carly said.

"Does it look like a bomb?" Quinn said, hope rising. If they'd found it, they could try to disarm it—or at least put it in a spot that would do the least damage to the aircraft.

Natalie took a step back at the word. "A bomb?" she said. "No . . . there's been another murder . . . two more murders."

"A woman and the attendant from the coffee station," Carly said. "Somebody killed them both. Juanita found their bodies down in the crew quarters below first class."

Quinn motioned Carly across the lounge, farther from Mattie. He kept his voice at a whisper. "Describe the woman to me."

Carly grimaced. "Juanita came up the stairs like she'd seen . . . well, two dead bodies. None of us went down there. We just came to get you."

Madonna Foss was sweating from the pain in her broken arm, but she was still coherent and looked like she wanted to punch Quinn in the face. That was good. He needed her mad and ready to fight if she was to protect his daughter. "I need to go check up front," he said. "You all right here for a minute?"

"We'll be fine." Foss put on a tight smile. "Mattie will look after me."

"I'll stay back too," Natalie said. "I still have the stun gun if I need it."

Quinn nodded. It killed him to leave his daughter, but if he didn't stop whatever was going on up front, it wouldn't matter who stayed back to watch her.

# Chapter 56

A balding flight attendant in his mid-forties named Andre stood guard outside the door to the crew rest quarters.

"Are you the one that found the body?" Quinn said.

"No, sir," Andre said. "Juanita found him. She's the senior flight attendant."

Before Quinn could ask anything else, the top of Juanita's head came up the ladder. Ebony eyes flashed at Quinn, daring him to get in her way. She'd been affected by the dead bodies, and though on edge, did not appear to be afraid. There was a fierceness about her that made Quinn wonder if she was afraid of anything.

"Looks like Paxton was beaten to death," she said. "The woman was strangled with some kind of cord." Hauling herself up the ladder with one hand, she passed what looked like a coffee grinder to Quinn with the other.

Quinn passed it to Carly and stepped back, helping the other flight attendant onto the deck.

"No one else is down there?" he asked.

Juanita shook her head. "Nope," she said. "Just poor

Paxton and the Chinese woman." She brushed a lock of hair out of her eyes.

"Wait," Quinn said. "The dead woman is Chinese?"

"I think so," Juanita said. "I couldn't find any ID, but that's what I'd guess. I'll keep watch if you want to go down and have a look."

Carly held up the coffee grinder. "What's this for?"

"That's the weird part," Juanita said. "Somebody plugged it in by one of the bunks. Looks like they used pillows to muffle the noise."

Quinn opened the grinder and ran a finger around the sides. It came back covered in silver gray dust.

Carly looked at his finger. "What the heck is that?"

"Aluminum," he said.

Juanita stepped away from the door leading to the crew quarters. "You want to go down and check it out?"

"No need," Quinn said. A feeling of dread washed over him. He had to get back to Mattie. "I know what's happening."

# Chapter 57

*The White House*

Baka, the derisive Japanese word for idiot, was nowhere near strong enough to convey Ran's contempt for Hartman Drake. She stood at the back of the cramped White House pressroom and watched as the president droned on and on about *his* administration and what *he* was doing to counter growing Chinese nationalism and a legion of other threats to the United States. As if this buffoon, this mindless lothario, could do anything but chase women and admire himself in the mirror.

Lee McKeon flanked the president, a few steps to the left, hands crossed at his stomach. He was taller than Drake by half a foot, slender—almost to the point of bony—where the President was husky and, Ran knew, McKeon was brilliant where the other man was overwhelmingly dim.

Few knew the truth, but McKeon might as well have had his hand up the back of the President's shirt, controlling him like a ventriloquist's dummy. But that was the thing about McKeon—he was happy to be in the shadows, working as the power behind the throne.

She'd asked him once, while he was still the governor of Oregon, if he did not wish to be the president. "Why waste time being the emperor?" he'd said. "When I can be the shogun?"

It was nothing short of amazing how he handled the fool—and Ran was not easily amazed. Though Drake strutted around as if he'd decided on his own to release the Uyghur terrorists in Guantanamo Bay to Pakistan where they could more easily escape and wreak more havoc against China, the idea had sprung from McKeon's fertile mind. It was all part of his larger plan to push America and China into a devastating nuclear war.

The Chairman of the Joint Chiefs, all his cabinet members, even close members of his West Wing staff, believed Drake was running the show. McKeon wanted it that way. He moved by suggestion and sheer force of will, rarely giving anyone more than a nod, or a word or two to nudge them in the right direction.

Drake was too shortsighted to see the larger picture. He wanted to open borders, allow members of al Qaeda, Lashkar e Taiba, and a dozen other terrorist organizations to slip through and put their little bombs in Disneyland and Times Square. But Lee McKeon was a big thinker. He'd inherited a sense of purpose and destiny from his father that the other man would never comprehend.

Under his quiet guidance, President Drake would chip away at the Chinese economy, throw the full weight of his support behind Japan and the disputed Senkaku Islands. He would start issuing a travel visa to the president of Taiwan and treat him like a head of state.

A cold war stalemate only worked if the US had someone at the helm who was willing to pull the trigger but hesitant to do so. A calculated overreaction, demanded by the American people for supposed atrocities by the Chinese government—like the bombing of an American airliner—would set off a chain reaction that would not stop until it was too late.

Lee McKeon foresaw how it would happen, and Ran had no reason to doubt him.

Chinese cyber experts would do their best to interrupt air defense systems. Ballistic missiles would be sent first, not to land- or sea-based targets, but to space, to destroy communication and military navigational satellites. The next barrage of missiles would rain down on American bases in Japan and South Korea. Chinese nuclear submarines would creep in close enough to fire dozens of Giant Wave nuclear missiles at cities along the west coast of the United States, while ICBMs arced over the North Pole toward New York, Baltimore, and Washington.

Of course, the US would not stand idly by. Theirs was the most potent and deadly air and sea war machine in the world. They would eventually "win," but it would prove a Pyrrhic victory. Like the great empires of Persia, Rome, Babylon, and Assyria, America was unbeatable—and like all the others she would fall. When she did, Lee McKeon would be there to stomp on her dying neck.

There was something about him, about his vision, that hypnotized Ran. He made her feel like a small child, full of wonder and amazement—the way her father had done, so many years ago when he was teaching her to kill.

She watched as President Drake began to take questions from the media and imagined the time when she could use those skills on him.

# Chapter 58

*Flight 105*

Tang steadied himself in the mid cabin lavatory, sifting the ground aluminum powder through the espresso sieve to remove the larger bits of foil. Rather than risk detection by staying in the crew quarters too long, he'd decided to finish the process in the lavatory.

He held up a sandwich bag containing nearly five tablespoons of the silver powder. Ma Zhen had assured him that would be more than enough, but still, he worried. Their device was so small for such a large aircraft. He agonized over the thought of merely damaging the plane and rotting in American jail where officious men would order him around all day. He might as well be back in China if that happened.

Crippling waves of doubt pressed him down, making it difficult to breathe. Hu had seen a man locate Gao in his seat as if it was known that he was the killer. This fact made Tang wonder if there were cameras on board. And if there were cameras, they might have noticed patterns in movement by now. In any case, there was some kind of policeman on board, possibly an air marshal. The way Hu described him, Tang was certain it was the *guizi* child's father. That made sense. He'd had the predatory look of someone who liked to be in charge.

Tang leaned against the counter, clutching the precious bag of metal in his fist as he stared into the mirror. Bloodshot, stricken eyes looked back at him—eyes that had seen death and knew there was nothing but more of the same in his future. There was no escape when he closed them, only the vision of his wife, strangled at the hand of another while he did nothing to stop it. Tang told himself it was for her own good, to stop her suffering, end her struggle—her jihad. But that did not matter now. Reasons were nothing to a bullet in a gun. He sniffed, steeling himself for what lay ahead, and pushed open the door.

Flight attendants seemed to be everywhere when he came out of the lavatory. He'd washed his face and left it damp so it looked like he'd been sick. A balding man met him mid-aisle and gave him an up-and-down look.

"Where are you seated, sir?" the attendant asked.

"Up front," Tang said. He let his voice tremble slightly. "Is something wrong? I heard there was a murder."

"We're taking care of it," the attendant said. "Return to your seat and stay there."

Tang nodded meekly, pressing past the much larger man. Ma Zhen had taken Lin's seat. It was only right. He was the most righteous, the most zealous. But more than that, he understood how the bomb worked. Now that Lin was gone, he should be the one to detonate it. Tang and Hu would act as guards to make certain he was not stopped.

Another flight attendant passed—this one shorter with dark, intrusive eyes. She moved quickly, counting heads and comparing them to a list in her hand. Not being Chinese, she wasn't likely to know if Lin was a masculine or feminine name. Tang waited until she hustled by, and then passed Ma Zhen the Baggie of aluminum powder.

Tang leaned forward in his seat, resting his head in his hands. They were so close . . . so incredibly close. He had to succeed now, for the sake of his wife, for the sake of their children. He had never been much of a praying man, but he listened to Ma Zhen's whispered prayer and found solace in that.

The bomb was brilliant in that it was so rudimentary. In theory, it was much too small to do much more than punch a small hole through the skin of an aircraft as large as the Airbus. But that was the beauty of it. A small hole would be large enough for his needs.

"Your wife destroyed the detonator," Ma said, nodding to the open backpack on the floor.

Tang's jaw dropped. "What?"

"Don't worry, my brother," Ma said. "I have another. I would never trust the success of this mission to a single point of failure. I must make one more trip to the lavatory." He held a flask discreetly so other passengers couldn't see it. He needed to mix the aluminum powder with the PETN and then fill the flasks with water—but that would take no time at all.

Tang craned his head around to look toward the back of the plane. All the flight attendants were still moving backwards, focused on their lists.

"Go now," he said. "I'll let Hu know to do his part."

Ma took a deep breath, his normal frown perking slightly. "In five minutes' time, our pain will be over," he said. "And I will see you in Paradise, Allah willing."

"Yes," Tang said. "Allah willing." But he could only think of getting to the back so he could watch the *guizi* child suffer the fate of his wife.

# Chapter 59

Quinn stopped at the aft lounge just long enough to make certain Mattie was safe before contacting the captain on the interphone. He explained the ground aluminum powder and its probable use in an explosive device, but went into less detail about the murders since he'd not seen them himself.

Listening in on the conversation with the captain, Gao began to laugh hysterically when Quinn mentioned that one of the victims was an Asian woman, likely Chinese. Half the passengers were of Asian ethnicity so it was hardly standout news.

"Two murders," Gao said in Mandarin, though he obviously understood English. "Two dead . . . Double Happiness . . ."

Quinn's mouth went dry when he heard the words. He dropped the phone, letting it swing from the cord as he wheeled and grabbed the cackling man by the collar. "What did you say?"

"Double Happiness," Gao said, quieter now but still grinning. His big head wagged stupidly back and forth as he spoke. "Lin is dead. I think double happiness is no happiness at all."

Quinn shoved Gao backwards, letting him fall against the stairs, and ran to fling open the curtain where Mattie sat with Madonna Foss. He knelt beside his daughter.

Gao's bellowing had been easy enough to hear. Quinn hoped the slurred Mandarin had been more difficult for Mattie to understand. The look on her face said he hadn't been that lucky.

"Is Lin all right?" Mattie said. "I heard that man say 'double happiness.' That's what I drew on the card I made for her. He said the word *dead*. Is she really dead?"

Quinn took her by the shoulders with both hands. "I don't know, sweetheart. What seat is she sitting in?"

Mattie closed her eyes, trying to remember. "It's upstairs, at the front. I remember she was two rows up from the bathrooms by the window on that side of the plane." She pointed to the left.

"Two forward of the lavatories and galley . . . That would be 12A," Carly said. "Business class."

Madonna Foss groaned. "That's near one of the emergency exits," she said. "Perfect place for a you know what."

"I already know you're talking about a bomb," Mattie said, shaking her head as if she had no time for secrets. "Really, Dad, do you think my friend is dead?"

"I don't know, sweetheart," Quinn said. "A Chinese woman has been killed, but we're not sure it's her." Blunt honesty had always been the best policy with Mattie. He nodded toward the handset. "Carly, can you get someone up front to take a look at 12A? Tell them not to make contact. Just see if anyone is sitting there."

Carly used the interphone to page Andre in the upper-deck business class and spoke with him for a short moment.

The captain's voice came across the loudspeaker.

"Ladies and gentlemen," he said. "We're approaching some extremely rough air. Please take your seats."

Handset to her ear, Carly's face grew pale as she listened to Andre report back.

"There's an Asian man sitting in 12A," she said. "And another two that refuse to take their seats."

"Refuse?" Quinn said. "Are they arguing?"

"Ignoring." Carly nodded. "According to Andre, one just ran down the front stairs."

That made sense, Quinn thought. Put the bomber in the middle while they had two men guard both sets of stairs on either side of him. "Tell Andre and whoever else is up there the bomb is probably in 12A. I'll be right there."

Quinn kissed Mattie on the top of her head, taking a short moment to smell her hair before he looked up at Foss. "Can you keep watching her for a few more minutes?"

"Goes without saying," the air marshal said.

Natalie stood, giving Quinn an uncharacteristic hug. Her perfume reminded him of his mother. "We'll take care of her."

"Thank you," Quinn said. He gave his daughter one last kiss on the head, wondering if he'd ever see her again.

Natalie pulled Carly to her, whispering something in her ear.

"Sit tight, sweetie," Quinn said to his daughter.

"Take the back stairs," Carly said. "It's quicker."

"I would," Quinn said. "But I need to grab something from my seat on the way."

# Chapter 60

Tang was standing just aft of the forward galley when Ma Zhen came out of the lavatory. He couldn't see the small plastic flasks full of water and explosive, but knew the device was ready from the look of relief on Ma's face. The men nodded, each dropping their shoulders in a half bow of respect and resignation. Then Ma disappeared behind the forward galley curtain toward what had once been Lin's seat.

Tang looked toward the back of the plane, watching for the American girl's father. Hu had already gone down the front stairs and was sweeping backwards on the main deck. They only had minutes left, but between the two of them, Ma would be protected.

"Hey," a woman wearing an Ohio State sweatshirt said. "Why aren't you in your seat?" Her voice held the suspicious edge of a mother with teenagers.

"Very dangerous man on board," Tang said, keeping up the image of frightened passenger for a few moments longer. "Crew say he come from there." He pointed toward the tail.

A burly man with a beard craned his neck to look behind him, and then stood. "I'm not going to sit around while someone is killing people on this plane," he said.

"Me neither." Another man, across the aisle and two rows back, stood as well. "What does he look like?"

A moment later, Tang had a group of six men who were spoiling for a fight. He described Quinn as best he could remember and started toward the back, leading his posse. He didn't have much time to make it to the *guizi* girl. Ma would detonate the device as soon as he attached the detonator—two minutes away at the most. The angry mob gave him credibility with the other passengers as he strode down the aisle. The irony of it all made him smile for the first time in months.

# Chapter 61

*Maryland*

Bowen ended the call with a frantic Joey Benavides and stuffed the cell phone back in his pocket. They were parked in the shadows on a side road off Rockville Pike, a block from the west side of Walter Reed Military Medical Center.

Bowen had never been much of a worrier, but sitting in a stolen truck with a member of a conspiracy to overthrow the president and now bent on breaking a federal prisoner out of custody ranked right up there with the activities that had caused his hair to go prematurely gray in the first place.

It was warm out, humid in the DC way that made clothes stick to skin and the odor of the last ten passengers rise up from the upholstery of vehicles left shut up too long in the sun. The concrete truck smelled like pastrami, overripe bananas, and half a can of Axe deodorant.

Bowen wore a short-sleeve sports shirt, plaid so it broke up the imprint of his Glock, unbuttoned and open over a black T-shirt. He'd left his ballistic vest in his Charger, which was still parked back at the strip mall, but consoled himself that getting shot was about to be the least of his worries.

"They're taking her to a ship anchored off Bloodsworth Island," Bowen said. "Some kind of old Navy gunnery range out in the Chesapeake."

"*Cocshons!*" Thibodaux pounded his fist on the steering wheel. "Don't tell me they're moving her by air." He had the Marshals Service short shotgun from Bowen's G-car between his knees, muzzle pointed toward the floor.

Bowen shook his head. "Not until they get her to Annapolis. You were right. Joey said they couldn't get a chopper here before General Hewn shows up, so they're taking her out by van. He says they're gearing up now to leave in fifteen minutes, give or take. They're running a lead and a follow. Ross will be in the middle, in a dark blue Suburban with blackout windows."

"Good deal," Thibodaux said, rolling his shoulders as he visibly relaxed a notch.

"So," Bowen said, "You said we have some kind of secret weapon. I get the basics of this plan, but now would be a good time to fill me in on the little details—before Joey calls back."

"We're gonna keep this simple. All gross motor skill stuff—"

A flatbed truck pulled up to park directly behind them, causing Thibodaux to stop in mid-sentence. Ronnie Garcia was behind the wheel. She jumped out as soon as she'd stopped and approached Bowen's window. A pimply kid Bowen hadn't seen before got out of the passenger side and came up behind her. He wore black-framed glasses the military called "Birth Control Goggles" for their propensity to chase away the opposite sex. He smiled meekly at Bowen and flinched a little when he saw Thibodaux, like a puppy afraid of being smacked.

"Staff Sergeant Guttman's a friendly," Ronnie said, introducing the kid. "He's helping us out with some of his tech."

Bowen couldn't help but smile when he saw the sultry Cuban. She wore faded jeans and a loose T-shirt that presumably covered a pistol. A Washington Nationals ball cap kept her hair pulled back out of her eyes.

"Jacques was just going over the plan again," Bowen said. "Our guy's going to call back with specifics of the move. We have about ten minutes."

Thibodaux followed a soccer mom with his good eye as she rolled by in a shiny minivan. He turned back to the others when she made the corner. "I was just telling the new guy that we're not going to get too intricate. Things will get dicey for a minute, but that's fine. We have to go fast for this to work. Staff Sergeant Guttman will put his bird in the air as soon as we get the call—"

"Bird?" Bowen said.

"Specifically a Schiebel S-100 Camcopter drone," Guttman said, pushing up his glasses. He was obviously proud of what Garcia had called his "tech." "She can fly over a hundred knots or hover in the trees until we need her. She's got a small Starepod on her nose so I can see what she's seeing on my iPad. Each of two hard points is equipped with a single LMM."

"'Lightweight Multirole Missile,'" Garcia offered as if she was used to translating military geek.

"Figured that," Bowen said. He'd seen his share of chopper-fired missiles.

Thibodaux took back control of the briefing.

"Guttman will work the drone from the passenger seat of your Charger. He'll take out any lead and follow cars with the LMMs. I'll pit the Suburban with Ross inside and pinch it into the curb. We put the smack on everyone inside that isn't Ross. You and Garcia get her the hell out of there in your G-ride."

"What if I get stopped?" Bowen asked.

"I'll be behind you in the concrete truck." Thibodaux shrugged. "But you're a damned United States marshal. Wave your badge and say, 'These aren't the droids you're lookin' for.'"

"Sounds like you have this all worked out," Bowen said. "Except for glossing over the part where we have a bloody firefight with the guys in the prisoner van."

"You forgot about our secret weapon." Thibodaux grinned. He seemed to thrive under the tension of impending battle.

"You said the drone only has two missiles," Bowen said. "What's its function with an assault on the prisoner vehicle after it's taken out the lead and the follow?"

Thibodaux shot a glance at Garcia. Both smiled broadly as a red Ducati motorcycle turned off the Rockville Pike and growled up next to them. A compactly built woman in jeans and a white leather jacket dropped the side stand and swung a leg off the bike.

"That drone ain't our secret weapon, son," Thibodaux said. "Not by a long shot."

Standing alongside her Ducati, the rider removed her helmet, giving her head a shake to free jet-black hair. Bowen recognized the woman immediately as Jericho Quinn's Japanese friend and teacher, Emiko Miyagi.

# Chapter 62

*Flight 105*

Captain Rob Szymanski weighed the risks of a possible explosive decompression at 40,000 feet versus keeping the altitude needed to make it to the only piece of rock between him and the western coast of Alaska if the bomb damaged an engine. He split the difference and set the bug on the autopilot to Flight Level 210 or 21,000 feet. Without turning into a lawn dart and frightening the passengers, a maximum rate of descent would get them there in a little over three minutes. The A380 was the quietest bird he'd ever flown, and being well in front of the engines, the cockpit was eerily silent but for the buzz of the electronics array and the occasional click of a keyboard.

First Officer Mick Bott sat in the right seat going over emergency procedures in a three-ring binder in his lap. A machinelike focus and bottomless levels of energy had earned him the call sign *McBott* as an F18 Hornet jockey in the Navy. The name had stuck and followed him into civilian life.

The captain looked out the side window, seeing miles

and miles of nothing in varying shades of blue. "What's our distance to Dutch Harbor?"

McBott looked up from his manual to consult the navigational display on the console of screens and buttons in front of him. "Two-seven-two miles southeast," he said. "Half an hour at this speed. Next closest is St. Paul Island at a hundred and sixty miles to our east. Neither runway is set up for heavy metal this big. I show Unalaska/Dutch Harbor at forty-one-hundred feet. St. Paul Island better at sixty-five-hundred, but still way too short."

Szymanski forced a grin. Over his thirty years of flying, he'd found smiling brought calm to situations that might otherwise melt into pandemonium. "I thought you Navy boys were used to carrier landings."

"You know I'm game, Captain," McBott said. "But putting this bird down on one of those little strips would be like landing a carrier on a carrier."

"Well, alrighty then," the captain said. "Let's hope it doesn't come to that. Start working through the checklist—and set the transponder to squawk 7700."

"Not 7500?" McBott asked. A transponder code of 7500 signified a hijacking. It could not be reset or denied in the air. Once activated, they'd be forced to land at the nearest airport and would be stormed by gun-wielding law tactical teams.

Szymanski shook his head. "Not yet. Considering the state of the world right now, I'm afraid they'd just shoot us down and be done with it."

"Squawking 7700. Roger that," McBott said, punching in the code. "I'd say three murders and a bomb on board qualify as an emergency."

# Chapter 63

Quinn had no idea if the bomb was on a timer or would be detonated by hand. Either way, he had to get up to 12A before he could do anything about it. Since the hijackings of September 11, 2001, airline passengers had taken on a new responsibility over their own safety. Gone were the days when a lone crazy man could stand and threaten a bunch of sheep that would stay obediently in their seats. Past disturbances had demonstrated that this new passenger mentality would not hesitate to run a would-be hijacker over with the drink cart or otherwise beat him to a pulp and restrain him with belts and neckties.

The problem for Quinn was that few people on the plane knew he was one of the good guys. They'd seen him running back and forth with Carly, but nerves were on edge and trust was at a premium. Without some form of help, there was a good chance he'd be stopped and pummeled in the aisle before he even made it to the stairs, let alone the bomb.

Carly, recognizable and trusted in her red-and-white Global Airlines uniform, walked up the right-hand aisle of the aircraft, a few paces ahead of Quinn, who moved up the left toward his seat. The captain hadn't announced an emergency but the seat belt sign was illuminated and everyone was aware of at least one murder on the plane. Now their stomachs told them the plane was diving toward the ocean. Hands reached out for Carly's attention, wanting an explanation. She did her best to wave them off, reassuring them everything was okay, and letting them know Quinn was on their side.

The noise of a commotion came from beyond the front bulkhead by the time Quinn neared his seat. A frenzied scream of "Fire!" sent a wave of panic up and down the plane.

Quinn knew better. A fire on a plane could be catastrophic, but the smell of it would be apparent pretty quickly. This was a diversion. He stooped next to his assigned seat, reaching under the tray table to remove the pins holding the metal arm in place. The commotion grew louder and Quinn glanced up to see a tall Asian man pushing a drink cart down the aisle as fast as he could directly toward him. A simple T-shirt showed the powerful arms and shoulders of a young athlete. A determined frown creased his lips.

Quinn yanked the metal tray arm, snapping off the last two inches but giving him a serviceable dogleg-shaped club nearly eighteen inches long. Not wanting to be in the aisle or crammed against the seat back in front of him, Quinn jumped up on his seat cushion with both feet, yelling for the young couple in the row ahead of him to move to the left. They complied, cramming themselves next to the window and giving Quinn room to shove the seat back forward and step around the cart as it rolled by. The Chinese man backpedaled when he saw Quinn's weapon, smiling maniacally as he produced a weapon of his own, a foot-long bread knife from first class. It was blunt on the end, but a middle-aged Russian man tried to grab the hijacker by the sleeve and got a quick lesson on how sharp the blade was with a deep gash that removed the top half of his ear.

Swinging the knife with his right hand, the hijacker unfurled a seat belt extender with his left, whipping the heavy buckle with great effect to strike any passengers that tried to stop him. Quinn had seen a *liu xing chui* or dragon's fist used in demonstrations by Shaolin monks before. A metal weight on the end of a chain, they could burst a skull like a melon in the hands of a skilled user—which this guy apparently was.

Another passenger tried to intervene as the hijacker went by. This one was a young African American. His bearing and the way he moved made Quinn think he might be a soldier. It didn't matter. The hijacker flicked the heavy buckle behind him, dropping the young man like a sack of sand with a deft pop to the temple.

Passengers fell like wheat before a sickle to the speed and precision of his weapons.

Quinn jumped into the aisle. The brakes on the cart had activated when the hijacker let go, causing it to stop directly behind Quinn's seat, blocking any chance of escape. Quinn shoved it backwards with his hip, giving himself a few extra feet of room to maneuver.

Popeye's mouth hung open. He looked like he wanted to crawl out the wall of the airplane when Quinn yanked up the seat cushion and slid it over his left arm, holding it in front of himself like a shield. The two fighters advanced on each other quickly, Quinn's club crashing off the hijacker's blade while the metal seat belt buckle pummeled the seat cushion shield, searching for an opening to Quinn's skull.

Rather than taking a defensive posture, Quinn attacked through his opponent, driving him backwards. Seemingly startled by Quinn's ferocity, the man retreated in the aisle. The soft foam of the seat cushion disrupted his timing with the makeshift dragon's fist. Focused on the moment of battle, he lost sight of Carly until she appeared behind the hijacker, directly in his path. Quinn kept up his assault, yelling for her to get out of the way.

The hijacker feinted with the knife, hoping to draw out the club. Instead, Quinn countered with the seat cushion shield deflecting the weapons long enough to chop downward with the metal club, smashing the bones in the hijacker's wrist and causing him to drop the seat belt extension. His wrist was badly injured, but he still had the blade.

He must have sensed Carly coming up behind him because he spun, grabbing her with the injured wrist and bringing the blade up toward her throat.

Fighting in the confined space of the aisle made any sort of strategy but direct assault nearly impossible. Over the years, Quinn had made every partner he'd ever worked with promise to come in with guns blazing if he or his family were ever taken hostage. He'd made a pact to do the same, not waiting for negotiators or SWAT teams and lengthy standoffs. Quinn had seen too many times to ignore that a lightning-fast counterattack on the heels of the first assault almost always beat prolonged peace talks. He could wait for the guy to get set with the knife to Carly's throat and then play a little game of standoff while both men postured and Carly fought a meltdown. Or, he could go all Samson on this guy and take his metal jawbone of an ass and beat the man's hip and thigh before he had a chance to settle.

He chose the latter—but before he could move, the sharp clap of an explosion shook the aircraft, causing it to shudder as if they'd hit another set of turbulence.

Quinn felt as if a sumo wrestler had jumped on his chest as the air was sucked out of his lungs. He exhaled instinctively, knowing there was a danger of an embolism if he held his breath. Books, napkins, and bits of clothing flew by on a great, sucking gust of wind that rushed forward in an explosive decompression. The air chilled in an instant. A thick vapor formed in the cabin, like the space in the top of a soda bottle when the lid is twisted half open. Plastic oxygen masks dropped from the ceiling, dangling like yellow ornaments amid an immediate heavy fog.

A half a breath later, the plane began to dive.

Quinn's stomach rose up with a chorus of screams from terrified passengers. He had no idea if the pilots would be able to regain control, but decided to continue fighting until they hit the ground. He didn't know their altitude, but guessed he had less than a minute before he blacked out from lack of oxygen. He'd performed well during hypoxia drills during pilot aptitude tests at the Academy, but naming face cards was a far cry from facing an armed hijacker.

One moment, Quinn found himself trapped in the aisle; the next he found himself in a zero-G environment, floating above the seats as his body fell at the same rate as the airplane. Kicking off the seat back beside him, he crashed into Carly, surprising the hijacker. The blade fell away as he flailed out, trying to grab something, anything to stabilize the falling sensation. Quinn peeled Carly aside and rained down blows with the tray table arm, knocking the man's jaw out of place and breaking his other arm.

The hijacker suddenly shoved Carly on top of a row of panicked Russians and lowered his hands to his sides. A resigned smile spread across his face. The bomb had gone off. His job was done. Quinn finished him with a blow to the temple.

Frantic cries of passengers mixed with the scream of rushing wind as the cabin pressure equalized through the hole torn somewhere up front by the bomb. The fog began to clear almost as soon as it had formed, revealing the scenes of panic and terror among the passengers.

The Airbus began to rumble louder, engines groaning as the pilot picked up the nose, arresting the dive. Quinn fell in the next instant as if dropped from invisible fingers, on top of a dazed Carly.

His face against hers, Quinn pushed himself upright, searching for a free oxygen mask. With all the air flowing out of the plane there seemed to be none left to breathe. They were still extremely high where the air was thin and cold. Quinn knew he would need oxygen in a matter of seconds. No amount of physical training could keep him from passing out if he couldn't breathe.

Behind him, above the fray of wind and terrified passengers, he heard Mattie scream.

# Chapter 64

Captain Rob took a long pull from his full-face oxygen mask once he regained control of the airplane. First Officer McBott did the same.

The concussion from the bomb had knocked out flight control, sending the plane into a nosedive until Szymanski had been able to wrestle her back into submission. There were redundant automatic systems, but the bomb had damaged those as well.

Every claxon, buzzer, and bell on the console had activated at once. A computerized voice, affectionately known as "Bitchin' Betty," warned of a pressurization failure in the hull.

"No shit," the captain muttered, and pushed the button to silence that little slice of noise.

Both men had their hands on the controls. Above even checking on the safety of the passengers in the back, their first priority was to make sure they didn't fall out of the sky. No amount of knowledge or radioing for help would do anyone any good if they stopped flying the airplane.

*Aviate, navigate—then communicate.* It was a pilot's mantra during an emergency.

"All engines are showing good," McBott said, running down the various systems to make certain they were functional.

"She's sluggish," the captain said, "but still responding. I'm taking her on down to one zero thousand."

His Air Force flight instructors had drilled into him the three most useless things to a pilot: altitude above you, the runway behind you, and fuel that was still on the ground. All of that was well and good until you were hurtling through the air in an aluminum tube with a hole in it—and that altitude was trying to kill everyone on board. Ten thousand feet would give him a couple of miles over the ocean to play with, but make the ride a hair less deadly.

"Flight level one zero thousand," McBott repeated, his voice muffled by the oxygen mask. He shot a sideways glance at Szymanski. "St. Paul Island is still 141 miles off the nose," he said.

"One-four-one," the captain repeated. "Roger that." Both men dispensed with any of their usual banter, not wanting to clutter up what they had to do with unnecessary words. And, Szymanski thought, depending on the size of the hole in his airplane, the odds were pretty high that their entire conversation would be played back off the flight data recorder after divers recovered it from the bottom of the ocean.

The plane shuddered again, as if to punctuate his fears. McBott's voice came across the intercom.

"We just lost number four," he said.

"Dammit!" Szymanski felt the airplane slow noticeably at the sudden loss of power. "Restart procedures," he said.

"Roger that," McBott said. "Doing it now." His voice was strained as if he were keeping the plane in the air by sheer force of will.

The captain pulled back on the controls to raise the nose slightly. Satisfied he'd slowed their descent rate enough to keep from ripping the wings off, he flipped the switch from intercom to radio.

"Mayday, Mayday, Mayday," he said, issuing his first emergency message roughly fifty seconds after the explosion. "Global 105 heavy—"

A second bang rattled the airplane, interrupting his transmission. A horrific clattering noise on the port side followed immediately on its heels.

"We've lost number three as well," McBott said, already running through the restart procedure.

The Airbus yawed dramatically to the left as the working engines on the right wing shoved her around. It took a moment for the computers to catch up and adjust the rudder and ailerons to compensate for the asymmetrical thrust. Szymanski checked his descent, leveling off at fifteen thousand feet, knowing he might need the extra altitude to make it to a runway now that he was crabbing along on two engines. It wasn't pretty, but they were still flying—for the moment.

Where there should have been the quiet roar of two powerful Rolls-Royce engines, there was only an eerie silence out the left side of the airplane. The smell of jet fuel permeated the cabin air, along with another odor that sent sweat running down Szymanski's back and caused him to gag in his oxygen mask. It was the smell of burning flesh.

"Okay," the captain said. "I have the airplane. Get on the horn and see if you can get anyone from the crew to give us a report."

Juanita's voice came across the interphone. She had to yell to be heard over the roar of wind. There was an incessant rattle in the background and Szymanski found himself wondering just how much of his airplane was falling off.

"The bomb took a twelve-foot section of the fuselage from front bulkhead on the upper deck to about row 10," she yelled. "A beverage cart and part of the floor went with it. I can see down to the main deck, but I'm strapped in so I'm not sure what the condition is."

"Injuries?" McBott said, looking across at the captain as they processed the idea that there was a gaping hole in the side of the plane.

"Five passengers on the upper deck went out when the bomb went off. I'm not sure about the main deck. Andre was standing in the aisle . . ." As strong and businesslike as Juanita was, her voice faltered when she spoke of the death of one of her crew. "Captain, I think he got sucked into one of the engines."

The term was FOD. Foreign Object Debris—like birds or a human body—entering a jet engine could trash the heavy blades, rendering them instantaneously useless. But it was the beverage cart that frightened Szymanski the most. The heavy chunk of metal and cans of soda could do a number on the skin of his airplane. He couldn't tell if the rip in its skin was making the plane shake so badly, or if it was something worse.

"Juanita," Szymanski said. "I need you to get where you can look out at the left wing and tell me what you see."

"Okay . . ."

There was an unearthly silence on the interphone as Juanita went to do as he asked. For a time Szymanski was worried that she had been sucked out of the plane as well.

"Captain." She came back on when he'd just about given up hope. "I'm not sure, but I think I'm seeing some pretty significant cracks in the wings."

Szymanski fought the urge to punch something. "Take the pistol," he said to McBott. "And go back and look for yourself. I hate to put this on you, but we've got a decision to make and we have to make it pretty damned fast. Do we keep flying until the wing falls off and have a hundred percent chance of killing every soul on board . . ."

McBott nodded, finishing his sentence. "Or risk a water landing while we still have a wing."

"There's no such thing as a water landing, son," the captain said. "Only crashing into the ocean. The odds are better than crashing with one wing, but not by much."

# Chapter 65

Quinn stood with his hand on the back of an empty seat at mid cabin, panting, terrified that he couldn't locate Mattie. Carly replaced the interphone at the bulkhead and gave Quinn a breathless nod. "She's safe on the upper deck on the other side of the plane, buckled in with the air marshal across from the rear starboard exit. Natalie thought it best to get her out of the tail section."

"Thank you," Quinn groaned. He'd gone to find Mattie as soon as they were at a low enough altitude to breathe without oxygen. Frantic when he'd not been able to find her, he circled back up the other aisle, making it all the way back to where he'd started.

Nearer the water now, they were experiencing severe updrafts that tossed the plane around like a rag doll. Carly convinced Quinn to buckle up beside her for a moment in the aft-facing seat along the mid-cabin bulkhead, reminding him that he would be of no help to Mattie if he was injured trying to get back to her.

"Ladies and gentlemen, this is your captain." Szymanski's voice came across the loudspeaker, incredibly calm under the circumstances. "We're about sixty miles from St. Paul Island, but as you know, we've lost both of the engines on our left side. Everyone put on your life vests, but *do not inflate them*. I repeat, *do not inflate them*. If we do experience a water landing, an inflated vest will make it difficult to exit the aircraft. . . . Take a moment to look over your safety cards. Find your exits and review the brace position. If we have to exit the aircraft, remember the slides are also rafts. Your crew are all professionals. Follow their lead. Remember to assist your neighbor. I'll do my best to get us down safely. And finally, if you are the praying sort, it wouldn't hurt my feelings if you prayed us to St. Paul Island."

Quinn ignored the bumps and sprang to his feet. He would get to Mattie if he had to crawl.

Carly seemed to understand. She nodded as she took the handset off the wall and interpreted the captain's message in Russian. Another crew member did the same in Mandarin as Quinn hurried toward the stairs.

Even amid the rattling bumps, a silent calm spread over the airplane as people contemplated their last few minutes of life. Some chatted with their seatmates; some held hands with people they'd only met a few hours before. Quinn passed a man who was scratching out a hasty note to his family. Others were doing the same up and down the rows.

The tail section took the worst of the bumping and threw Quinn around like he was on a carnival ride. He grabbed the handrail to steady himself as he bounded up the stairs, past the lifeless body of Professor Foulger.

The shaking on the upper deck seemed worse than below and Quinn staggered like a drunken man as he worked his way forward. He could see Mattie sitting beside Madonna Foss in the rear-facing crew seats at mid cabin. Farther forward, just past the bulkhead, and less than ten feet from Mattie, another man was on his feet and moving down the aisle. Quinn recognized him immediately as being with the woman Mattie had befriended—probably her husband, and part of the bombing plot. Quinn picked up his pace, screaming a warning to the air marshal.

Before she could react, the captain's voice blared across the speaker.

"Brace for impact. . . ."

A crew member shoved the Chinese man into an empty row, out of sight behind the bulkhead. Still a third of the plane away, Quinn knew he'd never make it to Mattie before they hit the Bering. He could see water out the window, blue-green and endless. Wearing a bright yellow life vest, Mattie bent forward at the waist, head down. She wasn't crying, but intently focused on doing everything by the book, as if she were in the middle of a drill. Quinn wondered if she knew he was near. Beside her, Natalie, the flight attendant and grandmother, shouted to those around her, "Get down and stay down!"

The turbulence stopped and the plane seemed to slow, floating like a kite before Captain Szymanski's voice came on again, still calm as if he was welcoming them on board for the first time.

"Brace, brace, brace . . ."

# Chapter 66

*Two minutes earlier*

Rob Szymanski took a deep breath and told himself to keep flying the airplane, no matter how terrified he was. A large crack had formed in the left wing. There was no way they were making it to St. Paul Island. If there'd been rough seas, he would have chanced it, but the great air traffic controller in the sky had seen to calm this little stretch of the Bering Sea to little more than a chop with long rollers that he hoped were spaced far enough apart that they didn't cartwheel the airplane. If Szymanski timed things correctly, he might be able to slow down enough to save a passenger or two.

Mick Bott covered his set of controls as a safety measure, but left the flying to the captain.

Szymanski eased back on the throttle, keeping the nose up as he neared the water. "You ever hear that death was nature's way of telling you to watch your air-speed?"

"I have heard that," McBott said. "Looking good, Captain." The first officer's voice was hushed, almost reverent. If he was afraid of dying, he didn't show it. "Airspeed is at one-eight-zero knots."

Szymanski kept the plane above the waves, taking advantage of ground-effect as he reduced the power a fraction at a time. Green water stretched out in front of him as far as he could see.

"There are three rules to a water landing," he said, dropping the tail. "Unfortunately, no one knows what they are."

Twenty feet off the deck, Szymanski gave the command to brace.

# Chapter 67

*Maryland*

Emiko Miyagi walked up to stand beside Garcia, giving Bowen a slight bow of her head. "Hello, deputy," she said before looking at the others. "Are we ready?"

Bowen could see the hilt of a short sword hanging upside down under her left arm, hidden by the white leather jacket. He'd seen some strange things, but a sword in suburban Maryland—Bowen shook his head in disbelief.

"Garcia told me you'd been killed in Pakistan," he said.

"That is not the case," Miyagi said. She tilted her head so the hair fell away from her neck. It was shorter than he remembered it from when he'd met her in Japan, barely covering what looked like a bad sunburn that ran from her right ear to disappear below the collar of her polo shirt. "I was able to jump into a well only moments before the missile's impact. Thankfully, all the brave men from the village ran for the hills at the first sign of attack. I remained underwater long enough for the drones that targeted me to move on, and then slipped away into the mountains before the men returned. Most people believe I am dead."

"Well, I'm glad you're not." Thibodaux shrugged big shoulders.

Miyagi's lips perked into the slightest of smiles. "We will see about that, Jacques san," she said.

Bowen's phone began to buzz. It was Joey Benavides.

"Showtime," Bowen said. "Joey's not on board any of the vehicles."

"That's a damn shame," Thibodaux said, starting the truck.

The assault worked as smoothly as Jacques had predicted. Staff Sergeant Guttman guided in his Camcopter drone from the tree line, using both LMMs to reduce the lead and follow SUVs to molten metal. North and southbound traffic along the Rockville Pike was effectively blocked by the two walls of fire, allowing Jacques to plow into the front fender of the Suburban carrying Ross and drive it into the curb.

The two ID agents that bailed out of the passenger side of the vehicle were met by a very angry Japanese woman with a flashing blade. She cut them down before they could bring their own weapons to bear. Guttman sent the Camcopter diving toward the driver's head, giving Thibodaux time to jump out of the concrete truck and finish him off with the short shotgun.

Bowen brought the Charger to a screeching stop between the two boiling fires. Garcia had the back door of the Suburban open a moment later. She dragged an unconscious Ross, dressed in an orange prison jumpsuit, back into his vehicle almost before he could throw it in park.

She beat her hand on his headrest before the door was even shut.

*"Go, go, go!"*

Bowen put the Charger in reverse, backing off Rockville Pike onto the residential street to the west, before whipping the wheel into a quick "bootlegger's" turn so he was facing the other direction.

*"Maldita sea!"* Garcia spat in the backseat. "I was sure hoping Walter would be in that Suburban."

The entire grab had taken less than forty seconds.

# Chapter 68

*Flight 105*

Quinn made it to an empty seat, halfway to Mattie before the captain's command to brace. His lap belt clicked into place a fraction of a second before the Airbus's tail touched the water. A frail-looking woman beside him leaned against the seat in front of her. A quiet prayer in Russian buzzed against her crossed arms.

A collective groan rose up from the plane and the passengers as spray flew past the windows. The aircraft wallowed in the water, nose still up, metal screaming as the icy waters of the Bering Sea tried their best to rip her apart. The captain did an incredible job of keeping the huge Rolls-Royce engines that dangled from each wing up and out of the water until the last possible second. Even so, they were sliding through the water at nearly a hundred miles an hour when the plane seemed to slump. Thankfully, Szymanski had continued to work the controls, even after he'd hit the water, and the engines on both sides impacted at roughly the same time, ripping them off, but keeping the plane from flipping one way or the other.

Quinn felt as if his head and shoulders were being

ripped from his body. A giant fist punched him in the belly as he was thrown against the lap belt with more force than he'd ever thought possible. He thought of Mattie and said a quick prayer of thanks that she was in one of the crew seats, and facing aft, her back to the bulkhead. He didn't think her little body could stand being thrown against the belt like that.

The plane continued to shudder and groan as it bled off speed, turning now as the left wing dug into the water and yanked them sideways.

The impact had damaged the support structure of the second deck and it now canted sideways, threatening to fall and crush the passengers below. Cries rose up from the main deck as the plane slowed and settled into the water, wallowing with the waves. The smell of burning electronics and urine drifted through the air.

Quinn looked up to see Mattie slouching forward against her belt. At first, Quinn thought she was unconscious. He nearly wept when he saw her lift her head. Screams and the sound of rushing water from below filled his ears.

Amazingly, the intercom still functioned and the captain's voice came across, shaken but still in control, giving the order to evacuate at all available exits.

Quinn was up and running before most passengers had even raised their heads. The Chinese man was up as well, and stepped around the bulkhead to pick up a shaken Mattie.

In the confusion of an evacuation, Natalie focused on opening the emergency door and deploying the inflatable stairs that would act as a life raft.

Foss saw the threat and grabbed for the man as he went by, but her shoulder had been knocked out of its socket in the crash. Along with her broken arm, it was impossible to defend herself against the man's elbow to her nose as he plowed toward the now open exit with Mattie in his arms.

Whatever the man's reasoning, he appeared intent on taking Mattie out of the plane with him. Others might think he was trying to help her evacuate, but Quinn could see the hate boiling in the man's eyes. Over his shoulder like a duffel bag, Mattie kicked and screamed to get away. Her eyes caught Quinn's as the man shoved his way past the other passengers gathering to evacuate and prepared to jump with the little girl in his arms.

Quinn slammed into him as he hit the slide, wrapping his legs around the man's waist and grabbing his head like a basketball as they all three bounced and tumbled down the slide toward the water. Whatever the man's intentions, he was no match for a father with Jericho's skill set, determined to save the little girl he'd abandoned one too many times. Half falling, half bouncing, Quinn sank both his thumbs into the man's eyes, ripping and tearing until he scraped bone.

The man screamed in agony, trying desperately to use Mattie as a shield as they hit the raft at the bottom of the slide and plowed over the side, still in a clinch, into the freezing water of the Bering Sea.

Shocked by the sudden onslaught of cold, the Chinese man tried to get away, but Quinn held fast, trapping Mattie between their two bodies. He took a deep breath an instant before they sank beneath the surface. Surrounded by green water, Quinn felt Mattie squirm in his arms. Fearful she'd taken a lungful of water, he pushed away with both thumbs, tearing her from the man's weakening grasp. Heart in his throat, he kicked toward the surface.

Madonna Foss was leaning over the raft when he came up, her nose dripping blood, but reaching for Mattie with her good arm. Her fingers wrapped around Mattie's shirt collar and she fell backwards, sloshing into the raft and the other passengers.

Quinn turned immediately, unsure if he'd see another attack. It was pointless. Lin's husband had surely sucked in a lungful of water when they'd hit the surface.

"He never came up," Foss shouted, extending her hand again.

"Mattie?" Quinn shouted, feeling his muscles begin to seize from shock and the chill.

"She swallowed some seawater," Foss said, "but she'll be fine when we get her warm." She reached for Quinn, assisted by a large man with the fierce eyebrows of a Cossack.

The raft began to fill as more and more passengers slid down from the groaning plane, crowding around Quinn and his daughter and helping to keep them warm.

Captain Szymanski's Mayday call was picked up by a passing FedEx 747 and relayed to Flight Following in Anchorage. The emergency locator beacon on the wounded Airbus began to transmit an emergency signal as well as their position as soon as she hit the water.

Two hours after the crash, three fishing boats from St. Paul Island, Alaska, arrived and began to take on the most seriously injured. Aircraft began to overfly the site and other boats arrived a few at a time. Scores of passengers had life-threatening injuries so Quinn and his daughter stayed on the raft and waited their turn. Jericho urged Foss to go on the third boat, but she refused.

A rusted green hulk that was a Russian fishing trawler

was the seventh ship to arrive. The name of the vessel was written in Cyrillic so Quinn couldn't tell what it said, but he recognized Carly the flight attendant riding in a dinghy deployed to ferry passengers from the damaged plane to the ship.

She waved at Quinn when she saw him, then leaned over to say something to the man at the helm of the dinghy. The man, a fisherman in a wool turtleneck and faded yellow foulies, turned the little boat toward their life raft.

His dinghy looked full, so Quinn tried to wave them on.

The driver said something in Russian. Carly shrugged, and then translated for him.

"Not sure what this means but he says your friend from Argentina said you should come with us."

"Tell him I knew her better in Bolivia," Quinn said, smiling at Aleksandra Kanatova's efforts to get him and his daughter to safety. Russian spy ships often masqueraded as fishing trawlers. She must have gotten word to one that was nearby when she'd heard that the plane had turned back toward the US, fearing an incident. When she'd found out the plane had gone down, she'd dispatched it to pick up Quinn.

He passed Mattie across the gunnel to Carly, and then helped Madonna Foss over before cramming himself in among a dozen shivering passengers.

Ten minutes later, Quinn stood along the rail of the Russian ship, beside Carly and Foss. He held Mattie in his arms. All were wrapped in wool blankets given to them by the crew. The ship's physician was seeing to a man with a compound fracture, but promised to look at Foss's injuries next.

"You did good out there," the air marshal said,

shaking her head as she looked across the gathering chop at the mangled wreckage. "I didn't realize what was going on until I saw you go all Hannibal on that dude."

Quinn looked down at Mattie, who slept against his chest, and shrugged. "Man's gotta do . . . Anyway, you know the rest." He looked over the side of the ship at the Cyrillic writing to change the subject. "What's the name of this ship?"

"*Retvizan*," Carly said. "I heard someone in the crew say it was named for an old warship. Fitting, from the other things I've heard them talking about."

Quinn gave a little shake of his head, but Foss saw it. "Come on," she said. "I got ears. I know you're not who you say you are. I don't care if you're a Russian spy. I'm just glad to be out of that airplane."

A Russian crewman brought out a satellite phone, and handed it to Quinn. It was his friend, FSB agent Aleksandra Kanatova.

"Would you look at that." He heard Carly laugh as he stepped away with the phone. "We're all missing our shoes. . . ."

# Epilogue

Vice President McKeon slammed the receiver down on his desk phone and buried his face in his hands. Winfield Palmer and Virginia Ross had both disappeared. Eighty-seven passengers on Global Flight 105 were dead or missing. Witnesses from the wreckage recalled seeing several men with children, but Quinn was still unaccounted for. McKeon would assume nothing until he had a body to prove the man was dead.

He snatched up the phone again, ordering his secretary to get him the commanding officer of the I Marine Expeditionary Force.

Thirty seconds later, Lieutenant General Race Craighead came on the line. He wasn't an "inside man" as McKeon had come to call the moles put in place by his father, but Craighead had his eye on a job with the Joint Chiefs, and wanted it badly enough to hop if the administration told him to.

"What can I do for you, Mr. Vice President?" the general asked.

"I'm aware of a certain gunnery sergeant," McKeon said, "whose skills are being wasted pushing papers at Quantico. I'd like to see him put to better use, say in some forward operating area in Afghanistan."


Two hours later, Jacques Thibodaux found himself standing tall in the colonel's office at Marine Corps Headquarters and Service Battalion at Quantico.

"I don't know who you pissed off, Gunny Thibodaux," Mike Wilde, the battalion colonel, said from behind the desk in his sparsely furnished office. Thibodaux's senior by only a couple of years, the commanding officer looked much older, with thinning gray hair and an even grayer disposition.

"Proud to serve, sir," Thibodaux said.

"Stand at ease, Gunny," Wilde said, getting up to shut the door. "I'm a friend of Win Palmer's, if that means anything."

Thibodaux nodded his head, but said nothing.

"The administration is trying to pull a little Uriah the Hittite shit with you. You know what that means?"

Thibodaux nodded. "My wife's a Bible girl," he said. "David sent Uriah into battle, and then withdrew in the heat of it, so he'd be killed and David could have his wife, Bathsheba."

"Exactly," Colonel Wilde said. "But Marines aren't that way. Are we, son?"

"No, sir," Thibodaux said, smiling. "I expect if Uriah would have gone to battle with a bunch of Marines, he'd have come back alive and kicked David's ass."

"Precisely," Colonel Wilde said. "So, we'll ship you off, just like the administration wants us to. According to Palmer, you have a friend over there who could use your help."

*  *  *

Glen Walter turned south off K onto 16th Street, heading toward an appointment at the White House. He was just a half a breath away from a bullet and he knew it. That Japanese girl was much more than McKeon's assistant. Walter could smell it on her. If anyone tried to kill him, it would be her. He'd managed to lose Virginia Ross and seven men on the same day. The men were of no consequence to the administration, but the media and his superiors had more of a conscience than the Vice President, so there would be a flurry of questions that could very well throw his anonymity, and thus his ability to do his job, in jeopardy.

He'd just passed the Hay Adams hotel and was approaching the back entrance to the White House grounds when his phone rang. He took the call via Bluetooth on the speaker of his Crown Victoria.

"Mr. Walters . . . I mean Walter," the voice said, shaky with tension and excitement.

"What is it?" Walter said. He took a left on H to make another block, in no hurry to see the Vice President and his little Japanese assassin girlfriend.

"Sir . . . this is Gant," the caller said. "You know that Cuban girl you're looking for?"

Walter slowed the car. His hands gripped the wheel until his knuckles turned white. "Go on."

"She's riding a motorcycle heading north out of Beltsville. . . ."

"Do not lose her again," Walter said, nearly coming out of his seat. "I'll get you some air support right away."

"I won't let you down, sir," Gant said.

Walter hung up, turning toward Logan Circle and Highway 1. The Vice President would just have to wait.

# ACKNOWLEDGMENTS

The list of people I need to thank grows longer with each book. I find myself returning to the same group of experts, and then adding more as I seek out help on more and more subjects. My friends Steve Arlow, Sonny Caudill, Nick Hefner, and John Janes offered tremendous help and insight into the mysteries and vagaries of flight and flying in large commercial aircraft as well as small bush planes. Steve Symanski helped me with mechanical aspects of airframes, FOD's and such. Arlis Hamilton let me bounce ideas about explosives off him and nodded quietly when I got something close to correct. As always, I have taken certain literary license with the specifics of things like security procedures, where to put a bomb on an airplane, etc. because I'm not in the business of writing how-to books for terrorists. There are already plenty of those on the Internet. I hope, though, with the help of all these great resources, I've been able to add enough verisimilitude that folks in the know will nod and say, "Yeah, that's pretty danged close."

As is my habit, I consulted with my friend and jujitsu sensei Ty Cunningham regarding the fight scenes. A big thanks to Ray, Ryan, Mike, Lori, Doug, and all the folks at Northern Knives for giving me a place to talk blades, guns, fighting, and war stories.

The Yup'ik Eskimos on the Yukon Kuskokwim Delta

in Western Alaska are a tough people with an incredibly rich culture. I am proud to have friends among them— Perry, James, Nathan, and Clayton to name a few.

My editor at Kensington, Gary Goldstein, my agent, Robin Rue, and her assistant, Beth Miller, continue to be great friends and mentors in this daunting business.

And, of course, my hat goes off to the men and women of the Air Force Office of Special Investigations and my old friends at the United States Marshals Service who provided me friendship and grist for the writing mill for decades.

And finally, to my dear bride, who gave me two gifts the first year of our marriage: a ballistic vest, and an electric typewriter, so I could chase after both of my dreams.